PROJEKT SAUCER 5: RESURRECTION

RESURRECTION

W.A. Harbinson

PROJEKT SAUCER: BOOK FIVE

Hodder & Stoughton

Copyright © 1999 by W. A. Harbinson

First published in Great Britain in 1999 by Hodder and Stoughton
A division of Hodder Headline PLC

British Library Cataloguing in Publication Data

A CIP catalogue record for this title
is available for the British Library

ISBN 0 340 71543 X

Typeset by Hewer Text Ltd, Edinburgh
Printed and bound in Great Britain by
Mackays of Chatham PLC, Chatham Kent

Hodder and Stoughton
A division of Hodder Headline PLC
338 Euston Road
London NW1 3BH

For Ken & Ann
and for
Ben & Marcos & Carina

Acknowledgements

This volume of the 'Projekt Saucer' series marks the completion of what is essentially a fully integrated novel of nearly 3,000 pages and approximately twenty years of work. Because a fifth volume was not envisaged for the series, a lengthy 'Author's Note', which detailed the factual background for the fiction, as well as an extensive bibliography, was included at the end of Projekt Saucer, Book 4: *Millennium*. While the 'Sources' included acknowledgements to all those who had helped me throughout the years of work on this epic undertaking, it would be remiss of me not to add my special thanks to a few without whom the project would never have been started in the first place or would not have been completed in its present state. Thanks, therefore, to:

Alan Earney, who commissioned the original *Genesis* way back in 1978; Nick Austin, who stepped into the picture at that early stage & stuck with it for the next 20 years; Meg Davis, my agent at MBA, who never lost faith; Stirling and Jeanne Weave, for last minute research in Washington DC; and to Mickey Newbury, a superlative singer/songwriter, for his endless inspiration regarding matters he neither writes nor sings about.

W. A. Harbinson
Paris, France
5 January 1999

31 December, AD 2000

The invasion began at midnight. The first sightings were made at precisely that time, on 31 December in the year 2000, over Washington DC. But other sightings were then made at midnight, local time, over every state capital and major defence establishment in the United States of America. While no one was yet to know it, similar sightings would be made right around the globe, all at midnight local time, until the whole world was covered.

The first lights appeared abruptly – and simultaneously – on the radar screens of Langley Air Force Base, Virginia, Andrews AFB, Maryland, and Washington National Airport. The unidentified objects were flying at approximately 500 mph, but they suddenly accelerated to fantastically high speeds, left the area and returned almost immediately. Startled air traffic control tower operators and the aircrews of several airliners saw unidentified lights in the same locations that had been indicated by the radar. They were flying to and fro at incredible speeds, making theoretically impossible turns, stopping abruptly to hover magically in mid-air, and in general creating a spectacular light show in the night sky.

Interceptor jets from Langley AFB were ordered out immediately to intercept the unidentifieds, but no sooner had they reached them than the lights blinked out and the blips disappeared from the radarscopes. The instant the jets left the area, the blips reappeared, in greater numbers than ever, and they had, by this time, moved into every sector covered by the radar, including the Capitol, the Pentagon, and the 'prohibited corridor' over the White House.

More UFO reports came in from Langley AFB, where the operators were now describing the unidentified lights as 'rotating and giving off alternating colours'. Another interceptor jet was despatched from Langley and visually vectored to the lights by the tower operators. However, as the pilot approached the lights, they blinked out, in the pilot's words, 'as quickly as light bulbs being switched off'. No sooner had this happened than the targets came back on the radarscopes at Washington National Airport. Again, interceptor jets were dispatched to locate them, but each time the aircraft were vectored in to the lights, the UFOs disappeared abruptly from the radarscopes and the pilots simultaneously reported that they had visually observed the lights blinking out.

Within five minutes, those unidentified flying objects, now numbering in their hundreds, were spread out in a huge arc around Washington DC, from Herndale, Virginia to Andrews AFB, Maryland.

In short, they had Washington DC boxed in.

Even as stunned workers in the White House, the Pentagon and other government buildings were pouring out onto the dark lawns to look up in disbelief at the many lights of various colours shooting to and fro, rising and falling vertically, making their impossible turns and hovering miraculously in the night sky and illuminating the wintry clouds, those same clouds began to boil and swirl, as if stirred by a giant spoon. Then something vast and terrifying took shape within them.

At first it looked like another cloud, though unusually big and too dark, but gradually it materialized as something round and flat-bottomed, definitely physical and truly enormous. It was perhaps three hundred feet wide, flat at the bottom and dome-shaped on top, the dome rising to a third of the base width, roughly a couple of storeys high. At first it was all dark — a deeper darkness than the night — but then the darkness was illuminated as if from within, a magical glowing that brightened rapidly to form a whirlpool of dazzling, silvery-white light that temporarily blinded all those looking at it. The immense object emitted a bass humming noise, an infrasound, almost *physical*, and then that almost imperceptible pressure became disturbingly palpable as lights suddenly blazed all over the great craft, illuminating the ground far below with their constantly flashing, rapidly spinning rainbow brilliance.

The UFO was an immense flying saucer.

Still high in the sky, at least a few hundred feet above the White House, the saucer was spinning rapidly around its axis: a gyroscopically stabilized fuselage shaped as an enormous silvery-white dome. The rapid rotation of the circular outer wings, or rings, slowed down as the saucer descended. But an electro-magnetic gravity-damping system was creating violent currents of air within a cylindrical zone the same width as the saucer, first flattening the grass on the lawns, then sucking up loose soil and gravel to make it swirl wildly, noisily, in the air as if caught in the eye of a hurricane.

Those watching started to panic, the men bawling, the women sobbing, many fleeing blindly, a virtual stampede, while the drivers of automobiles crashed into one another, turning the formerly quiet roads around the White House, the Ellipse and Lafayette Square into bedlam. Other spectators were too stunned to move and merely stood frozen where they were, mesmerized or terrified, looking up in awe as the gigantic saucer, a mother ship, continued descending, its outer rings still rotating and limned with an eerie, oddly pulsating whitish glow caused by the ionization of the surrounding air. This glow darkened to a more normal metallic grey when the saucer was just above the steel roof of the White House. There it stopped its descent and instead hovered magically in the air, blotting out the stars and dwarfing the building below with its immensity.

3

By now, disbelief and panic had also taken control of those inside the White House and, across the Potomac River, in the Pentagon. The switchboards of both buildings were being inundated with calls, both official and unofficial, reporting that similar sightings were being made over most of the top-secret military establishments and Air Force bases of Virginia and Maryland, that pilots could not get their interceptor jets to start, and that aircraft already in flight, including commercial airliners, were malfunctioning and crashing.

Already hundreds of lives had been lost.

Even as these reports were coming in, radarscopes and switchboards also began to malfunction. Communication was rendered chaotic and, within minutes, virtually non-existent. Automobiles and other forms of transport were coughing into silence and troop trucks trying to leave the Pentagon were also grinding to a halt, leaving the soldiers inside them baffled and terrified. Ordered out of the trucks, they spread across the grounds of the Pentagon with their weapons at the ready, though they hardly knew what to do with them. When they looked up at that great object in the sky, a floating cathedral of repeatedly flashing, spinning, multicoloured lights, filling the sky across the Potomac, its only sound a bass humming that seemed almost palpable, most of them could scarcely believe their own eyes. A few even threw their weapons down and ran away.

From the windows of the Oval Office in the west wing of the White House, above the unnaturally illuminated Rose Garden, the President of the United States also looked up – and was stunned by what he saw.

'Oh, my God,' he whispered. 'They've come back!'

With him in the Oval Office were the Vice President, two CIA agents and his personal bodyguard, Jack Benedict. As the latter – red-haired, grey-suited, normally fearless – frantically tried to contact the Pentagon, the CIA, Langley AFB – *anyone* – with a dead phone, the near-tactile bass humming sound faded away, the circular outer body of the great object above the White

4

House stopped rotating and the swirling debris settled back down. Then the coloured lights flashing above blinked out one after the other, plunging the night back into moonlit shadow.

Within seconds, however, those shadows were split by a thin column of light that burned down from the base of the flying saucer to the ground. As the base opened out like the lens of a giant camera, the column of light expanded until it was almost as wide as the saucer, nearly three hundred feet in diameter, forming a silvery-white pool on the Ellipse. An object emerged from the open base of the mother ship – another saucer-shaped craft – though this one was only fifty feet in diameter. With its outer body rotating rapidly, giving it a blurry, off-white, glowing outline, it floated down slowly, soundlessly, through the column of light, like an elevator in a brightly-lit shaft. While this smaller flying saucer was still making its slow descent, a similar craft emerged from the mother ship . . . then a third . . . and a fourth.

By now, the first fifty-foot saucer had almost descended to the lawns of the Ellipse. But instead of settling on the ground it hovered slightly above it, its outer body spinning rapidly, bobbing lightly like a cork in a pool of water, its eerie light illuminating the Zero Milestone while the currents of air caused by its rotation made the National Christmas Tree, a Colorado blue spruce, quiver violently and shed its leaves, though it did not topple over. Eventually, the outer body of the craft stopped spinning: its eerie, pulsating glow faded away, giving it a metallic, silvery-grey appearance, and then part of its base opened out, falling down at an angle, releasing a shaft of brilliant whitish light and forming a ramp that led down to the ground. The shadow of something large and inhuman fell over that ramp.

A giant insect emerged.

'What the hell . . . ?' Jack Benedict whispered, automatically feeling for the pistol holstered under his coat and then glancing sideways at the nation's Chief Executive. When he saw that the President was deep in shock, his own fear intensified.

'It's all over,' the President said, his stunned gaze focused on that . . . *thing* down there, illuminated in the light beaming out of the smaller saucer as it made its way awkwardly down the ramp.

It was not a living creature. It was, in fact, a robotic machine with a metallic body – twelve feet long, four feet thick, raised eight feet off the ground – guided by an insect-like head with a sealed snout for a mouth and two compound phototransistor eyes that resembled the headlights of a car. Various ultrasonic sensing devices, used to detect contact, pressure and slippage, protruded from its shiny black body. It also had four multi-directional robotic arms, each with two-fingered grippers like crabs' claws, and six hinged, fearsome-looking steel legs, resembling spider's legs, each possessing its own artificial nervous system and mounted on a large, square-shaped steel foot. The machine, which had a highly developed computerized intelligence, advanced across the Ellipse by using its left front, left rear and right middle legs as a stabilizing tripod while moving its remaining three legs, then reversing this procedure. It pounded the ground as it advanced to the north side, its robotic arms thrashing simultaneously, moving this way and that, its grippers uprooting and violently casting aside the National Christmas Tree before it moved on to the south lawn, approaching the central mansion of the White House. When it reached the columned and balconied south portico, stopped temporarily by the curved limestone wall of the Diplomatic Reception Room, laser lights shot suddenly out of its compound eyes – pencil-thin, pulsating, silvery-white beams filled with sparks, their output in the megawatt range – and a large section of the wall was blown apart, collapsing noisily in clouds of billowing dust.

'They're coming in!' Jack Benedict exclaimed, automatically withdrawing his pistol from under his jacket, then glancing in an embarrassed, confused and fearful manner at the others, including the stunned President, not quite knowing what to do with his weapon, which clearly would be, in these circumstances, useless. 'What the hell do we do?'

'We get the President out,' William Greenfield, the Vice President, replied sternly, his voice steady, even though he was wiping sweat from his furrowed brow.

At that moment, however, even as other fifty-foot saucers were either gliding off in all directions or disgorging more six-legged robots, which also scattered to surround and invade the White House, their black bodies gleaming in the pyramid of light still beaming down from the mother ship, different creatures emerged from the nearest, still hovering fifty-foot saucers.

'Oh, fuck!' Jack Benedict exclaimed. 'Cyborgs!'

The cyborgs, though much smaller than the robotic monster insects, looked every bit as nightmarish. Less than five feet tall, they were half human, half machine, the result of decades of secret prosthetic experiments. Originally designed for work on the seabed and in outer space, they had partially collapsed lungs and artificial breathing systems; so their mouths and noses had been surgically removed and that area of the face covered, instead, with a paper-thin cybernetic metal mask that had the appearance of wrinkled grey skin. Some of the cyborgs still had human eyes, though these were uncommonly narrow and see-mingly lifeless, while others had artificial compound eyes like those of a fly. In every case, the top of the skull had been surgically removed and replaced with a metallic stereotaxic skullcap embedded with minute electronic implants that con-trolled the cyborg's every function. The fearsome, inhuman appearance of the cyborgs was heightened by the fact that only a few of them still had their own hands: most of them had, instead, either two-digit or four-digit grippers similar to the steel claws of the robotic 'insects'. The 'palms' of these hands contained built-in small but immensely powerful laser weapons, producing megawatt beams that could stun, kill or demolish. The few cyborgs with ordinary hands carried holstered laser weapons that looked like silvery pistols. Every cyborg, no matter its individual characteristics, wore black coveralls and black leather boots.

Silent and implacable, they emerged from the still hovering, gently bobbing fifty-foot saucers to spread out in all directions, following the huge robotic insects. Some uniformed marines – White House guards – opened fire on them with rifles and submachine guns, but the bullets merely ricocheted noisily off them, apparently doing them no harm, and they responded by raising their artificial hands or their weapons and firing back with pulsating, hissing, spark-filled laser beams. Caught in light flickering in the dangerous alpha-rhythm range, between eight and twelve cycles per second, and also struck by powerful, physically destructive infrasounds, the marines screamed in agony, went into violent convulsions, then dropped their weapons and collapsed, some dead, others temporarily paralysed.

Suddenly, the telephone on the President's desk came back to life, ringing shrilly, shockingly, until Jack Benedict picked it up. After listening intently, Benedict held the phone away from his ear and stared with dazed blue eyes at the President.

'I've got General Samford on the line, Mr President, and he says the same thing's happening at the Pentagon.' Benedict let his gaze roam disbelievingly to the outside, where the great mother ship was still casting down its light, the smaller saucers were still hovering magically above the Ellipse and the south lawn, and the robotic insect creatures and cyborgs were surrounding the White House and, almost certainly, already entering it. 'According to the general, some of those . . . *things* . . . have already broken into the Pentagon and no one can stop them.'

'No one can stop them?' the President repeated like a man in a trance, turning Benedict's statement into a question.

'No. Right now some of them are making their way up the stairs of the building, zapping anyone who gets in their way.'

'Zapping . . . ?' The President was sounding more remote every second, doubtless fearful, among his many other concerns, for his wife and two children who were, right now, in the First Family's private living quarters on the second and third floors of the building.

8

'Right, Mr President. Those goddamned robots have laser weapons and they're either paralysing or killing outright the marines trying to stop their advance. Apparently, as they move through the building, they're somehow making the security and other electrical systems malfunction. The Pentagon switchboard has already malfunctioned once and it's behaving erratically again with various lines cutting out and the whole system threatening to collapse. Those robots, or the saucers they came out of – maybe even that great mother ship still hovering above them – have also managed to kill the ignition systems of every vehicle in the immediate vicinity, including those in the White House garage and the military trucks in the Pentagon's motor pool, leaving us without any form of transport. With those metallic legs, the robots can make their way up the stairs and that's exactly what they're doing right now. In fact, according to General Samford they've already reached the fourth-floor "B" ring of the Pentagon – our top-security ring – and have taken most of the people there captive. I think . . .' Suddenly distracted, he put the phone to his ear again, heard only static, and said, 'Hello, there. Hello! *Hello!* Damn it!' He slammed the phone down and turned to the other agents. 'The switchboard's down – either ours or the Pentagon's or both. I think it's time to get the President and his family out of the building.'

'How?' the Vice President asked, his green gaze bright with fear and disbelief.

'Pardon?'

'How do we get them out – or ourselves, for that matter – if we've no transport and those robots are taking over the whole building?'

'Jesus Christ!' Benedict exclaimed, agitatedly squeezing his temples between the thumb and forefinger of his right hand.

'I want to see my wife and children,' the President said in a dead tone, still staring in a daze at the bizarre *son et lumière* spectacle outside – that great pillar of light beaming down from the hovering mother ship; the thinner beams of light from the

9

smaller saucers hovering just above the south lawn and, beyond it, the Ellipse; the flaring compound eyes of even more robotic insects, now being followed by an ever-growing number of cyborgs – while listening to the increasing bedlam in the corridors of the White House – men bawling, women screaming, weapons being fired uselessly in long and short bursts, doors being smashed open, glass shattering, furniture breaking apart – as the robot insects and cyborgs already inside made their way relentlessly through the building. 'I don't care about anything else. I want to see my family.'

At that moment, however, the doors of the Oval Office were smashed open, torn shrieking off their hinges, thrown to the floor in clouds of dust, then ground into the carpet as an eight-foot-tall robot insect entered, its six legs and four arms moving rapidly, simultaneously, the floor shaking beneath it. Its mouthless head moved left and right, its compound eyes and sensors working, and then, when it saw the President and his men, it came to a halt.

The CIA agents had automatically drawn their pistols but none of them opened fire. They were either too shocked to do so or, as with Jack Benedict, had already gauged the hopelessness, the sheer *finality*, of their situation. They just stood around their stunned President and Vice President, looking up at that huge robot insect, and only lowered their collective gaze when half a dozen cyborgs, all with lifeless, chilling eyes, entered the room, holding stun guns in their hands. They formed a semicircle across the smashed doorway, taking aim with their weapons.

The men around the President let their weapons fall to the floor while slowly raising their hands above their heads. The President, who had no weapon to drop, simply raised his empty hands.

Even as the President of the United States was surrendering his once proud country, similar invasions were commencing elsewhere, all over the globe.

The world changed overnight.

Chapter One

wilson is back.

But who the hell is he? Gumshoe wondered, not for the first time, when he saw that cryptic message pop up as an anonymous e-mail on his permanently activated full-colour computer screen. That statement, or variations thereof *(where is wilson? who is wilson? r u lurking out there, wilson?)* had appeared out of nowhere a few weeks back and now seemed to be haunting cyberspace as surfers all over the country picked it up and passed it on, either for fun or hoping for a serious response. It was an odd little message, inexplicable, intriguing, with nothing to suggest who 'wilson' was or why he had suddenly sprung to life in the ongoing World Wide Web, which so far had not been taken over by the cyborgs. The message disturbed Gumshoe because it was leaving him out in the cold, presenting him with something that had come from somewhere he hadn't been — somewhere in cyberspace — and he couldn't bear the thought that there was anything out there — a scrap of information, a person, a mere shadow — that he hadn't known about and couldn't track down.

Was 'wilson' an invention? Almost certainly, Gumshoe thought. Probably a name snapped out of the blue by a resentful flame ghoul who'd been worked over in a thrash somewhere on the Internet, maybe kevorked – terminated – from his or her chat group and who had decided to haunt the system rather than confront the perns who'd done the damage. Maybe he, or she, was just inserting this 'wilson' into the thread in the hope of causing consternation, frustration and the total disruption of 'real time' which was, essentially, any time not spent on, or in (as some would have it), the Net. This was, of course, possible, but it still seemed strange to Gumshoe that this 'wilson' statement had persisted on the Net for so long and was now turning into a series of questions that no one, not even himself, could answer. At the very least, if wilson was an invention, he was likely to be based on a real person, a mere shadow in the system, in that great well of untapped data; and it was this possibility that was starting to nag at Gumshoe, who hated being toyed with by invisibles with good, bad or downright crazy intentions.

No doubt about it, whoever that flame ghoul was, he, or she, was doing a damned good job.

He or she? You never knew when a pern was just a post code and a date on an e-mail. So fuck wilson. He didn't really matter. What mattered was the pern. Was it male or female? That very question was what made sexual flirting on the Net so dangerous: short of inserting as an avatar into a 3-D environment (always dangerous itself: making you recognizable), you never knew if the lewd suggestions you were making through the keyboard were being made to a man or a woman. No wonder a lot of perns were scared of f2f (face to face) encounters or IRL (in real life) relationships. They could end up with *anything*.

'Fuck IRL,' Gumshoe said aloud, speaking to his monitor screen. 'I'd rather have cybersex. Besides, everyone says the real thing is disappointing and not nearly as good as the virtual other. No AIDS either, old buddy.'

In fact, AIDS was dying out, except maybe in places like darkest Africa or, possibly, Calcutta where, God help them, the technology was still retrograde and could not advance any farther, now that the cyborgs were in control. AIDS was actually in decline elsewhere because even as the cyborgs were keeping most sane and decent people off the streets worldwide, the World Wide Web was becoming more vital as a tool of communication: cybersex was replacing the real thing for an increasing number of those on-line – now more than half of the world's population. Naturally, though Gumshoe *did* still get occasional postings from darkest Africa, they were few and far between and, when they came, were often concerned with the fact that upgrading was practically impossible over there because the cyborgs, who otherwise weren't too interested in that vast territory, seemed determined to keep the situation static by allowing no technological imports. Yeah, and here in the US, as well as in Japan, Russia, China and the EU, the cyborgs, during what was now known as Year (#) I, had closed down the factories and research outfits producing *new* computers and other cutting-edge technology while not bothering to take action against the already established markets. So everything in the realm of technology – computers, biochemistry, the aerospace industry, even medical and surgical science – had been frozen since #I, the year Gumshoe had been born, which meant that places like Africa had remained in the technological Dark Ages (their AIDS figures, against the trend elsewhere, increasing) while here in the good old US of A the black market in computer equipment, albeit it was all stuff from circa AD 2,000, had become a thriving trade largely ignored by the cyborgs while being used increasingly as a means of continuing some kind of communication between humans (hence AIDS figures down). Kids like Gumshoe were therefore in great demand, despite, or possibly because of, the dominion of the cyborgs.

'Yeah, right,' Gumshoe said, again speaking aloud, without shame, to his monitor, which still contained its cryptic message about the unknown wilson. 'I got a lot to thank you bastards for; it compensates me for other things.'

Hearing a low rumbling sound coming from outside, which distracted him from painful thoughts about those other things, Gumshoe leaned sideways in his chair, pulled the curtain back and glanced down at M-Street in Georgetown, Washington DC. The street was in darkness, though erratically illuminated by rusty street lamps, many with broken glass, and a SARGE was moving steadily along it, looking like some metallic Neanderthal beast, the beams from its movable headlights sweeping both sides of the seemingly empty road, its wheels crushing the uncollected garbage as it moved past the house. Originally developed jointly by the US Army and the Marine Corps, it was one of the many military vehicles taken over by the cyborgs, technically upgraded by them, and now used by them in their constant war against the more rebellious members of the human community. The SARGE was, in fact, a Surveillance and Reconnaissance Ground Equipment vehicle, a small and highly manoeuvrable scout telerobot in the form of a four-wheeled, all-terrain frame that housed thermal imaging and zoom surveillance cameras. It also possessed dead-reckoning navigation and triangulation, along with a video camera for positioning, and it could calculate in advance where it needed to go, then head straight there, letting nothing short of a bomb stop it. The SARGEs were, in fact, often stopped by the home-made bombs of the new 'urban guerrillas', mostly teenage hot-rodders and bikers, the aptly named 'Speed Freaks'. But Gumshoe didn't want to think about them right now, nor about the cyborgs, so he let the curtain fall back across the window, blotting out real time yet again. Cyberspace was less threatening.

wilson is back.

So who the fuck was wilson and what was he doing here, sitting as e-mail on Gumshoe's monitor – and not for the first time?

'Yeah, right,' Gumshoe said, talking contemptuously to his glowing monitor and humming hard disk. 'I get the message, you fucking nerd. Are *you* wilson? Is that it? Is that the truth of it? Let's check it out right now.'

He dragged his cursor across the message, hit DELETE, clicked on another window and then keyed in his own e-mail.

From: <Gumshoe@rgf.com>
so what.
who the fuck is wilson and why should I, or anyone else for
that matter, be interested in him.
come clean poster or go back to being a lurker.
i await your response.

He clicked on SEND, then sighed wearily, not really expecting
an intelligent response (most responses so far had been asinine
jokes or outbursts verging on flaming). He sighed again, opened
a bottle of Bud (still in production and popular with the Speed
Freak gangs as an alternative to drugs) and drank it while gazing
in familiar disbelief at the state of his apartment.

The place was a typical on-liner's mess. Hardly more than a
living room with a bathroom, a mere part of his parents' old
brownstone in what had once been one of Georgetown's nob
streets, it was dominated by what Gumshoe had lovingly named
'the Tower of Babble': his six PowerMac 9500s with their eight-
gigabyte hard drives, 298 megs of RAM and PowerPC microprocessors. But the Tower of Babble, while being the dominant
item in the room, was also surrounded by stacked-up Radius
Pressview colour monitors, scanners, colour printers, digital
cameras, remote controls, mouses, boxes of floppies and loose
floppies, every other imaginable kind of software, and a veritable
junkshop of discarded modems and worn-out hardware. These
items were strewn across the room's only sofa, piled on top of
the old TV set and covered the table, lying there with the
unwashed cups and saucers and takeaway leftovers. They were
also stacked up on the chairs and littered the floor. There were
no books, magazines or normal CDs – only CD-ROMs –
because everything that Gumshoe wanted or needed came
through the Tower of Babble: music, movies, virtual-reality
games, cybersex, crank religions, world news (albeit news carefully monitored by the cyborgs) and even education, which for
Gumshoe mainly meant French lessons.

Gumshoe was determined to go to Paris, France, one day. Of course, the cyborgs had taken over that city as well (they'd taken over the whole globe) but apparently life in general was better over there and the Left Bank remained relatively untouched, either by the cyborgs or by passing time. The cyborgs were intelligent but they had no aesthetic sense and Gumshoe, who had studied Paris on every CD-ROM available, had been in love with the city since adolescence and was determined to go there eventually, when real time and circumstances permitted. Also, he thought the language was sublime, though he personally fucked it up when he spoke it, trying to follow instructions from the dark-eyed French babes on his CD-ROM programs – too often, alas, while mesmerized by their moist, glistening lips and masturbating until he practically came over them. Oh, yeah! Paris was great and so were the French babes, so he was determined to go there some day, despite the cyborgs and despite the fact that he'd never had a *real* babe, French or otherwise, in his life. Right now, however, he couldn't leave the US because the cyborgs had grounded all air transport – except their own, of course – thus kevorking world travel for the foreseeable future. Give it time, though. He'd get there.

Sighing, taking note of the mess around him, while automatically, nervously, lighting a cigarette, determined to add more smoke to his already cancerous room, he realized that he'd been collecting this garbage for years – from childhood, in fact – and that for him even the best was not good enough. No question, he would have updated the whole works if he could have. But nothing of note had been made after the cyborgs had taken over and the black market, though still functioning, was still glutted with stuff from the Old Age, which meant with anything from the year 2000 and before. Though ensuring that no new computers were made by humans, the cyborgs hadn't bothered to confiscate what had been out there already, thinking it not worth bothering about.

Mistake. *Big* fucking mistake. The cyborgs had obviously

reasoned that the Internet was only a game park, a primitive human fixation, a healthy distraction for a largely unemployed society, but they didn't know what was *really* going on out there. In fact, the whole fucking shooting match was out there – the hackers and the crackers, the flamers and the thrashers, the posters and the lurkers, the groupmind fundamentalists, chat-room ranters and cyber-terrorists, creating a new language with their acronyms and abbreviations and memes. Some of the perns were crazy, a lot were certainly dumb, but a fair number were as sharp as razors and determined to live their own lives, no matter how bizarre, despite (or *to* spite) the cyborgs. Yeah, they were all out there in cyberspace, communicating with each other, travelling the electronic highway, howling down the bandwidths, given a kind of freedom and venting their frustrations in that vast, disembodied world. Gumshoe loved it because he was part of it, had been practically born in it – and, in truth, because he was the best cracker in the business and did lots more besides.

Gumshoe. Nethead investigator. On-line in the New Age.

Randy 'Gumshoe' Fullbright, born in the year 2,000 and twenty years old next week, had picked that pern name, his signature for the Net, because he was a cyberworld researcher (an honest man) and a genius cracker (a criminal) but liked to think of himself as the kind of detective you could still see in downloaded old Hollywood movies. Humphrey Bogart for a start – Bogart in a gaberdine, flinty-eyed and deadpan – the private investigator, the gumshoe, to beat 'em all. Downloaded with Lauren Bacall, a sultry, wisecracking blonde, once his IRL wife, who could, even in black-and-white movies 'technically enhanced' with computerized colouring, also make Gumshoe come with a groan of pleasure in his well-worn desk chair. Naturally, though one of Gumshoe's many illicit lines of work was the breaking into of mainframes all over the world, he did it without actually having to leave his gloomy bachelor pad, so he met no sultry blondes and rarely got to walk those mean streets. (When he *had* to hit the streets, which he did with great reluctance, invariably he used his motorcycle.) Nevertheless, the essence of it, the meat and bone, as it were, was, in his view, pretty much the same and he felt like his monochrome heroes when he was having a good day, usually probing some company's system either to steal from it on behalf of another company or to insert something unpleasant – a malignant virus – into it. That was his work and he loved it. Most men just did what they had to do, but Gumshoe did what brought him satisfaction. He did just what he wanted.

Right now, however, it was evening and he really felt that he'd been at it too long, from dawn to dusk in fact. He had to get away from the glowing monitor screen, but each time he tried to get out of his chair another e-mail came in and he felt obliged to give an instant response. This worried him. A lot of those on-line became addicted to it – to the point where they could no longer interact f2f and positively dreaded IRL encounters. Gumshoe lived with the secret dread that he might become just such a nerd and often forced himself out of the building just to prove that he wasn't. He realized, of course, that the aversion of the nerds to f2f or IRL relationships, while certainly created by the lack of tactile communication on the Internet, the absence of real time and the basic inhumanity of the on-line situation, was also exacerbated to a great extent by a widespread fear not only of the cyborgs but also of the increasing violence and amorality of street life. This was now largely dominated by urban guerrillas such as the Speed Freaks as well as by the fearsome cyborgs.

'Aw, fuck it!' Gumshoe said, disgusted with himself. 'Let's get the hell out of here.'

However, just as he was about to make the supreme gesture of pushing his chair back and standing upright a response to his e-mail came in. Clicking on that window, he sat back expectantly, read what was there, then proceeded to interact via his keyboard with a cyberspace ghoul.

From: <Rawhide@wah.com>
where the fuck are you coming from.
why bother me with your shit.
i didn't post you with garbage about wilson or anyone else.
now i'm trying to get to bed, you fucking nerd.
who's wilson. go and ask your psychiatrist or dealer. put more
junk where your brain is.
over and out.

From: <Gumshoe@rgf.com>
if you didn't send it, who did, you fucking headcase. you got
someone else there, someone posting behind your back.
or are you just so fucking dumb you forget what you've posted
two seconds after hitting the send button. either that or your a
pitiful flame ghoul using wilson for mischief.
why not come clean, shitface.

From: <Rawhide@wah.com>
gimme a break, you jerkoff. i mean, I need to get some sleep.
i didn't post you about wilson though someone keeps posting
me with the same fucking sleep-denying shit. who's wilson. i
don't know. he's just a name on my e-mail.
you've now added to that pile of fucking e-mail with your own
and i don't like you for it one bit.
your the fucking flame ghoul not me.
beg off, buster. your wilson sucks.

From: <Gumshoe@rgf.com>
don't go to sleep yet. i'm not finished with you yet. you insist
your receiving e-mail about wilson but you haven't posted any.
well it came from your fucking address, baby, so why not
explain that.

From: <Rawhide@wah.com>
i can't. i can only confirm that i didn't send it. i can also

confirm that i've received the same message from a lot of
posters who insisted they didn't post anything.
maybe it's a worm in the system.
can i go to sleep now.

From: <Gumshoe@rgf.com>
sweet dreams, pal.
and think of this when you dream.
wilson is back.

Grinning, Gumshoe pressed SEND, then ran his cursor over the
text and pressed DELETE. 'Fuckin' A,' he said. Glancing at the
clock on his monitor screen, he took note of the fact that it was
indeed near bedtime for all good little boys and decided,
helplessly, against his better judgement and despite his leaden
eyeballs, to shelve for now any idea of going outside and instead
do a final bit of surfing and find out what else was going on in
cyberspace. He clicked his way here and there, raising and closing
windows, posting and receiving, vaulting over space and time,
creating on-line time that was nothing like real time, conversing
silently with some of the millions of ghostly voices out there,
either posting or lurking as newbies and perns, hackers and
crackers, surfers and flame ghouls in newsgroups, bulletin
boards, chat groups and mailing lists, or as avatars in 3-D
environments. He saw himself as an avatar – a digitalized image
of his own face in a chat room – just one of a group of similar
ghostly faces, all hoping to find some kind of spatial relationship
on-line. Uncomfortable with that, however, feeling unreal when
he saw himself, he clicked out of there and went elsewhere,
dipping into bits of this and that – cooking, gardening, bird-
watching, DIY, dress-making, child-rearing, shopping (everything except armaments, which had been banned by the cyborgs),
music, movies, pornography ('seduction' and 'rape' fantasies;
snuff movies and the like), mind-improvement, religion of all
kinds, New Age politics, millennial philosophies, subversion,

revolution and paranoid conspiracy theories, most relating to the rule of the hated cyborgs. The cyborgs, of course, took no notice of such theories, not concerned with the Net, a mere playground for fools as far as they were concerned; though they certainly monitored it and attempted, usually without success, to track down the constantly moving lurkers who generously, without charge, sometimes successfully e-mailed advice on bomb-making. But Gumshoe, who had reason to be concerned with the cyborg world, with what they were up to behind closed doors, in their enormous flying saucers, at the bottom of lakes and seas, on the dark side of the moon, was fascinated by the conspiracy theories and collected them avidly.

Nevertheless, every enthusiasm has its limits and when exhaustion finally claimed him, a few minutes before midnight, he clicked his way back to his Program Manager, unzipped his trousers and put a sensor-laden, penis-reactive condom on his cock. Thus prepared, he clicked on again, e-mailed one of his many faceless girlfriends, <Virgin@mm.com>, and engaged in a satisfying interaction.

Gumshoe: hi. are you sleeping.
Virgin: hi. no, obviously i'm not. but I was just about to go to bed, you fucking pervert and rapist.
Gumshoe: so what are you wearing. tell me in detail.
Virgin: ok u sleaze. a t-shirt, low-cut, real tight, and a zip-up, hip-hugging miniskirt. no shoes no panties and no bra. i mean i'm practically naked. you like what you see, don't you.
Gumshoe: i certainly do but i'd like to see more. why not take something off, but do it real slow. i mean give me a hard time. i'm hard already but you can make me harder. Come on, babe, make me feel good.
Virgin: ok. real slow. i'm taking the t-shirt off right now. it's off. now i'm unzipping my miniskirt. i'm wriggling out of my miniskirt. my miniskirt is off and i'm naked. do you like what you see.

Gumshoe: oh, fuck, yes. oh, fuck, i'm hard and ready for it. i want to suck your nipples and make them as hard as i am. i want to lick you all over. how would you like that.

Virgin: i'd love it. i love the thought of it. i'm wet just thinking about it. my nipples are as hard as you are and now i want you inside me. can you imagine yourself being inside me. do you want to come when you think of it. think of it. start coming.

Gumshoe *was* coming. He was exhausted and sleepily sensual and could imagine anything, so when he closed his eyes he saw Virgin at her monitor (he had to assume it was a 'her'), sitting naked in her desk chair, pubescent and slim and sweat-slicked, nipples hard and erect on full, heaving breasts, sultry lips moist and parted, long legs spread to receive him, fingering herself as she thought of him. He groaned aloud as he felt the tightening of the penile-reactive condom, his cock stretching it to its limits, his spine arching, groin heaving, then he gasped and groaned louder and shuddered violently and came, exploding into the condom, his insides spilling out, while his fingers frantically hit the keys on the much-abused keyboard, first five fingers, then four, then three, down to two and then one, typing out, 'oh my god ah fuck i'm coming, im coming, im comin, im aaaaaaaaaahhhhhhhhhhhhhhhhhhhhhhhhhh' until he couldn't make another sound and could barely think straight.

Barely, but enough. He clicked on DELETE and saw the screen going blank. Then he collapsed like a punctured balloon and just sat there for a very long time (not real time: on-line time) until his racing heart had settled down and his breathing was normal once more.

Relieved to be able to sleep at last, he removed the sensor-laden, penis-reactive condom from his flaccid cock and threw it into his rubbish basket where many more already lay forlornly. Then, leaving his computer on — he never switched it off — he finally pushed his chair back and went to the toilet. Emerging in the fullness of time, he slipped out of his clothes and crawled naked into the bed located against the wall facing his beloved Tower of Babble. After switching the light off, he lay there with his hands clasped behind his head, hoping to lull himself to sleep by gazing at the magically unfurling galaxy of his ancient but much admired Starfield Simulation Screen Saver. The light of the monitor screen filled the dark room with its eerie glowing, the unfurling stars projected on every wall, turning the room into an ever-expanding galaxy with him at its centre. Eventually his heavy eyes closed and he started drifting away.

Not to sleep.

Not just yet.

Just before sleep overcame him, he had a vision of his parents, the mother and father he could not recall consciously, and he imagined them, as he helplessly did so often, with pain and deep longing. He saw his mother as young and beautiful, her hair golden in the sun, and saw his father standing by her side, protecting her and their child. That child was himself, Gumshoe, now an orphan, dispossessed, a mere tenant in his own home, and he swelled up with the grief he had always tried to hide and with the rage – rage against the cyborgs – that could still give him nourishment.

Then, suddenly, he heard and felt the infrasound.

Fear rushed in to claim him.

Opening his eyes again, he saw another light in the room, a brighter, harsher light, pulsating oddly and rising up and down as it beamed in through a parting in the curtains. Even as he saw that light, he felt the almost imperceptible yet undeniably disturbing pressure of the infrasound and it made him jerk upright on the bed with his heart beating wildly. At first he could move no more, held there by his helpless fear. But eventually, impelled by the fascination that never left him, he rolled off the bed and padded on bare feet to the window, across which the pulsating light was passing slowly. He waited until the light had completely crossed the window and was moving away from his building. Then, cautiously, still fearful of being seen, he inched one of the curtains back and looked out.

A seamless, silvery-white, metallic sphere was drifting slowly in mid-air above the road. Spinning rapidly but silently on its own axis, it was giving off an eerie, pulsating glow and casting a thin, laser-like beam of light on the walls and windows of the buildings it was passing. It was, Gumshoe knew, one of the many remote-controlled self-regulating devices that the cyborgs in the White House used for observation of the capital each and every night. That beam of light, which was a sensor that could record the movement of solid bodies, including human beings, was also a laser weapon that could stun, paralyse or even kill. If it found a human being outdoors after midnight, it would stun him or temporarily paralyse him, then automatically call in a thirty foot flying saucer, a paddy wagon, to take him away.

Any human being taken away by one of those would never be seen again.

Watching the small, spinning disc as it moved away from his building, Gumshoe was torn between fear and rage, though the fear was much greater. Despising himself for this, though unable to control it, he let the curtain fall back and then gratefully crawled into his bed again. He stared once more at his monitor, at the Starfield Simulator, then let himself sink into the great silence of the galaxy that seemed to be expanding all around him where the walls of his room had been. He pretended it was real — that he was out there in the cosmos where nothing could harm him — but the fear was a long time subsiding and it kept him awake. When, finally, he *did* drift off to sleep, he was drawn down into that dark well on one lingering, inexplicable, haunting statement:

wilson is back.

Chapter Two

───────◦◦◦◦◦───────

Rebellious as always, Michael slipped out of the bunk bed in his room in the Quonset hut when most of the others in the building were still sleeping. Eager to get away, he washed by simply splashing warm water on his face, leaning over the steel sink. Then he cleaned his teeth and combed his hair. There was a mirror above the sink and Michael, like most eighteen-year-olds, could not resist studying his reflection. He saw there a young man, a stranger to him, with handsome, clean-cut features, almost golden-coloured blond hair cut short at the back and sides, and eyes as blue and clear as the Antarctic skies. That face did not reflect what he wanted to be (*too* young; too bland and immature), so he quickly turned away from it and proceeded to dress himself.

Already wearing his thermal underwear, consisting of tight cotton long johns that he loathed but always slept in, he put on over it a loose-fitting Gore-tex smock with hood and military-styled thick cotton trousers with Velcro pockets and large buttons. Although he had gone to bed wearing one pair of thick wool mountaineering socks, he now put a pair of nylon socks on over them, covered the top socks with Gore-tex seals that would allow perspiration to exit while preventing water from entering, then put on a pair of waterproof mountain boots to which he could fix snow shoes if necessary. Finally, after applying sunburn cream to his whole face, he put on a white nylon trouser-and-smock covering, a face mask that left only his eyes and mouth exposed, and two pairs of gloves, an inner pair of thin cotton and an outer pair of white nylon. If he had ventured outside without this protective clothing, his exposed flesh would have frozen within thirty seconds.

Now looking as white as the terrain he would soon explore, a virtual snowman, he opened his locker and pulled out a rucksack, followed by various separate pieces of equipment. To the webbed belt around his waist he attached a 6″ × 6″ microprocessor-based radio-telephone communications system and a hand-held GPS (Global Positioning System) receiver for communication with the base camp. He then packed the rucksack with high-calorie rations, drinking water, snowshoes, a powerful laptop computer, a pocket-sized digital camera and a portable tape recorder that used miniature tapes. When the rucksack was packed, he sealed it, humped it onto his back and then left his room, closing but not locking the door behind him, safe in the knowledge that nothing would be stolen.

The Quonset hut in which Michael lived was one of many packed together under the immense umbrella of a geodesic dome that glittered beautifully in the brilliant Antarctic sunlight. Situated at the base of the mountain where Freedom Bay was located, the dome contained living accommodations, a canteen, shops, self-generating power plants, garages, snow tractors, research laboratories for meteorology and atmospheric physics, a library, a radio station and a medical centre. Though part of the Freedom Bay colony, the geodesic dome was located outside it, at the base of the mountain that housed most of the community in its interior. As Michael walked across the floor of the dome, heading for the entry/exit point, he glanced up through the high, transparent roof and saw, in the towering cliff face above it, streaked with snow and ice, the honeycomb of tunnels that led into the mountain, with docking bays for the vertically-landing aircraft thrusting out from some of them and exterior elevators joining one level to another, some hundreds of feet above the ground.

Freedom Bay was not, in fact, located anywhere near an actual bay, but in a range of mountains situated in Queen Maud Land, approximately two hundred miles inland from the South Atlantic coast, along the zero meridian. Once claimed by the Germans, during the Nazi Period, and named Neu Schwabenland, Queen Maud Land was actually Norwegian territory – though, like the other claimed territories of Antarctica, it had been isolated from the global community when the cyborgs took over the whole world and used their technology to ground all air transport except their own. Most of the Antarctic bases extant in the year AD 2000 – Britain's Deception Island, the US's McMurdo Sound, the Norwegians' Cape Norvegia, the Russians' Novo-lazarevskaya – had been taken over by the cyborgs in #1. Their flying saucers now controlled most of the air space of the vast, frozen continent. However, the cyborgs had not been able to break through the force field protecting Freedom Bay and now, though clearly they were monitoring it, they largely left it alone.

As Michael had learnt in his history classes, Freedom Bay had originally been a secret Antarctic colony of masters and slaves, run by the legendary – or notorious – John Wilson. Its many levels had been hollowed out of the interior of a towering snow-and-ice-covered mountain in an area surrounded by other mountain ranges that soared up from a flat plain of snow and ice-filled lakes. The colony had been named 'Freedom Bay' by its present leader, Dr Lee Brandenberg, when the cyborgs took over the rest of the world and isolated this enclave from the United States. Elected in #1 as the new head of the besieged community, Brandenberg had announced that the colony would henceforth be devoted to protecting human freedom and to keeping the cyborgs at bay. Thus, though located inland, the colony had been whimsically – or ironically – named 'Freedom Bay'.

Now seventy years old, Dr Brandenberg remained as head of

the community and worked mostly out of Wilson's original office, located near the summit of the mountain. Michael revered him, even though they often fought, just as Michael fought constantly with his parents. When they and Brandenberg found out that he had gone off again on his own, they would be none too thrilled.

Leaving the dome by its single exit/entrance, located beside the larger steel doors for the snow tractors and motorized transport, Michael stepped into a vast, freezing world of snow and ice. All white. Everything. At least, everything but the sky, though even that was of a blue so clear and radiant that it merged into a reflective silvery whiteness. The land stretched out to the horizon, where gleaming, untouched snow merged with cloudless blue sky, its uniform flatness marred only by a line of eastward-facing mountain ranges, their peaks covered in ice that reflected the brilliant sunlight, and by the large blocks of pack ice and bizarrely shaped glaciers that drifted in unseen lakes far away. The landscape, in general, looked vast and its features stood out in breathtaking clarity.

This was what Robert Stanford would have seen when, in 1979, showing tremendous moral and physical courage, he had left Wilson's colony and walked out into the wilderness, fully aware that he was inviting certain death. Stanford was one of Michael's few historical heroes and now he wanted to follow in Stanford's footsteps and imagine how he had died.

Relieved to have escaped from the research station, the dome, without being stopped by anyone, he headed across the vast white plain. Glancing sideways while on the move, he took in the always stirring sight of the many aircraft resting on the landing zones located around the cave mouths at the base of the towering cliff, protected by overhanging ledges. The original aircraft had been flying saucers, but now, though the new aircraft could ascend and descend vertically, make extraordinary turns, and hover in mid-air just like the old flying saucers, they came in all shapes and sizes: disc-shaped, pyramid-shaped, pear-shaped and triangular; some, the sensing and anti-radar devices, as small as twelve inches in diameter, others, such as the 'mother' ships, as large as the commercial airliners that used to fly in 'the World' (the colony's term for the world outside Antarctica) before they had been grounded by the cyborgs. They were more highly advanced than the old flying saucers and, ironically, Freedom Bay had Wilson to thank for that.

Stopping momentarily to look beyond the many parked discs and other flying machines, Michael saw an immense hallway of unbreakable glass, thrusting out from a deeply shadowed hollow section in the base of the mountain containing Freedom Bay. A stone statue of Robert Stanford had been raised there in #1 on the orders of Dr Brandenberg. Its purpose, Brandenberg had stated, was to keep alive the memory of the man whose noble sacrifice signified what the colony was about: the fight for human freedom and, ultimately, the defeat of the cyborgs. According to Freedom Bay's history books, which had been written and were constantly updated by Dr Brandenberg, it was from that very hallway that Stanford, refusing the offer of life as a robotized slave-worker in John Wilson's vile 'scientific' community, had stepped forth to certain death. Now Stanford, carved in stone, looked out over the white wilderness he had died in as a proud, free man.

Michael, too, was a free man in Freedom Bay. But 'the World' had been stolen from him and he wanted it back. Stanford had refused to give in to Wilson and Michael, born long after Wilson's time, deeply resented the rule of Wilson's obscene offspring, the cyborgs, and was determined somehow to destroy it. Thus, now he was following symbolically in Stanford's footsteps and trying to imagine his final, lonely hours. Michael wanted to get closer to Stanford, to feel his essence, because he thought it would help him.

Given the layout of the mountain, Stanford could initially have walked out in only one direction, bringing him to where Michael was standing. After glancing down at his own booted feet, imagining them to be Stanford's feet, Michael convinced himself that Stanford would have walked in a straight line, not looking back, determined only to put as much distance as humanly possibly between himself and the colony. So Michael did the same, walking in a straight line, heading for the horizon straight ahead and hoping to come eventually to the body of water where Stanford had clambered onto the pack ice and been carried out to sea, gradually freezing to death.

Following actually as well as symbolically now in Stanford's footsteps, Michael gradually left Freedom Bay far behind him. He found himself on a vast white plain whose only guiding features were the thin ribbon of mountains to the north and the glaciers rising out of an unseen lake many miles ahead. There, in that exposed area, a strong wind was blowing and creating great curtains of swirling snow. It looked hellish out there. But that hell was what Stanford had experienced and Michael wanted to walk in his hero's footsteps. Within minutes, however, he was experiencing something else: the bizarre sensation that he was walking upside down and that the ground, with its green and purple vegetation, its glittering lakes and streams, was what he was walking on while the sky changed from azure-blue to pink and magenta. Had he not known of this phenomenon, he would have thought that he was going mad, but experience told him that he was seeing what the great Antarctic explorer, Rear-Admiral Richard E. Byrd, had described as the 'Avenue of Frozen Rainbows' – which was, in fact, a fabulous mirage created by the reflection in the sky of ice-free areas located perhaps hundreds of miles away. Stanford might have experienced exactly the same thing just before he died.

Michael had thought much about that subject and discussed it a lot with Dr Brandenberg, who had investigated the matter twenty years before the cyborgs took over the World. The story, as recounted by Brandenberg, still intrigued Michael.

While it was not known precisely how Stanford had died, in February 1980, approximately a year after he had stepped out of the Antarctic colony, the Coast Guard cutter *Amundsen* had come across his ice-encased body on a glacier drifting in McMurdo Sound. Subsequent investigations revealed that the ice-clad corpse had almost certainly started its long journey in an exposed water channel in the interior of Queen Maud Land, drifted along that channel to the Queen Alexandra Range, passing the Beardmore Glacier, then continued its journey under the Ross Ice Shelf to surface eventually, a year later, in McMurdo Sound with Stanford's body still frozen solid and perfectly preserved.

Most of the witnesses to that discovery had disappeared when the *Amundsen* itself either sank or inexplicably disappeared in a UFO-related incident that had occurred a few hours after the sighting. At the same time, in a similar UFO incident, Stanford's body had 'disappeared' from the room in McMurdo Station where it had just been surgically examined. All witnesses to that examination – except one – had also vanished. The sole remaining witness, an American travel photographer, Grant McBain, had left the *Amundsen* a few hours before it had disappeared without a trace. He had left the cutter in order to make a photo record of the autopsy conducted shortly after on Stanford's thawed-out body, but he had been absent from the operating theatre when Stanford's body and all personnel in the autopsy room had disappeared. Interrogated later by Lee Brandenberg, then a thirty-year old United States Air Force captain, McBain had confirmed that he had been in the toilet of the autopsy room when a UFO had come down over the building and strange beings, later revealed to be cyborgs, had taken away everyone in it, including the dead Stanford. None of them had ever been seen again – and now Stanford was history.

As he hiked deeper into that immense, snow- and ice-covered wilderness, frequently glancing back over his shoulder to see Freedom Bay receding, Michael began to run into the same weather that Stanford would have experienced once out from under the protective shadow of the mountain. Here, in this immense, flat expanse, the wind blew the snow in languid, glinting clouds across the plain, obscuring the line of the horizon where white snow met blue sky. Aware that his eyes could be damaged by such weather, as well as by the light, Michael put on his goggles. He did so just in time as, shortly after, he began seeing what Stanford might have seen during his fateful final hours: first an arch of light above a horizon that was forever receding, light flashing repeatedly and radiating outwards in arcs of dazzling phosphorescence, then a great balloon of light floating right there in front of him, a giant eggshell of light, transparent and shimmering, framing a sky that had turned a miraculous pink and was streaked with more lines of light.

I wonder if Stanford saw that, Michael thought. *If he did, he had a colourful death and might have died happy.*

The wind moaned louder, whipping up more snow. The swirling snow was now a white sheet that beat violently about Michael and stung his few areas of exposed skin. He ignored it and kept going. His teeth started to ache. The snow settling on his white thermal clothing soon formed a light frost. The beating wind grew stronger by the second and turned into a blizzard.

All white. Everything. Definition was lost. The wind moaned and the snow blew all around him and made him part of it. He stopped for a moment, shaken by the fierceness of it. He wanted to take off his gloves and goggles, to share Stanford's hellish experience fully, but he knew that if he dared to do so, he could be blinded and suffer from frostbite, losing his fingers entirely. Nevertheless, he kept going, heading into the howling wind. Here the whirling snow was forming immense dark portals that were luring him in. He stepped in and saw a light, moved forward and saw it brighten. The snow hissed and swirled violently and then the brightening light seemed to explode, temporarily blinding him. All white. Everything. He let the wilderness embrace him. Glinting glaciers and flashing pack ice and streams of yellow and violet. A great rainbow formed across the horizon to frame a blue sky streaked with silver. Then a luminous balloon. A mirage: a sun-dog. He saw miracles of blue ice and light, the dazzling wastes of the snowfalls.

Michael moved on, still determined, knowing that Stanford had come this way, that he could not have come much farther, that soon he, Michael, would reach the penultimate stop in Stanford's final journey. And true enough, when the blizzard eventually abated, letting the swirling snow settle down, he saw the glint of nearby water, blocks of drifting pack ice, bizarrely shaped glaciers, and knew immediately, with absolute conviction and a racing heart, that he had come to the place where Stanford had taken his last steps on Earth.

Approaching that broad expanse of ice-filled water, so deep that it looked black, flowing around towering glaciers and slabs of pack ice, an immense jigsaw of glittering, sun-reflecting black and white, he saw that it narrowed at its far end to become a channel curving away to the north. Studying the area intently, aware of the vast, eternal silence, feeling far too emotional, he realized that Stanford, still alive, would have stepped off from this very spot onto a drifting piece of pack ice, then deliberately stretched out on it and let it carry him away as he slowly, inexorably, froze to death. Gradually, as the block of pack ice drifted on, carried along gently on the waters of that distant channel, Stanford would have died: the snow falling on his dead body turning to frost that, over the weeks, then the months, of his long journey to the sea, would have turned to solid ice, a block of ice, growing thicker every day until, a year later, when it was spotted by the *Amundsen*, Stanford's body would have been completely encased in what had become a large, drifting iceberg.

That must have been an eerie, disturbing sight.

Glancing across the broad jigsaw of black water and snow-covered pack ice to where it narrowed down dramatically, Michael realized that he was looking at the same channel that had carried Stanford all the way from here to the South Atlantic coast. Fascinated by the thought of it, excited to be here, he slipped the rucksack off his shoulders, lowered it to the ice, then removed his laptop computer and digital camera. He spent the next hour taking photographs of the location, connecting the camera to his 1000MB laptop (designed and built in Freedom Bay, using Wilson's original technology) with its built-in full-colour photoprinter, and then examining the photos on his laptop screen for reasons he could not fully comprehend. In truth, while the photos showed little in themselves, he was hoping that they would stir his imagination and, perhaps, add a further dimension to his ongoing study of the history of Freedom Bay. Under Brandenberg's tutelage, he had been studying the history of the colony from its earliest days, when it had been set up by John Wilson as a scientific master-and-slave community, to its takeover by the United States in 1981 and, finally, its isolation from the rest of the world in the year 2000 when Wilson's offspring, the cyborgs, had taken control of most of Earth. Michael was studying the subject not only because of his personal fascination with it (it was, after all, his own history too) but also because Brandenberg was determined to rid the world of the cyborgs and he, Michael, was determined to help him do it.

He had just completed his work by the lake when he heard the buzzing of the radio-telephone system clipped to his belt. Removing it, fully expecting to hear one of his irate parents, he switched it on and said, 'Yes?'

'Michael?'

'Dr Brandenberg!'

'Correct.' Dr Brandenberg did not sound pleased. 'Where are you, Michael?'

'About five miles south, along the zero meridian,' Michael replied.

'You sneaked out again,' Dr Brandenberg said.

'Yes, sir.'

'If your parents find out, they'll be angry.'

'Yes, sir. I know that.'

'*I'm* angry, Michael.'

'I knew you would be, sir, but I couldn't help myself. I asked for permission and you refused. I couldn't take that – I just had to see the place – and I think I found it this time.'

'The place where Stanford took his last steps on Earth.'

'Yes, sir. Where he stepped off the mainland and onto that iceberg, knowing he was going to die. It had to be the first lake he came to and that's where I am now.'

'According to the meterological report,' Dr Brandenberg responded, not impressed, 'there was a blizzard in that area an hour ago.'

'Yes, sir. I came through it.'

'Braving the blizzard was an extremely stupid thing to do, Michael.'

'I think Stanford did it.'

'This obsession with Stanford is becoming unhealthy, Michael. Do you still have a sense of direction, or did the blizzard obliterate that as well as your common sense?'

'I brought a GPS receiver along and I can make my way back with that.'

Brandenberg took his time in replying, but Michael sensed that he was smiling despite himself. 'How bright you are,' Brandenberg said eventually. 'Still the brightest pupil I have. But what good did it do you to go out there, risking your own life and possibly, if they find out, frightening your parents, just to follow in your hero's footsteps?'

'It gave me a sense of him,' Michael replied without pause, with confidence, 'and I want a *living* sense of Freedom Bay's history – not just dry facts. When our day comes, when we take positive action with regard to the World, my sense of Stanford and the others from the World – Dr Frederick Epstein and the like – will help me to understand what I'm returning to.'

'You won't be *returning*, Michael,' Dr Brandenberg retorted drily. 'You've never *been* in the World.'

'Nevertheless, it was stolen from me,' Michael said. 'It was stolen from *my parents*. So when I think of entering the World, I can't help feeling that I'm actually returning home. Freedom Bay isn't my real home, Dr Brandenberg, and it isn't yours, either.'

He judged, from the ensuing silence, that his words had shaken Dr Brandenberg, making him dwell on the realities of their situation in general and of his own situation in particular. Before becoming head of the colony, in the late 1990s, Brandenberg, then still with the USAF, had kept his family in Dayton, Ohio, and had flown regularly back from Antarctica to see them. Unfortunately, the day before New Year's Eve in the year 2000, after spending Christmas with his family, Brandenberg had returned to Antarctica. He had therefore been in Antarctica when the cyborgs took over most of the World, thus cutting him and the others in Freedom Bay off from their families. Brandenberg had not seen his family since and the sadness that Michael sometimes glimpsed in him was almost certainly caused by that fact. Now Michael felt guilty for having reminded him of it.

'I'm sorry,' Michael said. 'I shouldn't have said that.'

'No,' Brandenberg replied softly, without anger, 'you shouldn't have said it. But then, you were always pretty quick with your tongue; you're too bright for your own good.'

'That's why you *have* to let me take part when you finally decide to go against the cyborgs and return to the World.'

'You'll take part in *nothing*,' Brandenberg said, 'if you don't learn to work in a team and do as you're told. Right now, you're the most troublesome pupil I have and I'm not sure that you're worth it.'

'I'm worth it,' Michael retorted. 'You told me so yourself. You said I'm one of the brightest brains of the younger generation and that out in the World I'd be considered a genius for my age. Will you now deny that?'

'No, I won't, but I don't respect your arrogance. Never confuse intelligence or education with common sense, which is largely to do with experience. You have a remarkably high IQ and very unusual gifts, but your knowledge of life outside academia is still extremely limited. Your arrogance is based on your ignorance and that makes you do foolish things – such as venturing out into the wilderness without telling anyone.'

'I'm perfectly safe,' Michael retorted, annoyed to be repri-manded even by this man whom he revered, possibly above all others living. 'And I'll be coming back soon.'

'You'd better come back immediately,' Brandenberg said, 'before your parents discover you're gone.'

'All right, I will.'

'Immediately?'

'I promise.'

'Good,' Brandenberg said. 'I'll try and protect your rear until you get back. Over and out.'

When the line went dead, Michael grinned, turned the phone off and clipped it onto his belt. Determined not to go back without a precise grid-coordinate reading of this place (an historic location as far as he was concerned) he removed the GPS receiver from his belt and turned it on. The Global Positioning System consisted of a number of satellites positioned above the earth – each one orbiting the globe twice daily – that transmitted precise time and position (latitude, longitude and altitude) information around the clock. The GPS receiver, listening to three or more satellites at once, picked up their signals to determine the user's position on Earth. By measuring the time interval between the transmission and the reception of a satellite signal, the GPS receiver could calculate the distance between the user and each satellite. It then calculated the position of the user by utilizing the distance measurements of at least four satellites in an algorithm computation. Thus, by using his GPS receiver, Michael could obtain a read-out of his precise location, accurate to a radius of 5mm. Now, after studying the liquid crystal display, he was able to mark on his map exactly where this lake was located, thus adding to his fund of knowledge about the Antarctic colony – Wilson's colony – before it became known as Freedom Bay.

Satisfied, he repacked his rucksack and took a final look at the lake with its drifting blocks of pack ice and bizarrely shaped glaciers, all being carried slowly on the weak current to the narrow channel on the lake's southernmost perimeter, from where it would travel all the way to the South Atlantic, as Stanford's body had done. Then he turned around and headed back the way he had come, across the vast, glittering white plain, towards the mountain range where Freedom Bay was located.

As he made the journey home, bathed in brilliant sunlight yet feeling the bitter cold (minus fifteen degrees Fahrenheit, he noted from the barometer on his wristwatch), he saw flying saucers ascending and descending vertically from Freedom Bay, continuing their round-the-clock patrol of the skies beyond the force field, which covered an area of fifty miles' diameter around the colony and was only turned off when craft were entering or leaving. The saucers of the cyborgs could not break through that force field and so they rarely ventured near Freedom Bay, though they certainly visited the Antarctic regularly: having taken over the original research stations of the humans, they now used them for their own dubious purposes. Those saucers never bothered Freedom Bay's saucers, nor were they bothered by them, but they often flew over the mountain, outside the force field, and Brandenberg believed that they were constantly probing for a way to break in. Sooner or later, if not stopped, they would succeed; but Brandenberg was convinced that the time was not yet right for Freedom Bay to take successful action against them. He was convinced that those in Freedom Bay, though in constant danger of being recaptured, should not act until they were certain of winning.

Michael, being younger, lacked Brandenberg's patience and when he saw Freedom Bay's flying saucers ascending and descending vertically over the mountain, the only home he had ever known, he yearned to be in one of them and see what lay beyond Antarctica, in what was known as 'the World'. That world had been stolen from him by the cyborgs and he wanted it back.

Even as he was thinking this, the laptop in his rucksack gave out a repetitive, high-pitched beeping sound. This being an indication of a rare incoming e-mail, Michael stopped walking, slipped the rucksack off his shoulders and knelt in the snow. He removed the laptop from the rucksack, turned it on, then hit the key that brought up his e-mail window. When he saw that single message on the screen, he could hardly believe his own eyes.

wilson is back.

Chapter Three

‹—————●○●————›

You cannot possibly know me because I do not know myself and I cannot even begin to explain it. I am the light and the resurrection, the beginning and end of all, and I exist where no laws can apply and where nothing can touch me.

I am here. I exist. This cannot be denied. They thought I was gone, but I have come back to haunt them and this is the record of my returning and of what I became. It was not what I had planned or even imagined but, clearly, given the trajectory of my work, it was inevitable.

Yet rebirth is a horror.

I swam out of the darkness of oblivion, a blank diskette waiting to be filled, not knowing who or what I was, as none of us do. I was, of course, unique, as I had been before, but this time even more so than before because I was the first. I had planned myself, of course, ordaining what was to be, but when my instructions were carried out, when the experiment was successful, the other me, the one who lived even as I died, could not know what had happened. Like you and your kind, like all the ghosts of human history, I remembered nothing about my own beginning and I only gazed outwards. Given awareness of myself by what was out there, I began to fill the blank spaces.

In the beginning was the light, the unimaginable first dawning, but even that is now beyond my recollection and I find it frustrating. My initial memories are of childhood, as they must have been the first time, though my recollections of the first time were obliterated when that one died at long last. I had to learn of the first time, to be force-fed my own history, but that did not come until much later, when I was ready to face it. First I crawled, then I walked, just like the normal do, then I spoke and observed and started reasoning, though that time, too, is lost to me. My first memories are of the water, the teeming depths of the seabed, the kind of fish that normal children never see, vividly coloured, grotesque, in a jungle of rocks, plants and plankton, illuminated in beams of light. Those lights were artificial, though I wasn't to know that then, and they beamed into the bottom of the ocean from the walls of my home. Out there, beyond the windows, held at bay by those immense plates of unbreakable glass, lay a world still largely unexplored and as alien as outer space.

My home was on the seabed. I was born and bred there. I had no parents, but many looked after me and each taught me something. I was revered from the start, cherished, held in awe, and never left alone for a second, because I, too, had my purpose. I recall the walls of the sea dome, gently curved, a white steel, punctuated with the panoramic windows that revealed the murky depths and with high consoles in which lights of many colours blinked repeatedly and computer screens, their windows overlapping, glowed like square eyes. There were maps on the walls, though they were not maps of the surface of the Earth; they were maps of the seabed, each one covering a different area as we, those who lived in the dome, systematically explored that vast, ever-shifting, unknown world.

Thus I learnt at an early age that the great dome in which I lived, the only world I had known so far, was enclosed and constantly on the move.

My world, that great dome of steel and glass, had no sky, no greenery, no natural air; instead, it had floors and ceilings, curving corridors and many rooms, manufactured air and artificial light, a closed-circuit ecology. There were animals in that dome, used for research and for food; there were humans used only for experimentation (often headless, without limbs) and there were others who at first I thought were just like myself, albeit different in appearance, but who I later learnt were not entirely human but only half so. They were, of course, cyborgs.

Yes, rebirth is a horror. Though there were other children, I was kept separate from them and made to understand that I was different. I ate and slept alone, had no free time at all, and studied mostly with the aid of an interactive computer system, my tutors merely selecting the software and offering general guidance. These studies kept me engaged (even my games were educational) and the thought of having nothing to do never entered my head. My earliest memories are of working, of learning: nothing else was permitted. Though my elders seemed to revere me, even to fear me, they made me work night and day. They were my rod and my staff.

I had no parents and did not know what parents were; ergo, this situation seemed natural to me and I never felt lonely. Sometimes, it is true, I experienced a fleeting sense of loss, a hollowness at my centre, as if part of me was missing, but invariably I shrugged the feeling off and returned to my work. My learning gave me my centre, my reason to be, and eventually nothing else really mattered. I thought my brain was my soul.

My world was the great dome and for years it was under water, but then I learnt that it was a gigantic submersible that could also take wing, though it did so but rarely.

On those rare occasions, the great dome would rise vertically, lifting off the sea bed, drifting up silently from darkness to light, first through striations that obliquely sliced the gloom, then into a dazzling explosion of sunlight as the sea, first dark green, then blue and foaming white, poured down the large windows, drummed against the metal walls, then turned into surging waves that eventually fell away, dropping out of sight, until the surface of the sea came back into view, this time as a vast sheet of blue far below, running out to the horizon, with the sky, either cloudy or bright, spread out all around us. Then, when we were so high that we could see the curve of Earth, the sky would also change, turning into a whipping, spiralling tunnel of shimmering white light streaked with silvery blue, a vertiginous well of brightness that gave no indication of which direction we were actually flying in: up, down or straight ahead. Then, abruptly, we would blast through the sky itself, a giant envelope tearing open to reveal a boundless, azure sea which would convulse and turn purple and then, just as abruptly, actually being the same sea, fill up with the burning radiance of a gigantic sun, even as the moon and stars also came out, now visible, with the sun, in an atmosphere so thin that even dust particles could not exist there. And seconds later (it always seemed that quick) we would be descending vertically over a different coastline, perhaps thousands of miles away, only to sink back into the sea, sinking down into the silent, eternal depths until we touched the seabed. And there we would remain for many months or, in some cases, years.

I have lived in the depths of many oceans and now I reach for the stars.

I was, of course, too young then to understand that we had been flying well beyond the sound barrier, over fifty miles up, on the very edge of space; just as I was too young to know that to live on the seabed was not normal. Nevertheless, my blank diskette, my young brain, was still being crammed full of knowledge, with languages, mathematics, geography, world history, astronomy and, most of all, with science, including aerodynamics, physics, biology, and computer technology. No literature. No art. Yet apart from that lack, I was, by my tenth year, as knowledgeable as the grown-ups who had taught me. A year later, with the aid of my computers, I began to outstrip them.

Now, as I write, in my fortieth year on Earth, I am so far ahead of my tutors that they seem like mere children. Now they fear me even more than they revere me. And that's as it should be.

In time you will fear me as well. But first you must find me. I am here. I exist. You simply have to accept who I am and how like me you are.

I will make sure you do.

Chapter Four

Gumshoe had to get out. This didn't happen often, but this evening he was feeling restless, as if he'd been flamed, and he needed air even more polluted than the air in his apartment. In fact, he needed action. He had been working for days now, breaking into the mainframe of a multinational pharmaceutical company on behalf of another multinational, stealing information and passing it on: the job had been more difficult than he had thought possible and had eaten up a lot of on-line time. Well protected with multiple passwords and a variety of traps for hackers and crackers, the mainframe had challenged Gumshoe's ingenuity for two days and most of three nights, driving him to a diet of home-delivery hamburgers, Chinese food, pizza pies, nonalcoholic drinks and cigarettes, all ordered up electronically as required, with him never having to go any farther than the front door downstairs. By the end of that lengthy period, when the mainframe had finally been broken into and the stolen data passed on electronically, Gumshoe's already cluttered room was dense with smoke and further messed up with cardboard takeaway cartons, styrofoam beakers and overflowing, foul-smelling ashtrays. To make matters worse, Gumshoe felt disorientated – nay, *lobotomized* – his brain consumed and drained by the bottomless pit of cyberspace, the glowing screen that sucked him in, surrounded him, eventually made him part of it, became his only world, down there in that howling electronic well with the perns, the flame ghouls, the lurkers, the other hackers and crackers. Now moved by the inexplicable urge to feel human again, which in truth happened rarely, he decided to tidy up his dump and go out for some action.

After cleaning his teeth for the first time in a few days, he stripped off his working clothes (plain white T-shirt, blue denims and baggy underpants), stepped naked into the shower – which, not working properly, was freezing cold – then dried himself and put on his Speed Freak clothing: tight, balls-hugging underpants, a bullet-proof vest, jet-black net-to-ankle zip-up coveralls and a sleeveless tropical jacket with a lot of pockets containing money in cash form (the credit-card economy had given way to electronic cash transfers), cigarettes, methamphetamine-based chewing gum, a wide variety of other drugs in pill form and a pack of cards to be used for gambling or simply to while away the time should nothing be happening. He put on a pair of black suede leather-soled boots, but as usual he eschewed the soft option of a helmet or other protective headgear. Finally, mindful of street crime, which was, these days, as bad as it could get, he strapped a Glock 19 semi-automatic handgun, conveniently small and light, to his waist, its holster positioned to the rear of his left side to enable him to cross-draw at speed. Thus prepared, he filled a black plastic bag with all the cardboard containers, styrofoam cartons, unfinished hamburgers and pizzas and cigarette butts, then hauled it out of the room onto the landing. After turning the keys in the three multiple locks on his reinforced room door, he humped the plastic bag down the stairs and out of the building.

It was late in the evening, which was warm this June day, and the few street lamps still working cast a baleful glow across the rubbish piled up on both sides of M Street. Though the city's infrastructure was steadily collapsing, neglected by the cyborgs, it still operated in certain areas and the rubbish *was* collected occasionally. Sometimes, however, it was so long between collections that the rubbish would turn to putrescence and be covered with swarms of fat black flies. That was the situation here and now: Gumshoe held his breath as he threw his rubbish bag on top of the others piled up on the sidewalk. Glad to be rid of it, he turned down the steps that led to the door of the basement. First using a confidential code number, then three more sets of keys, he let himself into the concrete-walled, gloomy basement where he kept his beloved motorcycle in a heavily padlocked and electrified steel-mesh cage. After turning off the electrical circuit, to avoid inadvertently giving himself a bad shock, he opened the four heavy padlocks, removed the immaculate silver-tanked Yamaha 400 from its protective cage, locked the cage again, then wheeled the motorcycle outside and humped it awkwardly up the steps to the sidewalk. He glanced left and right, always mindful of villains just like himself, then slung his leg over the saddle, started the motorcycle and burned off along M Street.

Crossing Wisconsin Avenue and continuing east in dense traffic, he was dazzled by the flashing bright lights of the noisy, neon-lit electronic games parlours, techno dance clubs and porno 'fun palaces' lining both sides of the road. Though the cyborgs had imposed a midnight curfew and were ruthless at enforcing it, they had shown supreme indifference to what human beings did for entertainment (the very concept was beyond them), so long as it was done before midnight. Indifferent, also, to everything but their own needs, the cyborgs had destroyed most import and export businesses by grounding all aircraft and stopping sea travel, had killed off the automobile, aircraft, shipping and computer industries as well as any other concerns that offered the chance of technological progress for humans, and had in general created unemployment on a scale never seen before in the United States. (And, according to Gumshoe's e-mail, things weren't much better elsewhere.) Perhaps in response to this, faced with no viable future, human beings, particularly the younger generation, had created an alternate world, based largely in cyberspace, which the cyborgs seemed to ignore, and had also thrown themselves wholeheartedly into every kind of hedonistic activity, including cybersex, virtual-reality adventures, 'real time' crime, heavy drinking and drug-taking, techno music and new forms of tribalism, as represented, in the case of Georgetown, by the growing number of motor-cycle-and-hot-rod gangs. At his tender young age, Gumshoe had never known a world without the cyborgs, so he was not to know that the electronic games parlours, techno dance clubs and porno fun palaces lining Wisconsin Avenue and M Street had once been more sedate bars and restaurants. What he *did* know was that the many kids of roughly his own age, now crowding the sidewalks and garishly neon-lit houses of pleasure, had a tendency to cram as much as they could into their evenings before the midnight curfew came into force, after which, if they were still on the streets, they would be in danger of being picked up by the cyborg watch patrols. No one knew what happened to those picked up; the only known fact was that, once picked up, you would never be seen again.

And that's the buzz, Gumshoe thought as he took the bridge over Rock Creek and burned along Pennsylvania Avenue, heading for Downtown. *The buzz is running that risk.*

Sweeping around Washington Circle and then continuing along Pennsylvania Avenue, he noticed how relatively empty the road was and was reminded that the better-off, the middle-aged, the kind still living in Foggy Bottom and clinging to their worthless fortunes, rarely ventured out at nights, being frightened not only of the cyborg patrols but also of the white teenage and ethnic Speed Freak gangs that swooped in most evenings from Anacostia or the north-east, defying the cyborgs, to rob, rape and kill. Studying the imposing government buildings as he burned past them, he noted that few lights were on inside them. This was yet another reminder that while the cyborgs had allowed a few, strictly necessary government administrators to remain in their jobs – mostly those dealing solely with the city's infrastructure, such as sanitation, local transport and what was left of law and order – these were few in number and so short of supporting staff that they could no longer do their jobs properly. They were, of course, further hampered in their work by the mass unemployment caused by the cyborgs' many restrictions and by an attendant lack of proper financing. The freezing of air and sea travel had led to the loss of revenue from imports and exports, including that from the all-important arms trade; while the mass unemployment had led to an even greater loss of tax revenue and, subsequently, the collapse of the IRS. Finally, that same mass unemployment had created an ever-growing crime wave based on the desperation of the rapidly rising number of jobless. So the few lights on in those government buildings were being burned by men with little actually to do – though some were still trying. There was a certain nobility in that and Gumshoe respected it.

As he approached the White House, which was brilliantly illuminated both inside and outside, he saw a couple of medium-sized flying saucers on the lawns in front of the building and cyborgs patrolling the grounds. The gates were guarded by a couple of SARGE robot scouts and by more cyborgs. Since his earliest memories naturally included the cyborgs and flying saucers, Gumshoe was neither repulsed by the former nor surprised by the latter, but he still found himself wondering just what the cyborgs got up to inside the White House, not to mention inside the Pentagon and other major government and military establishments.

According to what he had been told by his elders and had picked up in written histories available on the Internet, when the cyborgs had taken over at the end of the year 2000, the last year of the Old Age, they had arrived in truly enormous flying saucers, the so-called 'mother ships' of UFO legend. Reportedly, the mother ships had been seen emerging from various seas and lakes around the world: notably in the Bermuda Triangle in the west Atlantic, that area connecting Bermuda, Puerto Rico and the coast of Florida; the so-called 'Devil's Sea' bounded by the south-east coast of Japan, the northern tip of Luzon in the Philippines, and Guam; the Plata del Mar in Argentina; the Great Lakes of Canada – and even Loch Ness, Scotland, where, during the great age of UFO sightings between 1947 and 1999, many USOs (Unidentified Submarine Objects) had been mistaken for the Loch Ness Monster. Other massive 'mother ships' had been seen rising from well-hidden isolated areas in the Arctic Circle, the Antarctic and the wilds of Canada. Those mother ships had then come down over some of the most famous and important buildings in the world: the White House and the Pentagon in Washington DC, the Houses of Parliament and Buckingham Palace in London, England; the Kremlin in Red Square, Moscow; and the Forbidden City in Beijing, China. They had come down over similarly important buildings in the major cities of the former European Union (since broken up by the cyborgs and turned back into relatively harmless autonomous states). Additionally, they had come down over the world's top-secret defence and research establishments, including, in the case of the United States, the White Sands Proving Ground, New Mexico, and the US Space Command's Space Surveillance Centre in Colorado Springs, Colorado. In every case, the most important people found in those buildings, such as the President of the United States and the British Prime Minister, neither of whom had been given enough warning to make their escape, had been escorted out of their respective buildings and taken away in the mother ships. Neither the VIP prisoners nor the mother ships had ever been seen again and it was widely assumed that the giant saucers had returned to their underwater or mountain retreats, taking the VIPs with them, never to release them. The cyborgs had then taken over the buildings and remained there from that day to this. What they were now doing inside those buildings was anyone's guess.

Unable to continue along Pennsylvania Avenue because the stretch crossing the north side of Lafayette Square was constantly patrolled by cyborgs, Gumshoe took first a left and then a right, circling around the White House via H-Street, then went along G-Street, heading for the old Chinatown. Once exclusively Chinese, the area was now filled with previously well-off whites who had been forced out of their Capitol Hill or Downtown homes by criminal elements and now lived as poorly as the ethnic minorities. Ignored by the cyborgs, who did not differentiate between honest and dishonest humans, the criminal gangs had taken over the fine old houses of the middle and upper classes, turning them into cramped, though highly profitable, rooming houses or apartment blocks.

Though a kind of criminal himself, a cyberspace burglar, Gumshoe had little love of those particular criminals because the grand old Georgetown building in which he now had only a couple of cramped rooms had once been his parents' house and his childhood home. Even now it filled him with bitterness to recall that when he had been only fourteen, his parents (both physicists conducting important government-sponsored research out in Quantico) had been taken away one night by the cyborgs and had never returned. Gumshoe's grief had been monumental and had in no way been soothed when, a few weeks later, having deduced that the orphaned kid's parents would not be coming back, a bunch of hard men had taken over the house, generously offering to let Gumshoe stay on in his original bedroom with en suite bathroom so long as he paid them an extortionate rent, and had then converted the rest of the expansive, Federal-style house into similar, very cramped apartments. Unable to do anything about it, Gumshoe had paid his rent by exploiting his wizardry on computers to make money and had been doing the same thing ever since. Nevertheless, the situation rankled and was yet another reason for him to resent the rule of the cyborgs which had led to the breakdown of the old infrastructure and the rise of the new criminals.

Which was why he was going out for the night: to give the cyborgs some grief.

After roaring into Chinatown, where he saw no Chinese faces, he slowed down to avoid the rubbish piled up in the road.

Passing a row of dilapidated buildings that were, in fact, old Chinese restaurants that had been converted into dwellings by whites turfed out of better homes and now – having in turn turfed out the Chinese – living impoverished, gangster-dominated lives, he turned into Gallery Place, which looked like a war zone, and came eventually to the old MCI Center. Formerly a 20,000-seat sports arena for the city's basketball and hockey teams, it was now a disused, desolate gathering place for the teenage Speed Freaks.

Drawn in on waves of pounding techno rave music, Gumshoe found himself in the midst of friends. They were wearing work shirts, chinos, short-sleeved black leather vests, bandannas and sneakers or old Doc Marten boots with steel-reinforced toes. Some had short-cropped hair, others sported ducktails and pompadours 1950s-style. Many had tattoos on their arms, hands and faces. Their girlfriends were just as varied and bizarre. The Freaks were sitting in, sprawling upon or leaning against cars with after-market tail fins, aerofoils, skirts, spoilers and flashing purple police lights, low-riders with deep bucket seats and graphic equalizers that emitted waves of light, and garishly decorated, extremely powerful motorcycles.

Most of the Speed Freaks, whether hot-rodder or motorcyclist, favoured unmuffled engines and obscured licence plates. Weaving between them and performing daring acrobatics were kids on skateboards. A lot of them were drinking beer, popping pills, injecting methamphetamine with hypodermic needles or, if they couldn't afford that, sniffing glue instead. They formed a large, noisy, highly volatile and potentially dangerous tribe. Gumshoe was real glad to see them.

Sweeping up to his closest friends on his Yamaha 400, he went into a fancy skid, then came to a shuddering halt in a cloud of dust that made those nearest to him cough and curse.

'Fuck it, Gumshoe,' his best friend, Danny 'Snake Eyes' Knoke, said, waving the billowing dust from his face and spitting it out of his mouth. 'What a dumb thing to do.'

'Almost crushed your toes,' Gumshoe retorted, 'but decided to let you off light. The dust's sticking to the gel on your pompadour and it looks like a spider's web. You need another shower, hotshot.'

'You're fuckin' jokin',' Snake Eyes said, seriously alarmed and kneeling low to check his head in the offside mirror of his rainbow-coloured Mazda sedan, experimentally patting his greased pompadour. Heaving a sigh of relief to see that Gumshoe had indeed been joking, he straightened up, shook his head wearily from side to side, took a slug from his can of Bud and said, 'Very funny. Real smart. So what's cookin', dickhead?'

'Nothing much that I can see, Snake Eyes. I thought you might have some plans.'

'The only plan I've got is to go out and hassle some Full Metal Jackets. That's what we're all here for.'

By 'Full Metal Jackets' he meant both the cyborgs and the small, saucer-shaped sensing devices that glided eerily through the streets at night, always after the midnight hour, to spy on the human population and, if necessary, paralyse them and have them picked up by the dreaded paddy wagons. The nickname 'Full Metal Jackets' had been picked up from an old war movie that was still shown a lot on home TV and Internet channels. A lot of the kids freaked out on those old movies, just as they did on old music.

'*Bonsoir*,' Gumshoe said, nodding at the Long Hair who was leaning against the hood of Snake Eyes's Mazda sedan, wearing a ragged white T-shirt under a black leather jacket with silver chains, black leather hotpants, black stockings and high-heeled black leather boots that emphasized her long, shapely legs. She seemed, to Gumshoe, to have delicate features, though this was hard to confirm since, like the female punks occasionally seen on Internet documentaries about the legendary 1970s, she had hacked her hair short and dyed it a mixture of green and pink. She would, of course, still be called a 'Long Hair' as all the girls were these days. Also, to emphasize her archaic punk look, her eyebrows had been shaved off, painted stripes criss-crossed her pale face, and fake blood was trickling from the corners of her blue-painted lips. Chewing gum, she responded to Gumshoe's greeting with a superior look and mocking grin.

'So what's this *bonsoir* shit?' she sneered. 'What the hell does *that* mean?'

'It means "Good evening" in French,' Gumshoe informed her.

'You still trying to learn that shit?' Snake Eyes asked him, surprised.

'Yeah,' Gumshoe said, then returned his attention to the Long Hair. 'So who the hell are you?'

'She's my personal piece,' Snake Eyes informed him, 'and she's come along for the ride.'

'Bonnie Packard,' the Long Hair informed him, turning aside to spit on the ground. She looked up again. 'I'm the leader of the Wild Cats,' she said, 'so don't give me no shit.'

Gumshoe knew the Wild Cats. They were an all-girl gang of Speed Freaks who were as bold as the 'Short Hairs', the guys, when playing dangerous games with the Full Metal Jackets. Gumshoe had thought that Donna Prentiss, a butch bitch, was in charge of the gang – not this unknown, sneering slice of prime teenage ham.

'So what happened to the slippery cunt?' he asked, referring to Donna Prentiss, who was known to put out freely in real time, albeit with her own sex.

'She was zapped by a Full Metal Jacket,' Bonnie replied, 'and then taken away in a paddy wagon. We won't see her again.'

'That's for goddamned sure,' Snake Eyes said, grinning to reveal his bad teeth. 'No one comes back from that one.'

'Are you and her interacting?' Gumshoe asked of Snake Eyes while nodding towards the Long Hair.

'Only by e-mail,' Snake Eyes replied. 'I don't like that hands-on stuff.'

'I like it either way,' Bonnie Packard said, spitting once more on the ground, then looking directly, boldly, at Gumshoe. 'So what about you?'

'I don't like that real-time boogie,' Gumshoe informed her. 'Give me cybersex any day. I mean, it's cleaner and safer.'

'You ever had it real-time?' Bonnie asked, her purple lips crooked in a grin that would have been mocking had it not been for the dribbles of painted blood, which made her look like a vampire. 'If not, you might be missing something that's better than reported.'

'You can't miss what you've never experienced,' Gumshoe responded, not remotely embarrassed to be an IRL virgin, which so many of his friends were these days. 'I pick what I want and I choose my time and place and I don't have no Long Hair complications. I'll take that good old cybersex any day and I say it works fine. E-mail me and find out.'

'Go fuck yourself,' Bonnie said.

'He often does,' Snake Eyes said, grinning wickedly, glancing around him to see the other Speed Freaks, male and female alike, drinking beer, popping pills, sniffing glue and injecting methamphetamine in the moonlit darkness of the enormous sports arena which, with its 20,000 seats empty, looked haunted and eerie. The CD had been changed and now, replacing the techno rave music, Elvis Presley was singing 'Bossa Nova Baby' and the Speed Freaks were going wild, working themselves up to the song's relentless, percussive rhythm, blaring out of speakers rigged by some deejay genius to the rusty overhead arc lamps of the neglected stadium. 'Hey, dig this,' Snake Eyes continued, turning back to Gumshoe and Bonnie. 'Elvis is alive and well and has been seen coming out of the White House with some Full Metal Jackets of the more human kind, by which I mean cyborgs. He's producing something in there, some really big number, that'll let him make his second Comeback Special. That's why the Full Metal Jackets are here — they're here to resurrect Elvis. God, that Elvis, I love the fuckin' dude! Here, have some of these.'

As Gumshoe took, and swallowed, a couple of Snake Eyes's capsules of highly concentrated amphetamine, glancing sideways at Bonnie who was doing the same, he, too, was swept away by the voice of the dead hero and wished that Elvis was truly alive and well and preparing to make another Comeback. In fact, Elvis and Marlon Brando had come full cycle, first cult heroes of the Old Age, now the same in the New Age, having been resurrected as computerized holographic images that seemed as real as the originals when performing in virtual reality concerts on the Internet and in cyberdiscos. While Marlon Brando, in a digitally coloured version of *The Wild One*, had inspired a lot of the Speed Freaks, particularly the bikers, to imitate him in looks, dress and speech, it was Elvis who had really made the greatest comeback. In the new teenage world of cybersex, where e-mail relationships blurred the differences between male and female, it was Elvis, with his androgynous beauty, as well as with his transformation from uncouth teenage rebel to otherworldly Sun King, a Captain Marvel for the future, who had really caught the imagination of the younger New Age generation. Gumshoe knew all about Elvis, not only through the Internet, but because his mother had been fanatical about him, even though the so-called 'King' had died before she was born. Nevertheless, Gumshoe had, in a very real sense, been brought up with Elvis (a fairly unusual occurrence in a middle-class scientific Georgetown family) and now, with Elvis being so big with his own generation, he was fascinated by the question of why his mother, whom he had loved dearly, had, like him and so many others, revered the great rock 'n' roll performer.

Gumshoe had lost his mother when he was fourteen years of age (both his mother and his father, though he had felt her loss the most) and now wanted, with an unnatural passion, to know everything about her. Thus, as the amphetamine hit him, he wondered why she had loved Elvis and decided to ask the Cowboy about it.

'Fucking A,' he said aloud as the effects of the amphetamine rushed through his body, up to his neck, to his brain, making him reel from the force of it, his throat constricting from its biting, bitter taste. 'Do it, man! Talk to the fucking Cowboy. Find out where Mom came from.'

'What's that?' Snake Eyes asked.

'Nothing,' Gumshoe said.

'Who's the Cowboy?' Bonnie the Long Hair asked as she, too, reeled from the amphetamine rush. 'Are you losing it, man?'

'No, man, I'm not losing it,' Gumshoe retorted. 'I'm just airing my thoughts. Hey, Snake Eyes,' he said, turning to his old friend, bombed out, maybe psycho, 'have you ever heard of a dude called Wilson?'

'I got a couple of buddies by that name. Which one do you mean?'

'I mean the Wilson being brought up on e-mail. I mean a ghost out in cyberspace.'

'Don't know nothing about no ghost in cyberspace. Don't know no Wilson who ain't a Speed Freak. So who the fuck is *your* Wilson?'

'Never mind,' Gumshoe said.

'Come on,' Snake Eyes responded amiably, already forgetting the question, slipping down into the seat of his automobile, beside the vampirish Bonnie Packard. 'Let's go and tease some Full Metal Jackets and see how the cards fall. This is Viva Las Vegas time.'

'Wow!' Bonnie screamed.

Heart palpitating, head spinning, experiencing what seemed to be an abruptly heightened reality, Gumshoe cast a grin in the direction of Snake Eyes and Bonnie, now sitting side by side in the latter's tuned-up, rainbow-coloured Mazda sedan. Feeling a surprising spasm of envy for Snake Eyes, though instantly suppressing it, he kicked his silver-tanked Yamaha 400 into life, heard the awesome roaring of the many other Speed Tribe motorcycles and automobiles, then burned out of the sports stadium, into the dangerous night, preparing, as he choked in exhaust fumes, to hunt down the hunters.

So who the fuck's Wilson? he wondered as he raced into darkness.

Chapter Five

As Michael approached Freedom Bay, marching resolutely across the vast, snow-covered plain, the mountains of Queen Maud Land appeared to be shifting, riser higher, until, from being initially a thin inky ribbon on the otherwise white horizon, they had become a towering series of jagged, ice-capped peaks that dominated the unpolluted azure sky. Almost directly ahead, coming closer as he advanced, was the broad cliff face honey-combed with the tunnels that led into the community. Thrusting out from some of the tunnels were the docking bays for the vertical-landing aircraft. Exterior elevators joined one level to another, rising hundreds of feet above the ground.

As Michael came closer, he saw the many aircraft – disc-shaped, pyramid-shaped, pear-shaped and triangular – resting on their landing zones located around the cave mouths at the base of the towering cliff, protected by overhanging snow- and ice-covered ledges. The biggest craft, the 300-feet diameter saucer-shaped 'mother' craft, rarely used these days, seemed enormously and eerily beautiful from here, glinting a silvery grey in the brilliant Antarctic sunlight.

Michael kept walking, deliberately avoiding the immense glittering geodesic dome housing the research establishments in order to enter Freedom Bay proper, where he knew that his parents and Dr Brandenberg would be waiting for him – none of them too pleased with him. The final steps of his long journey brought him to an immense hallway of unbreakable glass extending from a deeply shadowed cavernous area in the base of the mountain, not far from where the saucers were parked. Just inside the hallway, looking out over the vast snow-covered plains of Antarctica, was the stone statue of Robert Stanford that had been raised there in #1 on the orders of Dr Brandenberg. Looking up at that statue, which showed a young, handsome man with a proud face, Michael felt a similar pride stirring in himself, making him even more eager to return to the World and wrest it back from the cyborgs.

Using a hand-held remote-control device, he opened the glass door and entered the immense hallway that led into the ground floor of Freedom Bay. The door closed automatically behind him as he walked past the statue of Robert Stanford and entered the great mountain complex through a steel door placed in the solid rock of the mountain's interior. Opening automatically, the door led into the expansive white-walled office, its walls lined with technical and scientific books, that had formerly been used by Robert Stanford's tragic friend, Professor Frederick Epstein, and that was now preserved as a memorial to him. Like Stanford, Epstein had spent many years back in the 1970s trying to unravel the so-called 'flying saucer mystery', only to end up here as one of John Wilson's brain-implant workers. Indeed, it was in this very room that Robert Stanford had bid his old friend farewell and walked out into the white hell of the Antarctic wilderness, preferring to die rather than stay here as a slave.

Crossing the office, Michael glanced at the central desk, imagining Dr Epstein sitting behind it and talking to the much younger, healthier Stanford. Erasing this vision from his mind, he entered the elevator at the far side of the room and pressed the button marked ASCEND. Like Epstein's office, the lift had white-painted steel walls, with only a small window in one wall to give a fleeting view of the various floors as Michael was carried up through the hollowed-out interior of the mountain.

Those glimpses were enough to remind him of the sheer size of the colony and of the fact that Wilson's technological and scientific work – though certainly not his hideous biological and other surgical experiments – was being continued under Dr Brandenberg's supervision for a more humane purpose. Out there, Michael knew, hacked from the interior of the mountain, were the original workshops and laboratories where Wilson's master-and-slave colony had created the first great flying saucers, produced an additional wealth of scientific innovation, and, less nobly, conducted gross experiments on human beings to create the cyborgs that now ruled the world. Thankfully, once the Old Age United States had taken over the colony, running it first under the supervision of their own scientists and then under that of Dr Brandenberg, the cyborg experimentation had been dropped. Wilson's medical and surgical innovations, once hideously misused, had then been used instead for good, alleviating pain instead of inflicting it and extending human life instead of creating monstrous cyborgs through the ghastly mutation of formerly normal human beings.

The elevator stopped one floor below the top level, where Dr Brandenberg had Wilson's old office, and Michael stepped out into a corridor that had been, like the rest of the colony, hacked out of the interior of the mountain. The corridor ran in a great circle around it, about thirty metres below the summit. Advancing along the constantly curving corridor, on a floor of smooth, tile-covered steel, between walls of white-painted, steel-covered rock, the outer wall bare, the inner one lined with off-white doors (the apartments of various members of the colony), he soon arrived at his own apartment, which he shared with his parents and younger sister. Opening the door with the same hand-held remote-control device that he had used to enter the hallway on the ground floor, he stepped into an apartment of softly rounded, high-ceilinged rooms, so designed because those harmonious shapes had been found to encourage feelings of peace and well-being. Indeed, Michael had such feelings as soon as he entered the apartment and took in at a glance its soothingly pale-coloured, body-moulded furniture, abstract, almost dreamlike paintings, soft wall-to-wall white carpeting, and potted plants and flowers that survived all year round in the gentle purple-red glow of fluorescent lamps that were radiating in the wavelengths necessary for optimum plant growth.

Hearing his mother and father talking in the kitchen, obviously preparing supper together, which was something they enjoyed doing, he let the door close automatically behind him, then made his way directly to his own room. Though softly rounded and high-ceilinged like the other rooms, it was much more cluttered. The pale blue-and-yellow walls were covered with shelves of books, the semicircular white-laminated desk was dominated by an advanced computer, printer and tall speakers, and the white-framed bed was littered with CD-ROMs and computer diskettes. One part of the gently curving wall was taken up with a wide-screen TV-and-video with attached music centre; a violin and guitar lay across a triangular, salt-covered table a few feet away, and a white-painted, metre-high cardboard pyramid stood on another table a few metres from the instruments.

After stripping off his arctic clothing, Michael showered, shaved and then put on casual clothing of the kind that had not changed since the colony had been taken out of Wilson's hands: blue denims, light green roll-neck pullover, socks and rubber-soled brown-leather shoes, all made in a Freedom Bay workshop and distributed free of charge. These clothes could safely be worn inside because the whole colony, including the living accommodations, utilized solar heat, drawing the sun's energy in through immense skylights placed strategically at various points in the mountain, storing it by means of solar-cell panels and heat-retaining eutectic salt containers, and distributing it via solar heat pumps designed by NASA way back in the mid-1970s and later utilized ingeniously by Wilson.

Before going in to see his parents, wondering if they had

found out about his absence, Michael distracted himself by checking the contents of his experimental preservation pyramid. Michael's work in the Parapsychological Research Department of Freedom Bay had indicated that just as the shape of a room could influence the human being in that room, so the shape of a container could influence an object placed within it. Studying the Egyptian pyramids as part of his research, he had learnt that the pyramid of Cheops, the Great Pyramid, was known to have unusual properties, such as the ability to promote rapid dehydration and thus preserve bodies in a mummified condition. This had been proven with experimental mice and other rodents deliberately left overnight in the Great Pyramid. Even more intriguing was the fact that blunt razor blades left overnight in the Great Pyramid would be sharp the next morning. This, Michael had deduced, was because the edge of a razor blade had a crystal structure: crystals grew by reproducing themselves, and the Great Pyramid, being itself shaped like a crystal or magnetite, acted as a resonator that encouraged crystal growth. Convinced, therefore, that there was a relationship between the shape of a space and the physical, chemical and biological processes taking place within that shape, Michael had constructed his own cardboard replica of the Great Pyramid, carefully making sure that the four isosceles triangles that constituted its sides each had the proportion, base to sides, of 15.7 to 14.94 and stood 10.0 of the same units high. When the structure was completed, he had placed the pyramid so that the base lines faced magnetic north-south and east-west. A stand 3.33 units high had been placed directly under the apex of the pyramid to hold the objects chosen by him for the experiment. Having placed a dead mouse and a used razor blade in the pyramid the day before yesterday, he now checked both and found that the mouse was mummified and the blunt razor blade was sharp again.

Satisfied, deciding to use the pyramid on a regular basis for the preservation of certain items, he threw the mummified mouse into his automatic garbage disposal unit, placed the newly sharpened razor blade on his desk, then picked up the violin standing beside the salt-covered table. Knowing that if his parents had found out about his absence they would not be pleased with him, he relaxed for fifteen minutes by creating a variety of visible vibration patterns. After laying the violin face-up on the table, he placed a thin metal plate on the instrument, spread a handful of salt on the plate, and then proceeded to create the patterns by drawing his bow across the strings. By falling only on those parts of the plate where there was no vibration, the salt arranged itself in a wide variety of beautiful patterns that had a soothing effect on the observer. Thus, after playing the violin for fifteen minutes, Michael felt relaxed enough to leave his room and go to see his parents.

He found them in the kitchen, having supper with his sister, Chloe. Two years younger than Michael and much loved by her parents and brother, Chloe, blonde-haired like Michael, but with porcelain skin, large blue eyes and delicate features, was just losing her baby fat and starting to develop into a shapely young lady. Michael's father, Joe Kimbrell, now forty-eight years old, had been a twenty-seven-year-old physicist working for NASA when, in 1999, he had been transferred to Freedom Bay, bringing his brand-new wife, Grace, with him. Grace had then been a meterologist, also working for NASA, and both of them were now doing the same work here in Freedom Bay. Three months after their arrival here, the cyborgs had taken over most of the world and, like most of the others here at that time, they had not been back to the US since. Michael, a planned child, as were all the children in the colony, had been born almost two years later, on 4 November #2, and Chloe, also carefully planned, had followed two years after. Dedicated to his work, which perhaps had kept him youthful, Joe was still a handsome man, looking about ten years younger than his actual age, with a thick thatch of reddish-blond hair and still-bright blue eyes. Grace, a rare beauty in her time, still with golden-blonde hair, was also dedicated to her work, which perhaps, as with her husband, had kept her looking much younger than she was.

On the other hand, Michael thought as he entered the kitchen-diner and caught his parents' disapproving looks, all those who lived in the colony did so under certain vitally necessary disciplines, including eating and drinking healthily, exercising regularly, having their health carefully monitored, and receiving medical treatment more advanced than anywhere else on Earth. For that very reason, most of them were more youthful and healthy for their age than they would have been out in the World. Ironically, this blessing was yet another of the fruits of John Wilson's hideous medical and biological experiments in the Old Age. Michael found this disturbing.

'Hi,' he said, taking the chair beside Chloe to face his father and mother across the table, its top covered with hot and cold vegetarian dishes made from high-yield crops matured in fluorescent-lit greenhouses right here in the colony and preserved by means of irradiation. The food looked and smelt delicious. 'Sorry I'm late.'

'I'll *bet* you are,' Chloe retorted, casting him a sideways glance and a mischievous grin.

'Are you?' his father said, not smiling at all. 'I seriously doubt that. I called you at your office in the dome and was told you had gone out. Did you leave the base again?'

Unable to tell a lie, Michael confessed, 'Yes, I did.'

His mother closed her eyes briefly, shaking her head disapprovingly from side to side, then opened her eyes again. They were blue, like Chloe's, and very steady.

'We expressly forbade you to do that,' she said.

Michael sighed. 'I know.'

'It's dangerous out there,' his mother said. 'You know you should never go out there unescorted and you promised not to.'

'No, I didn't,' Michael retorted. 'You and Dad insisted that I shouldn't go out there again, and though I listened to what you had to say, I sure as hell made no promises. I only listened. That's all.'

'Very smart,' Chloe said, again glancing sideways at him and grinning at his discomfort. '*I didn't promise; I just didn't reply* . . . I wish *I'd* thought of that one.'

'Shut up,' Michael said without malice.

'Not smart,' his father said, speaking to Chloe. 'Disingenuous. He uttered no lie, though he was planning to blatantly disobey us even as we were talking. Don't admire him for it.'

'You sometimes sound so puritanical,' Michael said, 'and it doesn't become you. You're not that kind of guy, Dad.'

'Smart with your tongue as well, are you?' his mother said tartly, though she, also, was too kind to carry off severity with any great degree of conviction.

'I'm not trying to be smart, Mom. I'm just stating a fact. From what I've heard about Dad, *he* wasn't a blue-eyed boy at my age. I mean, *you* told me that.'

'Oh, did she, indeed?' his father said, raising his eyebrows and glancing at his wife, clearly amused despite himself. Grace blushed and looked flustered. 'So what else did she tell you?'

'A lot,' Chloe chipped in, studying the spinach resting on her fork, all wide-eyed innocence. 'All those things you got up to in college, then later at NASA. She said you broke every rule in the book and were always in trouble. Real bright, Mom said, but pretty rebellious, refusing to do what you were told and always in hot water. Just like your son, Dad.'

'Thanks a million,' Joe said to Grace, who blushed a deeper crimson and became more flustered to see everyone staring at her.

'Well,' she stuttered, 'you *were* a little bit . . . And I was really just trying to amuse them with some . . .'

'Accurate recollections,' Chloe chipped in.

'Right,' Michael said.

'Wrong,' his father put in quickly, now finding it next to impossible to look stern. 'Your Mom was just winding you up. I may have done a few things here and there — what kid doesn't? — but I certainly wasn't as disobedient as you — and I did nothing dangerous.'

'Oh, no?' Chloe said tartly. 'What about the time you climbed the church tower at that military academy and stole the bell? You and some of your drunken buddies.'

'I might have told your mother that story to wind her up,' Joe said, 'but there's no proof that I was actually involved.'

'You were too drunk to remember, right?' Chloe said.

'You be quiet,' Chloe's mother said.

'Anyway,' Joe continued, turning to Michael, 'that wasn't quite the same thing. We're talking about the Antarctic wilderness here and, as you know damned well, *no one* is allowed to go out there alone. So why did you do it yet again?'

'I'm researching the history of Freedom Bay,' Michael began, 'and so—'

'You don't have to go out there to do that. We have all the historical records right here and—'

'I wanted to photograph the exact spot where Robert Stanford stepped onto that piece of pack ice, choosing his own way to die.'

'Hero-worship has its place in life, Michael, but not when it encourages you to go out there without an escort.'

'I was worried sick,' Grace said.

'You look fine,' Michael retorted.

'I was hoping you'd never come back,' Chloe said deadpan, 'so I could move into your bedroom, which is bigger than mine.'

'*I'm* bigger than *you*,' Michael reminded her, 'so I need more space.'

'Ha!'

'Let's stick to the point,' Joe said. 'More than once you've flagrantly broken the rules of this community and made even Dr Brandenberg angry. You're one of the best young men we've got, you'll be invaluable in the future, yet you're risking it all by ignoring what you're told and doing these crazy things. So why is that, Michael?'

'It's *because* I'm one of the best,' Michael said before he could stop himself, 'and that means I have a low boredom threshold.

Everyone tells me that I'm being prepared for the future, that some day I'll be used, but that particular day never seems to come and I'm growing frustrated. I've had enough education – I've done my work – now I need to do something more positive. Going out there, finding places like Stanford's departure point, gives me something to do other than study. Also, I go out there to meditate. You can't complain about that.'

'I'm pleased that you still meditate,' his mother said, 'but surely you don't have to do it out there.'

'The great silence of the wilderness is the best place of all for that purpose. My mind can roam in that silence.'

That statement made all of them, including Chloe, fall respectfully silent. Michael's meditation, for which he had been specially trained since childhood, had an almost religious importance in this community that otherwise was not religious. Though the meditation was used to gain temporary spiritually enlightening transcendence, it was also part of Michael's parapsychological training, undertaken to strengthen his skills in telepathy, telekinesis, thoughtography, psychometry and 'eyeless sight'. These skills would be needed for the fight against the cyborgs, many of which had developed certain parapsychological capabilities to replace the senses – hearing, taste and sight – that they had lost during their hideous surgical mutation. It was now known, for instance, that cyborgs whose mouths had been removed could communicate mentally, through telepathy, over great distances and that others, having lost their eyes, had developed eyeless sight: the ability to 'see' by sensing the force field around living creatures and 'feel' the colour of inanimate objects. (Though this seemed incredible, it was, Michael knew, no different from the way in which bats could 'see' with a sonar system that picked up echoes from other creatures or material objects and translated them into meaningful patterns.) Michael's abilities, however, did not stop there. He was also training himself, though meditation, in thoughtography (the ability to get thought images transferred onto photographic plates), which he could use for intelligence gathering from afar; and in psycho-metry, which enabled him to 'read' information from objects simply by handling them or to detect the traces of a person in a room long after he or she had left it. Last but not least, he was using the meditation to strengthen his abilities in telekinesis – moving objects from afar – so, all in all, the meditation was important and could not be ignored.

'All right,' his father finally said, breaking the lengthy silence, 'I'll accept that the meditation is important and that you may indeed be suffering from frustration and have other valid reasons for going out there all alone. So, despite the personal fears of myself and your mother, I'll support Dr Brandenberg if *he* gives you permission to go out there again.'

'I'll go and see him right now,' Michael said.

'You do that, son.'

'He gets away with murder,' Chloe said.

'Keep talking and I'll murder *you*,' Michael retorted as he pushed his chair back and stood up. 'I'll see you all later.'

Leaving the apartment, he made his way back along the same curving corridor until he came to the elevator. As the elevator carried him up to the very summit of the mountain, where Dr Brandenberg's office, formerly Wilson's office, was located, he thought of the conversation that he'd just had with his family and wondered if family life was as civilized out there in the World. He had thought about this often because he knew that Freedom Bay was something unique, a relatively small (pop. 587), self-sustaining scientific community isolated from the World and, so far as he knew, the only community on Earth that did not come under the rule of the cyborgs. For this very reason, Freedom Bay had been compelled to develop into an unusually disciplined society in which everyone played their part and certain rules of behaviour had to be strictly adhered to. Given the colony's isolation from the World, close family relationships were more important here than they were in the World and trust between the members of the community was equally vital. Thus, while Michael often felt frustrated, wanting to do more than Dr Brandenberg would presently let him, he felt secure here, at home, relaxed with his friends and family, and understood that not too many people out there in the World, particularly those his own age, could feel the same way about themselves. Their sense of community had been destroyed with the coming of the cyborgs and, according to what Dr Brandenberg had told him, they roved their cities in packs that preyed on one another. Having been born and bred in Freedom Bay, Michael could hardly conceive of such a society. But he still wanted to see it.

When the doors of the elevator opened, he stepped into a rectangular hallway, painted white and featureless except for the bay windows that offered a dizzying view of the various levels of the colony, hacked out of the interior of the mountain by Wilson's slave workers a long time ago. Glancing down, he saw the inner edges of the various floors that encircled the central well, one on top of the other, each linked to the others with catwalks and elevators, the various levels containing the workshops where the flying saucers and other forms of transport were constructed, as well as a wide variety of research laboratories, supply depots, administration buildings, a hospital, a school, a canteen, and everything else required for the maintenance of the colony. The central well itself, roughly hewn from the rocks, a good fifty metres wide and dropping all the way to the ground hundreds of metres below, would have been a black pit had it not been for the lights beaming out from the various floors to illuminate the darkness with an eerie, constantly flickering glow.

Looking down, Michael tried to imagine that great colony being built, the hundreds of slave workers starting at ground level and gradually making their way upwards over the years until the very summit had been reached. If anyone could have stood at the top of the mountain and somehow peered down through its untold millions of tons of frozen earth and rock as the slaves began their terrible task, the toiling figures would have looked like ants in an anthill down there, or like termites in a tree trunk. But they would have suffered like human beings, with blood, sweat and tears, many dying and being replaced by others as the work progressed. Michael thought of the ancient Egyptians, of the building of the pyramids, and realized that Wilson's achievement here was of a similar grandeur . . . and every bit as ruthless. Like the Pharaohs, Wilson had treated his labour force like pack animals, indifferent to their suffering, not counting the human cost; but now, a good seventy-five years later, his great bees' nest of a colony was still here and, more remarkably, still operating, though thankfully for a less obscene cause. This was a startling thought.

Turning away from the bay windows, Michael pressed the bell on the intercom fixed to the door facing the elevator.

'Yes?' a man replied, his voice trembling and electronically distorted by the intercom system.

'It's Michael Kimbrell. Can I come in?'

'Please do,' the voice said.

Hearing the lock click, Michael pushed the door open and stepped into what had once been Wilson's office and was now used by the present head of the colony . . . Dr Lee Brandenberg.

Chapter Six

———◦◦◦◦———

Roaring out of the MCI Arena on his silver-tanked Yamaha 400 motorcycle, just minutes before the midnight curfew imposed by the cyborgs, Gumshoe felt the hot rush of the amphetamine and was raised up high on a wave of druggy exhilaration. Hot on the tail of Snake Eyes's rainbow-coloured, souped-up Mazda sedan, he could see his crazy friend in the moonlit darkness and, seated beside him, bare arm thrown across his shoulders, the green-and-pink head of the short-haired Long Hair, Bonnie Packard.

Feeling a spasm of jealousy, which was not a familiar emotion and so left him confused, Gumshoe glanced back over his shoulder and saw the rest of the Speed Freaks coming up behind him, trying to overtake one another, dodging and weaving dangerously, engines roaring, horns honking, on their powerful motorcycles and souped-up, vividly painted automobiles. Meeting no resistance in Chinatown which was, given the midnight curfew, absolutely empty, Snake Eyes led them north, heading for Mount Vernon Square. Gumshoe knew just what Snake Eyes was doing. He was out for a long trip.

Following in the wake of Snake Eyes's Mazda, holding his position between it and the Speed Freaks coming up behind him, Gumshoe went with the amphetamine, letting it take him where it would, and saw the stars as enormous, glittering diamonds in the velvet sheet of the sky. The stars seemed to be alive, blinking on and off, pulsating, and Gumshoe longed to be out there in a spaceship, traversing the cosmos.

As he followed Snake Eye around Mount Vernon Square and into Massachusetts Avenue, as empty as Chinatown had been, he wondered what it would have been like to have lived here in the Old Age, before the coming of the cyborgs, when there was no such thing as a curfew and normal people, not just gangs like the Speed Freaks, stayed out to all hours. Nowadays, given the curfew, Washington DC was like a ghost town late at night, though other motorcycle and hot-rod gangs, the odd wino or crazy person, occasionally some rich folk from Foggy Bottom taking a chance by coming home late from a social gathering, and, of course, the constantly patrolling Full Metal Jackets, could produce a few surprises, good and bad, if you kept on the move. Feeling the wind beating noisily at his face, Gumshoe, boosted by the amphetamine, was certainly on the move.

Having seen nothing so far, the Speed Freaks behind him had started to amuse themselves by playing dangerous games. Gunning the engines of their vehicles, honking their horns, bawling obscene comments and grinning in drugged, beatific amusement, they were trying to overtake one another by weaving rapidly, driving along the sidewalks, forcing other drivers off the road by bouncing lightly against their cars, and even kicking out at other motorcyclists to make them careen and go into potentially dangerous skids.

Two came abreast of Gumshoe, a Skyline on one side, a Kawasaki 250cc on the other, both their Speed Freak riders grinning crazily. They tried forcing him off the road by cutting across in front of him, between him and Snake Eyes's Mazda, which was still out front. Gumshoe gunned his engine and roared ahead, spewing exhaust fumes over those left behind, and came abreast of Snake Eyes in seconds. He saw Snake Eyes's mad grin.

'Pretty nifty move, pal!' Snake Eyes shouted with Bonnie grinning sardonically beside him.

'Those dumb assholes,' Gumshoe bawled back. 'They're more dangerous than the Full Metal Jackets.'

'Fuckin' A!' Snake Eyes shouted.

Passing the National Postal Museum, approaching Union Station, they saw a BMW up ahead, coming towards them at a stately pace. Knowing that the driver could only be a government worker with special permission from the cyborgs to work late at night (his licence-plate number would be recognized by any remote-controlled SARGE, Prowler, or flying sensing device – a 'football' – sent out by the cyborgs), the Speed Freaks behind Gumshoe let out whoops of joy, like Indian war whoops, jerked the front wheels of their motorcycles up into the air like cowboys riding broncos, went into rapid 360-degree spins and came out of them again, still in the saddle, then spread out across the road and accelerated rapidly to block the path of the oncoming vehicle. Obviously shocked to see them, the driver of the BMW swung desperately to the side, bouncing up onto the sidewalk and coming to a grinding halt. But some of the Speed Freaks cut loose from the others to circle the stalled car on their motor-cycles and smash its windows with bricks that they swung above their heads in silk-stocking slings.

Glancing back over his shoulder as he continued along Massachusetts Avenue, Gumshoe saw the driver of the BMW, a portly man in a grey suit, stumbling out of his beat-up vehicle and attempting desperately to make a run for it. He had only taken a few steps, however, when one of the motorcyclists raced up beside him, leaned expertly to one side, and struck him on the back of the head with the brick in his sling. The man was plunging face first to the sidewalk as Gumshoe, feeling as high as a kite, looked to the front again.

In his urge to see what was going on behind him, he had slipped slightly behind and now a lot of the other Speed Freaks, still led by Snake Eyes, were spread out in front of him, their motorcycles and souped-up jalopies making a hell of a din. Reaching Union Station, which, though closed right now because of the curfew, was still more or less in operation with the consent of the cyborgs (since you couldn't import, export or leave the country by train), the Speed Freaks spread out even more to sweep across the plaza at the front of the building and circle the fountain a few times. The statue of Columbus and the Freedom Bell, once respected but now neglected, were badly chipped and covered in graffiti.

Following them on his motorcycle, observing everything with a drug-enhanced, vividly heightened perception, as hallucinatory as a dream, Gumshoe saw a couple of dishevelled winos raising their sleepy heads where they were sleeping under the triple-arched colonnaded entrance to the huge granite building. Seeing the Speed Freaks now roaring around the fountain, they jumped up with a surprising display of energy, fear being a strong incentive, and hurried into the main railway terminal, wanting to keep out of sight.

Holding his lead position, with Bonnie Packard still beside him, her bare arm around his unwashed neck, Snake Eyes led his bikers and hot-rodders south along First Street, which was empty, between the old Senate Office buildings, now being used by the cyborgs as some kind of workshops, and then past the Capitol, still dominated by the Rotunda, reportedly once illuminated every night but now completely dark.

Glancing up, Gumshoe was reminded by the many ugly cracks criss-crossing the ornate 180-feet-high dome that it, as well as other important buildings in the area, had been badly damaged by the infrasounds of the immense flying saucers that had descended vertically over the city on the first day of #I. That the occasional light still burned in the vast complex was nothing mysterious, since the cyborgs had made no attempt to interfere with the general running of the city's administration and, though abducting (along with the President) all of the leading senators, none of whom were ever seen again, they had let the less influential House of Representatives remain to run the country as best they could in the cyborg-dominated New Age. As the cyborgs, since abducting the President, had not permitted a new President to be elected, what was left of 'free' America was run from the Capitol with an ever-changing rota of representatives, both Democratic and Republican, approved by the cyborgs. It was widely believed that no representative received approval until he or she had been brainwashed by the cyborgs into being absolutely obedient. Certainly, since they slavishly toed the cyborg line, this could have been true.

A large flying saucer, rotating and glowing eerily, was hovering above the Rotunda as the motorcycles and souped-up cars roared past. When the Speed Freaks kept going, passing between the south wing of the Capitol and the Library of Congress, the flying saucer, which was there as a sentinel, did not descend to harass them.

Turning into Independence Avenue, a commercial corridor during the day but now dark and empty, the Speed Freaks accelerated, motorcyclists and car drivers alike, to take advantage of the long, straight road that ran west all the way along the Mall to the Washington Monument. Now racing each other with a reckless disregard for personal safety, they passed what had been, in the Old Age, some of the most famous tourist sights of the city. Formerly illuminated at nights to form a spectacular *son et lumière* display, they were now sadly neglected and, like most of the other buildings of the city, plunged into uninviting darkness. While lonely lights glowed from offices here and there, these were few and far between.

As they passed the overgrown lawns of the Smithsonian Quadrangle, its entrance pavilions in a shocking state of dis-repair, the iron gates covered in rust, Gumshoe accelerated to catch up with Snake Eyes, though he deliberately came up on the side where Bonnie Packard was seated. Noting that she still had her bare arm around Snake Eyes's unwashed neck, he came in close to the speeding Mazda, leaned sideways at a dangerous angle, the rushing wind beating at him, exhilarating him, and threw the short-cropped Long Hair a big grin.

'What are you doing with that fucking deadbeat,' he bawled, 'in that beat-up old jalopy? Why not transfer to the back of my bike and check out real life?'

Bonnie turned her head to give him a measuring stare. Her hazel eyes, brightened by amphetamine, looked unreal without eyebrows, in the painted stripes across her face, and the fake blood trickling from her blue lips made her seem even stranger.

'Real life?' she replied, shouting against the wind. 'That's what I'd find on your clapped-out motorcycle?'

'Better believe it, Long Hair.'

'You wouldn't know real life if it was shoved up your ass with a pitchfork.'

'That's it, babe! Shove it to him!'

Snake Eyes broke out in deranged laughter and slapped one hand on his steering wheel as Gumshoe, still grinning, straightened up and then shot on ahead of them. Still trying to impress the Long Hair, he leaned the bike hard to the right, sweeping around into 14th, catching a glimpse of the soaring obelisk of the Washington Monument as he headed deliberately for the most dangerous place you could be after the curfew . . . the cyborg-protected White House area. But this was exactly what they had come out for. This was the buzz.

Even before he had reached the area east of the Ellipse, Gumshoe saw that a dome-shaped flying saucer, over a hundred feet in diameter, its whitish-metallic body, not rotating yet, giving off an eerie, pulsating glow, was hovering directly above the White House and that a Prowler and a couple of SARGEs were patrolling the road straight ahead. The SARGEs were scout telerobots with thermal imaging and zoom surveillance equipment contained in four-wheeled, all-terrain frames resembling, and no larger than, the average dune buggy. The Prowler, however, was something else again. Originally built, like the SARGE, for the US Army and Marine Corps, it was a completely automated Programmable Robot Observer with Logical Enemy Response. The size and shape of a medium tank, a steel monolith on steel treads, it had sensors that enabled it to detect body or engine heat and movement, decide for itself whether the observed object – or person – was friendly or hostile, and act accordingly. If it attacked, its target didn't stand a chance, as the Prowler's former 105mm cannons and M60 machine-guns had been replaced by the cyborgs with powerful laser weapons.

Aware of this, Gumshoe deliberately raced straight at the approaching Prowler, as if about to ram it. Then, when he saw the snouts of the laser weapons turning towards him, which gave him a thrill, he grinned and made a sharp left, leaning the bike way over, turning into a deserted stretch of Constitution Avenue just as the lasers split the darkness behind him, hissing and crackling, their phosphorescent beams filled with millions of sparks. Whether or not the beams had struck anyone coming up behind Gumshoe he didn't know. But he certainly heard explosions behind him, indicating that the lasers had, at least, hit *something* solid – perhaps the road or a wall.

Exhilarated by the danger, burning up in the amphetamine rush, he glanced back over his shoulder and saw Snake Eyes's rainbow-coloured Mazda emerging from clouds of dust, obviously billowing up from pulverized concrete. As Snake Eyes, with Bonnie still beside him, raced towards Gumshoe, the rest of the Speed Freaks turned the corner behind him, also emerging from the swirling dust created by the explosions, weaving expertly left and right to make themselves difficult targets for the Prowler that had fired upon Gumshoe. Stoned out of their heads and therefore fearless, they were whooping and hollering.

Feeling like a kid, Gumshoe turned left again, into 14th Street, racing between the Department of Commerce and the Reagan Building. Then he circled back around the National Aquarium, deliberately heading for the White House Visitor Center. In his souped-up Mazda, Snake Eyes soon caught up with him. As they approached the junction at the eastern perimeter of the White House area, the Prowler that they thought they had left behind suddenly came around the corner to block the road.

'Shit!' Gumshoe exclaimed. Braking abruptly, he jerked his front wheel off the ground, went into a 180-degree turn, spinning around on his rear wheel, the tyre screeching like a stuck pig, and caught a blurred glimpse of Snake Eyes's Mazda slewing to the left. The motorcycle's front wheel slammed back to the ground, bouncing up and down, the spokes vibrating like crazy and making a shrill twanging sound as the Mazda mounted the sidewalk and crashed head-on into the wall of the National Aquarium, making a God-almighty din, with glass exploding and pieces of metal falling off it.

Gumshoe was heading back the way he had come, straight into the mass of oncoming motorcycles and hot-rod cars, already scattering to avoid him, suddenly roaring all around him. But when he glanced back over his shoulder and saw the Mazda crumpled against the damaged wall, clouds of dust swirling over it to slightly obscure it, he automatically turned back in a fancy, tight, screeching circle and went to the rescue.

Snake Eyes and Bonnie had already clambered out of the wrecked Mazda when the tank-like Prowler fired its front-mounted laser weapons. Two thin beams of hissing, crackling, dazzling light filled with sparks seemed to appear out of nowhere – they were just there, suddenly, illuminating the darkness: two phosphorescent cords linking the Prowler to the Mazda. The Mazda turned first red-hot, then white-hot, and then suddenly disintegrated, becoming a mass of boiling dust, until finally it exploded – a cloud of dust exploding – as Snake Eyes and Bonnie lay belly-down on the road, protecting their heads with their clasped hands.

Hardly knowing what he was doing but realizing that he was no longer high from the amphetamine, that it was starting to wear off just when he needed it the most, Gumshoe skidded to a halt between Snake Eyes and Bonnie as the former jumped back to his feet and stared – wide-eyed, outraged, disbelieving – at the dust settling down where his Mazda had once been.

'Oh, fuck!' he exclaimed as Bonnie, not getting up but staying belly-down on the road, started wriggling frantically towards Gumshoe. 'Those bastards have—'

'Get down!' Gumshoe bawled at Snake Eyes.

At that moment, however, as the other Speed Freaks on their motorcycles and souped-up jalopies boldly raced past the Prowler, then turned north to get away before they could be zapped by its lasers, a flying saucer about a metre in diameter, the kind known as a 'football', apparently seamless and rotating so rapidly that it radiated a white-hot glow, came down from the sky – probably from the larger saucer hovering over the White House – and abruptly froze in mid-air to hover a few metres above Snake Eyes. Not spinning now, hardly moving at all, merely bobbling lightly up and down like a cork in water, it shot a beam of light obliquely into Snake Eyes's surprised, upturned face. As Gumshoe looked on, horrified, wrenched back to earth from his drugged euphoria, Snake Eyes screamed and clutched his head, shaking it violently between his hands, staggering backwards, his knees bending. Then he shuddered as if having a fit, fell to his knees and keeled over. He hit the ground with a sickening thud.

'Oh, fuck!' Bonnie exclaimed. Jumping back to her feet, she raced up to Gumshoe, who was still in the saddle of his motorcycle, propping it up with his outspread legs and keeping the engine ticking over, preparing to take off. 'Get me out of here!' Bonnie bawled. She swung a leg over the pillion, came down hard on the rear saddle, then slipped her arms around him, clasping her hands across his belly, pressing herself tightly to him. 'Move it, dummy! she screamed.

Gumshoe took off. He was doing a tight U-turn, intending to go back the way he had come, as the Prowler and two SARGEs advanced along the street to pick up Snake Eyes's prostrate body. The other Speed Freaks had vanished, heading north, and Gumshoe went in the same direction, turning into 14th Street as the football pursued him. It moved so fast that it appeared not to move at all (it just blinked out behind him and then reappeared in front of him, spinning rapidly again on its axis, glowing eerily, a few metres ahead), but he shot under it just as its dazzling laser beam cut through the darkness like a shimmering sword, angled down to the ground.

'Fucker nearly got me,' Gumshoe said, speaking more to himself than to Bonnie.

'It got Snake Eyes,' Bonnie replied. 'We won't see him again.'

'That dumb bastard,' Gumshoe said.

But he wasn't too safe himself, he realized when he heard an almost imperceptible rushing sound overhead, coming from behind and racing on in front, slapping at him like a brief gust of wind as it passed – a Full Metal Jacket, the football, in flight. He was heading north along 14th, approaching Thomas Circle, when the football abruptly materialized again directly ahead, silvery grey and glowing with heat, hovering a few metres above the road and blocking his way, about to fire its paralysing laser weapon.

'Oh, fuck!' Gumshoe exclaimed, wrenching at the handlebars and cutting across to the opposite side of the road as the laser beam spat down through the darkness where he would have been if he hadn't changed direction. The footballs were certainly fast in flight, moving from one place to another in the blinking of an eye, but luckily they then took time to make their calculations, to ascertain with their thermal imaging and sonar sensors if the 'presence' within their range was a friend or a foe. Gumshoe took advantage of this knowledge to get around the football and continue along the road, turning north-west at Thomas Circle and burning into Massachusetts Avenue as fast as he could, which was, on his Yamaha 400, very fast indeed. He felt the pressure of Bonnie's body, her breasts and belly, against his curved back and it made him feel strange.

I'm coming down, he thought. *The amphetamine's wearing off. That usually means I'll feel depressed and panicky and this isn't the time for it. Stay cool. Think of Elvis. Go and see the Cowboy.*

Thinking of the Cowboy always gave him confidence, so he decided to head for where his weird friend lived, in a waterfront dive in Anacostia. Deciding that the safest way would be to go along the Potomac River, he turned left at Dupont Circle and headed down New Hampshire Avenue. The road wasn't empty. Straight ahead, the other Speed Freaks were weaving wildly left and right to avoid a Prowler that had blocked the entrance to Washington Circle and was firing at them with its powerful laser weapons. Those magical beams of light, which looked harmless in the darkness, could slice through human beings as if they were butter, punch holes in concrete walls, and disintegrate automobiles and motorcycles – as had been so graphically demonstrated back at the National Aquarium.

At that moment, even as Gumshoe slowed down, trying to decide what to do, he saw a couple of the Speed Freaks, caught in the laser beams, flying off their motorcycles, as if punched by invisible fists, and crashing down to the ground while their riderless vehicles careened wildly this way and that, then fell over, sliding and spinning along the road, making appalling screeching noises and sending up showers of sparks. At the same time, one of the automobiles was struck by a laser beam and instantly turned red-hot. In less than a second, it had gone from red- to white-hot, then it disintegrated while still on the move, weaving wildly left and right as the driver fried inside. Finally it exploded with an ear-splitting roar. The other Speed Freaks, coming down off their high, now clearly in a panic, were doing everything they could to get around the Prowler. But some of them crashed into others, causing even more madness and mayhem.

Gumshoe had slowed almost to a halt when the Prowler made an abrupt U-turn and turned into Pennsylvania Avenue, obviously about to protect the route to the White House by stopping the Speed Freaks heading in that direction. Grabbing this opportunity, he accelerated along the road, weaving left and right to avoid the smashed-up motorcycles and the remains of the dead Speed Freaks, some of whom were missing limbs that had been amputated by the laser beams. Then he swept around Washington Circle and continued on in the direction of the Potomac. He saw moonlight on the water, caught a glimpse of the few scattered lights of Arlington, but turned east before reaching the river and kept going until he came to the Lincoln Memorial. There he turned into Ohio Drive, running alongside the river. While he could see spherical lights gliding high in the sky – flying saucers on routine flights not connected with curfew breakers – there wasn't another vehicle in sight and that made him feel better.

'Where are we going?' Bonnie asked, resting her chin on his shoulder as she shouted into his ear.

'Anacostia!' he shouted back.

'This is the longest way round,' Bonnie informed him.

'It's also the safest, sweetheart.'

'I'm not your sweetheart.'

'That football,' he continued, ignoring her correction, 'must have sent a message to the other Full Metal Jackets, telling them what direction we were heading in. That's why they were waiting for us at Washington Circle. Now that whole area around the White House will be crawling with more of those bastards—'

'You bet!' Bonnie interjected.

'—so I figure it's best to keep as far away from there as possible. We'll take the next bridge across the river. That way we'll be pretty safe.'

'Right,' Bonnie replied, shifting in her seat to let him feel her warm, yielding breasts and belly. 'But why Anacostia? I thought you lived in Georgetown.'

'I do. But I don't think I should go back there tonight. That football might have identified me. So I'm gonna see an old friend instead. You wanna come or you wanna be dropped off somewhere?'

'I'll stick with you,' Bonnie said. 'I'm still shocked by what happened to Snake Eyes and I don't feel so good. I mean, I'm scared. I'll admit that.'

'The amphetamine's wearing off,' Gumshoe reminded her, 'and that never feels good.'

'Yeah, right. But what happened to Snake Eyes makes it worse. We won't see him again.'

'Probably not,' Gumshoe said.

As he took the bridge across the Anacostia River, he glanced down at the water, which was black, stippled with moonlight, and felt that he was staring into the black hole that would surely swallow up Snake Eyes. For indeed, though the football's laser beam was only a paralysing device – not as powerful as the beams that had killed the other Speed Freaks, slicing through them, cutting off limbs – the Prowler would have picked up the unconscious Snake Eyes and spirited him away with all the other still-alive unfortunates picked up the same night.

Where they were taken to no one seemed to know, though there *were* enough rumours to keep tongues wagging with nightmarish tales about hideous surgical experimentation and various forms of mind control. Though Gumshoe didn't give too much credence to such gossip, which also proliferated right across the World Wide Web, he wasn't about to reject it entirely and, in fact, thought about it a lot more than he wanted to. He really didn't want to brood over it because he had never fully recovered from the loss of his parents and was tormented with questions about what might have happened to them after they had disappeared. The very thought that they might have become the victims of some dreadful form of cyborg experimentation was more than he could bear, though certainly the possibility was real enough and had, in truth, given him many nightmares. Now, when he thought of Snake Eyes and what might become of him, his old fears for his parents were resurrected and made his post-amphetamine downer even more fearful.

Fuck it, Gumshoe thought, trying to defeat his fear with fake indifference. *We all take our chances and he took his. It's life and life only.*

He was now cruising through Anacostia, on the south-east shore of the Potomac, formerly a predominantly black area with a long history of social and economic problems that had only worsened with the arrival of the cyborgs and the breakdown in the city's infrastructure caused by their seeming indifference to it. Here, in the midst of the old low-income housing projects of the 1950s and 1960s, a lot of the houses had broken windows patched up with cardboard and newspapers, the shops had windows covered in protective mesh-wire cages, the pool halls were guarded by thugs, black and white, wearing T-shirts and denims, and the broken-down bars were used by hookers and their pimps, most of whom were poor whites who had been forced out of their homes across the river and who had landed up here.

'I don't like it here,' Bonnie said. 'This place gives me the creeps.'

'It's not as bad as it looks,' Gumshoe told her. 'At least the Full Metal Jackets don't come here, which means that life in these parts is more easygoing. That's why the Cowboy lives here.'

He had, in fact, reached the end of the old housing project area and was slowing down as he came to an isolated riverfront shack located about a mile out of town. Here he stopped the motorcycle and gazed at the shack. It stood in a small area of fenced-in lawn, set back about twenty metres from the river bank where a run-down rowboat was tied to a small mooring. Glancing across the river, Gumshoe saw spherical lights in the sky, eerily beautiful . . . deadly . . . the cyborgs' ever-watchful flying saucers. Shivering, he lowered his gaze again to study the shack straight ahead. Made of wood, with a corrugated-iron roof, it faced the river and had a porch running along it. Someone was sitting on the porch, silhouetted against the moonlit bend in the river, his booted feet up on the railing, a stetson hat on his head. Gumshoe nodded affirmatively and smiled.

'That's the Cowboy,' he said.

Chapter Seven

───────◆◦◦◦◆───────

You will come to me in time. You all do in the end. You will come to me, not knowing it is me you wish to find, because I represent what it is you most fear and yet desperately need. I am Evolution. I am what will be. I am the end of the long line that began in the cosmic stew and I will take you where it is you must go before the sun dies.

When the sun dies, the Earth will die also.

I understood this from childhood, my first childhood long ago, when I stood in the wheat fields of Iowa and studied the heavens. I was golden-haired then, as indeed I am again, and the sun was an immense silvery orb in a dazzling blue sky. I stood alone in a field of wheat, the stalks shoulder-high around me, and I squinted into the sun's dazzling striations, responding to them, even at ten years old, with one simple question:

When will the sun die?

That question turned me into a scientist and gave me my one religion. I realized that the sun would die eventually, taking with it Earth's heat and light, and that long before that happened every form of life on Earth would be extinguished. Man's time on Earth, therefore, would be brutally short if he simply followed Nature's course. Still an animal, he would die off like the dinosaurs as his life-giving sun died.

Something had to be done.

Thus that golden-haired boy, at ten years of age, found something to live for: the changing of man's destiny through science and, incidentally, the creation of a new kind of man as a means of continuance.

I have never strayed from that path.

Now, in my second coming, resurrected through my own genius, I am continuing the task I embarked upon in that wheat field in Iowa. I am golden-haired again, my skin unblemished, my health sound, and though regressive minds might view me as unnatural, I accept what I am without qualms. I am not who I was, since the dead cannot return, but I am a genetically identical human being and my original environment, experience and evolution have been carefully, rigorously implanted in me from the day I was born. Therefore, though I am not the original 'me', I know all that he knew and am impelled by the same drives and motives. Like him, I have only the one religion. That religion is science.

I am loved and loathed for this. The historical records prove this fact. Nevertheless, as I have no vanity, since personal feelings do not impinge upon me (as they did not for the original 'me') the responses to what I have done so far, the loving and the loathing, can have no effect upon my future decisions. I am what I am and I will do what must be done because I know that I was created for this purpose. The instructions left by my predecessor were followed to the letter and my rebirth was accomplished without problems.

I am here. I exist.

This is all that matters. Nothing else can be considered. What seems unnatural to some is perfectly natural to me and the evolution of man into machine is a natural, inevitable progression. I am different from the others in that I am not a cyborg, a man/machine hybrid, nor a clone like the other 'normal' ones, though like the latter I am certainly different and none the worse for it.

The cyborgs were once human beings, with human features and human thoughts, but now they are hardly human at all and their thoughts are strictly limited. They have artifical hearts, bionic audio transmitters for ears, sonar sensors for eyes, plastic arteries, synthetic bones and, where necessary, synthetic skin; thus some of them are more machine than man. Do they suffer horror and despair? No, they do not. In fact, their brains have been implanted with electrodes that control their every emotion, obliterate childhood memories, and keep self-awareness at a level shared by humanity's domestic pets.

No, I am not like them at all, being physically normal; but equally, though I may look the same, I am different from the clones, created from the DNA of *those now dead and used where a normal appearance is necessary: in the world of 'real' people. Unlike me, the clones were not born in the womb and this, more than anything else, makes them a different species. I am still of the human race.*

My surrogate mother is dead. I do not know who she was. By the early 1980s we were able to probe the double helix with powerful electron microscopes, then snip out sections of the chromosomal genetic programme and replace them with sections from another living organism — plant, animal or human. I was created, or re-created, with strands of my own DNA. Spliced out of the genetic blueprint for the original me, just before I — or 'he' — died, the microscopic strands of my DNA were kept in a culture dish in one of our many undersea laboratories until such time as my scientists, all brain-implanted and programmed to be loyal to me even after my death, had perfected the technique of creating an embryo and inserting it into a living womb. My mother, therefore, was a physically perfect female specimen abducted by one of my flying saucers and used solely as a surrogate womb.

Forty years ago, shortly after my Antarctic colony was taken over by the US, the embryo created from my DNA was inserted into that unknown woman's womb and I was born, nine months later, in the usual manner. Within hours of my birth, the woman was terminated and I was placed in the care of cyborgs specially programmed to think of nothing but my physical and mental well-being. The problem of the denial of the normal mother-and-child bonding, that could have led to serious emotional problems in later life, was solved by ensuring my creature comforts and by educating me, from my second year on, with a mass of information stored on vast databases and retrieved on interactive video disks. The information included not only history, geography, literature, philosophy, politics, mathematics and all the sciences, but also the history of the original 'me', including 'his' childhood and daily thoughts, the latter culled from his own writings, as well as countless subtexts that gradually erased the need for an emotional bond with a natural mother. Thus, by the time I was ten years old (the same age that the original 'me' had been when he first realized that the sun would die), I was by normal standards a genius, had no need for anyone other than myself, and was dedicated, as the other 'me' had also been, to the unfettered pursuit of knowledge and, ultimately, to the creation of a new human race — one that will take us to the stars before the sun dies.

The creation of that new race, a super-race, is now under way. My own rebirth took place during the relatively early days of eugenics, before the proper cloning of human beings had been perfected, but great progress has been made since then. Now test-tube clones, those born outside the womb, are a large part of our work force and are, indeed, in charge of the cyborgs, under my overall command. The cyborgs had their day but it was very short-lived and now, with the coming of the clones, they will be made redundant.

For the time being, however, they still have their uses, particularly because, being a man/machine hybrid, though now more machine than man, with many parts made of steel, they can withstand abnormal heat and pressure. Also, as their life-support functions of nourishment and waste-product removal are controlled by a central computer, they can 'exist' for as long as required without food or water. Thus, they are perfect for work on the seabed and in outer space; as workers or soldiers who virtually have no limits and cannot be killed.

The clones, on the other hand, though brought to life in test tubes and reared in artificial wombs, are still physically 'human' in most respects. For this reason, apart from their function as general supervisors, they are used mainly outside our colonies — on the seabed, on the dark side of the moon, and in the real world — for work that requires interaction with normal humans who, though willing to work with us, find it psychologically and emotionally difficult to interact with the cyborgs. In time, however, recombinant-DNA technology will enable us to cross-breed drone human beings in which all genetic disorders have been removed, total obedience has been instilled, and physical and mental capabilities have been carefully manipulated to suit our specific needs.

Those particular drone human beings, a product of the parallel evolution of machine intelligence and genetic adaptation, will be the first of the new super-race — the life form that will succeed the present human race and take us to the stars. Though looking like normal human beings, they will in fact be chimeras, cross-bred from a combination of DNA strands taken from different chromosomal genetic programmes and reassembled in any form required for the geneticist's purposes. Thus, though essentially 'human', they will be abnormally strong, exceptionally intelligent, emotionally neutered and motivated beyond reasoning. Further, by re-stimulating the genes controlling their own limb or organ development, they will be able to regrow lost limbs or, more important for longevity, regenerate failing internal organs. They will then, in effect, be supermen.

All of this will come about in the near future. Right now, however, the clones are physically 'normal' and only different in that they have been emotionally neutered: thus they can suffer no self-doubt or guilt, and have been programmed to do as they are told without moral restraint. They are out there right now, walking among you, unrecognized, and they are there, some in positions of great authority, to do only my bidding.

Who is a friend and who is a foe?

You cannot tell any more.

I am neither friend nor foe because such terms are meaningless to me. I am simply doing what I have to do and I will let no one stop me. There are those who would try because they think in terms of 'right' and 'wrong'. But I know that such concepts have no place in evolution, that only understands where it must go and takes the most direct route. I will follow that route, letting nothing stand in my way, because man is a primitive being filled with primal fears and only science can lead him out of the cave and into the heavens.

There is no right or wrong in this — the only moral law is progress — and those who must be used will be used, as we once used the animals: for all kinds of experimentation as well as for sustenance. The human race is merely evolution's tool, no more and no less, and soon it will be superceded by the fusion of genetic engineering and computers the size of molecules. When that happens, a new race will come into being and the old will die out.

I am here to hasten the advent of that great moment in history and I do so without personal feelings. I bear malice towards none. Nor do I bear good tidings. I merely state the facts as I see them and support them with action. My resurrection has ensured that I can do so and nothing else matters.

I am here to finish the task that I undertook in my former life. In order to do this, I will have to take you with me — and you will not, you cannot, refuse me. Already you are trying to find me — and that says it all.

I await your arrival.

Chapter Eight

'Wilson?' Brandenberg asked, looking perplexed. Formerly a captain with the USAF and now the seventy-year-old head of Freedom Bay, he sat behind Wilson's old desk in an expansive dome-shaped room that had windows running right around the white-metal walls, framing the view of the vast, snow-covered Antarctic wilderness. Between the windows there were doors, steel-plated, all closed, with control panels jutting out just beside them, their tiny lights flashing on and off. The desk was in the middle of the room and had a computer and various books piled upon it. Other books packed the shelves fixed to the walls between the windows. Brandenberg, now with a doctorate in physics, gained here in Freedom Bay where standards were much higher than they were in the World, smiled fondly at Michael out of a face that looked years younger than it was, though his hair was grey and thinning. With that slightly twisted lower lip, he could never have been too handsome, but the kindness in his gaze made him handsome in an avuncular kind of way. 'The message said "Wilson is back"?'

'That's right, sir,' Michael responded from where he was standing in front of Brandenberg's desk. 'The message just popped up on my e-mail when I was making my way back from Robert Stanford's burial ground, about thirty kilometres from here, along the zero meridian.'

'Stanford wasn't buried,' Brandenberg reminded him. 'He floated away on a slab of pack ice and then froze to death.'

'I know that, sir, but I like to think of that place, the last place he set foot on earth, as his burial ground.'

Brandenberg smiled and nodded. 'Why not?' He indicated the chair at the other side of the desk with a wave of his hand. 'You'd better sit down,' he said. 'You might be here a long time.'

Taking note of the remark, quietly spoken but still ominous, Michael sat in the chair facing Dr Brandenberg.

'Do you know where the message came from?'

'No. It had a code name for a Web poster that I know – a physics student in New Zealand with whom I correspond on a regular basis – but when I sent a message back, he insisted that he hadn't sent that message and had never heard of a Wilson. He *did* say that he had sent me another message, but it certainly wasn't anything about Wilson. He was adamant about that.'

'So someone hacked into your system and managed to rewrite your friend's message?'

'It would seem so, sir.'

' "Wilson is back"?'

'That's what it said, sir.'

'Wilson can't be back. Wilson's dead.'

'I know that as well, sir.'

Brandenberg sighed and sat back in his chair, gazing distractedly at the ceiling. He clasped his hands under his chin and remained silent for a considerable time. Eventually he lowered his gaze again.

'Is this the first time you've received the message?'

'Yes, sir.'

'Have any of your e-mail friends received it? I mean, is it some kind of bizarre Internet practical joke?'

'I ran an extensive check with my e-mail friends and none of them received that message. That's not to say that someone else hasn't received it, but certainly no one I know.'

'Mmmm.' Brandenberg glanced around the expansive white-walled office, perhaps thinking back to when he had first come here to take over Wilson's notorious master-and-slave colony and turn it into something considerably more civilized. Certainly he seemed lost in thought.

'You once met Wilson, didn't you?' Michael asked, hoping to break into Brandenberg's thoughts and learn more about the legendary creator of Freedom Bay.

'Yes,' Brandenberg said, pointing with his index finger to the high ceiling. 'Up there. In the only room above this one. The one we keep locked up. The one Wilson called his chapel. Almost certainly in mockery of religion; certainly not out of respect for it. He liked to say that his one religion was science and that room, which indeed has the appearance of a stark stone chapel, is where he went when he wanted to be alone. He also went there to die.'

'What was he like?'

Brandenberg shrugged. 'I can't really say. He was a very old man at the time. In fact, he was dying when I met him. He was stretched out on a stone bed in that stark stone so-called chapel with the sunlight beaming in over him, making him look like a ghost. More so because he was old – a hundred and twelve years old – though he looked about twenty years younger. Of course, he'd had, in his lifetime, a lot of surgical intervention to aid longevity, as well as plastic surgery. But although he didn't look quite as old as he really was, he was certainly old.'

'But what was he *like?*' Michael repeated with emphasis.

'Well, even though he was visibly dying when I saw him – practically on death's doorstep, with only hours to go – his eyes were bright, filled with a luminous, cold intensity, and his features, though wasted and yellowed with jaundice, formed what I later described for the historical records as, quote, *a mask of otherworldly repose.*'

'Otherworldly? What did you mean by that?'

'It was a face of unsurpassable intelligence and inhuman lack of emotion – the face of an alien.'

The description chilled Michael, though it also made him regret, as he had done so often, that he had not been born before his time, about fifty years ago, when he could have met the mysterious Wilson who had seemingly appeared out of nowhere to change the face of the world – just like an alien, indeed. The word 'seemingly' was appropriate in that *some* of Wilson's background was known, but the extent of his achievement, evil though it had been, when related to his obscure origins made it *seem* that he had appeared out of nowhere to create hell on Earth. Certainly, by any standards, Wilson's known background was sketchy, but it was enough to prove that he had been a human being, not an extraterrestrial. A mutant . . . possibly . . . but clearly one of the human kind.

Born John Wilson on July 6, 1870, in Montezuma, Iowa, to Cass and Ira Wilson, both local farmers. Attended elementary school in Montezuma, then high school in Des Moines where, according to his old school reports, he obtained straight A's in every subject, though he had problems interacting with the other students and was widely viewed as a 'loner'.

When Ira Wilson died, Cass moved back to his home town of Worcester, Massachusetts, and Wilson enrolled in the Massachusetts Institute of Technology (MIT), where he studied aerodynamics. In 1893, the year of his father's death, he was enrolled in Sibley College, Cornell University, New York, where he studied experimental engineering and was known as an unusually gifted student and, again, as a 'loner'.

In 1895 he obtained his bachelor of science degree (BSc) in aeronautics. His youthful brilliance was recognized when, shortly after his graduation from Cornell, he obtained work with an aeronautical company, Cohn & Goldman Incorporated, that was attempting to construct commercial airships in a plant in Mountain Pleasant, located near Montezuma, where Wilson had been born, on the border of Iowa and Illinois. Though relatively inexperienced, he was placed in charge of the project and brought it off successfully, designing and constructing the first airships to fly over the United States. The secret test flights of those airships led to the Great Airship Scare of 1896–1897.

Wilson's fanatical ruthlessness with regard to his work became evident when he gave Cohn & Goldman incomplete, unworkable drawings for the airships he had designed, blew up the airships he had already constructed for them, patented the proper designs in his own name and then sold them to Germany, thus enabling that nation to produce the airships that it used for its bombing raids against Allied troops during the First World War. Wilson then used the German money to finance his own aeronautical research plant in Illinois. There he secretly produced even more advanced aircraft, including the first turboprop biplanes to cross the Atlantic.

When the US government realized what Wilson was doing, they clandestinely financed him for even more daring, revolutionary research projects. These included the problem of the boundary layer and dangerous experiments with atomic propulsion. Again, Wilson was successful on both counts. But when, in 1908, his most secret experimental aircraft, reportedly using atomic propulsion, flew all the way to Russia but then crashed in the Tunguska region of Siberia, causing an explosion so big that some believed it had been caused by a crashing meteor or even an alien spacecraft, the US government backed out of the project.

Denied the funding that he needed for his work, Wilson spent the next two decades drifting incognito across the United States, from one small aeronautical company to another, keeping his light under a bushel but making a decent living by selling his less important innovations to commercial airline companies and aircraft construction plants.

Eventually, in the fall of 1930, when he was sixty years old, he turned up in Eden Valley, Roswell, New Mexico, to work with Robert H. Goddard, the controversial rocket scientist who later became known as 'the Father of the Space Age'. About six months later, shortly after Goddard had successfully launched his first liquid-fuelled rockets with Wilson's help, Wilson disappeared again.

In 1931, Wilson materialized in Nazi Germany, seeking the support that the US government had denied him. Admired by SS *Reichsführer* Heinrich Himmler, he was sent to work in a secret research establishment located at Kummersdorf West, about fifteen miles from Berlin and adjacent to Wernher von Braun's Rocket Research Institute. There, ruthlessly using slave labour, he experimented with a wide variety of highly advanced technologies, helped create the V1 and V2 rockets that devastated London, and eventually produced the first disc-shaped, vertical-rising jet aircraft, later to be termed 'flying saucers'.

Under no illusions about what would become of the so-called Thousand Year Reich, knowing that it would end in ignoble defeat and that he, Wilson, would be charged by the Allies as a traitor and war criminal, he used some high-ranking fanatical SS officers, who were already fired with the idea of creating an Aryan 'Super Race' in Antarctica, to continually send men and material to Himmler's secret underground complex in Neuschwabenland. When the war ended, Wilson went to Antarctica, took over the complex, and gradually created his nightmarish 'scientific' colony of masters and slaves.

Geared solely to ruthless scientific and surgical experimentation, the colony was soon using brain-implanted zombies to produce technologically advanced flying saucers, a wide variety of laser-beam weapons and, of course, cyborgs. The Great UFO Scare that began in 1947 with the Kenneth Arnold sightings and was accompanied by many tales of alien abduction was caused by Wilson's early saucers and cyborgs.

Wilson's aim was world domination and, through that, an unfettered exploration of the cosmos. But in 1981, an American travel photographer and UFOlogist, Grant McBain, accompanied by USAF Captain Lee Brandenberg, managed to destroy the Antarctic colony's defence systems, thus enabling US forces to fly in and take command of it. However, even as this was happening, a large flying saucer, the *Goddard*, named after Wilson's sole hero on Earth, the great American rocket scientist with whom he had worked all those years ago, Robert H. Goddard, was launched into space and deliberately blown up with the dead Wilson inside it.

Wilson's colony, without the robotized masters and slaves, was subsequently renamed Freedom Bay and dedicated to the overthrow of the cyborgs that, created originally by Wilson, had taken over the world to continue his diabolical work even after his death.

So that was Wilson . . . the evil or, as some would have it, just amoral genius, who had died forty years ago and had now returned as a name on Michael's e-mail. The thought that the message wasn't a practical joke was persistent and haunting.

'Anyway,' Brandenberg continued after his lengthy, thoughtful silence, 'Wilson is dead and that cryptic e-mail message can only be a little bit of mischief by a cyberspace lurker.'

'What lurker?' Michael asked. 'The only people who know about Wilson are right here in Freedom Bay. Out in the World, even before the coming of the cyborgs, the existence of Wilson was kept secret. As far as history in the World is concerned, Wilson doesn't exist. So what kind of lurker would even think to use Wilson's name?'

'We don't know that the message was referring to the same Wilson. It is, after all, a common surname. You're only *assuming* that it refers to "our" Wilson.'

'Don't you think it strange, sir, that I should receive that message when I'm actually at the spot where Robert Stanford, metaphorically speaking, turned his back on Wilson, choosing death as a free human being over life as Wilson's slave? Why should the message come to me there, of all places, if it doesn't refer to the same Wilson?'

Brandenberg nodded thoughtfully and pursed his lips. 'It certainly seems odd,' he said.

'And the phrasing: "Wilson is back." Back from where? It *could* be another Wilson who just went off somewhere and is about to return, but the name, the statement itself, the location and the timing, all make me think that it *has* to be about our Wilson.'

'Then it has to be some kind of joke,' Brandenberg insisted. 'It can't be anything else.'

'Even if we assume that it's a practical joke, that still raises the question: Who sent the message? Who's the hacker, out there in the World, who even *knows* about Wilson? The only known facts about Wilson, the only written records about him, are held right here in Freedom Bay.'

'Then we could have a practical joker right here in our midst . . . But I doubt it.' Brandenberg shook his head from side to side, convincing himself. 'Our people aren't that kind. They don't play practical jokes and certainly, even if they did, they'd never use Wilson's name. So it's possible, but highly unlikely, that the joker is here. It must have come from outside.'

'From where? To what purpose?'

Perhaps wearied by Michael's persistence, Brandenberg pushed his chair back, turned away and walked to the panoramic window. He stood there, framed by the Antarctic wilderness, silhouetted against its ice-covered mountain peaks and dazzling plains of virgin snow. His shoulders were bent. Indeed, he was almost stooped. Michael realized then that Brandenberg, despite his youthful face, was indeed an old man.

'Could Wilson still be alive?' Michael asked.

'Of course not,' Brandenberg replied, talking to the window, his back still turned to Michael. 'He was in the *Goddard* when it exploded – and I saw it exploding.'

'But did anyone actually see Wilson being carried into that flying saucer?'

Brandenberg turned back to face Michael, his brow furrowed, his gaze focused inward, travelling back to the past. 'No,' he acknowledged. 'Come to think of it, no one did. His body went missing and we were told by Dr Epstein, when he had been freed from the influence of his brain implants, that Wilson had died and that his body had been placed in the *Goddard.* I personally saw that flying saucer exploding and Epstein said it had been exploded deliberately, in order to scatter Wilson's remains through outer space. That was, according to Epstein, Wilson's final request, made just before he died in that room, his so-called chapel, located right above us.'

'Epstein might have lied.'

'He *might* have, but I doubt that he *would* have. He would have lied about it when he was still under the influence of his brain implants, but certainly not once he was freed from them, as he was when I spoke to him. Besides, even if Wilson *had* survived, he would now be over a hundred and fifty years old. Even with our present medical and surgical skills — the most advanced in the world — we couldn't keep a man alive that long. So Wilson, even if using the longevity treatments available in his time, wouldn't have lived much longer than he did. This is why I believe he died and was blown apart in the exploding *Goddard.* I don't think Epstein lied to me.'

Brandenberg returned to his desk, leaned back in his chair, clasped his hands under his chin and offered a slight, bemused smile.

'"Wilson is back",' he repeated, as if talking to himself, shaking his head in perplexity. 'It's a mystery,' he added.

They were silent for a moment, both thinking about the mystery, then Michael said, 'I still think there's something to it. I think it *is* about our Wilson and I don't think it's a practical joke. It came from the World, but it came from someone who knows about Wilson — a rarity out there — so if it's not a statement of fact, which surely it can't be, then it must be some kind of coded message.'

'Relating to what?'

'"Wilson is back . . ." Maybe that name is being used to suggest something *relating* to Wilson . . . Maybe the cyborgs. It could be a way of telling us that the cyborgs are about to do something special . . . something we should know about.'

'Which, if it were true, would still leave us with the mystery of the poster's identity and whereabouts.'

'Yes. So, at the very least, we should do our best to find out who this mysterious person is and then, if we can locate him, find out why he transmitted that message and just what it means.'

'How do you propose to do that? You've already traced the e-mail back to who you thought was the poster only to have him deny that he sent it. Clearly the real lurker is a hacker of the cleverest kind, maybe a flame ghoul trying to weave a disruptive thread. So even if he sends you another message, which he may not, you won't be able to find out where he's hiding because the details on the e-mail won't be his.'

'I wasn't intending to try cyberspace,' Michael replied, suddenly nervous. 'I was thinking of using my gifts.'

He was feeling nervous because the few who were 'gifted', as he was, only received advance training on the understanding that they would not use their 'gifts' without clearance from their superiors. Michael had not done that, but for him to even propose that he should use his talents for any purpose other than one of the first magnitude of importance made him feel that he had. His nervousness was only increased by the fact that as soon as he mentioned the subject to Dr Brandenberg the latter's eyes veiled over, indicating that he was either displeased or uncomfortable.

He stared steadily at Michael for a long time, his face grave. Then he took a deep breath and expelled it as he spoke.

'Your gifts,' he said simply.

'Yes.' Michael nodded.

'You believe that this message warrants that?'

'Yes, sir, I do.'

'To employ your gifts, as you know, can be dangerous, so I must assume you think it's worth the risk.'

'I do,' Michael said.

Now it was Brandenberg's turn to nod. He closed his eyes for a moment, thinking the matter through, deciding. Then, eventually, he opened them again and kept his gaze steady.

'Which particular gift are you planning to use?' he asked.

'Psychometry,' Michael replied, referring to his skill at obtaining information about a person simply by holding and focusing upon an object belonging to, or relating to, that individual. Like all of his parapsychological gifts, it was a useful talent, but one that could be dangerous: using it could place too great a strain on the heart and brain of the practitioner. For this reason, those with such psychic gifts could not use them without prior consultation with their superiors. 'I printed the e-mail out and I think I can use that paper to trace the poster.'

'You might only trace the original sender – your friend in New Zealand – since it was him, in fact, who sent the original e-mail.'

'I won't focus on his details. I'll focus on the message alone . . . on Wilson's name. I'll block everything else out.'

'Do you think that's enough?'

Michael hesitated, nervous again, then took a deep breath and plunged in with, 'No. I'm going to need something else.'

Looking even more concerned, Brandenberg straightened up in his chair. 'Oh? What's that?'

'I need to use Wilson's chapel,' Michael said. 'I think—'

'You know that no one's allowed in there,' Brandenberg interjected, sounding angry. 'You know I can't permit that. You have no right to ask.'

Michael did, indeed, know that traditionally no one was allowed into the room that Wilson had once described mockingly as his 'chapel' and that he had chosen to die in. Michael had never seen the room, but it had been described to him by Dr Brandenberg and he knew that there was nothing in it except the raised block of stone upon which Wilson had died. The room, unchanged, had been locked up by Brandenberg shortly after Wilson's death and had never been opened again because, as Brandenberg had said, 'It might be contaminated with Wilson's spirit, and that spirit is evil.' While this sounded, superficially, like an extraordinary attitude for a pragmatic scientist such as

Brandenberg to have taken, Michael knew, particularly given the nature of his own gifts, that Brandenberg had his reasons.

In Freedom Bay, parapsychology was accepted as a serious science and researches in the field had confirmed, among other things, that all human beings left some kind of psychic 'mark' on things around them and that information on an individual could be obtained by the concentration of mental energy upon an item touched by them or relating to them. It was this knowledge, therefore, and not primitive superstition, that had led Brandenberg and others in the colony to believe that traces of Wilson's personality could have been left in his chapel, particularly in the stone 'bed' upon which he had died, and that those traces could still contaminate, or corrupt, the person exposed to them. It was for this reason, then, that Wilson's chapel had been locked up shortly after his death and not entered by anyone since then.

'In asking for access,' Michael said, 'I know that I'm asking for a great deal. But I don't have a choice. I think I can trace the poster through the printed e-mail, but only if I can also use the unseen emanations of Wilson's deathbed. Please let me try, sir.'

Brandenberg stared steadily at Michael for a long time. Then he pushed his chair back, stood up and went again to the window overlooking the Antarctic wilderness. Michael sensed what he was thinking. He was thinking that the choice of the name 'Wilson' for that cryptic e-mail could not have been accidental and that it had to be some kind of coded message. He was thinking that the message, sent deliberately to the Antarctic, had to relate somehow to the cyborgs as well as to Freedom Bay. He was thinking that Michael's use of psychometry could be dangerous, particularly in Wilson's chapel, but that the possibility of the message being important made the risk worth the taking. He was thinking of saying 'Yes.'

And, indeed, he did. Turning away from the window, he nodded and smiled, this being a positive sign, then opened a drawer in his desk and withdrew a key that he handed to Michael.

'Be careful,' he said.

'I will,' Michael replied.

Smiling, he hurried out of the office, then made his way to the narrow flight of natural stone steps that curved up the short distance to the highest floor in Freedom Bay. The stairs opened out onto an expansive, pyramid-shaped hallway hacked crudely out of the mountain's rock and never properly smoothed. Small windows on either side of the hallway let striations of sunlight in, illuminating the stone-flagged floor – and the solid oak door to Wilson's chapel.

Hesitating only a moment, his throat dry, Michael turned the key in the lock and stepped inside. He closed the door carefully behind him and then studied the chapel. It was high and dome-shaped, built of rock hewn from the mountain and empty except for a six-foot-tall block of stone, Wilson's deathbed, that was resting in the middle of the vast, stone-flagged floor. The bed was hazed in a pyramid of shimmering light created by the shafts of sunlight beaming obliquely in through the windows. The silence was so complete that Michael could hear his own heartbeat. He found this disturbing.

Trying to keep his breathing even, he crossed to the centre of the room, withdrew the printed e-mail from his trouser pocket, then stretched out on the stone bed and laid the piece of paper on his chest with his hands clasped over it. He did not have to read it to see it: he could do that with his mind. Closing his eyes against the dazzling pyramidal web of light that fell across him, as it had once fallen across Wilson, he focused on the wording of the e-mail, on that one word, *wilson*, and soon saw it as clearly as if it was blazing in neon lighting inside his head. He breathed the presence of Wilson, felt the dead man's emanations, then rose out of himself, spiralling up into the light to gaze back down at the bed of stone – upon which he saw Wilson stretched out.

Michael knew with total certainty that it was Wilson. There could be no doubt about it. The man was very old, his skin yellowed with jaundice, but his gaze was still bright with a relentless intelligence and his features were so ascetic, so devoid of human emotion or warmth, that he seemed truly otherworldly. He was breathing harshly, clearly dying, dissolving into the shimmering light. But as he, the old man, was dissolving, another, younger man was taking his place.

This, too, was Wilson. Michael was sure of it. The younger man looked strikingly like the dying one but he was many years younger, about forty years of age. Though his features were hazed in the shimmering light, he seemed oddly familiar.

'You received my message,' he said, his voice ethereal, reverberating, ghostlike, 'and you cannot ignore it. Tell Brandenberg that I'm back and that you saw me and he'll send you to find me. When you do so, you'll know where your future lies and you will go to it willingly. I *am* Wilson. Come find me.'

The young Wilson dissolved also, fading into the shimmering light, back into the bed of stone. Then the old Wilson emerged from that same stone to die again before rebirth. He was there and then gone, dissolving like his younger self. Then the shimmering light brightened, became dazzling, phosphorescent, and Michael heard the pounding of his heart as a deafening thunder. His heart was racing and he was choking, breathing in harsh, anguished spasms: he knew that if he didn't get off the stone he would die just as Wilson had.

He tried to sit up, but failed; tried again and failed again. He felt the tightening of his head from the strain of concentration, his brain waves agitated, lightning tearing his mind's blackness, the alpha rhythms pushing him to the very edge of epilepsy while his heart raced so fast that he couldn't breathe and felt that the end had come. He saw the abyss just in time and jumped back before he fell, breathing deeply and rolling off the bed of stone, landing on his feet.

The piece of paper, Wilson's message, was on the floor and he bent down to pick it up. When he did so, his head started swimming and so he straightened up quickly.

Shocked and exhilarated, hardly believing what had happened, he hurried out of the room, Wilson's chapel, and went straight back to Dr Brandenberg's office. There he found the learned professor waiting for him, his ageing face creased by anxiety, his still-youthful eyes curious.

'Wilson's back,' Michael said.

Chapter Nine

'Hi, Dude,' Gumshoe said to the Cowboy where he was sitting in darkness on the porch of his Anacostia shack, silhouetted against the moonlit bend in the river, his booted feet up on the railing, a stetson hat on his head. Without otherwise moving a muscle, the Cowboy turned his head in Gumshoe's direction, then gave a big grin.

'Well, I'll be damned,' he said, 'if it ain't my old buddy, Gumshoe. How ya bin, kid?'

'Not bad,' Gumshoe said.

The Cowboy's shrewd gaze shifted, moving up and down, taking in the length and shape of the Long Hair standing silently beside Gumshoe.

'Mmmm,' he murmured appreciatively. 'And this is . . . ?'

'Bonnie Packard,' Bonnie said before Gumshoe could speak. 'And you can keep those fuckin' eyes in your head, 'cause I'm not into real time.'

The Cowboy's gaze shifted to Gumshoe.

'She means sex,' Gumshoe explained. 'She's not into real-time sex. I mean, she only likes cyberspace interaction. She doesn't like to be touched.' Realizing what he had just said, he turned to look into Bonnie's bizarrely painted eyes. 'Hey, didn't you tell me you liked it both ways? Didn't I hear you say that?'

'I only do it the other way occasionally and even then only

with Short Hairs my own age. No way would I consider it with that corpse. I mean, what age *are* you, buddy?'

The Cowboy wasn't offended. Cowboys took it all in their stride. He just grinned his lazy old grin, crinkled his prairie-green eyes, then took hold of the brim of his stetson hat to raise and lower it slightly. 'A man's only as old as he feels, Ma'am, an' I feel as young as you look.'

The bone-hard Bonnie almost melted. 'Oh, shit, man, that's great. I mean, the way you talk, man. The fuckin' Short Hairs I run with, those boondockers, they couldn't come out with somethin' like that to save their fuckin' lives. You're not as old as you look, man.'

'That's right kind of you to say so, Ma'am, but I sure don't deserve it.'

'Yes, man, you do. Just call me Bonnie.'

'Jesus Christ!' Gumshoe said. Disgusted, he spat in the grass around his feet, then grinned at the Cowboy and said, 'Okay, Dude, that's enough of that smooth shit. You got something to drink?'

'I sure do,' the Cowboy said. Swinging his booted feet off the railing, he leaned down to the side of his chair and picked up a couple of bottles of Bud. Straightening up again, he levered the caps off with his teeth, spat the caps over the railing, then held up the bottles. 'You gonna stand down there all day?' he said. 'Or are you comin' up here?'

'We're coming up,' Gumshoe said.

Motioning for Bonnie to follow him, he clambered up over the railing, onto the porch. When he turned back to help Bonnie up, she slapped his hand away and defiantly did it on her own. The Cowboy was sitting in an old rocking chair, but there were a couple of ordinary hard chairs beside him and Gumshoe and Bonnie sank down on them, then took the bottles of Bud from the Cowboy. He placed his booted feet back on the railing and sank back into the chair. When they followed his gaze, they saw spherical lights gliding across the night sky, silent and beautiful.

'Motherfuckers,' the Cowboy said. 'They're out patrollin' every night. They rise an' fall as straight as a die to pick up what they want from the American earth — animal, vegetable or mineral. The world's sure changed, all right.'

'You should know,' Gumshoe said. 'You were there at the beginning. What exactly happened that day, Cowboy? We wanna hear the full story.'

'You already know the full story.'

'I only know that the flying saucers came down and that the cyborgs came out of them. I only know that it happened all over the world and that now they're in charge. But I don't know *where* they came from or *why* they're here and I think you might have a clue. So what's the story, Cowboy?'

'Why should he know?' Bonnie asked with her customary belligerence. 'He's just an old guy who likes to wear cowboy clothes and get drunk on his porch. Hey, Cowboy, what were you in the Old Age? A Hell's Angel or somethin'?'

Grinning, the Cowboy leaned sideways again, picked another bottle of Bud off the floor, snapped the cap off with his teeth, spat it out, then had a good slug. He wiped his lips with the back of his hand and his smile was still there.

'Nope,' he said. 'I wasn't into motorcycles. I was a USAF orbital analyst working in the US Space Command's top-secret Space Surveillance Centre, hidden deep inside Cheyenne Mountain near Colorado Springs, Colorado. The locals called it Crystal City 'cause they didn't know exactly what went on inside that mountain and they imagined it was like those old movies you see on TV — *Star Trek* or *Star Wars* — with lots of space-age gadgetry.'

'Were they right?' Bonnie asked.

'They sure were. We had the most advanced space surveillance systems ever devised and they were pretty damned impressive to look at.'

'What did you do?' Bonnie asked.

'Knob turner,' the Cowboy said ambiguously, with a teasing

grin. Then he went on to clarify the picture. 'I worked on the third-level area, known as Box Nine, a good half-mile below ground level. It was a windowless, narrow chamber manned by half a dozen orbital analysts, including me. Known as knob turners, we spent all day or night, depending on the shift, seated in an eerie green glow in front of computer consoles that showed the curving ground tracks of the many objects floating in outer space, high above the Earth's atmosphere, just outside the US electronic defence perimeter, known as "the fence". The so-called fence was, in fact, the US Naval Space Defence System: a man-made energy field that stretched three thousand miles across the southern United States, extended a thousand miles off each coast, and reached out nearly fifteen thousand miles into space. It's still there, still checking what's out there, but now the cyborgs control it – that and the whole of Crystal City. Those bastards got everything.'

'So how did it work?' Gumshoe asked, always interested in technical matters.

'When an object passed through the energy field, the so-called *fence* was tripped and the invasion of our air space recorded on our radar screens. When that happened, receiver stations all over the country locked onto it. Within seconds, the computers would calculate the object's speed and size. That info was relayed immediately to the system's HQ in Dahlgren, Virginia, where the signals were processed by a high-speed IBM 1800 computer that determined the precise position and anticipated ground track of the object. That info was in turn relayed to us lowly knob turners in Box Nine where, based on the info we received, we'd be able to feed into our computers a mathematical description of the orbital elements of the object, including estimates of the time it would take it to reach Earth, its inclination to the equator, and the highest point, or apogee, of its orbit. From those computations, we'd be able to tell what was out there.'

'Shit, man,' Bonnie said, staring wide-eyed at the Cowboy, 'you're a pretty smart guy.'

'Thank you, Ma'am, for those kind words.'

'You ever catch anything up there?' Gumshoe asked, annoyed that Bonnie, who normally had no respect for anyone, was practically drooling with admiration for the Cowboy, now fifty-five years old.

'Yeah, lots of things, but nothing special. You gotta remember that even that long ago there were approximately *seven thousand* pieces of man-made debris floating out in space, including several thousand satellites and plenty of small items such as lost thermal gloves, screwdrivers, other tools, and even screws that had worked themselves loose and just drifted away. So they were all still up there, floating around, keeping our radar screens busy. Invariably, if we picked up an anomalous or unidentified object, commonly referred to as a *bogey*, it would turn out to be one of four types of item: a satellite whose orbital characteristics had changed, perhaps on command from the ground; a decaying object re-entering the atmosphere, in which case it was passed on to the TIP – tracking and impact prediction – teams; a newly launched object that had yet to be given an identification number; or simply one of the thousands of previously recorded objects floating around in space.'

'You never saw the flying saucers entering and leaving the atmosphere, tripping your fence?'

'We probably did,' the Cowboy said, 'and probably recorded them as unidentified flying objects – UFOs. But every time we vectored in aircraft to intercept them, they just blinked out on the screens and were never eyeballed by the pilots. Those sons of bitches were quick to disappear. So, though we recorded a lot of UFOs, that's just what they remained listed as: unidentifieds.'

'So what happened when the cyborgs invaded?' Gumshoe asked.

'We were caught with our pants down,' the Cowboy replied, 'and all that fancy *Star Wars* hardware didn't mean a damned thing. We didn't see their saucers coming until it was too late because they didn't come through the fence, from outer space.

They came from right here on Earth, from hidden bases in remote locations such as deserts and mountain ranges and, of course, from lakes and the seabed. So the flying saucers weren't seen as unidentified blips on the radar screens reading the man-made energy field; they didn't trip the fence. In fact, they weren't seen until they started *ascending* all over the globe, when they were recorded as unidentified blips on airport radars tracking known flight paths. So there we were in Crystal City, scanning outer space for signs of anything anomalous, while the whole show was taking place around us and we just couldn't see it. Not, that is, until a huge flying saucer, a mother ship, descended right over Cheyenne Mountain . . . and by then it was too late.'

'The Cheyenne Mountain complex,' Gumshoe said, 'was supposed to be the most secret base in the whole of the United States – and the most impregnable. I mean, it's buried deep in the mountain, it's protected by bombproof doors, and it had, at that time, every kind of electrical defence system known to man . . . So, given all that, how did the cyborgs get in?'

'They just walked in,' the Cowboy said. 'We couldn't do a damned thing to stop them. When that great mother ship came down, descending over Cheyenne Mountain and then hovering right above it as it released the smaller flying saucers, the ones containing the cyborgs and armed robotic machines – dreadful fucking things that looked like giant metallic insects – all our fancy hardware went haywire, blinking on and off, some smoking and even exploding, warning lights all over the place, sirens wailing and so on. Then the bombproof doors just opened and couldn't be closed again, the place was plunged into darkness – and just imagine that enormous place in pitch darkness with everyone in a panic – and then the cyborgs and the robotic machines just came in, swarming down through the whole complex, and no one could do a damned thing to stop 'em. Our weapons were useless against them. They had those laser weapons that could paralyse or kill. They simply zapped anyone who tried to resist, then they rounded the others up, marched them out of there, took them back to the mother ship in the smaller flying saucers, then took over the complex and soon had it operating again. A few days later, the technicians who'd been taken away were returned to their old jobs – but from what I hear, though they all *looked* the same as they'd looked before, they *weren't* quite the same. They were obedient and did exactly what they were told. They'd all had their minds tampered with.'

'I hear the cyborgs do that all the time,' Gumshoe said. 'Most of the humans who work for them, it's been said, have had their minds tampered with. There's a lotta talk of electronic implantation. Hairline fibres, so thin they're practically invisible, that are implanted in certain areas of the brain and can then control it. You think that's possible?'

'I know it is,' the Cowboy replied. 'They were doing it in our hospitals for years in the Old Age and the cyborgs were always well ahead of us, so no doubt they can do it. A lot of the cyborgs are remote-controlled that way – and so are the humans who work for them.'

'What about you?' Bonnie asked, pointing at the Cowboy with her unfinished bottle. 'You're sitting here right in front of us and you seem pretty normal. How come, big boy?'

'I got away,' the Cowboy said. 'A few of us managed to. We were able to make our escape in the darkness and we fled on foot from the mountain, still under cover of darkness. It was midnight, remember.'

'So how come you're here,' Bonnie asked, 'in Washington DC? Or, to be more accurate, in a shanty town in Anacostia?'

The Cowboy wasn't offended by Bonnie's directness. But he certainly looked less happy, his eyes narrowing as they gazed into the past. 'Well, now,' he said, as if not sure how to say it, 'I guess I'm here because I had to have some friends after I lost everything in Colorado, including my wife and kids.' He broke the shocked, uneasy silence by slugging some beer and clearing his throat by coughing into his clenched fist. 'That's one of the reasons I hate the cyborgs,' he said. 'They killed my wife and two kids . . . Not deliberately, mind you . . . But that don't matter a damn. I hate those bastards anyway.'

'What happened?' Bonnie asked with admirable bluntness.

'We tend to forget,' the Cowboy explained, 'that a lot of damage was done when the flying saucers descended. Those were big motherfuckers – the mother ships, I mean – and they gave off a kind of vibration, an infrasound, that sucked things up and knocked things down and cracked tarmac roads and short-circuited electricity systems and made engines malfunction. In other words, they caused havoc, with things – and folks – being smashed and crushed, falling into deep holes caused by splitting earth, dying in fires, by electric shock, and in automobile crashes or in planes that malfunctioned in mid-air and went down. There was that and then there was the general havoc caused by panic, when drivers and pedestrians saw those huge things descending.' The Cowboy sighed with genuine sadness, then continued, speaking more softly. 'So, when I escaped from the Cheyenne Mountain Complex, I made my way to Colorado Springs on foot. My house was fine, but it was empty, with all the lights still on. From where the house was, I could see that huge mother ship, hovering over Cheyenne Mountain with its lights flashing on and off repeatedly – a huge, lit-up cathedral, beautiful and terrifying at the same time. Wondering why the house was empty, I was just about to call the cops when a patrol car stopped out in front. A local cop and good buddy, Jim Baxter, got out to tell me that my wife and two kids, a boy and a girl, one twelve and one ten, had been killed in a car crash. His assumption, based on other crashes that he'd also attended over the past hour, was that my wife had seen that huge mother ship coming down over the mountain. In a panic because she knew I was there but she couldn't contact me, she'd put the kids in her car with the intention of driving them to her folks' place just a few miles away. In her panic – or possibly because the other driver had panicked – she crashed into another speeding car. The lone driver in the other car survived; my wife and kids were killed outright.'

'Aw, shit!' Bonnie exclaimed softly, with genuine sympathy.

The Cowboy merely nodded. 'Anyways,' he said, 'I was going to stay on in the house after the funeral, but one of the other knob turners who escaped from the complex with me came to tell me that the cyborgs were spreading out from Cheyenne Mountain into the surrounding area and that they were rounding up all the scientists and technicians who'd escaped from the complex, as well as others who hadn't been there at the time but who normally worked there. Those who were rounded up were, of course, returned a few days later when their minds had been tampered with. As for me, with my wife and kids gone and most of my friends in the hands of the cyborgs, I did the only thing I could do, which was to light out of there. I made my way to the only place I still had friends – your folks, Gumshoe, then living where you're living right now – and they let me hide out in your place until I arranged a new life, and a new name, for myself. I solved the problem by coming here, where only the deadbeats live, where the cyborgs never come, and I turned myself into the eccentric character you now see before you.'

'Jesus,' Bonnie said, 'that's all really sad. So how do you make a living these days?'

'I paint and decorate for the poor of this very area.'

'That's a hell of a comedown for a guy who used to do what you did.'

The Cowboy shrugged. 'Since the coming of the cyborgs a lotta folks have had to climb down a bit. A man's lucky to be makin' a livin' at all and I do okay.'

'You got no problem with the criminal elements around here?'

'Around here,' the Cowboy said, 'they think I'm weird, an alcoholic and a crazy, which means that they leave me alone and would never think that the cyborgs might want to find me. Of course, a good twenty years have passed since then, so the cyborgs really might have forgotten me by now.'

'Maybe' Gumshoe said. 'Maybe not. I think they might have long memories . . . and they still abduct people.'

'They sure do,' Bonnie said. 'So what happened to the President of the United States? Him and his Vice-President and the other political fat cats who were taken away that first day and never seen again?'

'I don't know,' the Cowboy said. 'No one does. All we know for sure is that the politicians left behind, the ones now running the country, are either too scared to take action against the cyborgs or have been brainwashed by them, electronically or otherwise. As for those picked up by the Paddy wagons, who knows what happens to them? They disappear. That's all we know. They disappear and they don't come back.'

'Yeah,' Gumshoe said, suddenly feeling a rush of pain and embarrassment. 'Like my parents disappeared and never came back – a few months after you fled to this place. I wonder about them all the time and not knowing what happened to them is more painful than actually losing them. It's kind of a torment.'

The Cowboy reached over to take hold of Gumshoe's shoulder and give it a gentle, compassionate squeeze. 'Yeah,' he said, 'I know what you mean. That must hurt a lot. No use telling you to not think about it, 'cause they were the kind of folks you remember.'

'They used to visit him in Colorado,' Gumshoe explained to Bonnie, 'when they went there as physicists on NASA business. That's how they became friends.'

'That's right,' the Cowboy said.

'I can't remember what they were like,' Gumshoe said, turning back to the fifty-five-year-old who was charming the eighteen-year-old Bonnie Packard. 'I only remember that my Mom loved Elvis Presley and I think he's great too.'

The Cowboy nodded. 'He sure is. That's why he's still so popular. Elvis was so unique, so off the wall, there was really no one to compare to him. You know why I think he's still so popular?'

'No, tell me.'

'I can't wait,' Bonnie added, rolling her eyes.

'He was everything rolled into one, you know? I mean, he did every kinda song you could do – the blues, country, gospel, rock 'n' roll, ballads, jazz, opera, kids' songs and novelty songs for the movies, an' he did 'em all like no one ever did. Then, of course, he was kinda androgynous: a real macho man on the one hand, kinda feminine on the other. You ever notice his face? One side of it, he looks like a hoodlum; the other side he looks like an angel – a real split personality. Then, to top it all, he wore those Captain Marvel capes and they made him seem almost godlike – or, at least, like someone from another planet. I think that's what did it. It's what your Mom used to say. She said that since the coming of the cyborgs and the growth of cybersex, with the differences between male and female being broken down on the World Wide Web, in all those e-mail transactions and virtual-reality sex parlours, Elvis had come to stand in for both sexes, offering something for everybody and making the unreality of the New Age seem perfectly normal. That Elvis, man, he's really fucking eternal and you'd better believe it.'

'They say he's been seen coming out of the White House with cyborgs and their human aides. Any truth in that, Cowboy?'

The Cowboy grinned at that one. 'Well, Elvis is alive and well and has been seen everywhere in the world, so I guess we'd better believe it. He also wanted to be a Messiah, you know, to change the whole fucking world, so maybe he's working on it with the cyborgs. For sure, they're doing *something* in the White House, so let's wait and see.'

'Maybe Elvis is really Wilson,' Gumshoe said.

'What? Who's Wilson?'

'You never heard of Wilson?'

'I've known a few in my time,' the Cowboy said. 'Which one do you mean?'

'I keep getting a message on my e-mail saying that Wilson is back. I don't know what it means and I can't find out who's sending it, 'cause the poster's details are always false. But I keep getting that message.'

'Cyberspace,' the Cowboy said. 'You're in a haunted world there. They're obsessed with all kinds of mystic shit and conspiracy theories. Maybe it's something like that.'

'You ever hear of a Wilson in that context?'

'Yeah, as a matter of fact, I did. Way back when I was working in Crystal City. Lots of whispers going around about a Wilson connected to flying saucer mythology – the old extra-terrestrial mythology, before the coming of the cyborgs, way back in the 1950s and 1960s – in the days of rock 'n' roll and Elvis, naturally. I can't remember much about what was said, though I do recall that *that* Wilson was kind of a cult figure in UFO mythology. It could be a practical joke based on that. Check him out on the Web.'

'I'll do that,' Gumshoe said. He glanced up at the night sky and saw the same spherical lights gliding to and fro high above Washington DC. Remembering what had happened to Snake Eyes, and recalling the SARGEs and Prowlers around the White House, he assumed that the cyborgs would be patrolling that whole area with even more than their customary thoroughness. They would be looking for anyone on a motorcycle and he was one of that breed. 'I think we'd better be going,' he said to the Cowboy, then indicated Bonnie with a nod of his head. 'I've gotta take this Long Hair home and that could give me problems.'

'Don't suggest I'm a fucking problem,' Bonnie retorted. 'I can make it back on my own.'

'Not recommended,' the Cowboy said smoothly, his grin as youthful as it was licentious. 'Stay here if you want to.'

'I'd be safe in your bed, would I?' Bonnie responded.

'Nothing'd happen that you didn't want to happen – you can be damned sure of that.'

'Let's go,' Gumshoe said, startled to find that he was con-cerned that Bonnie might actually decide to stay. 'I brought you here and I feel responsible for you, so I'm gonna take you back.'

'A real gentleman,' the Cowboy said.

'Ain't he ever?' Bonnie replied. 'You wouldn't think of it to look at him, would you?'

'He's a good kid,' the Cowboy said. 'Anyway,' he continued, turning to Gumshoe, 'you come back anytime and bring your lady. It always does me good to see you, dude, and your lady's a zinger.'

'Yeah,' Gumshoe said, hastily getting out of his chair and motioning for Bonnie to do the same. 'Right. I'll see you when I see you, Cowboy.'

'Make it soon,' the Cowboy said.

Gumshoe vaulted over the railing and Bonnie came over after him, again declining to let him help her and spitting on the ground near his feet to make him feel bad. *A real bitch in the making there*, he mused.

Gumshoe gave the Cowboy a big grin and waved his right hand. 'Adios,' he said. Then Bonnie waved and blew the Cowboy a kiss. The Cowboy blew one right back.

'Anytime,' he said, smiling warmly at Bonnie before turning his languid gaze on Gumshoe. 'And you watch out for those cyborgs when you're going back.'

'I will,' Gumshoe said.

Fearful that Bonnie might try being even friendlier towards the Cowboy, he hurried back to his motorcycle and waited patiently until she had climbed onto the pillion seat, with her arms and thighs pressed tightly to him.

'He called me a lady,' Bonnie said, whispering into his ear. 'That's some guy back there.'

'Yeah, right,' Gumshoe muttered. He kicked the motorcycle into life and shot off the way he had come, back through the dilapidated, often dangerous low-income housing projects with their smashed or caged windows, broken-down bars, and still highly active collection of thugs, pool-hall hustlers, pimps and whores, all surrealistically redrawn in the neon-lit darkness. Making it through without incident and soon approaching the bridge, he suddenly thought of something and braked to a halt.

'So where do you live?' he asked Bonnie.

'Nowhere,' she replied. 'I just got thrown out of my dive in Chinatown and now I've got nowhere to go. I was gonna go back with Snake Eyes, but now that's out of the question.'

With his heart sinking, though also oddly exhilarated (even aware, as he was, that the Long Hair behind him was not showing too much concern for the fate of her supposed boyfriend), he said, 'What the hell does that mean? I mean, where are your things?'

'What things?'

'Your possessions.'

'I don't have no possessions. The sons of bitches who threw me out kept my possessions in lieu of the unpaid rent.'

'Shit,' Gumshoe said. 'So where do I take you?'

'I'm not fussy,' Bonnie replied. 'Your place will do fine. Just don't expect no real-time interaction, 'cause right now I'm not into bein' touched.'

'Well . . .' Gumshoe hesitated, not sure how he should respond, preferring to be on his own but, at the same time, not really wanting to let her go, feeling . . . *something* for her and confused by the feeling. He wasn't into real-time interaction himself and that was the truth of it. So why, when he would get nothing out of it, should he give himself headaches? 'I mean . . .'

'Okay, just dump me,' she cut him short. 'You pick the spot. Just leave me and let the cyborgs pick me up. Say goodnight and sleep soundly.'

'Okay! Okay! I'll take you home for the night. You can stay there until you work something out. Just don't give me no hassles.'

'The Cowboy called me a lady,' Bonnie responded haughtily, 'and you *still* think you can talk to me this way? Where the fuck do you get off?'

'Okay! Okay! I'm taking you back. Now you hold on real tight.'

'Don't worry. I will.'

Gumshoe took her back to his place. They managed to get there in one piece. There were a few potentially nasty incidents – a SARGE here and there, a couple of Prowlers up ahead, a few remote-controlled flying saucers, or footballs – but he saw them all in time, from a good distance away, and managed to avoid them and keep going without being spotted. When eventually he reached Georgetown and had locked the motorcycle into its protective cage in the basement, he took Bonnie up to his apartment, switched on the lights, and was not surprised to hear her describe his home as a pigpen.

'But it's okay,' she added hastily. 'It's all right. I mean, I've lived in a lot worse.'

'Thanks a million,' he said.

They did not sleep together. Gumshoe slept on the sofa. He was gentleman enough to let her have the bed, though he deeply resented it. He did not sleep at all and Bonnie did not come to the sofa, made no attempt to join him, just snored softly all on her own, so he spent the night thinking of Wilson and wondering if he might drag up something about him if he trawled through the World Wide Web. He went to work first thing the next morning, while Bonnie was still asleep, pursuing Wilson – a phantom, a teasing riddle – through the teeming, abstract world of cyberspace.

Gumshoe found Wilson lurking there.

Chapter Ten

Michael was training himself with the rigour of an ancient samurai, honing his parapsychological skills for the day when he and others would move against the cyborgs – against Wilson – and wrest control of the world back from them. This course of intensive training had begun immediately after he had told Brandenberg about his extraordinary experience in Wilson's old chapel. Brandenberg had believed him and had accepted that the experience, if not necessarily meaning that Wilson was still alive or had been miraculously resurrected, certainly indicated that the demonic forces created by him were soon to be turned against Freedom Bay.

'We can't wait for that to happen,' he had told Michael. 'We must take the initiative – and that may mean returning to the World.'

'At last!' Michael had exclaimed.

Brandenberg had smiled bleakly. 'I know you've always been impatient to do this. But I didn't think we were ready for it, not quite advanced enough in our technology – in our flying saucers and laser-beam weapons; in the parapsychological skills of yourself and the other adepts. I'm still not a hundred per cent sure. But now, whether we're ready or not, we *have* to find out what the cyborgs are up to and somehow put a stop to them. Once we move against them, however, there'll be no turning back, because we'll either win for good or lose for good and it won't end until that's been decided. The cyborgs want us out of here — we're the only free men left on Earth; the only ones still standing against them — and once we go back into the World, they'll do everything in their power to keep us there.'

'What happens first?' Michael had asked, now more impatient than ever, excited by the knowledge that all his years of relentless work — the work that had begun early in childhood — were going to be put to good use at last. For the first time, he felt that it had all been worth it — and he was eager to prove it.

'The cyborgs, as you know, have developed a diversity of parapsychological skills to make up for the loss of their eyes, ears and mouths. Those skills include psychokinesis, thoughtography, eyeless sight, psychometry and various forms of telepathy. If we're to move against them, we need people the equal of them in those skills, which means that you and the other adepts will have to strengthen your skills even more, to the absolute limit, no matter how dangerous the attempt. You'll do that over the next few weeks, commencing straightaway, while I and the other elders of the colony discuss the situation and decide what steps should be taken. When we're ready to move, we'll inform you. Meanwhile, you must work at your skills night and day. As part of your training, you'll try to find out as much as you can about the cyborgs, particularly those in the White House. You can attempt this by astral projection, if you wish, but please do so with care.'

'I'll be careful,' Michael had said.

'Use any means at your disposal,' Brandenberg had continued. 'Isolate yourself from your family and friends. Meditate alone. The other adepts will be alone also, which is as it should be.'

'Can I venture into the wilderness?'

'Yes. Leave immediately, departing via the dome, and I'll inform your parents in your absence. Any questions?'

'No.'

'Good luck, Michael.'

Now Michael was far out in the Antarctic wilderness, well beyond where Robert Stanford had taken his last steps on Earth, in a vast, flat, glittering white plain surrounded by distant ice-capped mountains. He was sitting in the lotus position on the hardpacked snow, wearing only a loincloth, defying the freezing cold with the power of his will as he gazed wide-eyed into an immense, dazzling sun. He was practising a form of Tibetan *tumo*, defeating the cold through deep-breathing exercises and by focusing intensely on imagined inner fires, believing that in this way he could absorb *prana*, the life force, but also aware that it was dangerous in that it could cause hyperventilation and produce hallucinations or even unconsciousness, in which case his defences would be breached and he would freeze to death. At the same time, however, he was perfecting the skills that he had built up over the years, skills to do with controlling his pulse rate, digestion, metabolism and kidney activity while slowing his heartbeat almost to the vanishing point. In doing this, he was able to reduce himself, as an organism, to a condition similar to that of a hibernating animal. In fact, he could have been buried alive for several days without ill effects.

Concentrating on his inner fire, he saw it flickering in eternity, beyond time and space, in that interior self that few humans ever perceived, something separate from the blood and the bone of the frail, mortal body. Time stood still where the fire burned, or, more accurately, where it did not exist; and though one day passed into the next, Michael did not age a second. He lost himself in that inner fire, *became* the fire, burned as a flame, and in the heart of the flame his soul took wing and he rose out of himself. Looking down, he saw himself in the lotus position, almost naked, covered in snow, his eyes wide open, a mere speck in that vast white plain; then he turned away, spiralling up like a vapour, to project himself into the radiant, boundless sky and transcend Earth's dominion. He travelled through his mind, through the cosmos, to come down in another place.

He was back in the snow, still in the lotus position, still

almost naked, but now in front of the glittering geodesic dome that he had left many days ago. He had come here, he realized, not by astral projection, but by the Tibetan art of *lung-gom* that he had practised alone for years and that enabled him to travel at great, unnatural speed across the most inhospitable terrain, not by running like normal men, but by lifting himself magically from the ground and proceeding by leaps, endowed with the elasticity of a rubber ball and rebounding each time his feet touched the ground. In this way he would have covered any distance in less than half the time it would have taken him outside the trance state.

Aware that he had completed the first of his demanding exercises, he returned to his personal room inside the dome, the bleak abode of an adept, and refreshed himself by sleeping, eating and drinking regularly for forty-eight hours. His room, like all the other adepts' rooms, was dome-shaped (in fact, shaped like the interior of a flying saucer) and so spartan that it contained only a mattress on the stone floor, a blanket, some earthenware utensils for basic food and drink, and a low, glass-topped table holding items that could be used for his exercises in psychometry and thoughtography.

As part of their training, the adepts, all Michael's age, would often enter another adept's room and walk around touching various items, to leave traces of their presence in the room when they quit it again. These traces, invisible to the naked eye, could be 'read' by one trained in psychometry: it was part of the individual adept's training that, upon entering his own room, he would attempt to ascertain if anyone had been there in his absence and, if so, seek to identify that person by the traces of himself that he had left behind. Michael did this, walking around his room and lightly touching various objects while concentrating upon them with his eyes closed. His concentration was fierce, highly developed over years of practice, and soon he could sense that someone had indeed been in the room in his absence, touching various objects to superimpose his own presence, or leave his own traces, over Michael's. Once Michael had managed to confirm this, he picked up a CD-ROM diskette, the object upon which he had most strongly felt the traces of the other individual, and concentrated upon it, keeping his eyes shut tightly, until he could visualize that other person with his inner eye. Recognizing another adept, Leon Turturro, he called him on his cellular phone.

'Yes?' Turturro responded.

'It's Michael. Did you enter my room while I was away?'

'No.'

'Yes, you did.'

'I did not.'

'You did.'

'What makes you think that?'

'I checked a CD-ROM that I haven't used for months and I felt your personality all over it. Once I felt you, I saw you.'

'This must be love, Michael.'

'You should be so lucky.'

Turturro chuckled. 'You've traced the right man,' he admitted. 'Yes, it was me. Very *good*, Michael.'

'I might pay *you* a visit some day.'

'You do that,' Turturro said.

Pleased, Michael went to see Lee Brandenberg and found the old man seated behind his desk, studying the computer screen in front of him, framed by the windows that gave a panoramic view of Queen Maud Land. All white. Everything. Plains and mountains alike. When Michael approached him, Brandenberg waved him into the chair at the other side of the desk.

'So,' he said when Michael was seated, 'you've returned from the wilderness. How did it go?'

'Excellent,' Michael replied, thinking (as he did every time he entered this room) of how Robert Stanford, Dr Frederick Epstein and the legendary John Wilson had all been, at one time or another, in this very same place. He was awed by the thought. 'I meditated there for many days, almost naked, yet the bitter cold didn't bother me at all. Nor did I have the need for food and drink from start to finish. When I returned, I ran all the way as if my feet had wings, completing the journey in less than half the normal time. I was in the trance state.'

'You suffered no ill effects?'

'None.'

'Are you continuing with your training?'

'Yes.'

'So why are you here?'

'Though I've managed in the past to project myself as far as the moon, I've never been able to get into any of the buildings being used by the cyborgs . . . places like the White House and the Pentagon, right here on Earth. I'm going to try again – I'll try to access the White House – but first I wanted to ask you about something that I've never quite understood.'

'What's that, Michael?'

'When they first arrived, the cyborgs took over every major government building in the world and most of the top-secret research establishments. While their reasons for taking over the latter were understandable – they wanted to use the facilities and labour of those establishments for their own research projects – their retaining of places such as the White House, Buckingham Palace, the Kremlin and the whole of the Forbidden City in Beijing seemed pointless to me.'

'Why?'

'Apart from the Forbidden City, most of those buildings are relatively small and not suitable for massive technological research.'

'So?'

'What do the cyborgs want them for?'

'Psychological warfare,' Brandenberg said without hesitation. 'They're using their possession of those places as a constant reminder to us of just how much the human race has surrendered to them. Those particular buildings represent the highest author-ity in the country they belong to, so by taking them over and remaining in them, by throwing out the monarchies, the presidents, the political leaders, and by continuing to use the buildings for their own purposes, the cyborgs are depriving the humans of their greatest symbols of national pride and unity. The possession of those buildings is, in fact, a slap in the face to the people; a constant reminder that their leaders couldn't defend them and that the cyborgs are now in charge.'

'But we don't really know what the cyborgs are getting up to in those buildings.'

'No, we don't. As you said, most of them can't be used for large-scale technological research, but they could be used for medical, surgical and computer research – all areas that we know they're obsessed with. Certainly, they won't be wasting the space provided – but God knows what their projects are. So please try again to access the White House because we *have* to get in there.'

Returning to his room, Michael squatted in the lotus position on the cold stone floor and placed himself in a 'receptive' state by first attaining complete relaxation, then, in that unnatural condition (complete relaxation being alien to the human condition), concentrating intensely on his inner self. Eventually, after hours that seemed like days, with the physical world dissolving around him and his spirit in free fall, his brain was producing a steady alpha rhythm that enabled it to have telepathic communication over vast distances – a form of astral projection. Once in this state, he prepared himself for his mental assault on the protected White House by concentrating on something easier to get at – the unprotected moon – and in this he succeeded.

The cyborgs had taken over the dark side of the moon and Michael, through astral projection, saw their self-repairing robot moon-miners digging for plagioclase and anorthosite, which were a source of uranium, and ilmenite, containing titanium and iron. These substances, Michael knew, were used for the building of the cyborgs' flying saucers and other spacecraft. Realizing through this that the cyborgs were still involved in the building of spacecraft, doubtless of a kind even more advanced than those they already had, Michael cast his thoughts farther afield and saw that the moon's surface was now crawling not only with robot moon-miners but with fuel-cell, hydrogen-burning tractors, mass drivers and soil blowers. Its once barren valleys and plains were now peppered with cyborg-constructed nuclear power plants, ninety-foot antennas with aluminium reflectors for the transmission of electric power obtained from microwave beams in space, 1000-foot-diameter radio telescopes that constantly scanned the cosmos, and immensely powerful radio beacons that were sending signals into space non-stop. Letting his thoughts travel on, he saw that various cyborg satellites and space stations, the latter shaped like great wheels and spinning constantly to produce artificial gravity, were in orbit around the moon. Carried up there, sometimes in their separate constituent pieces, by flying saucers, they were assembled and maintained by a combination of cyborgs and robot workers. Human beings, as Michael knew, had no place up there because every space project of the Old Age had been brought to a halt.

With his telepathic powers now at full strength, and so feeling more confident, Michael returned his thoughts to Earth and concentrated intently on the White House. After his success in reconnoitring the moon, he was initially frustrated when, as had happened so often in the past with this target, he now came up against a wall of impenetrable darkness.

He fought to break through this wall, but it constantly pushed him back, and he realized that the cyborgs, highly advanced in parapsychological skills, had created a mental barrier to prevent telepathic intrusions into their space. This time, however, Michael refused to give in: instead, he focused even more intensely on what he was doing, first *imagining* the White House, then *willing* it into being as a visible entity in his head. It materialized eerily, reluctantly, out of that unreal wall of darkness until it was clearly there before him. First he saw the eighteen acres of flower gardens, lawns and trees around the whitewashed sandstone building, then the balustraded roof-line, and then, finally, the Ionic pilasters and windows with alternating rounded and triangular pediments.

At this point, he felt a fierce resistance, a great mental force pushing against him, and the image of the White House wavered and grew dim as the barrier created by the combined mental telepathy of the cyborgs tried to keep him outside. He refused to retreat, instead concentrating still more intently, feeling that his brain was bursting, aware of his racing heart, the agitated alpha rhythms – and was relieved when he saw the image of the White House becoming three-dimensional, seemingly solid, growing larger each second.

From high above the building, where his astral projection had placed him, Michael saw the Prowlers and SARGEs parked in front of the North Entrance, with cyborgs patrolling back and forth. He glided across the building, as if his thoughts were borne on wings, eventually descending over the lawns of the Ellipse. Once there, he willed himself to the southern side of the White House, melted into it, was surrounded by it, and emerged into what he assumed by its appearance was the Diplomatic Reception Room. He could see this room clearly, as if in broad daylight. It was empty, but when he tried to go through it, to explore the rest of the building, wanting to check all three floors, the light abruptly dimmed, the walls appeared to vaporize, and he found himself drifting through a darkness filled with flickering, silvery-white fireflies, which reminded him, rightly or wrongly, of the electrochemical signals, the neurons, that pass information from one point in the brain to another.

Where am I? Michael wondered. *In the White House or not? Is this the White House or the interior of someone's brain? Someone or something? What's happening here?*

He was being blocked again but he willed himself onward, letting his memory guide him, recalling the diagrams he had studied to familiarize himself with the building, and glided upwards, over stairs he could scarcely see, to what he assumed was the East Room on the first floor. Now, though he saw little, the darkness being even deeper, he heard a bass humming sound, almost *felt* it, an infrasound. As the sound grew louder, as the pressure increased, the silvery-white fireflies multiplied dramatically, flickered on and off more rapidly, then started streaking this way and that, at incredible speeds, now here and then there, living and dying on the instant, creating countless lines of light that criss-crossed repeatedly until they formed an immense, glowing, constantly changing web, the strands of which were joined by a distant, rhythmically pulsating, mesmerizing dark core.

Suddenly terrified, imagining that he was approaching a monstrous, steadily breathing, all-devouring spider in the centre of its immense web – a virtual cosmos of darkness and streaming light and infrasounds that could be *felt* – Michael almost lost control and felt his concentration weakening. But he managed to hold on long enough to convince himself that what he feared could only be an illusion.

Gliding forward again, surrounded by the darting fireflies, the criss-crossing silvery-white lines, an abyss of darkness on all sides, up and down, beyond time and space, he approached that pulsating dark core at the heart of the great web and felt the bass humming sound, the infrasound, as a palpable presence, moving in on him, crushing him.

At that moment, for no reason that he could comprehend, even as he felt that he was suffocating, Michael thought of Wilson.

He sensed that Wilson was *here*, right in front of him, all around him, somehow part of that pulsating dark core at the heart of the immense glowing web that now filled his whole view.

Fear rushed back to hammer down his defences and smash his concentration.

Everything dissolved around him, the great silvery-white web turning back to light-flecked darkness, the fireflies then disappearing to leave only the darkness, and the darkness receding to let the walls of the White House reappear, albeit vaguely, and finally the White House itself dissolving as he returned (or, more precisely, as his thoughts returned) to his room in the glittering geodesic dome outside Freedom Bay. His heart was racing and he was trembling, sweating profusely, as if about to collapse.

He did not collapse. Instead, he stretched out on his spine, placed his hands behind his head, spread his legs and practised deep breathing until his racing heart had slowed down and he was breathing normally again. Back in control of himself, but still shaken by what he had experienced, feeling older than his true age yet somehow more prepared for the future, he hurried out of his room. He left the geodesic dome and crossed to Freedom Bay, passing the parked flying saucers and other vertical ascending craft, all created by the legendary John Wilson, then took the lift up to Dr Brandenberg's office near the mountain's summit. No appointment had been made, so Brandenberg looked up, surprised, when Michael walked in and stopped in front of his desk.

'Wilson's back,' Michael said without preamble but with absolute confidence. 'And he's in the White House.'

Chapter Eleven

──────◆◆◆◆──────

Gumshoe's personal space had been well and truly invaded by Bonnie Packard and he was having trouble coming to terms with it. If Bonnie had been a saint sent down from heaven to look after him, Gumshoe would have still had problems because he had lived by himself for so long and didn't know how to compromise with the habits and foibles of the other human being now sharing, supposedly temporarily, his small, cluttered apartment in Georgetown. The problem was exacerbated by the fact that Bonnie was *not* a saint sent down from heaven to look after him, but was, instead, a noisily opinionated Long Hair with the domestic skills of an orang-utan. Given her state of impoverishment (also temporary, she had informed him), Gumshoe had bought her a lot of clothes to compensate for the ones she had lost to her unpaid landlord and already they were strewn all over the apartment to add to Gumshoe's normal state of disorder. As for the bathroom, he could hardly find his own toothbrush in the clutter of hair gels, hairclips, combs, brushes, lipstick, phosphorescent make-up, unwashed knickers and discarded bras left there by his disorganized female guest.

Not that she wasn't trying. It was quite touching, really, the way she would mutter, 'Oh, for Christ's sake!' when Gumshoe feebly complained about the mess and then melodramatically tidied up, picking her things off the floor and chairs and out of the sink only to dump them in some other equally messed-up area. Then, as she discarded what she was wearing or made herself up – the purple lipstick and painted face and gelled hair – she would drop things all over the place again, obviously not used to drawers or cupboards. In truth, she drove Gumshoe mad.

'So what's happening to this other place you're trying to find?' he asked her when she'd been in his place a fortnight, instead of the one night he had planned.

'Why? You want rid of me?'

'I didn't say that. I merely—'

'I'm a nuisance now, am I?'

'I didn't say that, either. I merely—'

'I made your breakfast the other morning,' she bitterly reminded him.

'Cornflakes.'

'What's wrong with that?'

'Nothing. They were great. But—'

'You didn't even say thanks.'

'I made breakfast all the other days,' he reminded her. 'Toast and boiled eggs.'

'I hate boiled eggs.'

'You never mentioned that fact before. Now about this apartment you're trying to find . . .'

'I'm looking! I'm looking! It just isn't easy. I mean, I don't have a dime to my name and they aren't into charity.'

'I lent you the money for a deposit,' Gumshoe reminded her.

'You really *do* want rid of me, don't you?'

'What happened to the deposit?'

'I mean, it's not that I'm any kind of trouble. All I do is watch TV.'

'That's true enough,' Gumshoe said.

And it *was* true enough. From the moment she slipped out of his bed to the moment she slipped back into it, leaving him to sleep on his lonesome on the settee, she did little other than watch the TV, with the external speaker turned off and earphones on her head, her jaws mangling chewing gum, purple lips blowing bubbles. He desperately tried pretending that she wasn't in the room, right there behind him, her legs long and practically naked except for the hotpants, moving restlessly this way and that, making suggestive rustling sounds, exciting his seemingly constant erection, while he worked in growing despair at the twenty-eight-inch computer screen of his Tower of Babble, either hacking into someone's system on behalf of a rich client or trying to track down some references to the mysterious 'Wilson'.

So far he hadn't managed to find anything on Wilson, though he had, given the constant distraction of Bonnie's presence in the same room, fucked up more than one professional hacking job in a way that he had not done before. This frustrated him greatly. Even more frustrating, however, was the fact that he found her undeniably attractive, despite the ghoulish make-up, and that even as her presence here was preventing him from engaging in cybersex (she would be right there behind him, watching his every move), it was also increasing his sexual desire and making him think helplessly of her as a potential source of real-time relief. Given his former love of cybersex, he was shocked to find himself feeling this way and as a result was even more keen to get rid of her. When it came to the subject of her imminent departure, however, he could not pin her down.

'Any luck today?' he asked when she had returned from yet another jaunt around the seedier, therefore cheaper, residential areas of Washington DC, supposedly looking for somewhere cheap to rent.

'No.'

'Nothing available?' he said, knowing damned well that there was plenty of accommodation available in the only areas she could possibly afford, if she could afford anything at all, which he was beginning to doubt, though she insisted she would be all right once she had been able to put down the deposit he had given her. The situation, she had explained, blinking her big star-painted eyes, was that her friends would help her out on a weekly basis once she had her own place, though they couldn't cough up the three-month deposit demanded in advance. Making good money from his hacking work, Gumshoe had given her that deposit but was convinced that she had, in fact, already spent it on clothes or, just as likely, on drugs. He suspected the latter because of her ability to watch the TV all day long as if in a trance, only moving enough to cross and recross her long legs to encourage his distracting erections. His distraction was, of course, even more acute because of the lack of cybersex due to her constant presence on the settee right behind his work desk and his ever-engaged Tower of Babble.

'I saw a few places,' she confessed, sighing and stretching out on the settee to watch the TV with spaced-out eyes, 'but I wouldn't expect a pig to live in 'em.'

'Maybe you haven't spread your net wide enough.'

'Are you suggestin' I'm not takin' this seriously?'

'I merely——'

'You think I want to stay *here*, is that it?'

'I only meant——'

'You think I'd rather stay with someone like you, a cyberspace ghoul, when I could be living my own life with friends who know how to live?'

'I'm not a cyberspace ghoul.'

'You're not much better, that's for sure. You spend all your waking hours on that goddamned computer and you hack into other folks' systems for dubious reasons. Go out! Get a life!'

'I'm happy with the life I've got,' Gumshoe said, 'and I do go out on occasion. I met *you* when I was outside, after all.'

'Big occasion! Big deal! The ghoul goes out once or twice a year and thinks he's living a life. Now do you mind? I'm tryin' to watch TV.'

'You watch TV a lot,' Gumshoe reminded her.

'So as not to distract you,' she retorted quickly. 'That's the only reason. I mean, a girl can't make a sound in this dump because the maestro's at work, so I watch TV instead – when I'm not out looking for a decent place to stay, which is exhausting, believe me.'

'Regarding a place to stay . . .'

'Stop nagging me,' Bonnie said, picking up her headset to cover her ears and concentrate on the TV while stretched out, very attractively, on the settee, her long legs sensational as always in the hot pants, agitating Gumshoe's neglected loins. 'I'm doin' the best I can. Now why don't you just go back to work and leave me alone? Lose yourself out in cyberspace.'

Gumshoe did so, not knowing what else to do, distracting himself from his unusual yearnings for real-time sex with Bonnie by hacking into the computer systems of major companies on behalf of other companies, either to steal something from them or to insert a destructive virus: both kinds of job paid well. Or he pursued his present main obsession – apart from Bonnie – to track down info on the mysterious Wilson.

For a while it looked like nothing was going to come up, that the Wilson he wanted was a cyberspace ghoul's invention. But eventually, after a whole week of searching, he found him under an obscure posting entitled UFOs – MAN-MADE, put out by a now-defunct flying saucer organization way back in the early 1980s. Scrolling down through the text, Gumshoe, initially bored, found himself gradually straightening up in his chair with growing excitement.

This was his man all right.

The term 'UFOs', as used in this particular article, referred to unidentified flying objects in general rather than flying saucers in particular. After yawning his way through an interminable, often subliterate essay on biblical UFOs and other historical sightings – clearly misidentified sightings of comets, meteors, solar flares, noctilucent clouds, plasmoids, corona discharges, ball lightning, temperature inversions, and the planet Venus – he reached the Great Airship Scare of 1896–1897 and became *really* excited.

According to the article, that particular scare, the first of the modern UFO flaps, had been caused by a number of 'mystery' airships that were seen flying over the United States between November 1896 and May the following year. Those sightings took place five years before the first aeronautical experiments of Orville and Wilbur Wright; and though there were, by that time, various airship designs on the drawing boards or in the Patent Office, none were known to have been constructed. Nevertheless, hundreds of perfectly sane United States citizens saw airships flying overhead and reported that they were mostly cigar-shaped, that they frequently landed, and that the pilots often talked to the witnesses, usually asking for water for their machines.

The only pilot who ever gave his name was a man who called himself 'Wilson'. He never gave his first name.

Now really excited, Gumshoe read on . . .

The first 'Wilson' incident occurred in Beaumont, Texas, on April 19, 1897, when one J.B. Ligon, the local agent for the Magnolia Brewery, and his son Charles noticed lights in a pasture a few hundred yards away and went to investigate. They came upon four men standing beside a large, dark object which neither of the witnesses could see clearly. One of those men asked Ligon for a bucket of water, Ligon let him have it, and then the man introduced himself as Mr Wilson. He told Ligon that he and his friends were travelling in a flying machine, that they had taken a trip out to the Gulf — presumably the Gulf of Galveston, though no name was given — and that they were returning to the quiet Iowa town where the airship and four others like it had been constructed. When asked, Wilson explained that electricity powered the propellers and wings of his airship. Then he and his crew got back into the airship and Ligon watched it ascending.

The next day, 20 April, Sheriff H.W. Baylor of Uvalde, also in Texas, went to investigate a strange light and voices in back of his house. He encountered an airship and three men —

and one of the men introduced himself as Wilson, from Goshen, New York. Wilson then enquired about one C.C. Akers, former sheriff of Zavalia County, saying he had met him in Fort Worth in 1877 and now wanted to see him again. Sheriff Baylor, surprised, replied that Captain Akers was now at Eagle Pass, and Wilson, apparently disappointed, asked to be remembered to him the next time Sheriff Baylor visited him. Baylor reported that the men from the airship wanted water and that Wilson requested that their visit be kept secret from the townspeople. Then he and the other men climbed back into the airship and 'Its great wings and fans were set in motion and it sped away northward in the direction of San Angelo'. The county clerk also saw the airship as it left the area.

Two days later, in Josserand, Texas, a whirring sound awoke farmer Frank Nichols, who looked out from his window and saw brilliant lights streaming from what he described as 'a ponderous vessel of strange proportions' floating over his cornfield. Nichols went outside to investigate, but before he reached the large vessel, two men walked up to him and asked if they could have water from his well. Nichols agreed to this request – as farmers in those days mostly did – and the men then invited him to visit their airship, where he noticed that there were six or seven crew members. One of those men told him that the ship's motive power was highly condensed electricity and that it was one of five that had been constructed in a small town in Iowa with the backing of a large stock company in New York.

The next day, on April 23, witnesses described by the *Houston Post* as 'two responsible men' reported that an airship had descended where they lived in Kountze, Texas, and that two of the occupants had given their names as Jackson and Wilson. Four days after that incident, on 27 April, the *Galveston Daily News* printed a letter from the aforementioned C.C. Akers, in which Akers claimed that he had indeed known a man in Forth Worth, Texas, named Wilson; that Wilson was from New York; that he was in his middle twenties; and that he was of 'a mechanical turn of mind' and was then working on 'aerial navigation and something that would astonish the world'.

Finally, early in the evening of 30 April, in Deadwood, Texas, a farmer named H.C. Lagrone heard his horses bucking as if in stampede. Going outside, he saw a bright white light circling around the fields nearby and illuminating the entire area before descending and landing in one of the fields. Walking to the landing spot, Lagrone found a crew of five men, three of whom engaged him in conversation while the others collected water in rubber bags. The men informed Lagrone that their airship was one of five that had been flying around the country recently; that theirs was in fact the same one that had landed in Beaumont a few days before; that some of the airships had been constructed in a backcountry town in Illinois and that they were reluctant to say anything else because they hadn't yet taken out any patents.

By May that same year, the wave of sightings ended . . . And the mysterious Mr Wilson wasn't heard from again.

Completing his reading of the unsigned article, Gumshoe was so excited that he temporarily forgot the presence of Bonnie, still stretched out on the settee behind him. Now with the other lead he had needed – the UFO phenomenon of the so-called Post-war Years, meaning the years after World War Two – he started surfing the Net to find anything else relating to man-made flying saucers. As he did so, he found Wilson's name popping up repeatedly, letting him gradually piece together a life that seemed, even with hindsight, to have been truly incredible.

The 'Wilson' who featured so strongly in the Great Airship Scare of 1896-1897 had repeatedly stated that he had con-structed his airships – either five or six – in Iowa and Illinois. Taking those locations as leads, Gumshoe ran a search for a

Wilson who had either come from or worked in one of those two areas. It did not take him long to find a John Wilson, born 6 July 1870 in Montezuma, Iowa.

Montezuma, Gumshoe noted, was located near the border with Illinois, which the 'Wilson' of the Great Airship Scare had also given as a location for at least one of his airship-construction plants.

A further trawl through the Net produced extracts from an obscure out-of-print non-fiction book, *Project UFO: The Case for Man-Made Flying Saucers* (1995), written by a British author, W.A. Harbinson, covering the whole history of man-made flying saucer projects, and giving Wilson's history in more detail. Most of that history was included in the Net posting and when Gumshoe read it, the hairs on the back of his neck stood up. He read it all three times, trying to take it in: Wilson's career at MIT, his responsibility for the Great Airship Scare of 1896–1897, his work on liquid-fuelled rockets with Robert H. Goddard, his subsequent covert career with the Nazis, his designing and building of the first flying saucers and, finally, his flight to, and death in, Neuschwabenland, Antarctica. It was fucking mindblowing.

'The son of a bitch!' Gumshoe muttered without thinking as he studied his glowing screen.

'What's that?' Bonnie Packard called out from her supine position on the settee behind him. 'Did you say something, shithead?'

Startled to be reminded of the presence of the short-haired Long Hair behind him, reminded in turn by this fact that he no longer had any privacy, he called over his shoulder, 'No!' and then went back to his reading, only to find that he had reached the end of the book extracts about the mysterious Wilson.

'Shit!' he exclaimed.

'What's that?' Bonnie Packard called out, her vacant gaze still fixed on the silent TV screen, getting the sound through her headset. 'Did you speak again, dumbo?'

'Not a word,' Gumshoe lied.

He spent the next half an hour surfing the Net for anything else he could find on Wilson, but came up with nothing until, on an impulse, he keyed in FICTION/WILSON, and found himself trawling through every character named Wilson in English-language literature.

Voilà! He hit the jackpot.

Way back in 1980 a British author named W.A. Harbinson – the very same hack who had penned the factual tome on man-made flying saucers – had published a 600-odd page novel, *Genesis*, that was, he insisted in a lengthy Author's Note, fact disguised as fiction. The novel's theme was that the flying saucers sighted since the end of the Second World War were actually man-made craft and that the mastermind behind them was the same mysterious 'Wilson' who had first come to light during the Great Airship Scare of 1896–1897.

Published as an original paperback, *Genesis* became a cult success on both sides of the Atlantic and remained in print for almost two decades. In 1995, however, the author published another fact-based novel, *Inception*, which was a 'prequel' to *Genesis*, covering Wilson's life in greater detail, including his work for the Nazis, and suggesting that at the end of the war he had fled with other Nazi scientists to a secret base in Neusch-wabenland (Queen Maud Land), Antarctica. There he had completed the construction of his first successful flying saucers and had used them as weapons in his battle to gradually, scientifically, take over the world.

Inception was followed by another so-called 'prequel', *Phoenix*, that brought Wilson's story up to the beginning of the original *Genesis*. The latter then became Book Three in the novel-sequence known as the 'Projekt Saucer' series. A fourth novel, *Millennium*, was published in 1996, completing an epic work, totalling about 2,300 fact-filled pages, based on Wilson's extraordinary life and including . . . his death.

For indeed, according to Harbinson, Wilson *had* died in his

Antarctica base just before it was captured by US military forces and turned into a legitimate research centre called Freedom Bay. There, according to Harbinson, Wilson's tale had ended.

Yet, according to what Gumshoe was now finding on the Net, Harbinson himself was something of a mystery . . . as was the fate of his epic series based on Wilson's life.

Though the series was essentially an epic *American* story, only two of the books had been published in that country – inexplicably, the first and the third. The fact that the second and fourth books had not been published in the US, though they had been published in Great Britain, had led to suppositions on the Net that those particular volumes had been suppressed. As for the author, though he had written 2,300-odd pages of fiction based on the known facts of Wilson and his flying saucers, as well as a voluminously researched non-fiction book on the subject, he had not been known personally to anyone in the UFO-research community and had never been seen at any UFO convention, any science fiction convention or, indeed, any kind of authors' convention. His final novels – not about Wilson or man-made flying saucers, though on marginally related subjects – had been released in 1999. Then he had dropped out of sight almost as completely as Wilson had done many years before.

Nevertheless, given the odd fate of his epic series, particularly in America, where two of the volumes had possibly been suppressed, and given that no one in the UFO community of the time had ever met the author of that voluminous flying saucer research, by the time his epic series about Wilson had gone out of print completely, in #4 of the New Age, when the arrival of the cyborgs had perforce increased computer interaction and devastated conventional book publishing, there was widespread speculation on the Net that Harbinson might have been a member of the National Security Council (NSC), which was then communicating with the 'aliens'; that he might have been abducted and brainwashed by the 'aliens' into writing his books to spread disinformation about man-made flying saucers to detract from the real, alien saucers; and, finally, that he might have actually *been* Wilson and that *the latter* had been using the novels for a different kind of disinformation. So the Net of the late 1980s had speculated.

Gumshoe wondered if there was any truth to it. Certainly the author, clever bastard, whether Harbinson or Wilson, had constantly, blatantly, stolen from himself, moving text, mainly factual, from one book to the other, obviously to ensure that even if one volume in the series went out of print, the next would still carry the factual, as distinct from the fictional, material. He had therefore written the series with clear, ruthless intent before dropping out of sight.

Gumshoe was fascinated. Having lost the trail of Wilson, he now tried to find Harbinson in the hope of discovering just how much of what he had written about Wilson (assuming author and character were not one and the same) was true and how much was false. Alas, after many more hours of surfing the Net, he learned only that Harbinson had travelled a lot and otherwise had led a carefully anonymous life. Net press cuttings and reproductions of the blurbs of various dustjackets showed that while born in Belfast, Northern Ireland, Harbinson had lived at various times in Australia, the United States, Spain, London, Cornwall, the Republic of Ireland and Paris, France. *Millennium*, the final book in his epic 'fictional' series, had been completed in Paris, but some time after that he had moved back to West Cork, Ireland. Finally, in the year 2001, or #1, the year the cyborgs took over, he had disappeared for good.

Had the cyborgs taken him? Gumshoe wondered, leaning back in his chair and staring in a daze at his computer. Or had he disappeared for his own good reasons when the cyborgs took over?

'What the fuck . . . ?' Gumshoe muttered.

'What's that?' Bonnie Packard said from behind him, where she was still stretched out on the settee, mesmerized by some mindless quiz show on the TV. 'Did you say something to me?'

'No,' Gumshoe said.

'You said something,' Bonnie insisted.

'Just talking to myself,' Gumshoe said.

'That's a real bad sign, buddy.'

Gumshoe distracted himself from her increasingly trouble-some presence (troublesome in the sense that he was starting to have sexual fantasies about her and was troubled by this fact) by punching some more keys, interacting with his mouse, and commencing another search across the Net, this one designed to find out if there was any recorded date for Harbinson's death. He had, after all, been born on 09 09 41 and would therefore be nearly eighty years old this year.

Even after a search that took him two hours, Gumshoe came up with zilch.

So clearly, if Harbinson *wasn't* Wilson, he was possibly still alive somewhere.

Where?

Determined to track down the British self-plagiarizing hack — *if* he was still alive — Gumshoe used his considerable skills and a lot of expensive on-line time to hack into the computer system of the royalties department of his last recorded publisher, located in London, England. Though worldwide book publishing had been devastated by the cyborgs' takeover and a subsequent leap in home entertainment that included downloaded fiction and interactive comic books on CD-ROMS, which in turn had dramatically reduced sales of printed volumes, a few of the original publishers had managed to survive in a rocky fashion and clearly Harbinson's publisher was one of them. Luckily for Gumshoe, given the publishing company's pitiful output these days and its consequent dire financial straits, it had an antiquated computer system that he was able to penetrate with relative ease. It had obviously been a long time since the publisher had been able to afford expensive security-program updates. Or had needed them.

Bringing the list of authors up onto his screen, he scrolled down to 'Harbinson, W.A.' and was pleased to note that the old goat was still being mailed royalty statements – though most of them, he also noted, were for minus payments, which confirmed that his books were out of print. He was, however, still receiving the statements and the last one, only four months old, had been mailed to him at an address in . . . Holy shit! . . . Right here in Washington DC.

Now so excited that his heart was racing slightly, Gumshoe scribbled down the address, then swivelled around in his chair to look at Bonnie Packard, where she was still lying supine on the settee, staring with stoned eyes at the same mindless TV quiz show, listening through the headphones. Her long legs were raised, one crossed over the other, and in hot pants they looked pretty sexy. Taking a deep breath to control his rising excitement, which now included a rising cock, Gumshoe slipped out of his chair, walked up to the settee, raised the earpiece off Bonnie's right ear and said, 'Hey! You wanna go out?'

The stoned dullness instantly left her painted eyes as she rolled them up to take him in.

'You mean . . . *outside?*'

'Yeah, I mean outside.'

'Hot dog, man, let's go!'

Galvanized back into life, she jumped to her feet and followed Gumshoe out of the apartment. Gumshoe led her down to the basement, removed his motorcycle from its cage and wheeled it out into the street. Then, when Bonnie was sitting behind him, he burned recklessly out of Georgetown, heading for Mount Vernon.

The sunlight was dazzling.

Chapter Twelve

You know who I am, but you cannot accept that it is me, because I died a good forty years ago when you took over my world of snow and ice. But time marches on, science opens new doorways, and the work I began in the Old Age has led to my rebirth. This was the reward for my foresight and a devotion to science, the purpose of which was to forge a new future for mankind. Your kind think of me as evil when in fact I am a redeemer, returned to correct the ills of mankind, painful though the process may be. As a child in my first incarnation I already knew that I was destined to do this.

I succeeded.

I am.

Naturally I was always a man out of my time, far ahead of my own time. And now, in my second incarnation, nothing has changed. Indeed, the world I inhabit, the world begun by the other me, is so far more advanced than your own and has a clearly defined purpose. It is a world devoted to science, to the pursuit of knowledge above all else, and everyone in it has their place, chosen for them at birth. From their first breath to their last, from the light of birth to death's darkness, they are taught to think only of their work and are shaped by that work. They are brought up in a closed system, cut off from the outer world, on the seabed, in underground complexes, in spaces so confined that you would not think it possible, though it certainly is, and there they live a life that has meaning and leaves no room for doubt.

With regard to our state of advancement, our young receive their education through interactive media systems and computer technology with heightened sensory stimulation, including 3-D sound and wraparound vision. Though our body of knowledge keeps expanding, we have no problems with the storage of printed books as our libraries store everything in computers with memory crystals that can compress whole encyclopedias into the space of a grain of sand. Instead of sprawling campuses, we have small student meeting rooms fitted with video-conferencing terminals, e-mail systems and database access. Chemical, biological and physics experiments are simulated electronically, doing away with the need for space-consuming laboratories. Erotic needs also are met electronically, with teledildonics simulating sex with sights, sounds and tactile input of the real thing: thus potentially messy human interaction is kept to a minimum. Our advances in medicine and surgery, gained through my so-called 'obscene' experiments on human beings in the Old Age, have enabled our surgeons to operate on patients without actually touching them, without the need for making large, bloody abdominal incisions, since the body's interior can now be viewed holographically and telepresence allows operations to be performed by remote control only after the exact cause of the trouble has been located.

All of this, and more, takes place in our large flying saucers, in our domes on the seabed, and in our hidden bases in isolated areas all over the world.

The Earth is our oyster. With our saucers, we can go anywhere, from the bottom of the oceans to the peak of the highest mountain, from dense forest to desert plain, and pick up anything we require for our own maintenance. From ordinary soil and sea water we extract aluminium, magnesium, titanium and cobalt; from seabed nodules we process pure gold; from acid-rain-producing high-sulphur coal we produce pure carbon cubes. With biofabrication techniques, in which the fundamental DNA codes in living tissue are altered, we can produce any kind of material we require from standard protein building blocks. Once these materials were used for the building of more saucers, but our most recent saucers are made of etherium which is as light as a feather yet extraordinarily strong and capable of withstanding up to 4000 degrees Fahrenheit — a temperature that melts all other known materials. Thus, we are virtually invincible and we now rule your world.

Your kind resent this, I know, but your resentment is ill-founded as the world we took over is one that could not have survived without us. Thus, while we are doing what we have come here to do, we are also cleaning up the mess we inherited.

What mess? you ask.

Let me tell you.

The earth contains six billion people and a quarter-million more are added to that figure every day. Those people now produce, consume and dispose of more material than in all the rest of history combined. Indeed, even as I dictate this, rubbish sites worldwide are overflowing and no room can be found for any more. The atmosphere is polluted. Right around the globe, waste incinerators and industrial processes are spewing deadly toxins into the sky and every year the Earth is poisoned with an additional 2.5 million tons of pesticides. Your creation of chlorofluorocarbons through the use of refrigerators, aerosol cans, gas emissions from automobiles and circuit-board fabrication is destroying the ozone layer and letting more ultraviolet light through to reach the Earth to cause sunburn, skin cancer, cataracts and crop damage, even as it drastically affects the world's forests, plankton and weather patterns. The ozone hole over Antarctica is now the area of the United States and the height of Mount Everest and more ozone holes are presently appearing over Europe and Canada. The continuing destruction of the remaining ozone will dangerously reduce still further our protection against solar radiation and lead to even higher levels of skin cancer, cataracts and other diseases. The increase in global warming due to the presence in the atmosphere of industrial greenhouse gases will cause drought on a massive scale and a drastic rise in sea levels, bringing about widespread famine, the flooding of major cities and, parodoxically, the terrifying possibility of a new Ice Age of the kind that may have wiped out the dinosaurs.

Were you doing anything to stop this? No. Instead you were producing even more deadly pollution with your ruthless pursuit of various forms of energy. Your hydroelectricity required the blockage of mighty rivers, your need to grow crops led to the destruction of tropical forests, your industrial areas were choking with smoke, your oil refineries filled the air with poisonous gas, your nuclear waste contaminated the earth and sea, and your thermal pollution was reaching appalling, potentially destructive levels.

We, on the other hand, those you would view as evil, are already taking this problem in hand.

By taking over the world, by stopping international travel and isolating each individual country from all the others, we have frozen mankind's state of technological advancement back where it was in the Old Age. Thus, if not stopping global pollution altogether, we have certainly ensured that it will not increase as rapidly as it had been doing before we took over.

We stole your freedom? What good was your freedom to you? By the time we took over the world, that world was not only destroying itself with global pollution but heading towards unprecedented conflict and bloodshed. Islamic fundamentalism had spread outward from the East to engulf Europe, the Mediterranean, the United States, and virtually the whole of the developed world. The Flame of Allah scorched all those it touched, with Islamic terrorism causing widespread destruction. The Middle East remained in turmoil and elsewhere anti-Semitism was flourishing and was the cause of more violence. In Bosnia, formerly Yugoslavia, in the very heart of a supposedly civilized Europe, rape, torture, murder and genocide were continuing with a barbarism not seen since the dark era of Nazi Germany. Terrorism was rampant on a global scale and terrorist atrocities were occurring more frequently and noted for their worsening brutality. Eco-terrorists, bio-terrorists and religious terrorists were bombing buildings with women and children inside them, ramming and sinking ships at sea with the crews still on them, releasing poisoned gas in subways, pouring toxic chemicals into reservoirs and aqueducts, practising even more hideous forms of biological warfare, destroying whole ecosystems by infecting their monitoring structures with computer viruses, and even using genetic engineering for the creation of biological weapons that could target their diseases on specific racial groups. On top of all this was the rise of extremist violence among every imaginable self-styled minority group, including Christian fundamentalists, Millennialists, doomsday cults, radical Blacks, and even the more rabidly active feminists and homosexuals. In fact, the world we took over was about to explode. But by isolating one country from another, by making it more difficult to transport armaments and explosives worldwide, we stopped the explosion.

Nor was that the only explosion threatening the world we took out of your hands. The population explosion was out of control and starting to make the whole world ungovernable. I repeat: six billion people and a quarter million being added to that figure every day, all with different, often conflicting, religions and political creeds. In India alone, twenty million Sikhs were fighting to form an autonomous Punjab nation, millions of Muslims in Kashmir were seeking *independence, Hindu fundamentalists were attacking those of other faiths, and bloody riots and slaughters were commonplace. In Africa, the population doubled in two decades and its billion citizens, divided by ethnic, tribal and linguistic barriers, ravaged by drought, famine and environmental degradation, waged bloody war against each other, paving the way for continent-wide disintegration. In China, the pressures of a 1.2 billion population were leading to the unravelling of that vast country's national fabric with social disorder, lawlessness, widespread political corruption, increasing unemployment and a dramatically rising suicide rate. Even the United States was spinning apart, with its fifty states competing fiercely against each other, disunity spreading, national allegiances decaying, unemployment rising, crime increasing, extremist movements demanding regional autonomy or actual secession, and racist and millennial groups of all kinds causing destruction and death on a grand scale. And everywhere in the world at the time we took over it was the same, with the gap between rich and poor increasing, refugees flooding the globe, ethnic tensions mounting, the arms trade booming; and drugs, genocide, plagues, starvation, pollution and terrorism rampant.*

We cannot solve this problem immediately, but we can, and will, in the long term. We took the first steps in population control shortly after we arrived and projects relating to other aspects of Earth control are under way. We aren't moved by altruism, but by healthy self-interest, being aware that the world, though only a temporary abode for mankind, has to be prevented from self-destruction at least until we can leave it. That time will come eventually — it is what we are striving for — but until it does we have to ensure that the Earth remains manageable.

This is why we have taken over, why we abduct in our flying saucers, why we have to enslave so many of you and keep those still free terrified. Because of these acts, you think of us as evil, as being beyond the pale. But we are merely pragmatic, impelled by pure reason, our pathways not cluttered with primitive emotions, our intentions clear and resolute. We have come to drag you out of the dark cave and let you reach for the stars.

In time, as the sun dies, the Earth will die as well. But long before that happens, before the dying Earth becomes no more than a barren cinder, before the human race dies off like the dinosaurs, like so many other species, we must leave it and travel on to our destiny.

We, you and I, having emerged from the primordial slime before our brothers, are engaged in this task.

This is what binds you to me.

Chapter Thirteen

Michael was dreaming. He was a golden-haired boy standing in an immense field of wheat, gazing up at the sun and wondering when it was going to die, as he knew that sooner or later it must. As he gazed at that silvery orb, squinting against its dazzling light, it expanded to cover the whole sky and let him dissolve into its shimmering haze. That haze had a dark core, an oddly pulsating light-flecked mass at the centre of which, very far away, as if viewed through the reverse end of a telescope, was a circular patch of slowly spinning stars. Michael was drawn towards those stars, through the tunnel of the infinite, and emerged to another cosmos, an immense web of flashing lights – not stars, but lights, flashing on and off rapidly, all around him, above him and below him, and he knew that he was inside a huge brain and being consumed by it. Then he saw himself up ahead, a mirror image of that golden-haired boy, but even as he was drawn towards the boy, either himself or another, the boy dissolved briefly and materialized again, this time as a full-grown man with the same golden-blond hair.

'This is what binds you to me,' the man said, indicating with a nod of his head the thousands of lights flashing rapidly on and off in that immense, pulsating darkness. 'You and I, despite our many differences, are one and the same.'

'No!' Michael protested, suddenly filled with a revulsion that consumed him and made his heart race.

He tried to turn away, but there was no direction home, just that universe of neurons flashing on and off, racing to and fro, up and down, and he felt himself dematerializing, being sucked into it, to become a part of it as the golden-haired man, his smile slight and chilling, looked on without blinking. That look terrified Michael, making him cry out as the darkness swiftly melted away and the sunlight returned . . . then he awakened, being shaken by his sister, whose smile was infinitely more human than the smile of the man in his dream.

'Hey, hey,' Chloe said, still shaking him awake where he lay on his bed in his parents' apartment in Freedom Bay, his eyes filled with the lights of the room, not with the sunlight. 'Wake up. You were crying out in your sleep. You must have been having a bad dream. Come on, wake up, handsome.'

Michael rubbed his eyes, then sat up on the bed. 'Yes,' he agreed, 'I was having a bad dream. What are *you* doing here?'

'I've been sent to fetch you,' Chloe said, brushing blonde hair from her large blue eyes. 'Dr Brandenberg urgently wants to see you.'

'Dr Brandenberg?'

'You heard me,' Chloe said. 'He called ten minutes ago and talked for a long time with Mom and Dad. I don't know what he said, but whatever it was it seems to have upset them both, so it must be pretty serious. They told me to come and fetch you immediately, so you'd better get out there real fast.'

'I will,' Michael said. He started to pull the sheet off him, but remembered that he was naked under it so instead he raised his eyebrows while still looking at Chloe. She looked back, smiling slightly. 'Well?' Michael asked.

'You want me to leave?'

'I want to get out of bed.'

'We're brother and sister,' Chloe said. 'No secrets between us.'

Michael pulled a pillow over his shoulder and swung at her with it. She ducked and sprang away from him, giggling as she made her way to the door. 'I bet you look *awful* naked,' she said.

'Get out of here,' Michael said.

'I am on my way, brother.'

When Chloe had left the room, Michael slipped out of bed and went for a shower. As he was washing, he recalled his dream and realized that he had been dreaming about Wilson, that unknown man with whom he was beginning to feel an inexplicable, faintly disturbing familiarity. Nothing that he had heard about the mysterious Wilson had made him seem appealing and, indeed, Dr Brandenberg had described him as a mutant – brilliant but inhumane and, given his absolute, thoroughly ruthless pragmatism, almost inhuman. Yet, despite this, there could be no denying that Wilson had also been a scientific genius and a genuine visionary, his technological innovations reshaping the world and leading, in the end, to the rule of the cyborgs, a tyranny for which he had also been responsible. Therefore, if Michael shared anything with Wilson, it was a visionary outlook on the future. Wilson had, after all, worked to circumvent the eventual death of the sun and the consequent obliteration of Mankind. Despite everything else he now knew about Wilson, much of it despicable, Michael had to admire him for that at least.

Drying himself off and dressing, Michael wondered what Dr Brandenberg had said to his parents and why he so urgently wanted to see him. Clearly, the call was related to what he had told Michael's parents, which strongly suggested that it was serious. Realizing this, Michael alternated between dry-throated nervousness and excitement as he left his bedroom and went into the living room, where he found both his parents and his sister seated around the table, just finishing breakfast. Before he could say a word, his father indicated that he should sit at the table, which he did. He saw the anxiety, carefully suppressed, in his mother's face and was struck by how much like Chloe she looked, right down to the blue eyes and golden-blonde hair.

Wilson had blond hair, he thought obliquely. *And I have blond hair. The boy in my dream had blond hair and I felt, in the dream, that it was me, though he seemed to be Wilson. No wonder I feel strange.*

In fact, as he studied his mother's face, noting how concerned it was, he wondered crazily if he was Wilson's doppelgänger, or vice versa. It was certainly a crazy thought in that Wilson, whether or not he was still present in some form right now, had originally died about forty years ago. Nevertheless, Michael could not shake off the feeling that he and Wilson were somehow connected. The very idea was disturbing and he was relieved to turn his attention on his father, who was looking both concerned and proud as he distractedly ran his fingers through his thatch of reddish-blond hair. He, at least, did *not* remind Michael of Wilson and that was a blessing.

'You can have your breakfast later,' Joe said. 'Right now, you have to go and see Dr Brandenberg. He wants you there straightaway.'

'Can you tell me what it's about?' Michael asked.

'Yes.' Joe glanced at Michael's mother, Grace, then returned his gaze to Michael, letting his breath out in an audible sigh. 'You're going out into the World,' he said, 'and you're leaving today. Dr Brandenberg asked for our permission and naturally we gave it.'

Michael's nervousness gave way to pure excitement tinged with disbelief. He had been waiting so long for this, preparing for it most of his life, and now that the moment was here he hardly knew how to react. His parents and Chloe, he knew, would be upset by his departure, concerned for his welfare, knowing how dangerous it would be out there, and this knowledge made him feel a bit selfish, even as his excitement increased. Nevertheless, he desperately wanted to go and nothing could change that fact.

'Thanks,' he said, not really knowing what else to say. 'I suppose I'd better get up there. I'll see you all later.'

'Not until you return,' his mother said, the pain of loss already in her blue gaze. 'Not until you return from the World, I mean. Brandenberg told us that we had to say goodbye now because you're leaving immediately.'

Despite Michael's enthusiasm, the speed with which this was all happening took him by surprise. 'Immediately?' he said. 'What about clothes and things?'

'You're to go up to Brandenberg's office as you are,' his father said. 'Everything, including your clothing, will be taken care of after he's spoken to you. You won't be seeing us again until you return from the World.'

Michael nodded, pushed his chair back and stood up. 'Right,' he said, preparing to leave the apartment, now wanting to leave as quickly as possibly and get this painful farewell over with. He had never left home before, apart from his treks into the nearby Antarctic wilderness and it took some getting used to. His mother and father stood as well, but Chloe remained seated, trying to smile and failing. His mother and father walked around the table to stand in front of him. Everyone was speechless for a moment. His father took hold of his right hand, shook it vigorously, then tugged him close for an emotional embrace.

'I'm proud of you,' he said, patting Michael's back, 'but you take care out there. You've worked for this all of your life and we appreciate the importance of the task you've been given. But the World is very different from Freedom Bay and certainly, these days, extremely dangerous. So be very, very careful out there and make sure you come back.'

'I will,' Michael said.

His father stepped back to let his wife embrace her son. Grace gave him a lingering hug and kissed him on the cheek, whispering, 'God bless you. I love you. Now, please . . . Go quickly.'

Michael pulled her back into his arms and kissed her on the cheek. 'I love you, too,' he said. Then he released her and went to the table to lean down over Chloe. She turned her big blue eyes, slightly moist, up towards him, still trying to smile, but still failing. He placed his hand on the back of her neck, then kissed the top of her head. 'Look after Mom and Dad for me,' he said.

'Yeah, right,' Chloe said, managing this time to grin, though her voice sounded shaky. 'See you soon, brother.'

'Absolutely,' Michael said. Then he turned and waved at his parents as he walked to the door. Once outside the apartment, after closing the door behind him, he took a deep breath, then proceeded along the gently curving white-walled corridor until he came to the elevator. Entering the elevator, he pressed the button for the penultimate floor and let himself be carried silently upwards, feeling that he was rising to the heavens to face Judgement Day.

Stepping out onto the floor containing Brandenberg's office, he thought of Wilson's chapel on the floor directly above, the top floor of the whole complex, on the very summit of the mountain, and recalled his experience there with a mixture of awe and fear. He had somehow made contact with Wilson there – or, at least, with Wilson's spirit – as he had done later, when he had astrally projected himself into the White House. The explanation for this foiled him for the present, but he would soon find out more. He would find the truth, or certainly attempt to find it, out there in the World. His fate awaited him out there.

Crossing the rectangular hallway to Brandenberg's office, he glanced down through the large bay window at the various inner levels of Freedom Bay, hacked out of the interior of the mountain by Wilson's slave workers a long time ago, each floor linked to the others by catwalks and lifts, the darkness of the central well eerily illuminated by the constantly flickering lights of the separate levels. Farther down, hundreds of metres below, was the docking area for the flying saucers, but these could not be seen from up here, being obscured in a pit of pitch-dark blackness. Slightly dizzied by what he was looking down upon, overwhelmed, as he always was, by the sheer magnitude of it all, he turned away from the window and pressed the bell located beside the intercom fixed to the door of Brandenberg's office.

'Yes?' Brandenberg said through the intercom.

'It's Michael.'

'Good. Come in.'

Michael entered. He found Brandenberg seated, as always,

behind Wilson's old desk, framed by the panoramic windows and their stupendous view of the vast, snow-covered Antarctic wilderness. Brandenberg indicated the chair at the other side of his desk with a wave of his hand. Michael sat facing him.

'You spoke to your parents?' Brandenberg asked rhetorically, since the answer was obvious.

'Yes,' Michael said. 'Clearly, you've decided to move against the cyborgs and you're sending me. I'm deeply gratified, sir.'

'Be just as deeply cautious,' Brandenberg responded sardonically, 'because what you're going to attempt will be extremely dangerous.'

'I always knew that,' Michael said.

Brandenberg nodded affirmatively, his slightly crooked lower lip curving into a slight smile. 'So,' he said, 'I take it you're prepared to leave immediately.'

'I'm prepared and keen.'

'Try not to be too enthusiastic, Michael. Try, instead, to remain distant and objective, thinking calmly at all times. You're not doing this for personal glory, but for the good of this colony and, ultimately, for the good of the whole world. Keep this firmly in mind each time you have to make a decision. By this I mean that what might help you in the short term could be detrimental to Freedom Bay, thus the world, in the long term. Instant victory isn't always a good thing and can often be deceptive. Think coldly and clearly.'

'Like Wilson,' Michael said.

Brandenberg smiled again. 'Yes, like Wilson. At least, as pragmatically as Wilson. Whether Wilson's alive or dead we still can't say for sure, but he's certainly the guiding light for the cyborgs, the spirit behind them. So think like him and try to anticipate what he'd be planning in any given situation. Do that and you might survive.'

'I will,' Michael said. 'So what have you planned?'

Brandenberg sighed forlornly, as if not sure that what he had planned would actually bear fruit, let alone be feasible in the first place. 'Your task is to insert yourself into Washington DC and then somehow get into the White House. Once inside, you're to ascertain if Wilson is actually there, either in body or in spirit, then somehow put a stop to him or, if he isn't actually there, put a stop to the work of the cyborgs and free the White House. If you succeed in doing that, we can follow you in and gradually wrest control of the whole country out of their hands. Whether or not this is possible is, of course, an issue of debate. In all fairness, I must remind you of this fact.'

'Can I ask why you decided to move at last? Was it because of my belief that I'd made some kind of contact with Wilson?'

'Or with some *manifestation* of him,' Brandenberg emphasized, then sighed again. 'Yes. I find it difficult to accept that myself, but the possibility remains that, given Wilson's state of scientific advancement at the time of his death, he *could* have somehow put himself back in circulation, either in the body of someone else – a human brain-implanted to such an advanced degree that he virtually *is* Wilson – or as a clone brought up from birth to be as near to an exact replica as possible. It is, after all, only a matter of time before the biocomputer combines with the cyborg to produce a clone that not only *looks* like the original person but also thinks and feels like him. This could be the case here.'

'Yet this Wilson – or this person . . . this manifestation . . . this *presence* that I assumed was Wilson – seems to be making telepathic contact with me, as if he knows me and has a reason to draw me to him. How do we account for that?'

'How, indeed?' Brandenberg responded, again sounding sardonic. Then he shrugged, slumping deeper into his chair. 'We have no way of knowing that yet – and your confusion as to how to describe him is understandable. All we can say for certain is that *you* have the gift for telepathic communication and it's known that biocomputers will, sooner or later, communicate the same way. If this . . . this Wilson is some kind of resurrected persona, some marvellously recreated facsimile of the original, either in a physical body or as some kind of bio-electronic entity, then his influence could be as strong now as it was when he was still alive – certainly with the cyborgs. In fact, the cyborgs could have *created* this Wilson from instructions left by him before he died, which was just before cloning became possible and well before biocomputers came into being. A biocomputer would be as alive as a human brain, with all its reasoning powers, and this . . . this Wilson communicating with you could be something like that. If this turns out to be the case, I've no idea how you're going to deal with it. But since you're the most advanced adept we have, having – as far as we know – all the parapsychological skills required for what you may be confronted with, naturally you were our first choice.'

'You're flying me to Washington DC?' Michael asked.

Brandenberg shook his head. 'No. That would be too dangerous. The cyborgs control the whole of the country, but they're particularly vigilant over important areas – and Washington DC is one of them, obviously. None of us here have left Antarctica since the takeover because of the cyborgs' control of the skies, but in this case we don't have a choice. We're going to fly you in to a pretty remote area, hoping that our own saucer – the most advanced we've so far developed – will get there unimpeded, perhaps being mistaken for one of their own or simply blocking their radar scans, which we can now do. But given our lack of experience in this area, we can't guarantee success. To be blunt about it, we might not even get you as far as the United States.'

'And if you do?'

'We're going to drop you off well away from Washington DC, well away from that whole area, in an isolated location in the Great North Mountains that divide West Virginia from Virginia. Depending on what route you take, that's about ninety miles, or nearly a hundred and fifty kilometres, from the heart of Washington DC. We'll drop you off near Wood-stock, which will enable you to make your way across the Shenandoah Valley. It's heavily forested and will give you good protection. From there, you'll have to make your own way to Washington DC, playing it by ear the whole time. *Don't* travel by night. Though the cyborgs' surveillance flights don't bother too much with that area, the odd ones almost certainly fly over it occasionally and chances are they would do so at night, after the midnight curfew. So, surprising though it may seem to you, daylight travel is safer. Also, don't necessarily trust anyone you speak to. While just about everyone you speak to may seem normal, an awful lot of people in the World have had cyborg brain-implants — and that makes them as close to an alien being as you're likely to get. In other words, though they might seem perfectly normal, they're controlled by the cyborgs and will instantly report back to them.'

'The walking dead,' Michael said.

Brandenberg smiled. 'When I was back in the World, as a young man, as an Air Force Captain, I saw an old black-and-white movie called *Invasion of the Body Snatchers*. The plot seemed a bit far-fetched at the time, but it wouldn't be these days. When people receive cyborg brain-implants, they *do*, in effect, become zombies who, though looking and behaving perfectly normally, have no will of their own and live only to spy for the cyborgs. You have to watch out for them.'

'Is there *anyone* I can trust?' Michael asked, becoming aware that the World he was going to visit was more treacherous and dangerous than he had imagined.

'Yes. There are plenty of people out there who are actively fighting the rule of the cyborgs and you'll probably need some of them to help you survive in Washington DC and even assist you when it comes to getting into the White House. The question is: how do you find them? Concerning this, I can only say that you should look, in particular, to people your own age — young people — the kind who most openly revolt against the cyborgs. Many of them, I have to tell you, aren't worth their own spit and only do what they do for vicarious thrills. Many of them are into drink and drugs, playing dangerous games with the cyborgs only because, like the disenfranchised of any society, they've nothing better to do and are dumb enough to think they'll always get away with it. Nevertheless, they're probably the only age group you can approach with any confidence: it'll be up to you, if you make contact with some of them, to use your own judgement as to their reliability. Certainly, you've got to get some help from somewhere, from streetwise kids, even if only for survival in the city until such time as you can infiltrate the White House. Just be careful who you trust, is all I'm saying. Apart from that, I can't help you.'

'I haven't packed anything,' Michael said. 'My parents wouldn't let me. They said you'd take care of that.'

'Yes,' Brandenberg said. 'I will. You can't wear your own clothes because all our clothes are made right here and would be instantly recognized as not having been manufactured in the US. As there are no imports or exports any more in the World, any clothing not made in the United States would instantly draw unwanted attention to you. So we've manufactured some clothing especially for you, based on designs found on the Internet, styled to suit someone of your age in present-day America, and with local labels prominently displayed. Likewise with your shoes, comb, toothbrush and other personal possessions.'

'Identification if I'm stopped?'

'The cyborg patrols only stop people to abduct them, so if you're stopped by them you'll be finished – you'll disappear and not be seen again – so just keep out of sight if you see a flying saucer or ground-based cyborg vehicle. You will, however, need new identification to show to local police, supermarkets, normal people who may imagine that *you're* a cyborg spy; and, of course, you'll need the plastic cards of a "real" person in order to obtain money from cash dispensers.'

'That's surely impossible,' Michael said.

Brandenberg smiled triumphantly. 'No, it's not,' he said. 'In preparation for this day – and for the day when, hopefully, we can send more men back there — we've spent the last few years hacking into various computer systems in the World and inserting the details of fictitious people, giving them full backgrounds and personal histories, then opening bank and shopping accounts for them. The hacking also enabled us, for instance, to make regular electronic deposits and withdrawals from those accounts to ensure that they would, if checked, look like they were being used all the time. Since all statements in the World are now sent by e-mail, we were able to make up false e-mail addresses for the automatic sending of those statements. Those addresses, however, while seeming to be in the US, all originated here and the statements come in on our own computer screens. So you'll be given the detailed history and documentation of one of those fictitious US citizens, one based in Washington DC: that means you can withdraw money, pay rent for accommodation and, of course, buy anything you need for as long as you're there.'

'How do I communicate with Freedom Bay?'

'You'll be given a 1000-megabyte notebook computer that you can use for e-mail that can't be intercepted or received by anyone but us. Your fellow adept, Leon Turturro, has been instructed to keep track of your movements telepathically and you can, should circumstances prevent the use of the notebook, try to contact him by telepathic means. You can also use the notebook for hacking into other computer systems, notably those of the cyborgs, but including the banks and retail outlets with which you'll be dealing on a daily basis. Okay?'

'Sounds great.'

'You sound like a child,' Brandenberg said testily, 'and that means you're too excited for your own good. *Stop* being excited, Michael. This isn't a childish game. It's an important job that could, if you happen to get caught by the cyborgs, lose you your liberty, your mind, or even your life. So keep your ego out of this. Think of yourself as a machine. Don't be swayed by vanity or childish pride, which could lead to mistakes. What we're doing, we can only attempt once – and we can't afford to foul up. Now, are you ready to leave?'

'Yes,' Michael said.

He was ready for anything.

Chapter Fourteen

Gumshoe crossed the 14th Street Bridge, took the exit for the National Airport, then burned along George Washington Memorial Parkway, passing the occasional SARGE or Prowler. He glimpsed the occasional flying saucer gliding overhead, ascending or descending vertically, or simply hovering over a stalled car, preparing to abduct the unfortunate driver who, once taken, would never be heard from again. Knowing this, Gumshoe detoured every time he saw anything relating to the cyborgs, though he always came back to the route that took him to Mount Vernon. It only took him twenty minutes. Once there, he continued another three miles south until he reached the expansive, well-kept grounds of Woodlawn Plantation.

Formerly the property of the National Trust for Historic Preservation, the late-Georgian-style mansion, surrounded by green lawns, rose gardens, large trees and boxwoods, all resplendent in late afternoon sunlight, had fallen into neglect with the coming of the cyborgs. It had then been rescued by a charity organization that had turned it into a nursing home for hard-pressed artists, musicians and writers – a desperate last gasp for the preservation of culture in a society now controlled by the cyborgs and hence devoted almost totally to scientific advancement.

'Jesus, man, this is some joint!' Bonnie Packard exclaimed

when Gumshoe had brought his motorcycle to a halt in the curved driveway in front of the riverside entrance.

'It sure is,' Gumshoe said, waiting until Bonnie had slipped off the pillion seat before swinging his right leg over and propping the motorcycle up on its support. 'Maybe we can find you a room here. I mean, it's used as a nursing home.'

'Up yours,' Bonnie said.

Standing in front of the portico over the entrance to the elegant building, which had symmetrical one-storey wings connected to the two-storey main house, Bonnie looked even more bizarre than she actually was, with her short-cropped pink-and-green hair, shaved eyebrows, striped face, blue-painted lips with fake blood, and, of course, her black-leather jacket with silver chains, skintight white T-shirt, black stockings, hotpants and high-heeled black leather boots. Nevertheless, there was something sweet about her, something soft behind the hardness, a suppressed sensitivity, and Gumshoe was increasingly taken with her, despite his own reservations.

'*Venez avec moi,*' Gumshoe said, starting towards the entrance.

'What the fuck's that mean?' Bonnie retorted, stopping him in his tracks.

'Sorry,' he said. 'It just slipped out. A little bit of the old *parlez-vous français.*'

'Think that makes you smart, do you?'

'I'm only taking lessons. Certain phrases just keep popping out before I can stop them.'

'Bullshit,' Bonnie said. 'You're just showin' off, that's all. You think that Frog language makes you somethin' special, but it doesn't, believe me.'

'You don't think I'm something special?'

'No, I don't.'

'My heart's breaking,' Gumshoe retorted as he turned away from her and walked up to the entrance, leaving her to follow him, which she did. Stopping behind him as he rang boldly on the doorbell, she said, 'So what are we here for?'

'I want to talk to someone,' Gumshoe replied, 'and this is where he's staying.'

'Who is he? Some kinda geriatric?'

'I suspect so,' Gumshoe said.

The door was opened from inside and an overweight middle-aged woman with a severe face under pinned-up greying auburn hair stared grimly at him. She was wearing a black blouse, black skirt and flat-heeled shoes.

'Yes?' she said flatly.

'This is the Woodlawn Rest Home?' Gumshoe asked.

'It sure is.'

'I'm Randolph Fullbright,' Gumshoe said, using his best speaking voice, 'and this is my friend, Belinda Packard, made up and dressed in that peculiar outfit because we're on our way to a kid's party where she'll be entertaining them later this afternoon.' He caught Bonnie's sharp glance, but ignored her and turned back to the grim-faced housekeeper, smiling pleasantly at her. 'Do you have a resident here who goes by the name of Harbinson?'

The woman glanced suspiciously at Bonnie, taking in her bizarre apearance, then returned her unflinching gaze on Gumshoe.

'Why do you want to know? Are you related?'

'That means he's here,' Gumshoe said.

'That's no secret,' the woman responded. 'He's been here for years. So are you related?'

'No,' Gumshoe said, deciding to start his lies with a truth. 'My dad's an old friend of Mr Harbinson and he just found out he's here. He phoned me from New York, where he lives, and asked me to drop in and pass on his regards. Is this a good time to see him?'

'You should have phoned in advance,' the woman said.

'Sorry,' Gumshoe said, feigning contrition. 'I just never thought. I mean, I'm only in Georgetown and this place is so close, I just jumped on my bike without thinking. Any chance of seeing him?'

'Well . . .' The woman glanced again, this time with open distaste, at the gum-chewing Bonnie.

'It's just to say hello,' Gumshoe said pleasantly. 'I'm sure he'll be real thrilled to hear from my dad.'

The woman shrugged indifferently, then stepped aside to let him and Bonnie enter. 'Well, I guess it can't hurt. I'm Mrs Weatherby, the housekeeper. Okay, come on in.'

They both stepped inside. Mrs Weatherby closed the door behind them, said, 'This way,' then led them across a central hall with nineteenth-century furnishings and paintings, a drawing room on one side, a smaller sitting room on the other, then up the stairs to the central hall of the second floor.

'Nice house,' Bonnie said.

'It used to be nicer,' Mrs Weatherby responded, leading them across the hall towards some closed doors, 'when it was open to the public and was the same as it had been when its former owners, the Lewises, lived in it. It only had four bedrooms up here then, but they've since been divided up into smaller rooms to accommodate more guests. Mr Harbinson is only one of those guests and he's quite a handful.'

'How do you mean?' Gumshoe asked.

'You'll find out,' Mrs Weatherby replied, stopping in front of one of the doors and hammering on it with the knuckles of her clenched fist. 'Mr Harbinson!' she called out. 'Are you decent? You have visitors!'

'What's that?' a quavering male voice responded.

'I said you have visitors! A Mr Fullbright and a Miss Packard. Can I show them in? Are you decent?'

'I never have visitors,' the man, Harbinson, replied, his voice quavering and rasping with age, 'and I don't want any now. Send them away . . . No, wait! Did they bring anything with them?'

'Pardon?'

'Any presents . . . Cigarettes? Whisky? Liquorice Allsorts? Oh, what the hell, I'm fart-bored again. Send them in anyway!'

Rolling her eyes, the woman opened the door and nodded for

Gumshoe and Bonnie to enter, which they did, finding themselves in a small room, practically touching the end of the bed
upon which, propped up against three or four pillows, an old
man in striped pyjamas was resting.

'My office is in the drawing room downstairs,' Mrs Weatherby said. 'Please let me know when you leave.'

'I will,' Gumshoe said.

When Mrs Weatherby had closed the door, Gumshoe and
Bonnie stared at the man propped up on the bed. He was gaunt
and lined with age, but had clearly once been handsome. He still
had a fine head of silvery-grey hair and surprisingly bright,
searchingly perceptive blue eyes that, right now, were taking
Bonnie in from tip to toe.

'Mmmmm,' he said. 'Tasty . . . If a bit on the odd side.'

'What's that?' Bonnie responded, stepping forward to the end
of the bed, about to give the old goat a sharp retort.

'So,' the old goat said, turning his bright, questioning gaze
upon Gumshoe, 'who are you? Did I know you once? Perhaps
when you were children? Otherwise, I can't imagine who . . .'

'I'm Randolph Fullbright,' Gumshoe said quickly, 'and this is
my friend, Bonnie Packard. No, Mr Harbinson, you don't know
us. We're just fans of your work and we heard you were here and
decided to come out and see you. We thought you might tell us a
bit about how you came to write your "Projekt Saucer" series
and . . .'

'Fans?' the old goat interjected, smiling to reveal a set of sound
teeth. 'Did you say you were fans?'

'Yes, sir,' Gumshoe said.

'Please, please.' Harbinson waved to the wooden chair beside
the bed, indicating that Gumshoe should sit on it, then he patted
the other side of the bed with the flat of his hand and nodded
to Bonnie. 'And you sit here, my dear,' he said, his voice turning
as oily as it could, given his advanced years. 'Right here, beside
me.'

Looking sceptical, Bonnie sat on the edge of the bed while

Gumshoe took the chair at the opposite side. The old goat immediately patted Bonnie's bare thigh, saying, 'That's it, my dear. How nice to see you. What a sweet girl you are.' He studied the length of her bare thigh with his roaming gaze, then gave it a gentle squeeze. 'It's so nice to have visitors.' When Bonnie gently removed his hand from her thigh, he smiled and turned his bright gaze on Gumshoe. 'So, did you bring me any presents?' he said. 'Any cigarettes? Whisky? Liquorice Allsorts? I *do* love the latter, but they say they're bad for my cholesterol and they won't let me smoke or drink either. This place is a prison.'

'Seems like a nice rest home,' Bonnie said. 'It was once a real fancy joint. How long have you been here?'

'Five years,' Harbinson said, his bright gaze roaming lecherously over her body, his smile clearly wicked. 'I need to be looked after and I came here when my last woman left me. It doesn't cost much to stay here.'

'How come you're here?' Gumshoe asked. 'I mean, you're British, right?'

'Right,' the old guy said, reluctantly removing his gaze from Bonnie. 'From Northern Ireland, actually, which means I'm a British citizen. I was in New York, researching a book, when the cyborgs took over and, of course, then I couldn't leave the country: no one could. I was trapped in America.'

'That must have been pretty rough,' Bonnie said. 'Losing your family and friends in England.'

'We lose everything in life,' the old man responded, smiling, 'so I've made a point of never expecting anything to last and I don't miss anyone or anything – apart from booze, cigarettes and sweets.' He shrugged his shoulders, which were frail in the striped pyjamas. 'What did I leave behind me? I wasn't married at the time, my children were grown up, living their own lives, and I'd spent most of my life travelling anyway, so I was used to being alone. Of course, I always needed looking after. I mean, all writers do. We need to be royally fucked – in the most positive sense – and mothered and in general spoilt rotten. So, when I realized that I was trapped, almost broke, in a foreign country, I nosed around for an unattached woman who had her own income. The one I found was from Washington DC and I moved there to live with her, hopefully for good. But, of course, she let me down badly. She'd thought I was famous, you see – and what woman can resist that? – but then, when she found out that I was broke, that my career was virtually over, she used her influence to have me placed here, thus artfully removing me from her life. So, here I am . . . No Liquorice Allsorts?'

'What are they?' Bonnie asked.

'Candy,' Gumshoe explained. 'British candy. No, sir,' he added, turning back to the ancient scrounging author, 'we've got no Liquorice Allsorts.'

'Whisky?'

'No.'

The old panhandler pouted sulkily at him, then whined, 'It's not nice to visit someone in a hospital and not bring them something.'

'This isn't a hospital,' Bonnie said.

'It's a home for geriatrics,' the old guy responded, 'and that makes it the same as a hospital. No grapes either, I gather.'

'No grapes,' Bonnie said.

Looking even more disgruntled, the aged writer sank deeper into the pillows and gazed forlornly at the lithograph adorning the wall above Bonnie's head. The lithograph showed the French Marquis de Lafayette on a visit to Woodlawn in 1824. The old writer lowered his gaze until his eyes were travelling once more along Bonnie's bared thigh. That sight made him suck his breath in. He raised his gaze to smile at her, then reached out to squeeze her thigh again. 'Still,' he said, now practically ignoring Gumshoe, 'it *was* nice of you to come and see me. I miss the company of young women, even in my advanced years. My, what a nice, fleshy thigh you have!'

Bonnie smiled, patted the old rogue's hand, then gently

removed it from her thigh as Gumshoe distracted him with, 'You don't write any more?'

'Of course not. I've written all I was ever meant to write and my time as an author is long past.'

'*Meant* to write?' Gumshoe asked, recalling those Net speculations that Harbinson might have had an electronic brain-implant and been compelled to write his epic series about Wilson and man-made flying saucers as a form of disinformation to protect the real, extraterrestrial saucers and their alien occupants. Or, conversely, that Harbinson was a covert member of the NSC and had been spreading disinformation on their behalf to draw attention away from their supposedly ongoing interaction with these same aliens. In an insane world anything was believable, so both possibilities remained open and Gumshoe wanted the truth of it.

'Yes,' the old man said. 'I wrote what I was meant to write – what came into my head – and then I ran dry and that was it. After that, I could only live off various women, as many male writers do. The women, you see . . .' Here he cast a lewd grin in Bonnie's direction . . . 'The women have always had a soft spot for writers, thinking of them as bad boys who can be converted, ho, ho, or as children who need looking after, so of course any writer worth his salt will not disappoint them. Don't you think that's wise, dear?' His hand crept back towards her leg.

'You were probably a bloodsucking lecher,' Bonnie said. 'Now get your paw off my thigh.'

'So sorry,' the sly old bastard said, unperturbed, though he did at least remove his hand. 'It went there of its own accord.' He turned back to Gumshoe, smiling brightly. 'So, no Liquorice Allsorts and no whisky. What about cigarettes?'

'You shouldn't smoke,' Bonnie said. 'It's bad for your eighty-year-old heart.'

'You don't smoke?' the former writer said to Gumshoe, ignoring Bonnie for now.

'No,' Gumshoe said.

'Too bad. I am perishing. I might as well roll over and go back to sleep.'

'You wrote a lot of books,' Gumshoe said, hoping to appeal to the old bastard's vanity, 'not all of them about flying saucers. How did you get into that?'

'It just seemed like a good thing to write at the time,' the old bastard said, now glancing uneasily about the room, as if the walls had suddenly started to close in on him. 'It was nothing mysterious. I mean, the subject was popular at the time, so I just picked up on it. God, I'd kill for a smoke!'

'Books about *extraterrestrials* were popular at the time,' Gumshoe reminded him. '*Not* books about man-made flying saucers. You were the only one who wrote about man-made saucers and your books soon disappeared. In fact, you wrote four massive novels on the subject, as well as a nonfiction book, and only the first and third books in the series were published here in the States. How did that come about?'

The old man shrugged. 'Who knows about the ways of publishers, dear boy? They don't belong in the real world. They live in a world all their own and it defies comprehension.'

'What I'm trying to say,' Gumshoe said loud and clear, 'is that I could understand it if they dropped the series halfway through because the first couple of books didn't sell enough. But why in hell would they publish the first and *third* book in a four-book series? That just doesn't make sense. Were those particular volumes suppressed?'

'I really can't say. I can't remember. It was so long ago . . . Are you sure you don't smoke?'

'What was in books two and four?' Gumshoe asked, ignoring the old goat's 'Let's change the subject' question. 'Did they include material that had to be suppressed? More detailed stuff about Wilson?'

'Wilson?' Harbinson's head suddenly jerked up, his gaze startled, his wide eyes flitting fearfully left and right. 'Wilson?' he repeated, licking his dry lips. 'What about Wilson?'

'You wrote about him,' Gumshoe said. 'You wrote an awful lot about him. You wrote two and a half thousand pages of fact-based fiction about him, so I'd like to know if he existed in real life or not. Did he?'

'Of course not. I wrote fiction – as you have, indeed, just noted – and Wilson was only one of the many characters in that fiction, another product of my rich imagination. Why think anything else?'

'Because you claimed at the time to have based him on an historical figure of that name – the Wilson of the Great Airship Scare, remember? – and newspaper reports of the time support your contention.'

'Never believe what you read in the papers,' the old man said dryly. 'Not even the papers of 1896 and 1897. Newspapers *invent* things.'

'But you quoted those newspapers in good faith and also wrote a non-fiction book on the subject of man-made flying saucers, giving Wilson as the originator of them. Are you now saying that it was all a fabrication?'

'A writer has to eat,' the venerable W. A. Harbinson said, 'and Wilson was my meal ticket for a while . . .' At this point he yawned ostentatiously. 'I feel so tired. Can I sleep now?'

He was starting to snuggle down deeper into the bed, obviously planning to pull the sheet up over his pale, craggily lined face and blot out the real world – but Gumshoe didn't let him. The sheet was practically up to the old goat's panicky eyes when Gumshoe jerked it down again and stared directly at him.

'Wilson existed, didn't he?'

'No!'

'Yes!'

'No!'

'Tell the truth!'

'Yes, yes! He existed! I want to sleep now! Where's Mrs Weatherby? She'll tell you I have to sleep.'

'This old bastard's senile,' Bonnie said. 'You're wastin' your time talkin' to him, Gumshoe. He'll tell you anything you want to hear, but that won't mean it's the truth. You're wastin' your time here.'

'Is Wilson still alive?' Gumshoe asked, ignoring Bonnie.

'Of course not. He died years ago. Mrs Weatherby? Where are you, Mrs Weatherby? I want to sleep, Mrs Weatherby!'

'Mrs Weatherby's in her office downstairs and can't hear a thing you say,' Gumshoe informed the increasingly disturbed old man. 'So why don't you just answer a few more questions. Like are *you*, in fact, Wilson?'

'What? *What?* Are you *crazy?* Why should *I* be Wilson?'

'Because you wrote two and a half thousand pages about Wilson and man-made flying saucers, yet no one ever found out where you got all that research from.'

'Dear God,' W. A. Harbinson – formerly successful author, now potential graveyard material – said despairingly. 'What are you talking about?'

'I'm talking about two and a half thousand pages and an enormous amount of research about man-made flying saucers by a man who wasn't known by a single soul in the UFO-research community, who hadn't approached any UFO-research organization for assistance with his research, and who was never seen at any UFO convention or any kind of convention related to that subject. I'm talking about a writer who produced a tremendous amount of flying-saucer research and whose sources for that information remain unknown. So where did you get your information from, Mr Harbinson?'

'Libraries!' Harbinson snapped defensively. 'Read the bibliographies in my books. The sources are all in the bibliographies. I read hundreds of books.'

'Those bibliographies were bullshit,' Gumshoe said. 'They sure as hell were extensive, very impressive to glance at. But when examined more closely they turned out to be composed of books that gave no information about Wilson or man-made flying saucers. They were books on the Nazis, on aerodynamics, on rocketry, on so-called "extraterrestrial" saucers — but not one of them could be seen as a proper source for the facts that you cleverly disguised as fiction. That had to wait until you wrote your non-fiction book on the same subject. You wrote about man-made flying saucers for fifteen years without turning to any known specialists for help. So I ask you again, Mr Harbinson: where did that fifteen years of research come from?'

The old man clutched his head in his hands and shook it from side to side. 'I don't know! I can't remember! My head hurts! Why won't you give me a cigarette?'

'I'll give you something better than a cigarette,' Gumshoe said, 'if you answer my questions.'

'What?' Harbinson's head jerked up again, his eyes wide and greedy. 'What will you give me?'

'Why did you suddenly start writing about man-made flying saucers,' Gumshoe asked, 'when you were already successful as a writer of general fiction? And where did your information come from? Those two questions need answering.'

'You said you'd give me something.'

'Answer the questions first.'

'Give me something first.'

'No.'

'Yes!'

Gumshoe sighed. 'You have to earn it,' he said.

The old man started whimpering, then he rolled away from Gumshoe, pulled the sheets up to his shoulders, stared at the opposite wall and said, whispering, 'I can't, I can't, I can't. I *don't want* to remember. I don't want them to come here and see me again—'

'Who?'

'The men in black . . . I just want to be left alone and to die in this bed. That's not much to ask, is it?'

'You get visits from men in black?' Gumshoe asked, aware that men in black, widely believed to be human beings with brain implants, were often seen in the company of cyborgs, going in and out of the White House.

'I've got a headache,' the old man responded. 'That's because we're talking about it. I get headaches when I'm just thinking about it, so please leave me alone now . . . Who are you, anyway?' He back to gaze up at Gumshoe, his eyes now wide with fear. 'Are you one of . . . them?'

'No,' Gumshoe said, realizing just how frightened the author was and knowing that there was only one way to get him to talk. 'No, I'm not one of them . . . and neither is she.' He indicated Bonnie with a nod of his head, then slipped his right hand into his jacket pocket and withdrew a capsule of methamphetamine. 'This is better than a cigarette,' he said, lying blatantly. 'It'll help you get rid of your headache and make you feel good. Just wash it down with some water.'

'Ah, bless you, my boy, bless you,' the old man garbled, taking the capsule from Gumshoe, popping it into his throat, then washing it down with a tumbler of water and laying his grey head gratefully back on the pillows. 'I knew, from the minute I saw your face, that you had a kind heart. So what will it do to me?'

'It'll get rid of your headache, make you feel good, and loosen your tongue.'

The old man closed his eyes. 'Just what I need,' he said.

Gumshoe glanced at Bonnie, who shot back a look of disgust at what he assumed she viewed as an immoral act. Then he studied the old man, the writer W. A. Harbinson, sly and slightly crazy, perhaps becoming senile, but certainly very frightened by his own recollections. Gumshoe sat there by the side of the bed, waiting patiently for his victim to feel the rush of the methamphetamine. When he saw that the rush had hit him, when the old goat sighed and smiled, Gumshoe leaned across him to whisper into his ear.

'What started you writing about man-made flying saucers?' he asked him. 'And where did you get your information from?'

The old writer sat up stiffly in bed, fixed his stoned blue-eyed gaze on Gumshoe – and told him everything.

Chapter Fifteen

Michael and Dr Lee Brandenberg took the lift down through the bowels of the mountain, passing the various levels of this great hidden complex originally created by Wilson, and emerged to the cleared area on ground level that had become a landing bay for the flying saucers. Here, beyond the parked saucers, the sky was a silvery-azure sheet that stretched over the flat, snow-covered plain and fell away to the distant ice-capped mountains farther along the zero meridian.

Michael was going to be flown out on one of the smaller saucers, a fifty-foot transport, that was resting on its four hydraulic legs with its exit door tilting down from the base to form a short ramp to the ground. Though in many ways more advanced than the saucers inherited from Wilson at the time of the takeover of his colony, its means of flight and underwater movement was essentially the same, being powered by a highly advanced electromagnetic propulsion system that ionized the surrounding air or sea, combined with an electromagnetic damping system that aided its lift and flight capabilities. The bodywork, Michael knew, was made from an electrically charged magnesium orthosilicate so minutely porous that it managed to be essentially waterproof while ensuring, in flight, an absolute minimum of friction, heat and drag. The raised transparent dome was uncovered and Michael could see the crew inside, preparing for take-off. Had it not been for that uncovered dome and the ramp, the saucer would have looked seamless, a gigantic whitish-grey metallic egg that had been moulded miraculously in one piece. In fact, the saucer, like most aircraft, had been made in separate pieces and the divisions between them were indeed there, but joined together so precisely as to make them virtually invisible.

'That's a beautiful sight,' Michael said, meaning it, as he and Brandenberg stopped at the foot of the ramp.

'It depends on how you look at it,' Brandenberg said. 'When I see the saucers, even our saucers, I tend to think of Wilson and that does much to mitigate their beauty for me . . . But I know what you mean. Now, are you sure you're ready?'

'Yes,' Michael said, adjusting the straps on the rucksack that contained everything he would need in the World, including his 1000-MB notebook, new identification and plastic cards for financial and other transactions.

Having spent the last three days in almost total isolation, not allowed to go back and see his family, wired into an interactive multimedia system with 3-D sound and wraparound vision that had pumped into him everything he needed to know about one Michael Johnson, the person he was to impersonate should he be interrogated by the cyborgs or anyone connected to them, Michael felt that he was now ready to make his way in the World, dangerous though it might be.

'I don't think you could teach me anything else before I go out there,' he went on, 'so I'm pleased to go now.'

'Good,' Brandenberg said. 'No point in saying that we're all depending on you; I'm sure you know that already.'

Michael grinned. 'Yep.'

'Any message for your folks and Chloe?'

'Yes. Tell them that I'll be back without fail and I'll bring them the key to the United States. Tell them I love them.'

'I will,' Brandenberg said. Then he sighed and looked up the ramp at the open doorway leading into the flying saucer. He looked back at Michael and held out his hand. 'Good luck,' he said.

They shook hands, then Brandenberg stepped back to let Michael enter the saucer.

Nodding silently in acknowledgement, trying to still his excitement and stay cool, Michael went up the short ramp and found himself in a brightly lit white-painted hallway, completely featureless, but with a low, dome-shaped ceiling and a corridor curving away to his right. To his left was a white-painted steel door that was obviously blocking the 'end' of the same completely circular corridor that, Michael knew, ran around the outer perimeter of the craft, just above what would soon be a revolving disc-shaped lower wing.

As there was no other way to go, Michael entered the corridor to his right. The instant he did so, he heard a bass humming sound and turned back to see the short ramp lifting off the ground and moving obliquely back up into the side of the sloping fuselage, locking into it so tightly that the joins around its edges could not be seen, making the wall once more look perfectly seamless.

Impressed by the precision of the construction, Michael continued along the curving corridor, which likewise appeared to be seamless and was certainly featureless, containing no windows on either side. In less than a minute, however, he came to a doorway, located on the inner side of the corridor, and found himself looking into the central cabin of the craft, clearly the control room, that had about a dozen reinforced viewing windows around its circular wall and a dome-shaped ceiling of heat-resistant reinforced Perspex, giving the crew a 360-degree view from any part of the flight deck. This was the same transparent dome that Michael had seen from outside.

Having been thoroughly trained in flying-saucer technology and flight skills, he recognized from the intricate control panels, in which small lights of many colours were flashing constantly on and off, the standard hardware for a normal airliner, including switch panels, pitch-trim controls, autopilot-engage switch, inertial navigation, navigational radio selector, weather radar, radio equipment, intercom switches, a highly advanced brand of ADF (automatic direction finder), computer selection switches, and an unusually small but exceptionally powerful computer that controlled most of the flight deck functions and could be activated by an electronic 'voice' composed of minute vibrations transmitted at varying speeds and frequencies. However, the flight deck did *not* contain such standard aircraft controls as thruster-reverse lights, nose-gear tiller, speed-brake handle, or even brake-pressure or aileron-and-rudder trims, as these were not required for the unique propulsion systems of this kind of craft.

Though relatively small and, from what Michael could see, relatively unsophisticated in comparison with the great so-called 'mother ships', this transport craft actually possessed a variety of large and small CAMS (Cybernetic Anthropomorphous Machine Systems) or metal arms with remote-controlled claws, which were used to scoop up exotic marine life and a wealth of normally unavailable minerals from the ocean bed and the soil of Earth. It could also release and receive much smaller saucers, a mere metre in diameter, that could be used as radar-blocking devices or, with their electronic 'seeing' and 'hearing' capabilities, as advance 'scouts', sending back details of any other aircraft in the vicinity. They could also make the engines of other aircraft and even automobiles malfunction; and they were, as well, capable of stunning or hypnotizing human beings with their flickering strobe lights. Those dangerous lights, used extensively in Wilson's day, had not so far been used by the aircrews of Freedom Bay.

Because the transport saucers were almost completely computer-automated, the aircrew in this case consisted of only two men, captains Arnold Jessup and Des Clinton, both in their late thirties, both wearing open-necked shirts and blue coveralls. Jessup was the first pilot while Clinton was there as the navigator and to stand in for Jessup should something disabling happen to him, such as a stroke or heart attack. Otherwise, the saucer was run by a computer system that could not only maintain itself but could also, in most cases, repair itself.

When Michael entered the flight deck, both crewmen turned to face him.

'Captain Jessup,' Michael said by way of greeting, nodding with a smile first to one man, then to the other. 'Captain Clinton. Good to see you both.'

'Hi, Michael,' Jessup said. 'Good to see you. All set for the trip?'

'I think so,' Michael said.

'You think so?'

'I *know*.'

Jessup grinned. 'We're taking off in a couple of minutes, so you'd better strap yourself in.'

'Here,' Clinton said, indicating the rucksack on Michael's back. 'Let me take that. You can't sit in a chair with that on your shoulders and you have to sit in a chair. You can have it back when we drop you off.'

Michael nodded agreement, slipped the straps off his shoulders, then handed the valuable rucksack to Clinton and watched him put it into a locker. He then followed the others by strapping himself into a vacant seat at the control panel. Even as he was doing so, the saucer throbbed with a bass humming sound, almost an infrasound, then vibrated slightly.

Instantly, the lower wing-plates began to spin around the static central dome, at first slowly, then more rapidly, and the saucer, swaying slightly from side to side, lifted a few metres off the landing pad. As the saucer hovered in the air, now bobbing gently like a cork in a mildly turbulent sea, its circular wing plates rotated ever more rapidly until they became no more than a silvery-white blur with a pulsating whitish glow, or corona, around their rim, and the saucer began its steady, vertical ascent. Simultaneously, two meniscus-shaped sections of what looked like white steel, but which was actually magnesium orthosilicate like the fuselage and wings, slid up from the bottom of the Perspex dome to fit into each other at the top, forming an umbrella-shaped protective covering and blocking out the sky. At the same time, rectangular plates of magnesium orthosilicate slid down to cover the many windows, turning the inside of the cabin into a perfectly sealed, apparently seamless whole that offered no outside view of anything whatsoever.

Being already in the air, the saucer did not follow the customary two-stage pattern of flying saucer lift-offs: instead, it made a tentative vertical ascent to what Michael judged to be about sixty metres, hovered for a few seconds, then climbed abruptly to a high altitude, almost certainly just below the stratosphere. There it levelled out sharply, before shooting suddenly, horizontally, to the north, heading for the Weddell Sea and the South Atlantic Ocean.

Though Michael knew this was happening, he didn't feel a thing because the saucer was utilizing a gravity shield that came on automatically when required. For this reason, once the saucer was in proper flight, he and the others, now needing no protection against G-forces or decreased outside air pressure, were able to release their safety belts and move about the flight deck without fear.

Michael crossed immediately to Captain Jessup who was now taking command, speaking his instructions into the pinhead microphone strapped to his throat as part of a communication system that also included a covert ear piece for receiving. His spoken instructions were being converted by the computer into an electronic language understood by the saucer's control console, which would react accordingly. When he had given the computer its latest instructions, he turned and grinned at Michael.

'Enjoying it?' he asked.

'Yes, but it's a pity we can't see outside.'

'You can when we slow down,' Jessup replied. 'When we're

entering United States air space. I can open the shutters then.'

'When will that be?' Michael asked.

'About an hour,' Jessup told him. 'We're flying over the Antarctic Circle, the Falkland Islands, Brazil and Guyana, across Haiti and the Bahamas, then on to the east coast of America, descending over Newport News, coming down in Virginia.'

'We'll do that in an hour?'

'You can bet on it,' Jessup said.

'Do you think we'll get through without being seen?'

'I think so,' Jessup said.

In fact, they had only been flying for about half an hour, which placed them approximately over Rio de Janeiro, when the saucer's radar screens showed the blips of other moving objects. Checking the flight characteristics, Clinton was able to ascertain that the blips indicated large objects flying too quickly to be normal aircraft – in other words, they were cyborg flying saucers.

'Nothing to worry about,' Jessup said. 'We know what frequency their radar works on, so we're using a frequency that renders us invisible to them. They'd have to eyeball us to know we're here and we'll never get that close to them. Bless the wonders of science. Nevertheless, we'd better take evasive action just to be sure.'

Even now, in mid-flight, with Jessup talking the saucer into ascending and descending repeatedly, making sheer, abrupt turns of the kind that would once have seemed impossible, there was, for Michael, absolutely no sensation of movement. However, when Jessup opened the shutters around the circular wall as they flew across the Bahamas, thus obtaining a 360-degree view without breaching the upper protective covering of the dome, the saucer was still flying so fast that all Michael saw was what appeared to be a rapidly whipping, frantically spiralling tunnel of shimmering white light streaked with silvery blue, a vertiginous well of brightness that gave no indication of what direction they were actually flying in: up, down or straight ahead.

It was, of course, the latter. Flying at a speed far beyond that of sound, over fifty miles up, on the very edge of space, the saucer appeared to be blasting through the very sky itself, into another world, a great white sheet tearing open to reveal a vast azure sea that instantly convulsed and turned purple, then, just as abruptly, being exactly the same sky, filled up with the dazzling radiance of a gigantic sun. Miraculously, the moon and stars then appeared, clearly visible even in the middle of the day, rendered so by an upper atmosphere so thin that even dust particles could not exist there.

Perhaps just to please Michael, Jessup slowed down to hovering speed when directly over Bimini, in the Bahamas. This location could be seen both as a densely packed collection of glowing dots on the radar screen and as it actually was on the TV monitor wired to a high-powered aerial camera. What the monitor was showing was, in fact, a photomosaic of the western end of the Bermuda Triangle where the Gulf Stream flowed northward between Florida and the Great Bahama Bank and, in the exact middle of the picture, Bimini itself, mono-chrome on the screen but actually a ravishing tapestry of green and blue streaked with so-called 'white water' containing sul-phur, strontium and lithium which often made it glow eerily.

'In the Old Age,' Jessup said, 'before we took over Freedom Bay, lots of people saw flying saucers over this area and even, in some cases, rising up out of the sea itself. For years those sightings were explained away officially either as natural phe-nomena caused by the unusual weather characteristics of the area or as the eerie glowing that comes naturally from the water itself. Then, of course, it transpired that flying saucers *were* emerging from the Bermuda Triangle — Wilson's saucers — and those bastards are almost certainly still down there, exploring the sea bed. It's a hell of a thought.'

'We'll put a stop to them eventually,' Michael said. 'That's why you're flying me in there.'

'Let's hope you succeed,' Jessup responded pragmatically. 'But I wouldn't bet on it.'

'Bet on it,' Michael said.

Amused by Michael's youthful confidence, Jessup grinned and turned back to the control console, speaking into his throat mike, giving instructions that would make the saucer take them on to the east coast of America. When the instructions had been given, the saucer ascended vertically about fifty metres, then shot off in a westerly direction, heading for Norfolk, Virginia. With its gravitational shield also functioning as an inertial shield, the mass of the craft in relation to gravity was reduced to a minute fraction of its former value. This permitted exceptional buoyancy for the craft in the atmosphere, extremely high accelerations (so fast, indeed, that the human eye could not detect the saucer's acceleration from its hovering position in the sky and would imagine that it had abruptly disappeared) and the capability of coming to a remarkably fast stop or going into abrupt right-angle turns without harming those inside.

Given instructions by Jessup and now flying on autopilot, the saucer knew where it had to go. So, approaching the mainland, it stopped abruptly, made a sharp, right-angled turn, then shot off to the north-west, automatically following the topography of the land below by means of a control system that bounced radar-like signals off the ground and back again for instant computer analysis and constantly changing flight directions. Because of this, as well as the weakening and strengthening of the gravitational pull of the Earth when the saucer dropped low enough, it appeared to be bobbing repeatedly as it sped on a horizontal trajectory across Newport News and on to Richmond, Virginia.

With the shutters still open and the saucer's speed greatly reduced, Michael could look down and see the vast sweep of the Shenandoah Valley with its rich profusion of forests, orchards, and pastures, criss-crossed with rivers, all illuminated in daylight, moving past in a blur far below. However, before he could blink, the Great North Mountains heaved into view, expanding at a breathtaking rate. Then, suddenly, the mountaintops were spread out below and the saucer, which had come to an abrupt halt that had not been felt by Michael or the other two crew members, was hovering directly over their drop zone, about five thousand metres above the highest peak, just north of a clearly visible small town that nestled in the emerald-green foothills.

'Is that Woodstock?' Michael asked.

'It sure is,' Jessup replied. 'So prepare to land.'

'What does that mean?' Michael asked.

'The gravity-damping system will automatically turn itself off before we reach ground level, so you'll need to strap yourself in again until we touch down.'

'Just like driving a car,' Michael said.

'You got it, kid.'

The descent commenced as soon as Michael and the others had strapped themselves back into their chairs in front of the constantly blinking control console. At first the saucer vibrated slightly and wobbled a little, its lights flashing on and off. Then, with its circular wings still rotating around the gyroscopically stabilized central fuselage, though now at greatly reduced speed, it steadied and dropped vertically, first through the military and civilian flight paths, its radar checking for oncoming aircraft, then through the scattered clouds, and finally all the way down, past the mountain peaks and sheer and shallow cliff faces.

Though not hindered by normal heat and drag and thus giving off no sonic booms or other noises except for its almost tangible bass infrasound, the saucer, as it reached ground level, was nonetheless creating violent currents of air within a cylindrical zone the same width as its rotating wing-plates, making the grass and plants flutter wildly, noisily sucking up loose soil and gravel, and causing them to whirl in the air. As it reached ground level, swaying gently from side to side, the rotation of its wing-plates slowed gradually and the whitish glow of its electrically charged, minutely porous magnesium orthosilicate, which was ionizing the air surrounding it, darkened to a more normal metallic grey.

Another bass humming sound coming from under the floor of

the control room indicated to Michael that the four hydraulic legs were emerging from the base of the saucer. When the saucer touched down, it bounced lightly a few times, then became perfectly still as the wing-plates ceased their rotation. Then the wind created by the craft's electromagnetic gravity-damping system faded away, letting the swirling soil and wildly fluttering uprooted plants fall back to the ground. A brief silence reigned.

'Home and dry,' Jessup said at last, breaking the silence. 'You can unstrap yourself now.'

Michael unclipped his strap as the others did the same. Then all three of them stood up. Clinton removed Michael's rucksack from the cupboard it had been placed in and handed it to him, saying, 'Have a good hike down to Woodstock, kid, and watch out for the walking dead.'

'You bet,' Michael replied, putting his arms through the straps and hoisting the rucksack onto his back. Hearing another bass humming sound, by now a familiar noise, he knew that the panel at the end of the corridor was falling down to form a ramp to the ground outside.

Captain Jessup placed his hand on Michael's shoulder and said, smiling, 'Let's go. We can't hang around here.'

He led Michael out of the control room and back along the curving corridor until they reached the open door formed by the falling-away of the panel that now sloped down to the ground as a short ramp. Feeling very strange, like someone setting foot on an alien planet for the first time – feeling this way because he had never been in the World before – Michael looked out.

He saw what he had never once seen on the snow-covered plains of Antarctica: rolling hills covered in trees, verdant pastures and, in the distance, a glittering, winding river and, beyond it, the red-tiled rooftops of a small town. The sky seemed much lower than he was used to and the clouds were more grey than white; nevertheless, it looked beautiful.

Michael turned back to Jessup and held his hand out.

'Thanks, Cap'n,' he said.

'My pleasure,' Jessup said. 'Now you be extremely careful out there. Good luck and God bless.'

'Thanks,' Michael said.

He stepped down the ramp into the warmer air of the World. He had never been here before and the air smelt different. At the bottom of the ramp, he looked back up at the saucer, waved to Jessup, then walked a good distance away, surprised at how hard the ground felt under his feet with no snow to soften the impact. Once he had gone what he felt was a safe distance, on the edge of a densely forested area, he turned back to watch the flying saucer ascending.

The panel that had acted as a ramp had already been with-drawn, all the shutters had been closed, the metallic covering remained over the transparent dome, and the saucer looked, all in all, like a seamless, whitish-grey eggshell, though of imposing dimensions. It emitted a bass humming sound, an infrasound that Michael could feel even where he stood, and then the multicoloured lights around its rim began to flash on and off, one after the other, to form an increasingly blurred kaleidoscope. The circular wing-plates began rotating, first slowly, then much faster, again creating violent currents of air that made the grass and plants flutter wildly, noisily sucking up loose soil and gravel and causing it to spin in the air. Seconds later it was lifting slowly off the ground to hover mere inches above it. It hovered there for a brief moment, bobbing like a cork in mildly turbulent water. Then, abruptly, faster than the eye could see, it shot up vertically and appeared to blink out, like a light bulb being switched off.

When the swirling gravel and foliage had settled down again, Michael turned away from the clearing and headed into the forest.

Chapter Sixteen

'Life is dreadful, dreadful, dreadful,' the formerly well-known British hack W.A. Harbinson declaimed melodramatically in the nursing home in Woodlawn Plantation as the methamphetamine sang in his varicose and other coarsened veins while Gumshoe and Bonnie Packard listened intently. 'Life is so dreadful that only old age, or, perhaps, your average publisher, can reveal its true awfulness. "The horror, the horror", as Kurtz cried out in that excellent work by someone other than my good self . . . Mmmm, *nice* . . . What was *in* that excellent little capsule?'

'Never mind,' Gumshoe said. 'Just lie back and enjoy it. So what made your life so damned dreadful?'

'Publishers,' the old goat said. 'Those who make us and break us. They have us on the rack night and day and few of us survive. Of course, *I* survived, not being precious like some, but the price – well, what can one say? – here I lie in my penury. The writer's life is precarious.'

'You don't seem to be doing too bad,' Bonnie said, never quick with the sympathy. 'I mean, bein' in this fancy joint an' all. All those broads who looked after you. I'd say that's a pretty sweet way to sneak into your cranky old age. No offence meant, pal.'

'And none *taken*, my dear.' Revitalized, at least temporarily, before the sweats started in, as surely they would, the licentious old dog let his rheumy, lustful gaze roam over Bonnie again, taking in every curve and hollow. Then he smiled, showing that he still had good teeth. 'Point taken, my angel. Every nightmare has its bright side. It could have been worse, of course – the British National Health Service and so forth – but here I am, lying in this comfy bed, with my hand on a youthful thigh.'

'Take it off,' Bonnie said. She didn't wait for him to do so, but removed the hand herself, then crossed her long, shapely, stocking-clad legs to give the old lecher something to latch onto and keep his tongue wagging. 'So what *else* gave you heartache?'

'Disappointment,' he lied. 'You don't get here without being there. You two are too young to know it – nothing wrong with that, I'm sure! – but life is a process of disillusionment and you can't get away from it. I so wanted to write, you see, to be better than I was. Yet when I succeeded, when I had Andy Warhol's fifteen minutes of fame, I realized, as the good Dorothy Parker said, that there's no *there* when you get there. So I went for the money. What else is there when you're nowhere? And so I wrote all those books about flying saucers and reaped the whirlwind.'

'You mean *money?*' Gumshoe asked.

'That and heartache,' the old guy said. 'All the treacheries of success. Vindictiveness from the critics, petty jealousy from fellow scribes, envy from former friends, begging letters from total strangers, nasty claims from the Inland Revenue, then, to cap it all, being cheated out of most of my income by publishers and agents and movie producers and every woman who ever warmed my bed. The price of fame, please believe me, is extortionate, so don't even try for it.'

'I won't,' Bonnie promised.

'You wrote those books just for money?' Gumshoe asked, not believing a word of it.

'Oh, yes, I did. I sold my soul for what I thought would be a fortune and it turned out to be no more than a pittance. I will never forgive myself.'

'He's a moralist,' Bonnie said.

Secretly wishing that Bonnie would shut up for at least a few seconds, but not about to risk her wrath, Gumshoe threw her a pained grin, then returned his attention to the bright-eyed old faker on the bed. Mr Harbinson, it seemed to Gumshoe, was playing a role, that old Eccentric Writer number, in order to avoid answering questions that he did not wish to answer. He had slipped up, however, by mentioning visits from the Men in Black. Although he had then wriggled out of that subject, Gumshoe fully intended to return to it, slowly but surely. Mr Harbinson had written hundreds of thousands of words about man-made flying saucers, about the mysterious John Wilson, and just about everything he had written had turned out to be true. More remarkably, he had somehow managed to write all those words and gather in all those facts without any assistance from anyone in, or related to, the UFO organizations of his time. So where had his information come from? So far, the old rogue wouldn't say, but Gumshoe was now ready to push him as hard as necessary.

'Okay,' he said, 'so you wrote the books for money—'

'May God forgive me!' the old man interjected, as hammily as any actor projecting to the balcony.

'—but how did the ideas actually come to you? I mean, what made you think of that particular subject, which was way, way out of your normal field?'

'Nothing mysterious there, dear boy. About 1980, one of my readers and regular correspondents, a German engineer living in Frankfurt, had attended a scientific exhibition at the Hanover *Messe* Hall and picked up what at first sight appeared to be an orthodox newsletter devoted to the futuristic sciences. That newsletter contained two seemingly unrelated articles: one on the scientific future of Antarctica, the other about Germany's Second World War flying saucer construction programme. The latter article was concerned mainly with a *Luftwaffe* officer, *Flugkapitän* Rudolph Schriever, stating that this officer had designed, in the spring of 1941, the prototype for a so-called "flying top" and that the device had been tested in June 1942. The article went on to say that this same *Flugkapitän* Schriever had gone on to construct, in August 1942, a large version of his original flying disc – yes, it was now called a disc – but that in the summer of 1944, in the East Hall of the BMW plant near Prague, he had updated the original model, replacing its original gas turbine engines with some form of jet propulsion. As I recall, that flying saucer was described as a large ring-plate with a wing-disc that rotated around a fixed, cupola-shaped cockpit. The wing disc had adjustable jets inserted all around it and could itself be adjusted to various angles to give it its manoeuvring capabilities. It had a diameter of about forty-two metres and a height from base to canopy of thirty-two metres. When tested, it reached a flight speed of two thousand miles per hour.'

'That's a hell of a good memory you've got there,' Bonnie said tartly, 'for such an old guy.'

'Thank you, my pet. In fact, I've always had a very good memory for facts and figures. The writer's gift, don't you know. Anyway, the article went on to suggest that Schriever's flying saucer, or a more advanced version of it, ended up in a secret Nazi base in Antarctica, having been shipped there in pieces, probably in submarines, throughout the war years. Indeed, the article also stated that Operation Highjump, the massive US Antarctic expedition led by Admiral Richard Evelyn Byrd in January 1947, had actually been a military operation disguised as a scientific expedition and designed to root the Nazis out of their hidden lair in Neuschwabenland. That operation failed, according to the article, because Byrd's assault force was repulsed by the superior capabilities of the German flying saucers. The United States then withdrew from Antarctica for almost a decade.'

'And the other article?' Gumshoe reminded him.

'This was clearly a newsletter with National Socialist leanings and the second article was, therefore, a rather crude propaganda statement masquerading as a scientific review of Antarctic potential. Dusting off the already well-known topographical facts, what one was left with was an insistence that the Democratic Republic of Germany should claim back their rights to that part of the Antarctic that the Nazis stole from the Norwegians and arrogantly renamed Neuschwabenland. The two articles combined, then, were suggesting that a Nazi scientific community was still hiding out in an underground base in Neuschwabenland, Antarctica, that it was responsible for the flying saucers then being seen all over the world, and that it should be allowed to remain there in what should be German territory.'

'So this friend in Germany, this engineer,' Gumshoe said, 'sent you those articles.'

'The complete newsletter containing them,' Harbinson said. 'Clearly, or so I thought then, he felt that he'd found the answer to the UFO problem and he wanted me to write a factual book about it. I checked the material out and thought that it would make good commercial fiction. *Voilà!* My career turned in a completely different direction and brought me, if not lasting success, my fifteen minutes of fame.'

'Who was this correspondent?' Gumshoe asked.

The old man shrugged and licked his drying lips. 'I forget his name,' he said. 'Just one of my many readers who liked to correspond with me. I never met him personally.'

'Did he keep in touch?'

'No. Surprisingly, he didn't. More surprisingly, he stopped communicating shortly after I published the first book in the series. I haven't heard a word from him from that day to this.'

Gumshoe was growing excited, though he tried not to show it. He had just remembered that more than one of his trawls through the Net had produced unsubstantiated reports of a secret flying-saucer base in Antarctica, though one run by a bunch of *American* scientists. According to word on the grapevine (the historical facts being scanty and now erased from computer records by the cyborgs), that base had once belonged to another, unnamed nation, but had been captured by the US shortly after the close of the Second World War, then isolated from the international community when the cyborgs took over the whole world. The location most often given on the Net for that real, or imagined, flying-saucer base was Queen Maud Land. Now this deceptively eccentric old goat, W.A. Harbinson, was talking about a supposed Nazi base in Neuschwabenland, which was, in reality, Queen Maud Land. More interestingly, Harbinson had received his original information from someone who had then disappeared from the scene as soon as that information was published in book form. Which suggested that the man who had encouraged him to write the books had had his own reasons . . . This was something to think about . . .

'So when you researched the subject—'

'From books!' the old hack interjected abruptly, his eyes widening with what seemed to be panic. 'All from previously published books!'

'Right,' Gumshoe said to the shameless literary thief, 'from other books . . . So when you completed your ten years or so of research, what was your conclusion?'

'About what?'

'The reality, or the non-reality, of man-made flying saucers and the German connection.'

'My conclusion was that the Germans had indeed been involved with fairly primitive flying-saucer construction projects, that the Americans had later continued that research in the United States, that the American flying saucers did not fly very well, and that the secret test flights of those saucers – notably the Flying Flapjack, the Avro Car and, perhaps, some early disc-shaped moon-landing prototypes – had led to the outburst of so-called *UFO* sightings of the 1950s and 1960s.'

'Yet you went on to write hundreds of thousands of words suggesting the very opposite: that the Nazis *did* have a secret flying-saucer base in Antarctica, that it was run by a brilliant, renegade *American* scientist called John Wilson, and that when Wilson died, in the early 1980s, the US took over his base and continued to work on even more advanced flying saucers. Why did you do that?'

The old man sighed, shrugged again, licked his dry lips, then wiped some beads of sweat from his forehead, coming down from his high. 'I told you,' he said. 'Money. It just seemed like a good idea at the time and it certainly worked for me.'

'That's all?'

'That's all . . . God, I don't feel good any more. I have a blinding headache and the effects of that excellent capsule are wearing off already. Would you happen to have another one?'

'They're bad for your heart,' Bonnie said.

'I don't have a heart, honey.' Harbinson gave Bonnie a brief, lascivious smile, but stopped smiling when he turned back to Gumshoe. '*Please,* dear boy, just one more . . .'

'Well, now,' Gumshoe responded slowly, deliberately, 'I'm not so sure about that . . .' He leaned back in his chair as if deep in thought, as if deciding whether or not he should give the old fart a second capsule. Of course, he fully intended doing just that – he wanted Harbinson to talk – but first he wanted him to sweat a little and yearn even more for that little capsule. Considering this, Gumshoe felt like a sadist, but he really had no choice in the matter. He was a guy who liked answers. 'Well, okay,' he said, leaning forward again and producing another capsule of methamphetamine from his pocket. 'I guess I can let you have one more, though you've got to promise to keep talking to me.'

'I will!' the old man exclaimed, his rheumy eyes brightening greedily at the sight of the capsule held up before his nose like a dangling carrot. 'I'll talk your head off, dear boy.'

'Good,' Gumshoe said. As he gave Harbinson the capsule, he knew that this one, on top of the other, would loosen his tongue more than he realized and possibly get him to reveal what he had so far concealed. So he gave the old guy his capsule and then watched him swallow it. When he had done so and seemed more relaxed, Gumshoe leaned forward again.

'How do you feel?' he asked.

'Much better,' Harbinson said. 'An *awful* lot better, in fact. I feel as bright as the sun.'

'Thinking more clearly, are you?'

'Oh, yes! Age normally dims the mind, destroying memory, but now my mind is an ocean.'

'Got your memory back, right?'

'Most assuredly so, young man. Old friends and enemies are parading through my brain as if they were in this very room. Those capsules are *wonderful*.'

'What was the name of the German who first sent you that information about Nazi flying saucers?'

'Kruger,' the old man said without hesitation. 'Hans Kruger — a regular correspondent . . . until I published those books, of course.'

'Ah, yes,' Gumshoe said, 'the books! Let's talk about the books. Where did you get all your background information? Do you remember that now?'

'Yes,' Harbinson said.

'So where did the information come from?'

'From my dreams,' the old man said.

'What?'

'It all came from my dreams,' Harbinson repeated, dreamily indeed, closing his eyes and smiling a little. 'I would go to sleep and dream about a flying saucer descending to pick me up and . . . and . . .' He stopped smiling and tossed on the bed, then moaned softly and held his head in his blue-veined hands. 'They were dreams,' he said. 'Only dreams . . . I always thought they were only dreams . . . Until later, when . . .'

'What were the dreams about?' Gumshoe prodded him when he moaned again and stopped talking.

'The Men in Black,' the old man said, regaining control of himself. 'Flying saucers and Men in Black. The flying saucers would descend and pick me up and take me away . . . Sometimes over my car when I was driving at night . . . Sometimes over the house when I was sleeping in bed . . . The flying saucers would descend, over my car, over the house, and these creatures would emerge . . . *alien* creatures . . . some as small as children, though with very large heads; sometimes cyborg creatures with no noses or lips . . . and they'd either pick me up and take me away in their saucer or simply surround my bed and communicate with me there.'

'Communicate?' Gumshoe prodded him. 'You mean talk?'

'They talked to me, yes . . . No, they didn't *really* talk. I thought I could hear them speaking, but they didn't have lips, yet they somehow put those voices into my head and I couldn't get rid of them. In my house, around my bed, they talked to me for hours . . . *communicated* for hours, filling my head with all those facts . . . but when they abducted me, taking me up in their saucer, it was all very different . . . They did things to me . . . Sometimes painful things . . . They injected me, put things into my skull, sometimes made me wear earphones and fed me the information that way . . . They did all of this in my dreams – and I had dreams for ten years.'

'The dreams stopped eventually?'

'Yes, they stopped.'

'When?'

'When the publishers stopped commissioning my books; when my career went downhill . . . When everything seemed to go wrong.'

'What way? How did things go wrong?'

'My books were selling so well, but then things just went haywire. I received visits from Men in Black – government officials, they said – and they told me that I was putting things in my books that were not permitted. They told me to stop writing them . . . If I didn't, I'd be in trouble. I didn't – I wrote the third and the fourth, but then more things happened . . .'

'Such as?' Gumshoe prompted him.

'The whole four-books series was published in England, but only two volumes were published in America. The Americans had contracted for all four books, so they were obliged to *start* publishing, but inexplicably they dropped volumes two and four, which made one and three incomprehensible to the reader, thus vastly reducing their sales . . . Naturally, I demanded an explanation from the publisher, but no one there was willing to talk. They refused to communicate on any level, either to me or to my agent, then they quietly dropped the whole series and pulped what was left of books one and four . . . Those books have never been published since.'

'In America,' Gumshoe corrected him. 'They were published in England.'

'Yes,' the old man said. 'All four books *were* published in England but, I repeat, only the first and the third were published in America before being pulped.'

'What was in volumes two and four?'

'American-related material,' Harbinson said. 'It was practically all American. The complete story of Kruger's work for the Nazis; his hidden base in Queen Maud Land, Antarctica; Rear Admiral Byrd's failed attempts to get him out of there; his post-war dealings with the Americans, covertly trading with them throughout the years of the Cold War; his contribution to NASA and other US military projects; his death in Antarctica and the secret takeover of his base by the US in the early 1980s. Volume four completed the story and I think that explains it. They didn't want that distinctly American material published in the United States and so those volumes were dropped, then the rest of the series was killed off. That's when my troubles began.'

'Wait a minute,' Gumshoe said, now so excited he could hardly breathe, since clearly the original encouragement of Harbinson to write those books had been intended to leak at least a certain amount of the truth about the source of the man-made flying saucers. 'Who the hell was Kruger?'

'Kruger was Wilson. That was the name he used in Germany:

the name on the German passport that he obtained from the Nazis.'

'So Wilson really existed?'

'Yes, God help us, he did.'

Gumshoe glanced at Bonnie who, though giving a laconic shrug, was clearly intrigued. Gumshoe turned back to Harbinson.

'So what happened when the books stopped being published? Did the dreams stop as well?'

'Not dreams . . . I thought they were dreams . . . But, no, they weren't dreams . . . I kept thinking they were dreams for years after, but then I found out they weren't.'

'How?'

'Hypnosis . . . When my flying saucer books were dropped, I turned to other subjects, but every time I tried to sell one of those books, they were rejected for ambiguous reasons. Soon, editors and other former publishing friends were refusing to answer my calls. Incoming calls did not get through. I bought one fax machine after another, but none of them worked . . . I was convinced that my phone was tapped . . . My house was burgled and my papers stolen . . . All those years of work, all those facts and figures about Wilson and his flying saucers, disappeared overnight . . . Eventually, it all collapsed . . . my career and my marriage . . . I kept having the dreams . . . the flying saucers and Men in Black . . . Then the dreams stopped at last, but instead I started having blinding headaches and thought I was going mad . . .'

'But you didn't go mad.'

'No. I went for a physical, but they found nothing wrong with me . . . I then went to a psychiatrist and he put me on to a hypnotist . . . That's when I learnt that the "dreams" were *real*.'

Gumshoe glanced at Bonnie and noted that she was leaning closer to the bed, studying Harbinson intently. She didn't look laconic any more and her big eyes were bright. The old man had slipped down under the blankets and his eyes remained closed. He did not seem too happy.

'Go on,' Gumshoe said.

'Under hypnosis,' the old man said, 'I was taken back to those early days, to the time of my first dreams, and relived them exactly as I had dreamed them – or as I *thought* I had dreamed them. I also relived for the hypnotist the visits I'd had from the Men in Black. According to the hypnotist, these were genuine experiences that could not have been falsified in the trance state . . .'

'And?' Gumshoe prompted him when he tapered off into a soft groaning followed by silence.

'He later played back the tapes of what I'd said in the trace state and they revealed that the Men in Black, who always came to my house at night and entered my bedroom to surround me in my bed, were normal human beings in normal black suits who insisted that they were government secret agents. The tapes also revealed that during their final visit to me – after which, of course, what I had thought were only dreams had ended – they warned me that if I ever talked about my experiences with them, they would come for me and take me away for good. I knew for sure that they meant it.'

'Anything else?'

'Yes. They said that they might one day want me to write another, final book for them, but that when and if they did, they would pick me up and take me away to work on it in complete seclusion and secrecy. Until then, they said, they'd leave me alone – as long as I kept my mouth shut . . . But dear God, now I'm talking.'

'They'll never know,' Gumshoe said.

The old man's eyes opened to look thoughtfully, perhaps cynically at Gumshoe, though also with fear in them. 'They know everything,' he said with conviction. 'I don't know how, but they do. Maybe because they put something in my head that enables them to read my every thought or, at least, know where I am. Either way, when they used to pay their visits to me, they seemed to know everything.'

Gumshoe glanced at Bonnie and saw the nervousness in her eyes. Like him, she was thinking of the unusual powers of the cyborgs and relating them to the Men in Black. All things were now possible.

Turning back to the old man, who seemed to have told the truth for once, he said, 'They won't know a thing about this visit. You can take that as read.'

'I hope so,' Harbinson said, no longer casting a lascivious eye upon Bonnie, no longer smiling, simply looking exhausted as the effects of the methamphetamine wore off. He also now looked truly old. 'I live in dread of their coming.'

'They won't come,' Gumshoe said. He pushed his chair back and stood up, indicating that Bonnie should do the same, which she did. 'Thanks,' he said to the old man. 'You've sure given us a lot of useful information and we're both grateful for it.'

'My mistake. I'll regret it.'

'No, you won't,' Gumshoe said.

He shook Harbinson's hand and then led Bonnie out of the room and back down the stairs. Locating Mrs Weatherby's office just off the central hallway, he told her that he was going and thanked her for letting him see Mr Harbinson, who had turned out to be a great character. Receiving only a glacial smile and a curt nod, he grinned brightly and led Bonnie out of the building. The sun was sinking behind the green hills of Virginia and the afternoon light was quietly darkening.

'Hop aboard,' Gumshoe said, swinging his leg over his motorcycle and kicking its steel support up. When Bonnie was on the back, he revved the bike into motion and headed along the curving west front driveway, between the smooth green lawns and whispering trees. He was just turning out of the estate when he saw the flying saucer.

'Holy shit!' he exclaimed.

Shocked both by the speed of the flying saucer's approach and by the unexpectedness of seeing it out here, where the cyborgs rarely patrolled, he swerved off the road and braked to a halt in the shadows beneath the tall trees. The saucer had appeared out of nowhere, in the blinking of an eye, coming from the direction of Washington DC, and now, before Gumshoe could blink twice, it flashed over the top of the trees as a ball of light – no more than that – and suddenly reappeared over the front lawn of the house as a solid, silvery-grey, domed craft, about fifty feet in diameter and hovering magically.

Remaining on the bike with Bonnie still behind him, her thighs pressing tensely against his hips, Gumshoe looked on in mounting despair as the flying saucer, a transport, descended languidly to the lawn to settle mere centimetres above it, still hovering magically. This saucer had no old-fashioned hydraulic legs, but merely hovered just above the ground, swaying gently from side to side, while one of its side panels fell outward and down to form a ramp sloping to the ground.

Two cyborgs emerged from the saucer, both as small as children but with exceptionally large heads and only a smooth metal mask where their nose and lips should have been. Both were carrying stun guns in perfectly normal hands. They were followed out by three normal human beings, all wearing ink-black suits with plain white shirts and narrow black ties: the notorious Men in Black. All five entered the Woodlawn Nursing Home and emerged a few minutes later, surrounding Mr Harbinson, frail in his striped pyjamas and obviously distraught, and the housekeeper, Mrs Weatherby, who walked between them like a woman in a trance. Harbinson and Weatherby were led up into the flying saucer by the cyborgs, followed by the Men in Black. Then the ramp moved back into its original place, forming part of the seamless, circular main body, and the flying saucer took off again.

Spinning rapidly and silently, but sucking up gravel and loose leaves to make them swirl violently, noisily, in the air, the saucer ascended leisurely, vertically, to an altitude of about a hundred metres, well clear of the treetops. Then it hovered briefly again before abruptly shooting off at a right angle, back in the direction of Washington DC.

It disappeared as quickly as it had appeared, in the blinking of an eye, as if it had never been.

'Those poor bastards,' Gumshoe said, blaming himself for what had happened and feeling thoroughly ashamed . . . even as fear for himself and Bonnie crept coldly over him. 'Let's get the hell out of here.'

With Bonnie clinging tightly to him, he shot off down the road, back along Route 235, heading for the George Washington Memorial Parkway and the deepening darkness.

Chapter Seventeen

I was twenty years old when we took over the world, but, educated and matured well beyond my years, I was already our leader. Like an Egyptian prince, I had been born and raised for this task, but with a singular difference: the instructions for my resurrection had been written out by myself. Before I died, in the Old Age, in that colony in Neuschwabenland, Antarctica, I knew that we were on the verge of creating new life, creating and growing a DNA chain, and I arranged for a clone of myself to be the first one created. By that time, no one in the colony had a mind of their own: they had all been electronically implanted and programmed for absolute obedience, total loyalty. And so, before my death, I arranged for them to clone me when the breakthrough in cloning, which we were rapidly approaching, finally came. In fact, it came the next year.

I am a product of parthenogenesis, self-cell-division, the real form of virgin birth.

Like the rest of the world, we had started off with other, less successful forms of life creation, such as artificial wombs and in vitro fertilization to produce embryos that could be implanted in the wombs of women. Naturally, our first artificial wombs were primitive, with the foetus being removed from its mother's womb a few weeks before natural birth was due and suspended in an artificial chamber filled with a solution of sugars and salts. The premature child was fed and supplied oxygen via its umbilical cord, which was attached by plastic tubes to a heart-lung machine, but such children invariably died from their own waste products. We did, however, move on to pressurized steel chambers containing an oxygen-rich saline solution that could push oxygen through the body of the foetus, but these foetuses, like the others, also died from their own waste products. Nevertheless, the day came when we produced living, perfectly normal human beings in artificial wombs, through in vitro *fertilization and, finally, embryos created through parthenogenesis and placed in a natural womb for full development.*

Once it was clear that we could do this successfully, we experimented with the creation of slightly abnormal, though more intelligent, human beings. Having discovered that the sole limitation on the size of the human brain is the diameter of the female pelvic girdle, we experimented surgically on a wide variety of abducted females until we were able to enlarge the pelvic girdle without killing the subjects or damaging them in a way that rendered them useless to us. When the operation was completed, we then made them pregnant with in vitro *fertilization techniques and artificial wombs to produce babies with unusually large brains contained in large heads. Brought up in isolation, these children were indoctrinated or electronically brain-implanted to behave exactly as we wanted them to. They were then allowed either to grow into normal adulthood, albeit with unusually large heads and enhanced intelligence, or were surgically mutated into cyborgs.*

The misinformed, when observing such creatures emerging from our flying saucers, invariably assumed that their abnormally large heads were proof that they had to be extraterrestrials. This aided our programme of disinformation for a great number of years.

To early parthenogenesis experiments we added a variety of recombinant-DNA techniques, or gene surgery. I personally had become aware of the striking resemblance between the way computers operate and the way the deoxyribonucleic acid (DNA) double helix controls all known forms of life. By this I mean that the DNA double helix, like the computer, stores information in a coded form and the on-off structure of the DNA chain of molecules, shaped like a ladder twisted about its own axis to form the double-helix shape, is remarkably similar to the on-off switchings in computer memories. The complexity of DNA foils your world's still relatively primitive computers, but aware of the similarity between the operation of computers and that of the DNA double helix, I was able to develop a twenty-trillion-byte computer. Given that one neuron of the human brain roughly equals one byte of a computer, our computers, based on my original prototype, now rival the human model, the DNA double helix, in complexity and in ability. This in turn has enabled us to advance our recombinant-DNA technology to an unimaginable level of accomplishment.

You will never catch up with us.

With our new computer-controlled, exceptionally powerful electron microscopes, we were able to more fully probe the structure of the double helix, the key to life, then isolate sections of the chromosomal genetic programme of living organisms — plant, animal or human — and insert other, replacement sections. In this way we were able to create cross-bred animals, chimeras, blending two completely separate species that could not mate, thus creating a sheep with a goat's head, a dog with a cat's body, two-headed mice, and even rats with fish gills and fins instead of legs and a tail. From these primitive early chimeras, we moved on to cyborg-animals created for specific tasks: for example, headless cows as drug factories, producing a variety of genetically engineered drugs from their milk; and meat cattle that are themselves no more than large lumps of meat that seem alive and are indeed so, having a heart and circulation though no head or brain because, in both cases, their biological nervous systems are linked to a central computer system that controls all their functions.

From these useful, genetically engineered cyborg-animals, it was but a step to the genetically altered human being.

First, we abducted human beings suffering from genetic disorders and injected them with DNA material that carried the correct version of their malformed gene. Or, conversely, we changed their structure for the worse by mixing malformed genes with their healthy genes and letting them breed and multiply until the original, healthy genes had been replaced entirely by the malformed ones. During those early years, the abductees whose structures were genetically altered for the worse, giving them some disease or making them criminal or psychopathic, were terminated once the experiment had succeeded. Where the abductees were genetically altered for the better, we either kept them for further experiments or used them as workers who would never complain or cause any problems. Finally, when we saw how successful the recombinant-DNA techniques were, we started using them on a regular basis to produce perfectly healthy, mentally superior, totally obedient workers.

In this area of research, we have long been using the amniocentesis procedure, in which the mother's womb is examined for markers indicating the extra *chromosome that causes mental retardation and the physical abnormalities of Down's Syndrome. Advancing from this innovation, we learned to scan for literally hundreds of other diseases and defects, including criminal or psychopathic tendencies, while the child was still in the womb. At first we aborted any foetuses with such abnormalities, but now we simply alter the genetic structure of the growing foetus to ensure that it is, when born, perfectly normal and healthy.*

This is, you will realize, a form of eugenics, the control of human breeding, a concept long reviled and feared by liberal thinkers. Most notorious as something cruelly used by the Nazis of the Old Age (including myself in my first incarnation), it was actually first practised in the United States in the 1930s with official sterilization programmes that were used to prevent the so-called 'unfit' from breeding. The 'unfit', according to US policies of the period, included the feeble-minded, the epileptic, the blind, the deaf, the deformed and those crippled or merely suffering from what were considered, at the time, to be socially unacceptable diseases.

So do not express revulsion at what we do. What we do, your kind did first.

Thankfully, the state of your genetic engineering is still retarded whereas ours is in what would be, to you, an awesome stage of advancement. As long ago as 1984, bio-engineers in the Arizona Genetic Laboratory caused a rat to regrow a lost limb by restimulating the genes controlling limb development. While nothing much was heard after that particular experiment, we capitalized on their research and now our genetic-engineering techniques enable to us regrow corrupted internal organs and lost limbs. The genes that cause growth in the foetus remain in place throughout adult life and by stimulating them with our advanced recombinant-DNA techniques, we are able to regenerate amputated hands, arms or legs. This is particularly useful when it comes to replacing the ageing human parts in the early cyborgs.

Is this your Frankenstein nightmare? Fear not: you will get used to it. Soon, when you join us, it will seem as natural to you as shaving or clipping your nails, in both of which cases you are destroying some of your own genetic chromosomes. Indeed, to shave or clip your nails is to engage in genetic engineering, albeit of a routine kind. What we were doing, however, was essentially no different. But what we were doing, good or bad, right or wrong, was merely the prelude to our penultimate achievement: the cloning of human beings.

I was the first.

Just before my death, at my command, my bio-technicians extracted minute samples of my original genetic blueprint from a piece of my skin tissue, then cloned and grew the DNA string from it to create another 'me' in a test tube. Naturally, I was only a replica *of the original me, a physical mirror image, while otherwise being a blank diskette waiting to be filled. So it was that the thoughts and experiences of the original John Wilson had to be implanted in me, virtually imprinted upon me, and this process, which began from my first months, continued until I knew everything that John Wilson had known and virtually felt all that he had felt. I was given the same name, the same background and memories (the wheat fields of Iowa; the knowledge that the sun would die; the construction of airships and jet aircraft and flying saucers; the Second World War and the flight to Antarctica; the exploitation of the Cold War to get the most out of the Soviets and the Americans; the death at an unnaturally old age and the subsequent cloning), forced to read his diaries daily and learnt, with the aid of interactive media systems and computer technology with heightened sensory stimulation, including 3-D sound and wraparound vision, to relieve his whole life, study his life's work and in general become virtually the same man that he had been. Now, to all intents and purposes, I am John Wilson.*

How do I feel about this? A parentless child, the product of a true virgin birth, in a brave new world. Someone shaped by the experiences of another and carrying on his life.

Nothing. I feel nothing. By which I mean that I feel normal. Knowing nothing else, possessing no memories other than his, those memories are as real to me as is your past to you. I take pride in my own history, which is, of course, his history, and strengthen that pride with the knowledge that I am carrying on his work. I believe in what I am doing, as he believed, and this is enough to sustain me.

Wilson's goal was the creation of the Superman and we, his successors, in creating men through cloning, in making them physically perfect and intellectually superior, have in fact turned them into Supermen. This, our penultimate achievement, has already been accomplished.

So, you might well ask, if this was our penultimate *achievement, then what was our* ultimate *achievement?*

Alas, we have not yet attained it. But we are here, in your cities, running your world, in order to do so. We will soon succeed.

Come and join us.

Bear witness.

Chapter Eighteen

Making his way through the forest, Michael was filled with a sense of strangeness and wonder, never before having been surrounded by trees, in a gloom criss-crossed with striations of sunlight in which motes of dust were at play. Mentally attuned to the vast skies and dazzling light of Antarctica, to a feeling of boundless space and clarity, he felt slightly claustrophobic in the forest, with the branches of the trees blocking out the sky except for cloudy patches here and there. From what he could see, the sky looked low, unnaturally so, and this only heightened his feeling that he was a stranger in a strange land, though he knew that this was simply the world that his parents, and most of the other adults in Freedom Bay, had originally come from.

This is where I truly belong, he thought, *so I'd better get used to it.*

Leaves tumbled down around him, rustled around his feet, and there were many other unfamiliar sounds that distracted him constantly. Luckily, he'd studied the area on his computer before coming here, learning all he could about it, and he knew that most of the unfamiliar sounds he was hearing were being made by animals and birds of the forest, none of which were dangerous.

As he walked, he found himself stroking the barks of the trees, bending the branches, stroking the leaves, picking up plants and flowers, just for the unfamiliar tactile sensations they gave him.

There were no trees around Freedom Bay, no leaves, plants or flowers, so he explored the forest as he walked through it, marvelling at its many colours and shadings, taking them in with deep pleasure and gradually losing his initial feeling of claustrophobia.

Nevertheless, despite the novelty of this new experience, he tried not to lose his concentration, keeping firmly in mind the knowledge that this World was ruled by the cyborgs and that even out here, in the mountains and valleys, they could have a presence. It took him an hour to get clear of the forest, passing repeatedly from gloom to striations of sunlight, and each time he saw a patch of sky above he looked up automatically, fully expecting to see a flying saucer, though in the event he saw none. When eventually he emerged from the forest, to the wide-open spaces, the sun was sinking and casting great shadows over the land.

This was a rural area of orchards, pastures, hamlets and small towns. White-painted wooden fences divided the land, separating one field from another where the farmers were growing maize, wheat, oats and groundnuts. A line of mountains – not the ones he had come from – ran along the south-western horizon, dividing the valleys from the darkening sky; a broad, glittering river snaked south of where he was standing; and directly in front of him, to the east, was a small town of mostly white-painted houses with roofs of red tiles, where lights were winking on, one after the other, as the sun went down.

Between the town and where Michael stood was a winding stream. A boy wearing coveralls and a soft peaked cap was fishing in it, sitting on his backside on the far bank, gazing distractedly in Michael's direction, using a rod and line. Realizing that the boy had seen him, though he didn't seem too concerned, Michael ambled towards him, suddenly feeling nervous but trying not to show it, waving his right hand as he approached the near bank. The boy saw him waving and waved back, then jabbed his finger to his left, indicating some stepping stones that crossed the stream. Nodding to show that he had understood, Michael headed in that direction, crossed the stream by way of the stones, then walked along the bank until he came to where the boy was sitting. Up close, he saw that the boy was about twelve years old, his face freckled and sunburnt.

'Hi,' Michael said. 'Catch anything yet?'

'Nope. Never do.'

'So why are you fishing?'

''Cause I like it,' the boy said.

Michael smiled and knelt beside him. 'There are no fish in this river?' he asked, just to make conversation and gain the boy's confidence.

'I don't think so,' the boy replied. 'My Dad and me used to go fishing in Chesapeake Bay. Lots of fish there, lots of big boats, and we used to have a great time. That doesn't happen any more, so I come here instead. Who knows? I caught a lot of fish in Chesapeake Bay, so sooner or later I might catch one here. A guy lives on hope.'

'Chesapeake Bay's a good distance from here,' Michael said. 'Why did your Dad take you there?'

'He didn't. We lived there. In Annapolis. My Dad was a Drill Instructor at the Naval Academy and one day last year he went to work and didn't come back. He'd been picked up by a flying saucer. When we were told that by the police, my Mom got real scared and sold the house practically overnight and moved us out here. So that's why I'm fishing here.'

'You haven't seen your Dad since?'

'Nope,' the boy said, looking hurt but resigned. 'And I don't expect to, neither. No one picked up by a cyborg saucer has ever been seen again — not unless they've been brainwashed. I guess my Dad's gone for good.'

Sympathetic to the boy, but relieved to know that he had no fondness for the cyborgs, Michael said: 'So your mother brought you here because she thinks you'll be safer here than in Annapolis.'

'Right,' the boy said. 'As my Mom said, Annapolis, the whole of Maryland, the whole way from there to Washington DC, is filled with air force and naval bases, so the cyborgs are all over those areas. She brought us here 'cause this is mostly rural and the cyborgs don't come around much. Short of climbing Mount Everest, she said, we couldn't be safer.'

'She sounds sensible,' Michael said.

'She is. So what are you doing out here, Mister? You don't come from here.' He glanced at the rucksack on Michael's back. 'You hitch-hiking around?'

'That's right,' Michael lied. 'Hitch-hiking. I've come from Cincinnati and I'm trying to make my way to Washington DC.'

'That's a bad place to go,' the boy said, obviously thinking about his father and looking forlorn. 'The cyborgs are all over that place and the closer you get to it, the more saucers you'll see. If they stop you, you're finished.'

'Yes?'

'Yeah,' the boy said. 'You'll just disappear.'

Michael nodded towards the nearby town, the nearest buildings of which were only a few hundred metres away, at the other side of a road that snaked through rolling, shadow-covered pasture lands. 'You live there?' he asked.

'Yeah,' the boy said.

'It looks like a nice little town.'

'It's a morgue,' the boy said.

'Well, I guess I'd better be moving on,' Michael said, standing upright.

'You really shouldn't travel at night,' the boy advised him, speaking with the gravity and authority of a mature man. 'Though there aren't as many saucer patrols here as there are in Washington, they still fly over occasionally and nearly always at night. That's mostly when they abduct people. You'd be better off staying here for the night and moving on tomorrow.'

Michael glanced automatically at the clapboard houses of the small, pretty town. 'Do you know of anywhere there I can stay?' he asked.

'Sure,' the boy said, grinning happily and clambering to his feet to stand in front of Michael. 'At our place. My Mom does bed and breakfast for the odd traveller to supplement her income. She offers dinner as well. There's no one there at the moment, so the bedroom's available. You can stay with us, then light out in the morning. If you get a couple of decent lifts – and avoid the saucers – you'll be in Washington before tomorrow evening. What about it, mister?'

Studying the boy's bright blue eyes and big grin under his mop of wind-tossed blond hair, Michael realized that he was desperate for company in this beautiful though isolated place.

'Sounds good,' he said.

'Great! I'm Jim – Jim Pendleton.'

The boy held out his hand and Michael shook it. 'Mike Johnson,' he said, using the name on his false identification papers and plastic cards. 'Nice to meet you, Jim.'

'Same here,' Jim said, kneeling briefly to pick up his fishing tackle, then straightening up again. 'God, I'm hungry!' he exclaimed, revitalized by the very thought of company. 'I didn't realize how long I've been out here. I'm *starving!* Let's go, Mike.'

Walking energetically, he led Michael across the road, then on to the western edge of town, a short distance away. As they approached the nearest houses, the sun started sinking in a darkening blue sky tinged with crimson, casting great shadows over the lush green pasturelands, criss-crossed with white-painted fences, sometimes hemmed in with orchards, dotted here and there with yellow tractors and other vehicles on the move in the distance. Again, Michael was struck by the richness of the unfamiliar colours and by what seemed like an unusually low sky, though the latter was, he knew, an illusion, since that same sky also covered Antarctica. He realized, then, that he felt comfortable with the boy because he too *felt* like a boy, seeing everything as if for the first time – which was what he was, in a real sense, doing.

'Nice evening,' he said when they reached the outlying houses and started wending their way between them.

'It's not bad,' Jim replied. 'Hi, Mister McCloud!' he called out, waving to a man who had been mowing his lawn and was now relaxing with a cigarette before darkness fell. The man, who was tall and skinny, wearing coveralls, with thinning hair and a face dried out by too much sunshine, grinned and waved back.

'Evenin', Jim!' he shouted.

'Got a visitor,' Jim said, indicating Michael with a backward jab of his thumb.

'You won't starve in Jim's house,' the man said, speaking to Michael. 'His Mom lays a good table.'

'I'm pleased to hear it,' Michael said.

Jim led him on, going along a couple of narrow lanes between the clapboard houses, waving to other friends and neighbours who were still outdoors, some sitting on porches and watching the sun go down. After turning a couple of corners, he arrived at his own home which, like most of the others, was a two-storey, white-painted clapboard house with a porch running along its front, overlooking the well-kept grass of its front yard.

'This is it,' Jim said, bounding up the steps ahead of Michael, laying his fishing gear on the floor of the porch, then opening the front door and sticking his head in. 'Mom!' he called out.

'Yes!' a woman's voice responded from inside.

'I got a visitor wants to stay for the night,' Jim said.

'I'm coming right out, son.'

As Michael mounted the steps to join Jim on the porch, a thin woman with a gaunt, attractive face and short-cropped blonde hair came to the door, drying her hands on the white apron tied around her loose lime-green cotton dress. She was smiling in welcome, but she studied Michael with slightly suspicious eyes.

'Hi,' Michael said. 'Mike Johnson. I'm making my way from Cincinnati to Washington DC. Hitch-hiking. Jim says you can put me up for the night.'

'Well . . .'

'He says you do bed and breakfast occasionally and that's what I'm after. Only for the one night.'

The woman continued to study him thoughtfully and he knew what she was thinking. *Is he one of us?* she was thinking. *Or is he one of them?* Given what had happened to her husband, she would be thinking about the cyborgs night and day; and, just as often, about those people who'd had brain implants before being sent back out as programmed zombies to spy on family and friends. Those people were widely known as 'the living dead' and this woman, whose husband had been abducted, would be wondering if Michael was one of them.

'Just this one night,' Michael repeated to reassure her, 'and then I'll be moving on.'

Having decided, for whatever reason, that Michael was normal, the woman nodded assent. 'A hundred dollars for dinner, bed and breakfast,' she said. This figure, as Michael knew from his research, was generous to a fault in these days of rampant inflation. 'We all share the bathroom.'

'That's fine,' Michael said.

'Okay. Come in.' As young Jim beamed with pleasure, the woman stepped aside to let Michael enter. Before going in, he removed his rucksack from his shoulders and held it down by his side. Entering the house with Jim close behind him, he found himself in a medium-sized living room, tidy and cosily furnished with soft armchairs, a sofa, potted plants and flowered curtains framing a view of the distant, purple-shadowed mountains. There was a large TV-and-video set in one corner, though it wasn't turned on, and there were a couple of bookshelves filled with books. The latter were a surprising sight to Michael because, according to his research, very few people read print on paper these days, getting most of their information and relaxation from computers and CD-ROMs instead.

As he was surveying the room, the woman stepped around in front of him and offered her hand. 'The name's Mary.' Michael nodded and smiled. 'Dinner's almost ready,' Mary said, 'so let me show you your room. You can have a quick shower or bath before eating. Dinner's ready in half an hour.'

As the flight from Freedom Bay to Virginia had only taken about an hour and he had only walked for ninety minutes since then, Michael nearly said that he didn't need a shower or bath. Remembering, however, that he was supposed to have hitch-hiked all the way from Cincinnati, he nodded agreement and said, 'Great. I could do with freshening up.'

'I'll bet,' Mary said. 'And you,' she added, turning to young Jim with mock severity. 'You come up as well and make sure you wipe that mud off your hands.' She had said it with great affection and Jim spread his two hands in the air, palms upward, to study the mud from the river bank with a big grin.

'Gee,' he said, 'where did that come from? A guy just can't keep clean out here.'

'Up you go,' Mary said.

Jim bounded up the stairs, with his mother following him and Michael going last. There was a short landing upstairs with a couple of bedrooms and a bathroom running off it. As Jim rushed into the bathroom to wash his hands, Mary stepped aside to let Michael enter his bedroom. It was small and homely, with flowered wallpaper, a big fluffy quilt on the bed, pine wardrobes, and a window offering a good view of the pasturelands. It was almost dark by now and the stars were coming out over the distant mountains, slightly dimmed by a full moon.

'Very nice,' Michael said, resting his rucksack on the floor and turning back to face Mary where she stood in the doorway.

'Thanks,' she responded. 'You'll find towels in the top drawer of that chest-of-drawers. Come down when you're ready.'

When Mary had turned away and was going back down the stairs, Michael placed his rucksack on the bed, opened it and withdrew his toilet bag. He was pulling a large towel from the chest-of-drawers when Jim rushed out of the bathroom, shouting, 'I've finished. All clear!' When Michael grinned and waved at him, the boy beamed again and went clattering down the stairs, leaving Michael free to have his shower. Twenty minutes later, showered and changed into fresh clothing, he was sitting with Mary and Jim at the dinner table, experiencing the kind of food he had never eaten before.

Because of Lee Brandenberg's insistence that Freedom Bay had to stand as a living rebuke to John Wilson's extraordinary cruelties, particularly his nightmarish surgical experiments on both humans and animals, the colony produced and consumed only vegetarian food. Michael, therefore, had never eaten meat, fowl or fish in his life. He had, however, been forewarned that most Americans were carnivorous and viewed vegetarians as 'cranks'. For this reason, Brandenberg had recommended that Michael force himself to eat meat when in the company of World people and not draw unwanted attention to himself as someone who was 'different' or 'eccentric'. Now, as he shared his first World meal with Mary and young Jim, he had to use all the will power at his command not to feel nausea as he cut up, chewed and swallowed his grilled steak. The rest of the meal, however (mashed potatoes, boiled carrots and green beans; dessert of apple pie with ice cream) was, while certainly unfamiliar, absolutely delicious, as was the smell of it.

Still trying to get used to the fact that he was actually in the World, where he had never been before, Michael was not at ease when it came to making casual conversation over the table, but he tried his best.

'This is a pretty nice area,' he said. 'It has a nice feel to it. I've always liked travelling through Virginia. It still looks unspoiled.'

'The Old Dominion,' Mary said sardonically. 'Mother of Presidents.'

She was referring to the titles given to a state that was historically the most important in America. As Michael knew from his research into Virginia, the first permanent English settlement in the country had been made at Jamestown in 1607; Virginia was one of the original thirteen states of the USA and the tenth to ratify the Constitution; and it had espoused the

Confederate cause during the Civil War and was readmitted to the Union in 1870.

'Right,' Michael said. 'An awful lot of history in Virginia. A lot of famous men came from it.'

'Washington, Jefferson, Monroe and Robert E. Lee,' young Jim said, showing off and smiling cockily. 'I learnt that in school.'

'What else did you learn?' Michael asked to keep the conversation going. 'About Virginia, I mean.'

'Everything,' Jim responded, his cocky grin even broader. 'It consists of an area of 105,710 square kilometres, it has a population of slightly under five million, its major industrial centres are in Norfolk, Richmond, Portsmouth and Newport News, its most important mineral's coal and its leading commercial crop's tobacco. Pretty neat, eh?'

'Pretty neat,' Michael agreed. 'What are its main rivers?'

'The Potomac, the James, the Roanoke and the Rappahannock.'

'Correct,' Michael said. 'So where's the Dismal Swamp located?'

'South-east,' Jim responded proudly.

'And the Piedmont plateau?'

'West,' Jim said. 'Right?'

'Right. And the Blue Ridge?'

'Further west,' Jim said. 'Extending north-east, south-west across the state and rising to Mount Rogers and the Appalachians. I'm right again, ain't I?'

'You sure are,' Michael said.

Yet he still felt uneasy, nervous of saying the wrong thing, letting something about Antarctica slip out. Luckily Jim kept talking, obviously thrilled to have someone new in the house, telling him all about school, his new friends, his favourite TV programmes and movies and computer games, only being interrupted by his mother when he became too excited or came out with some spontaneous childish fantasy. Inexorably, however, his conversation wound back to his earlier days in Maryland, where clearly he had been much happier until the disappearance of his father.

'That's why I hate the cyborgs,' he said. 'They took my Dad away and ruined our life. I'll hate 'em forever.'

'Stop this,' his mother said abruptly, standing up to clear the table. 'I've told you before to stop thinking about it. Thinking about it's not good for you.'

'I can't help thinking about it,' Jim replied. 'It's just there, in my head. I think about it every night in bed and I can't help that either.' He looked up at Michael. 'Are there cyborgs in Cincinnati as well?'

Michael nodded. 'Yes. The cyborgs are everywhere.'

'When I grow up,' Jim said, 'I'm going to form my own gang and then go to war against the cyborgs. I'm gonna get rid of all the cyborgs and track down my Dad.'

'Shut up, Jim,' his mother said, returning to the table and lighting a cigarette. Aware that cigarettes caused cancer, Michael was slightly shocked to see Mary smoking, though he tried not to show it. 'Cincinnati,' Mary continued, turning to Michael. 'Surely there can't be as many cyborgs in Cincinnati as there are in Washington DC. I mean, there's nothing as important as the White House or the Pentagon in Cincinnati. Not many air force or naval bases, either.'

'No, nothing that important,' Michael agreed, speaking purely from his research, since he had never been to Cincinnati in his life, 'but we *do* have a lot of chemical plants and factories producing machine tools, so the cyborgs *do* have an interest there. Obviously, they're not as strong a presence in Cincinnati as they are in Washington DC, but they're there all the same.'

'I'm gonna get rid of 'em when I grow up,' Jim repeated. 'You better believe it.'

Mary smiled, though there was pain in her eyes and, as Michael noticed for the first time, her face, which must have been pretty once, was now gaunt from stress. 'He's obsessed with the cyborgs because of his father,' she said to Michael.

'I don't blame him,' Michael said.

'So why are you going to Washington DC? Given the strength of the cyborg presence there, it must be one of the most dangerous cities in the United States.'

'I'm trying to find someone,' Michael said, not quite lying, since he was, indeed, trying to find Wilson. 'An old friend who used to send me e-mail on a regular basis, then just suddenly stopped doing so. I've sent message after message but he doesn't reply, so I think something's wrong.'

'What did he do?' Mary asked.

'Software for computers. He specialized in keeping the old systems going. It made him good money because with the production of new computers banned by the cyborgs, the old ones are now more valuable than ever.'

'The maintenance of old computers,' Mary said, exhaling a cloud of unhealthy, polluting cigarette smoke. 'That's enough to get a man into trouble in Washington DC. He might have been picked up for that.'

'By the cyborgs,' Jim clarified.

'And if that's the case,' Mary said, 'you'd better be careful about going to his place. It might still be under cyborg surveillance.'

'I'll be careful,' Michael said, then ostentatiously yawned and stretched himself in the chair. 'Boy, I'm really pooped. Did a lot of walking today and I want to light out early in the morning, so I'd better get a good night's sleep.'

'What time do you want to be wakened in the morning?'

'Seven,' Michael said.

'Jim will knock on your door on the dot of seven and I'll have breakfast ready.'

'Great,' Michael said, standing up. He walked around the table and mussed Jim's blond hair. 'Thanks for the help, kid.'

'No sweat,' Jim said.

Wishing them both goodnight, Michael went upstairs to his bedroom, undressed and stretched out on the bed. Looking through the window, he could see a full moon shining its light on the dark mountains and valleys, beaming out of a sky drenched with stars. He felt far from home now, a long way from Freedom Bay, and realized that, apart from occasional expeditions into the Antarctic wilderness, he had never left home before, nor been separated by such a great distance from his parents and Chloe. It made him feel grown up, but it also made him feel lonesome, more so because of the warmth he had sensed between Mary and Jim. And, of course, when he thought of Mary and Jim, he also thought of the cyborgs and the grief that they had brought to so many.

The cyborgs are Wilson's children, he thought. *The offspring of Frankenstein.*

This was a chilling reminder of what he was doing here and he fell asleep on it.

The next morning, after a hearty breakfast of cereal and toast with honey, having politely declined ham and eggs, Michael said goodbye to Mary and Jim. Then he set out again, walking carefully along the side of the sunlit road that snaked through the green pastures and rolling hills in the direction of Harrisonburg, trying to wave down any vehicle that passed.

He did not walk for long.

Chapter Nineteen

The Cowboy was, as usual, sitting in darkness on the porch of his Anacostia shack, silhouetted against the moonlit bend in the river, his booted feet up on the railing, a stetson hat on his head. Gumshoe and Bonnie approached him in that darkness, having managed once more to get through the low-income housing project without mishap. Without otherwise moving a muscle, the Cowboy turned his head in their direction, then gave a big grin.

'Well, lookahere!' he exclaimed. 'My favourite couple's come back to me. How are you two?'

'Fine,' Gumshoe said, stepping up onto the porch with a grinning Bonnie beside him. Gumshoe was reminded by that smile that the Cowboy, during their previous visit, had charmed the not-easily-charmed Bonnie. It made Gumshoe feel jealous.

'We're not a couple,' Bonnie corrected the Cowboy. 'We're just buddies, is all.'

Which proved, if Gumshoe had any doubts, that she'd been charmed by the Cowboy.

God protect me from my friends, Gumshoe thought. *Not to mention older men. These old guys are seductive.*

'You don't have to be shy with me,' the Cowboy drawled, his eyes twinkling at Bonnie. 'I think you make a great couple.'

'We're *not* a couple,' Bonnie insisted. 'We're just runnin' around together at the moment.'

'Pretty neat,' the Cowboy said.

'Have you two finished?' Gumshoe asked, raising his hands pleadingly in the air and staring aggressively from one to the other. 'I mean, I've come here for a *purpose.*'

'What's that?' the Cowboy said. 'Here,' he added before Gumshoe could answer, turning to Bonnie, taking hold of her shoulder and tugging her down onto the chair beside him. 'Take this chair, young lady.'

'Gee, thanks,' Bonnie said, clearly not used to such gallantry but charmed by it all over again. She settled into the chair and crossed her long legs to give the Cowboy a good look. The Cowboy had a good look.

'This is serious,' Gumshoe said, glancing about him for a chair and finding only a wooden crate to sit on. He sat on the wooden crate. 'You hear me, Cowboy?'

'What's that?' The Cowboy dragged his eyes away from Bonnie's legs and fixed them on Gumshoe. 'What was that you said, Gumshoe? Here,' he added before Gumshoe could reply, reaching down into the cardboard box at his feet and pulling out a bottle of beer, which he uncapped with his teeth and then handed to Bonnie. 'Have a beer, sweetheart. It's real hot tonight.'

'Gee, thanks,' Bonnie said, smiling sweetly as she took the bottle of Bud from the Cowboy. 'That's a real nice thought.'

'I like to see a lady smile,' the Cowboy said.

'I'm sure you do,' Bonnie rejoindered.

'Thanks a million,' Gumshoe said.

'What for?' the Cowboy responded, reluctantly dragging his eyes away from Bonnie's breasts and looking at Gumshoe instead.

'For the beer.'

'Hadn't forgotten you at all,' the Cowboy drawled, unperturbed, grinning as he reached into the box again and pulled out another bottle of Bud, which he handed, unopened, to Gumshoe.

Gumshoe stared at the bottle for some time, then said, 'How do I open it?'

'With your teeth,' Bonnie said.

'I can't do that,' Gumshoe admitted.

'That's the way real men do it,' Bonnie informed him. 'Just like the Cowboy, here.'

'I'd break my teeth,' Gumshoe said.

'Yeah, probably,' Bonnie agreed.

'Here, give it to me,' the Cowboy said. 'I just wasn't thinking, kid.' He took the bottle from Gumshoe, uncapped it with his teeth, then handed it back. 'There you are, pal.'

'Thanks,' Gumshoe said.

The Cowboy had a long swig of his beer, then, wiping his lips with the back of his hand, said, 'So what are you here for?'

'What?' Gumshoe said.

'You said you'd come here for a reason.'

'Oh, right, that's correct, I've come for a reason.'

'What reason?'

Gumshoe had a slug of his beer, stared stonily at Bonnie, who was being far too friendly with the Cowboy, then turned back to the handsome object of her admiration. Gumshoe admired the Cowboy as well, but he was, to his surprise, resentful of the fact that Bonnie felt the same way.

I must be losing my mind, he thought.

Clearing his throat by coughing into his fist, he began, 'Well, I've just been to see a pretty interesting character called W.A. Harbinson and—'

'Who?'

'W.A. Harbinson. So—'

'What are his Christian names?'

'I don't know. He—'

'Why doesn't the son of a bitch use his first names?'

'I don't know. It's probably just a professional thing. You see, he's a writer and . . .'

'You mean books?'

'Yeah, right.'

'Don't know nothin' about books. Hardly ever read.'

'Who does, these days?' Bonnie said, not only approving of the Cowboy's lack of literary leanings but also clearly wanting him to know it.

'Yeah, right,' the Cowboy said, throwing her a smile like the rising sun.

'Thing is,' Gumshoe said, glaring at Bonnie and trying to regain the Cowboy's attention, 'that this guy told us an awful lot of stuff that I think you might know about, you having worked in the Space Command Centre in Colorado Springs and being privy to things that the average Joe wouldn't have been informed about. I think that most of what this old guy – this Harbinson – told us was true and I want you to confirm it.'

'I mightn't be able to do that,' the Cowboy said carefully. 'Classified information and so forth . . .'

'You haven't worked there for fucking years,' Gumshoe reminded him, 'and now the place is being run by the cyborgs. So unless you've got something going for the cyborgs, you've nothing to hide.'

The Cowboy grinned slyly. 'Okay, shoot.'

Gumshoe passed on what he had been told by the old British writer. It took a long time to recount, but the Cowboy listened patiently, slugging his beer methodically and occasionally giving Bonnie a friendly smile. Bonnie sat quietly, her painted face in the shadows, her rainbow-coloured hair limned by the moonlight. In her own bizarre way she was attractive and Gumshoe was drawn to her.

Eventually, when he had finished with Harbinson's story, Gumshoe had a slug of his beer, wiped his lips on his sleeve, and waited patiently for the Cowboy's response. When the Cowboy just gazed thoughtfully across the glittering, moonlit river, not saying a word, just softly humming to himself, Gumshoe, running out of patience, decided to prompt him.

'So,' he said, '*did* you hear anything about it? Did Wilson actually exist, was he responsible for the flying saucers, and did the US take over his colony, hidden in Antarctica?'

The Cowboy sighed. 'I never heard of a Wilson,' he said. 'That's why, when you first mentioned his name, I didn't connect it to what I'm about to tell you.'

'What's that?' Gumshoe asked.

'The truth of the matter is that when I worked at the Space Surveillance Centre, before the cyborgs took over, we were told to *ignore* all sightings of any flying object not instantly identifiable and certainly any that appeared to be *controlled* — in other words, flying saucers. We knew that the saucers were up there — a lot of our pilots had even eyeballed them — but we couldn't do a damned thing about them, though we could track where they came from and returned to.'

'Antarctica,' Gumshoe said.

'Right. Most of them from there, though there were also some that ascended and descended over our own top-secret air force and naval bases. Rumour had it that those were our own and I was willing to believe it 'cause they never showed the same extraordinary capabilities as those that came from — and returned to — Queen Maud Land in Antarctica.'

'You could track them that accurately?' Gumshoe asked.

'Sure. Our spy satellites out in space could pinpoint a single individual on the ground. So, yeah, we were that accurate and we could tell exactly what part of Antarctica those saucers came from . . . And they came from a specific location in Queen Maud Land, that was damned sure.'

'And that was a secret colony run by Wilson?'

'Yeah, I presume so. The talk about a secret colony became more voluble every year and we knew it was being run by a single individual, though we never did know his name — that's why I didn't think about it when we last talked.'

'Good one,' Gumshoe said.

'Anyway,' the Cowboy continued, grinning, 'we learnt through the grapevine that the colony had originally been run by the Nazis but that at the time the flying saucers were becoming big news, just after World War Two, the same place was being run by a brilliant renegade *American* scientist – and he was the brains behind the flying saucers. As I said, we never did learn his name, though we gradually learnt that he was an extraordinary guy who had, single-handedly, turned his small Antarctic colony into a major contender on the world stage and was, in fact, becoming even more powerful than the United States and the Soviet Union. In fact, it became pretty widely known, though never officially acknowledged, that he was *negotiating* with us and the Soviets, playing one against the other, and that he'd been personally responsible for some of the major innovations – and disasters – of the early space age.'

'The disasters as well?'

'Yeah. Wilson was responsible for the death of Captain Thomas F. Mantell, way back in 1947 – the first case of a pilot being killed while pursuing a UFO. In fact, Mantell was deliberately shot down by one of Wilson's saucers as a warning to the US Air Force that they weren't to pursue him. However, that was small potatoes compared to what came later.'

'Such as?'

'Wilson would make certain demands on us and the Soviets and, almost certainly, the Brits and other major powers. If his demands weren't met, he'd arrange some kind of spectacular demonstration or so-called accident. The biggest spectacular, though not the first, was in 1952 when a great number of UFOs – actually Wilson's large and small saucers, both manned and remote-controlled – virtually invaded Washington DC and surrounded the White House when President Truman was resident in the building. That invasion couldn't be stopped and it scared the shit out of everyone who experienced it, so Truman, who'd tried to block Wilson's plans, played ball with Wilson after that. As for the so-called accidents – disasters actually threatened and then carried out by Wilson – they included the explosion on Project Vanguard's first rocket at Cape Canaveral, Florida, which caused the death of three astronauts, and the killing of President Kennedy by a frustrated communist sympathizer who Wilson picked up and turned into a brain-implant patsy. In all of these cases, and others, Wilson's motive was to remind the superpowers of his own far superior technology and make them do his bidding. Invariably, they did.'

'Wilson was actually negotiating with the superpowers?' Gumshoe asked in disbelief.

'He sure was. In fact, with regard to the good old US of A, he negotiated covertly with every President from Harry Truman to Ronald Reagan — and he kept them in line.'

'How?'

'From what I picked up, your Wilson, for all his technological superiority, still needed a lot of things he could only obtain outside Antarctica and he got them by trading with the outside world. Bear in mind that this was the time of the Cold War and the Space Race, when the US and the USSR were both terrified that the other side would win and so were willing to do just about anything to keep ahead of the game. To do that, they needed Wilson's technology and Wilson, aware of this, ruthlessly played one side against the other. Since his technology was so advanced, he could afford to give both the US and the Soviet Union what was, to them, highly advanced technology because it was, to him, already obsolete. So that's how the son of a bitch negotiated — repeatedly giving them a little bit of what they needed while always remaining ahead of them. Pretty smart, right?'

'Right,' Bonnie said.

'When did you join the Cheyenne Mountain Complex?' Gumshoe asked the Cowboy.

'About 1992.'

'So the American, Wilson, would have been long dead by then and the colony would have already been in US hands.'

'Right. It was taken over by us in 1982, placed under the command of a former USAF captain, Lee Brandenberg, who'd been instrumental in breaking the Wilson case, kept top secret, run by volunteers instead of slaves and, finally, renamed Freedom

Bay. As such, it carried on Wilson's work, exploiting his extraordinary technology, but using it for the defence of the West.'

'If it was top secret, how did you know about it?'

'Those of us working at the Space Surveillance Centre had to be officially informed about the existence of Freedom Bay because it was assumed that with Wilson out of action, most of the flying saucers picked up by our defence systems would be our own. What we hadn't counted on, of course, was the fact that Wilson – if such was his name – had spent most of the post-war years, the best part of four decades, abducting and brain-washing people all over the globe while making ever more advanced flying saucers and hiding them in remote locations or even on the seabed – in the Bermuda Triangle, in the so-called Devil's Sea bounded by Japan, Luzon in the Philippines and Guam, in the coastal waters off Argentina, particularly near Plata del Mar, and even in the Great Lakes of Canada and in Loch Ness, Scotland – waiting for the day, even after his death, when his cyborgs and computers would be so advanced that they could operate on their own, multiply and grow, and take over the world when the time was ripe, to continue his work. As we now know – to our cost – that's exactly what happened . . . Now you tell me that the guy was called Wilson. Well, whatever he was called, he certainly existed. You can take that as read. What's *your* interest, Gumshoe?'

Gumshoe didn't reply immediately because in truth, when he actually thought about it, he *didn't know* what his interest was. This had all started, as he now recalled, with that deceptively simple but actually extremely ambiguous e-mail popping up on his computer screen saying *wilson is back*. That message had, of course, aroused his insatiable hacker's curiosity and sent him on this intriguing chase. In fact, the chase was becoming obses-sional, more so than normal, and Gumshoe had often found himself wondering why. Now that the Cowboy had put the question into words, he tried to come up with an answer.

'I think it's to do with my parents,' he said, glancing uneasily, maybe with embarrassment, at Bonnie. 'Since the abduction and subsequent disappearance of my folks, I've secretly hated the cyborgs and wanted to somehow bring them down. I'm not alone in this. A lot of the kids my age, a lot that I know personally, lost their folks the same way and now want to strike back at the cyborgs. That's what motivates the likes of the Speed Freaks when they play their dangerous games with the cyborg patrols – and that's exactly why I do the same.'

'Right on!' Bonnie whispered.

Oddly pleased by the remark, Gumshoe threw her a quick smile, then turned back to the Cowboy. 'When I first saw that e-mail message about Wilson, I was merely amused, then I became intrigued and then I decided to check it out – all pretty normal so far, given my normal hacker's curiosity, the need to know what kind of flame ghoul was trying to do some damage to some thread somewhere in the Net. 'Course, at first I'd assumed that this Wilson was just an invention, a name picked at random, as anonymous as Smith. Then, when I discovered that he'd actually existed and may have been responsible for the creation of the first flying saucers and, later, the cyborgs . . . well, when I came to that possibility, I just had to go farther, find out more, confirm or deny. Now that I *can* confirm and know what Wilson was up to, what the cyborgs are almost certainly still doing behind closed doors, in the White House and the Pentagon and elsewhere, I'm more determined than ever to help put a stop to their rule.'

'How?' the Cowboy asked, quietly implacable.

Gumshoe sighed. 'I don't know.'

'They took that writer away,' Bonnie cut in, 'so they might find out that we were talkin' to him – if, of course, they didn't already know, maybe reading his goddamned mind, and took him for that very reason. If that's the case, then for sure they'll come for us. This is real heavy rock 'n' roll.'

The Cowboy turned his head to stare at her, smiling again,

though this time it wasn't seductive: it was more of a kindly smile. 'So what's the story behind *you*?' he asked. 'Do you have a cyborg background as well?'

'Yeah, I do,' Bonnie said, glancing from the Cowboy to Gumshoe, suddenly looking distraught. 'Same as Gumshoe,' she said, turning back to the Cowboy. 'Same as all of us. I was thirteen at the time. I had a kid sister, Marie, two years younger than me. My Mom and Dad went out one day, just goin' to see some relatives, and I said I didn't want to go; instead, I wanted to look after the apartment, just like an adult. So they humoured me, right? We were livin' in Chinatown — we'd only moved in a few months back, when some Chinese were still livin' there but movin' out quickly — and the relatives that my folks were goin' to visit were in Greenbelt, Maryland. So they went in our car, taking Marie with them, and that was the last I ever saw of any of them. No one even knew they were missing — at least, no one but me. I was thirteen years old, in that apartment on my own, and when my folks didn't come back that evening, I was pretty damned scared. They didn't come back the next day, either, and that scared me even more, but I had the sense to pick up the phone and call the relatives that they'd said they were gonna visit, way out there in Greenbelt. The man who answered was my uncle. I'd never liked that son of a bitch. He said that my folks had been, that they'd had a nice visit, and that they'd left about eight that same evenin'. When I told him my folks hadn't come home, he became scared as well — more scared for himself, though — and told me that if my folks didn't turn up, I wasn't to call him about it again 'cause he just didn't want to know. So my folks never returned. I never called that bastard again. I just stayed at home, day after day, night after night, praying every day and night that my family would reappear and eating everything I could find in the kitchen until I'd cleaned the place out. After that, it was go out or starve, so I got up and went out.'

She glanced from the Cowboy to Gumshoe, as if uncertain that she should continue, looking a lot less hard than she normally did, looking almost childlike. Gumshoe felt his throat tighten.

'I just wandered around Chinatown,' Bonnie continued, 'desperately hoping against hope that I'd see my family, though I knew in my heart that I wouldn't, 'cause when people just upped and disappeared, it meant the cyborgs had got 'em. So I just wandered around, thinkin' about Mom and Dad, thinkin' about my kid sister, only eleven years old, already taken by those damned cyborgs for God only knows what purpose, an' I cried an awful lot as I walked, growin' even more scared, until I was picked up by this guy six years older than me. I was nicely built for my age. I had the body of someone older. This guy charmed me an' asked me about myself and I gave him my story. When he heard that my folks were gone, that their apartment was empty, he suggested that I take him back there and said he'd look after me until my folks returned. So I did – I took him back there – and nat'rally he seduced me. He took me over completely – and took over the apartment. Then, after a couple of months, he threw me out in the street. I survived as best I could, drifting from one man to the next, a whole stream of benefactors, until, when I was fifteen years old, I found this nice steady guy who loved me and really looked after me. That lasted for three years. It was the best time of my life. Then my guy went out on his motorcycle with a bunch of his biker friends and he was zapped by a football and picked up in a paddy wagon and taken away. He hasn't been seen since.'

She glanced at Gumshoe, as if nervous about his reaction to her past history. When she saw that he was sympathetic, not angry, she returned her gaze to the Cowboy.

'So,' she said. 'I have my own reasons for hating the cyborgs an' that's why I hang out with the Speed Freaks and why, if you really want to know, I'm now hanging out with him.' She nodded in the direction of Gumshoe. 'I'll hang out with anyone who hates the cyborgs so much that they'll actually try goin' against them – guys like the Speed Freaks. In the eyes of some, that makes me a lowlife, but I don't give a damn.'

The Cowboy stared thoughtfully at her for a moment, a small, admiring smile playing on his lips. Then he said, 'You ain't no kinda lowlife, that's for sure. You can play in my ball park any day.'

'Hear, hear,' Gumshoe said.

Bonnie stared from one to the other, then grinned from ear to ear. 'Oh, boy!' she said softly. 'A gal's got it made here.'

The Cowboy nodded, then turned to Gumshoe. 'So,' he said. 'Now you know that Wilson existed, that he did some nasty things and that his cyborgs are carrying on his work. What's the point, Gumshoe?'

'It's not a point,' Gumshoe replied. 'It's one lingering, unanswered question. Was that e-mail message a sign that Wilson's somehow come back?'

'Come back? From where? You mean from the grave?'

'I'm not sure what I mean, but I think that message had a purpose – and the purpose was to remind us of Wilson. Who would send it and why?'

'Might've been Wilson's ghost,' Bonnie said, 'floating out there in cyberspace, tryin' to make his way back into real time. You never know about these things.'

'Might be Wilson for real, in some other shape or form,' the Cowboy added, 'given the advanced state of his technology even before he died. Might be Wilson's brain resurrected through a goddamned computer or Wilson cloned and now flesh and blood again.'

'Right,' Gumshoe said. 'From what I've learnt, his technology was getting there before he died and it may be there now. He might have had his cyborgs programmed to bring him back when they had the technology. Given the advanced state of the cyborgs of today, I'd say they could possibly do that. In fact, the Men in Black are widely believed to be clones and I for one believe that they really are. So Wilson, either as flesh and blood or as some kind of vastly advanced computer intelligence, could indeed be with us again.'

'Jesus!' Bonnie whispered.

'He won't help us,' the Cowboy joked. 'But that gets me back to my original question. What, assuming that Wilson's back with us, can we do about him?'

'We can worry about that,' Gumshoe said, 'when we know if he's really come back. Right now, I want to know if he has or has not, so I'm making that my next job.'

There was silence for a moment as they all gazed at the night sky, thinking of what was up there: spy satellites and flying saucers and space platforms and the cyborgs' ongoing Moon programme – a constantly growing, interlinking intelligence with a mysterious purpose. None of them liked what they saw up there, so they all lowered their eyes again.

'Anything else I can help you with?' the Cowboy asked eventually, obviously not too keen on this type of lengthy silence.

Gumshoe sighed. 'No.' He glanced at Bonnie, then put his empty beer bottle down and climbed to his feet. 'You've told me more than enough. Now I'll have to try to track Wilson down – find out if he's truly back – and you can't help me with that.'

'Get in touch if you find him,' the Cowboy said, 'and need some kind of back-up.'

'I will,' Gumshoe said. 'Come on, Bonnie, let's go.'

Looking more agreeable than she'd ever done before, her features softened by the moonlight, her bizarre make-up less unsettling, Bonnie pushed her chair back and stood up. She smiled at the Cowboy, then at Gumshoe, giving each equal measure, then said, 'Okay. See you soon, Cowboy.'

'I sure hope so,' the Cowboy said, waving his right hand in languid farewell and grinning lazily at both of them. 'You two take care out there.'

'I'll try,' Gumshoe said.

He jumped down off the porch with Bonnie close behind him. Then they both clambered onto the motorcycle and burned out of there, heading back to the low-income housing project running along the east branch of the Potomac. Again they managed to make it through the dubious stretch of houses with boarded-up windows, caged-in shops, heavily guarded pool halls and broken-down bars without being hauled off the motorcycle by some of the dangerous thugs who ruled this area. After passing through that stretch safely, Gumshoe took the first bridge across the Anacostia River, intending to avoid the Mall and the White House area where the cyborg patrols would be out in force, looking for those breaking the midnight curfew.

This was no help to him.

He was burning along Ohio Drive when a small, silver-white disc, a so-called football, spinning rapidly on its axis and giving off an eerie glow, shot so quickly out of the darkness of West Potomac Park that it was hovering in mid-air right in front of him before he could avoid it.

Startled, he wrenched on the handlebars of his motorcycle, intending to go around the football. But it cut abruptly across his path, stopping in front of him again, and made him take an even sharper turn. He heard Bonnie scream as the motorcycle went into a spin, and he bawled 'Jump!' when he knew he had lost control and was braking to slow it down.

The bike went into a screeching slide, spinning along the side of the road, hurling up a shower of sparks. As it toppled over, making an awful din, Bonnie jumped off and rolled over the ground. Gumshoe let go, following Bonnie's example, and then also rolled over the ground, putting space between himself and the crashing bike. The bike bounced up onto the sidewalk, smashed down onto its side, shuddered violently and eventually was still – though the front wheel kept turning.

Gumshoe jumped to his feet and saw Bonnie up ahead, shaking her head from side to side, trying to clear it, as the football, no longer spinning or glowing, now a clear metallic grey, glided towards her.

'Watch out!' Gumshoe bawled.

He rushed up to Bonnie, pushed her violently sideways and screamed at her to run for it as the football made a half-turn towards him, attracted by the sound of his voice. A hole opened up in the sloping top half of the football and a laser beam shot out of it, a thin beam of silvery-white pulsating light filled with sparks, hitting him fully on the face to temporarily blind him, then making his vision explode into a subjective cosmos of spinning stars.

He felt himself falling, thudding onto the ground, and managed to raise his head just enough to see Bonnie running away, losing herself in the darkness of the park.

'Good girl,' Gumshoe whispered.

He tried to sit upright, but he seemed to be paralysed, every bone in his body frozen. As he lay there, filling up with helpless dread, another flying saucer, a much bigger craft, one of the fifty-foot manned saucers known as a paddy wagon, descended upon the road just ahead of him. It stopped just above the road, mere inches from its surface: then a metallic panel swung down from the paddy wagon's side to form a ramp to the ground.

Two cyborgs emerged and walked directly towards him. They were less than four feet tall, had metallic masks instead of noses and lips, and were dressed in silvery-grey coveralls and black leather boots. They both had normal hands, though neither held a weapon.

They stood over Gumshoe who remained paralysed, in despair, awash with horror and dread. Then they leaned down to grab him by the shoulders and jerk him upright.

Gumshoe stood on his own two feet, though he couldn't feel a thing – not those feet, not his hands, not his arms, not even his lips. Then he found himself moving towards the hovering saucer, either being carried or dragged there by the cyborgs.

He moved up the ramp – by what means he could not tell – and then entered the dazzling light of another world. That was when the real nightmare began.

Chapter Twenty

The old beat-up truck rattled and rolled beyond Harrisonburg as the sun climbed higher in the sky and Michael coughed to clear his throat of the cigarette smoke filling the cabin from the countless cigarettes of the driver. A sun-withered, rheumy-eyed old farmer wearing a bib-and-brace, he was grilling Michael because he was a stranger hereabouts.

'Could tell that straightaway,' the farmer, who had introduced himself as Ira Fisher, said. 'I knows 'em all, north and south, east and west, an' I could tell right off that you wasn't from Virginee. That's why I picked you up.'

'Because I wasn't from here?'

'Right,' Ira said. 'Livin' here, a man gets bored right quick, so a talk with a stranger is edifying. You understand?'

'Yes, I do,' Michael said.

'So where's you from?'

'Cincinnati,' Michael replied, deciding to stick to his original story.

'Never been to Cincinnati,' Ira informed him. 'Never had the inclination. Too big a place for the likes of me. So what did you do there?'

'Lecturer at the Xavier University,' Michael lied blandly. 'I was there for a year. My first job after graduation.'

'Lecturer? Sounds like a cushy number to me. You like teaching, do you?'

'It's okay,' Michael said, now getting into his role-playing and feeling more comfortable with it. 'It's not exactly what I wanted to do, but things aren't easy these days.'

'Damned right, they're not,' Ira said. 'Ever since those lousy cyborgs took over, it's been pretty hard all round. Not that it affected me much, me bein' a farmer and all. The cyborgs ain't really interested in rural matters, particularly if you ain't into exports. I mean, me, I deal in oats and groundnuts, selling 'em in places like Alexandria, so I don't have a problem. It's the bigger fish, like them in the tobacco industry, them dependin' on exportin', that was hit hardest when the cyborgs took over. When those cyborgs grounded the aircraft and docked the ships, they put a stop to exportin' and that ruined a lot of folks. Not me, though. I'm purely local deliveries.'

'Lucky you,' Michael said.

'Yeah, lucky me. So where's you headin' for, kid?'

'Where you're going,' Michael said, deciding not to mention Washington DC again since clearly, given the reaction of young Jim and his mother, people wondered about someone wanting to go there.

'Alexandria?'

'Right. I got a job teaching there and I start next week. Do you go there a lot?'

'Once a week,' Ira said. 'Sell my stuff to the restaurants and shops and there's still a lot of those there.'

'Nice town?'

'Yeah, right pretty. Located right there on the Potomac and the Old Town still stays pretty nice 'cause there's nothing there to really interest the cyborgs. Used to have lots of tourists, but that's all died out, of course, since no foreign tourists can get into the goddamned country and American tourists don't wanna go near it 'cause it's too close to Washington DC, where everyone knows the cyborgs are thick on the ground. So it's mostly residential now, though it costs a fortune to live there. But that money can still buy good amenities, such as clean roads and street lights. So, yeah, Alexandria's not bad. You could do worse, kid. Just stay out of Washington DC and you should be okay.'

Mindful that Ira could be one of the walking dead, softening him up to loosen his tongue, Michael glanced sideways at him, saw his rheumy, bloodshot eyes and assessed him as a bit of an old soak, not brainwashed at all. Relieved, but still not certain, he said, 'Have you ever had any close encounters with the saucers or cyborg ground patrols?'

Ira shook his head, then spat out of the window of the truck. 'Naw, not me. Not way out there in Shenandoah. See the odd saucer flying overhead occasionally, but usually pretty high up and obviously on its way to somewhere else. They're not really interested in rural areas, from what I've heard; they're more interested in industrial zones and them secret research places and, of course, anything to do with what used to be our national defence – air force bases and so on. That's why they're so thick in Maryland, as well as in the capital. 'Course, you *do* hear stories, even way out here in Virginee.'

'Stories?' Michael was gazing out of his window, still trying to get used to the sheer beauty of the World: the rich pastures and orchards, the soft browns of the tree trunks, the golden leaves of the trees themselves, the vivid green of the grassy slopes, the silvery, glittering streams, the white-painted houses and fences, the different, deeper blue of the sky. Used to the vast, relatively featureless whiteness of the Antarctic, he was having problems in taking in all this detail, though he was getting used to it. 'What kind of stories?'

'Well, as I say, I've personally only ever seen the saucers flying up real high, on their way to some place else, but I'm told that they even come down over Virginee, mostly at nights, and that occasionally people disappear and ain't ever seen again. Sometimes their cars or trucks are found – the doors open, the key still in the ignition – but other times the vehicle vanishes as well. Then, of course, the farmers sometimes talk of cattle and other animals being found dead and mutilated, cut up with surgical skill. The say the cyborgs are doing it – cutting up the animals for spare parts; sometimes draining their blood. I don't know if those stories are true or not, but they sure make a man think.'

Michael believed the stories. He knew from his research that even as far back as the 1960s and 1970s, way back in the Old Age, Wilson's air crews, some human, others cyborg, had been landing in their saucers to butcher animals, drain them of blood and remove their organs for use in their surgical experiments or as spare parts for more cyborgs. According to what Michael had read, those animal mutilations had terrified the populace even more than the human abductions had, striking some primitive nerve that made them think of ancient, diabolical rituals instead of the ruthless march of an all too human science, which was what it actually was. Even Michael, when he thought of the animal mutilations, found himself shivering inwardly at the thought of what that butchery signified, of what possibly still went on behind the closed doors of the cyborg community. The cyborgs were half human, half machine, and a lot of butchery had been practised to make them that way. The very thought was nightmarish.

'Are we getting near Alexandria?' he asked.

'Yep,' Ira said. 'About another ten minutes.'

Michael checked his wristwatch. It was just after eleven in the morning. He had hit the road at eight, walked for about thirty minutes, then was lucky enough to have been picked up by Ira, who was going all the way to Alexandria. The whole journey, from start to finish, had only taken three hours and would have been even quicker if Ira's truck hadn't been so slow. Now, looking out of the truck at the outskirts of Alexandria, he saw tree-shaded brick walks and a mixture of colonial clapboard houses and Georgian mansions. Glancing up at the sky, which was blue and streaked with white clouds, he saw no flying saucers. Looking out again as they entered the Old Town quarter, he glimpsed a waterfront lined with restaurants and boutiques. The women on the sidewalks were elegant and the men all looked prosperous.

'It all looks pretty normal,' Michael said. 'No flying saucers, no cyborg patrols.'

'Like I mentioned before,' Ira said, turning away from the waterfront and slowing down to stop in front of a colonial clapboard building in what Michael noticed was King Street. Ira turned to stare at him with his rheumy, bloodshot eyes, jabbing his finger at the attractive building they were parked beside.

'The old Ramsay House Visitors' Centre,' he said. 'Not too many visitors these days, but they still give you information about how to get where you want to go or where you can stay.' He hesitated. 'Where *are* you going?'

Michael momentarily went blank, then, to his horror, instead of visualizing where he was going, he had a vision of the Freedom Bay mountain, soaring white and craggy above the vast snow-covered plains of Queen Maud Land in Antarctica. He was shocked that this should have happened when he had so carefully worked to ensure that all such thoughts should be blocked from his mind, this being a major part of his parapsychological training. Yet he felt that some outside force, perhaps someone else with similar training, had actually broken into his mind and wrenched from it what he had been suppressing. He found himself staring at Ira Fisher with a new and disturbing perception.

The eyes of Ira Fisher were no longer rheumy and bloodshot but clear and hard, as if a sudden surge of energy had burned out of his brain to clear them. He was staring steadily, unblinkingly at Michael as if looking deep into him.

'Mount Vernon College,' Michael said, at last recalling his research and picking a location outside of the capital.

Fisher continued to look steadily, searchingly, at him, then said, 'Nice job you got there.'

'I hope so.' Michael opened his door and started sliding out of the truck, letting the rucksack, which had been resting on his lap, down first.

'You got somewhere to stay?' Fisher asked him, his voice suddenly flat, without timbre.

'Not yet,' Michael replied as he dropped down out of the truck. Sliding the straps of his rucksack back over his shoulders, he looked up at Fisher and saw those unnaturally bright eyes studying him coldly.

Fisher nodded in the direction of Ramsay House. 'They might be able to help you over there,' he said, still speaking in the flat monotone that seemed oddly inhuman.

'I'll try them,' Michael said. 'Thanks for the lift.'

'Don't mention it,' Fisher said, not smiling at all.

Michael turned away and walked across the sidewalk to Ramsay House. When he reached the entrance, he glanced back over his shoulder and saw that Fisher was still staring steadily at him. Michael waved and entered the colonial clapboard building where he found a small office staffed by a middle-aged woman. The walls were covered with racks of information booklets but there was room for a couple of public telephones. Instead of speaking to the woman behind the counter, he went to the window and looked out. He saw Ira Fisher driving off, but Fisher had only gone about twenty metres when he stopped again, clambered down from his truck and entered a public phone booth, where he could clearly be seen punching in a number. At the same time, the phone rang on the desk of the small office behind Michael. Michael glanced over his shoulder to see the middle-aged woman behind the counter picking up the phone, listening, then putting the phone down again and raising her eyes to stare directly at him. Looking through the window again, Michael saw Fisher leave the telephone booth, clamber back into his battered old truck and drive off, this time turning the corner at the far end of the road, obviously continuing his journey. Turning away from the window, Michael saw the middle-aged woman fix him with a glacial smile and a searching gaze.

'Yes?' she said. 'Can I help you? With accommodation, perhaps?'

'No, thanks,' Michael said.

Convinced that the woman had been the recipient of the phone call made by Fisher and that Fisher, contrary to Michael's initial belief, was a brainwashed former cyborg abductee, Michael hurriedly left the building and asked the first person passing by outside where he could find the westbound DASH bus. Given instructions, he made his way to the station and boarded the first bus leaving Alexandria. The bus took him into the capital via the George Washington Memorial Parkway and deposited him shortly after outside the King Street Station Metro. During that brief journey he saw cyborg flying saucers hovering in the sky in the direction of the National Airport, the Pentagon and, across the Potomac, the White House area and Capitol Hill. He took the Metro from King Street Station to Gallery Place, being careful to meet no one's gaze, and emerged into the old Chinatown, which was now in a dilapidated state of repair and filled, as he knew from his research, with relatively cheap accommodation run by hoodlums and taken up mostly by hard-pressed people of his own age group. As he would be searching for people his own age, this was where he would stay.

The place looked like a war zone. Spread around a vast, clearly neglected sports arena, the old MCI Centre, it was a wasteland of dilapidated buildings that had once been Chinese restaurants but were now living accommodations for the new, mostly white, disenfranchised. Drunks and drug addicts were standing forlornly around the doorways of what Michael assumed were bars for the consumption of alcohol (which, as a Freedom Bay adept, he had not yet tried) or squatting or lying shamelessly on the sidewalks in the light of the noonday sun. Young people of both sexes were also crowding the sidewalks, many near their motorcycles, most of them wearing a wide range of unsophisticated clothing, the kind that was a throwback to the Old Age with its emphasis on black leather jackets, decorative chains, hair of many colours and weird styles, plus bizarre make-up that included stripe-painted faces and rings through ears, noses and lips.

Michael saw no policemen. This, he knew, was due to the fact that since the arrival of the cyborgs – who now controlled everything but only sanctioned what was in their own interest – social matters such as local law and order, transport, sanitation, the financing of City Hall, and the general welfare of the populace had been more or less ignored. The human beings nominally in charge were, because of financial restraints imposed by the lack of commercial enterprise, rendered virtually helpless. The cyborgs had a programme of their own and, though its purpose was as yet unknown, it certainly did not appear to include the everyday welfare of those they had conquered. That was clear here in Chinatown.

Flying saucers, Michael noted, were hovering above China-town almost constantly, though he saw none descending. He was becoming used to the fact that he was a stranger in a strange land and was also aware that the so-called walking dead, as perso-nified by Ira Fisher, could disguise themselves perfectly well. He was pretty certain that Fisher had almost certainly read his mind and had reported him to another of his own kind – the woman in the information centre at Ramsay House – as someone worth watching. Michael used all of his parapsychological skills to tune into the thoughts of others as he looked for a reasonably decent place to stay while avoiding the more dubious types loitering about the place. Eventually, after walking the streets for about an hour and talking to a few people, some of whom were against the cyborgs while others had clearly been brainwashed by them, he found an old Federal-styled building located almost directly opposite the sports stadium. It looked considerably better than anything else he had seen, with no drunks or drug addicts cluttering up its doorway. Taking a deep breath, reminding himself to stay cool, he entered the building.

It wasn't exactly a palace inside, but it was in a better state than most of the buildings Michael had previously checked out.

Though it was certainly faded, there was actually carpet on the stairs and the paint on the walls had not yet started peeling. A small room at one side of the entrance hall, probably a walk-in cloakroom in the Old Age, had been converted into a desk clerk's room and a young man was standing behind the raised counter, checking his books. He was wearing a T-shirt with FUCK YOU printed across it and he had shoulder-length hair, a drooping moustache and a ring through his nose. He looked up when Michael entered and his gaze was suspicious.

'Yes?' he said curtly.

'I'm looking for somewhere to stay,' Michael said. 'Do you have anything?'

'Where do you come from?'

'Cincinnati.'

'What are you doing here?'

'Look, I just want a room and—'

'We like to know who we're taking in,' the young man interjected bluntly. 'Particularly when people are coming from elsewhere. I mean, what makes anyone want to come to Washington if they don't work for the cyborgs? So what are you doing here?'

Michael was already working, using his powers of telepathy, breaking into the young man's thoughts, and he sensed the fellow's instant revulsion at the very thought of the cyborgs. Also, he felt no drawing upon his own thoughts, which indicated that the young man had no parapsychological skills, which in turn meant that he had not been brainwashed and was perfectly normal. For this reason, Michael decided to tell the truth.

'I'm looking for someone,' he said, then added his next lie. 'A girlfriend. She comes from this area but was sent to Cincinnati by her mother after her father was abducted. I met her in Cincinnati. We became involved and then her mother got sick and she had to come back here to look after her. They both disappeared a couple of weeks back and I want to find them. At least, I want to find her.'

'They were probably abducted as well,' the young man said, now looking a lot less aggressive, sounding sympathetic. 'And if that's the case, you haven't a prayer. They'll be gone for good, pal.'

'I've been told that some of the abductees are released eventually.'

'Some of them,' the young man agreed. 'But if your girlfriend's released, you probably won't want to know her. She'll be one of them.'

'I have to know one way or the other,' Michael said, 'so I'm determined to find her. Now what about that room?'

The young man studied him thoughtfully for a moment, then grinned and shrugged. 'Why not?' he said rhetorically, then he pushed his register across the counter. 'Here, you have to sign the book. Don't use your own name if you don't want to. So long as I get you to sign, I'm perfectly legal and that's okay with me.'

'Do the cyborgs come around here to check?' Michael asked as he entered his false name in the book.

'Not the cyborgs – the walking dead. The ones they've brainwashed to do menial tasks for them. They make surprise visits now and then, just like the old IRS guys. So if you see anyone checking my books, just stay out of sight.'

'I will,' Michael said.

The young man held out his hand. 'Ben Wilkerson,' he said, introducing himself.

Michael shook his hand. 'Mike Johnson.'

Ben gave him the room key. 'Room four, second floor. You want anything, check me out first. I'm pretty cool about Chinatown.'

'I will,' Michael said. 'See you around.'

'*Ciao!*' Ben responded, winking, grinning and forming an 'O' with his thumb and index finger. 'Relax and enjoy.'

With his rucksack still on his back, Michael made his way up to the second floor and then let himself into his room. It was small and spartan, with an old pine chest-of-drawers, a pine wardrobe, a steel-framed bed and a double-ring electric hob. The toilet facilities, he knew, would be communal, but the room was at least clean, as were the bedclothes. Removing the rucksack from his shoulders, he placed it on the floor, then proceeded to unpack it and place its contents, mostly clothes and toiletries, either in the chest-of-drawers or in the wardrobe. There were no maps or reference books about Washington DC in the rucksack as he now carried all that information in his head. The only unusual item was his high-powered notebook computer, which he placed on the cabinet beside the bed.

By the time he had finished unpacking, which took about fifteen minutes, it was still only two in the afternoon, so he spent the rest of the afternoon in meditation, seated in the lotus position on the floor and concentrating intensely on his inner self. In this way he was able to keep a sharp edge to his various parapsychological skills and, at the same time, roam telepathically over the capital, checking it out. In his mind's eye, he saw the flying saucers hovering over the White House, the Pentagon, Capitol Hill, the cyborg patrols all around them. But, try as he might, he still could not break into those buildings and was forced to accept, once more, that they were being protected by parapsychological skills far stronger than his.

The only way he would be able to enter the White House would be to go in in person.

Time passed quickly in meditation, in what was virtually a trance state, and when he came back to Earth, to his material shell, evening had fallen. Now being too tired to eat, not wishing to begin his work until the next day when he would be fresh and fully alert, he decided to sleep. He deliberately left the curtains open and, once he had stretched out, fully clothed, on the bed, he kept his eyes open as well, letting himself be lulled by the moonlight.

As he lay there, he thought of Ira Fisher and gradually realized just how cleverly the cyborgs could brainwash their victims. At some level of his consciousness, Fisher had remained exactly the same as undoubtedly he had been before being brainwashed: a heavy drinker with rheumy, bloodshot eyes and a normal human aversion to the rule of the cyborgs. Thus, he could talk to truly normal human beings without making them suspicious. On another level, however, when it seemed that there might be a need for it, such as when talking to a stranger, the brainwashed part of his consciousness took over and turned him into a robotized worker for the cyborgs. More interestingly, he had clearly deployed parapsychological skills, telepathic skills, in order to break into Michael's thoughts. The cyborgs, therefore, when brainwashing their victims, were now implanting at least some of the parapsychological skills that they, the cyborgs, possessed themselves. This, Michael realized, would make the walking dead more dangerous than ever.

Closing his eyes, he tried to sleep, but oblivion did not come easily. Eventually, just as he *was* falling asleep, he was awakened by the almost imperceptible pressure of what he knew to be an infrasound of the kind made by many flying saucers. Opening his eyes again, he saw a small, circular light, like the beam of light from a large lamp, but in this case pulsating rhythmically, passing slowly across the dark room, obviously beaming in from something that was gliding by just outside the window. Even as he saw that light, he felt the infrasound still more strongly. It made him jerk upright on the bed.

Forcing himself to control the fear that had swept instinctively over him, he rolled off the bed and padded on bare feet to the window, across which the pulsating light was still passing slowly. He waited until the light had completely crossed the window and was moving away from the building. Then, cautiously, still fearful of being seen, he peered around the curtain.

A seamless, silvery-white, metallic sphere was drifting slowly in mid-air above the road. Spinning rapidly but silently on its own axis, it was giving off an eerie, pulsating glow and casting a thin, laser-like beam of light on the walls and windows of the buildings it was passing. It was, Michael knew, one of the many remote-controlled, self-regulating devices that the cyborgs in the White House and elsewhere used for observation of the capital each and every night. That beam of light – a sensor that could record the movement of solid bodies, including human beings – was also a laser weapon that could stun, paralyse or even kill.

Watching the small spinning disc as it moved away from his building, Michael was torn between fear and rage, though thankfully the healthy rage soon took command. Returning to his bed and sitting upright against the headboard, he opened his notebook and sent an e-mail to a false Cincinnati address, which was actually a home page in Freedom Bay. The message, which could only be read on Freedom Bay's computers, was to Dr Lee Brandenberg.

The bird has found a nest.

Message sent, the bird closed his eyes and slept.

Chapter Twenty-one

The first nightmare was the paralysis. One of Gumshoe's adolescent fears had been the thought of having a stroke and being paralysed completely, not able to move a muscle, while still being highly active mentally. Now, as he moved up the ramp of the flying saucer, a paddy wagon, either dragged by the cyborgs, though they appeared not to be touching him, or propelled by some means beyond his comprehension, he was living that nightmare: completely paralysed from head to toe, but still mentally active. In a weird way, he felt that he was *floating* up the ramp, though this might have been due to his complete lack of tactile sensation. This feeling persisted as he reached the top of the ramp and entered the saucer.

All white. Everything. At first he was almost blinded by the light. Then his eyes, which were all he could move, adjusted to the brightness and he saw that he was surrounded by walls of what looked like white steel, perhaps a combination of magnesium and titanium. In his desperate attempt not to panic from fear of his paralysis, he tried as best he could to focus on what he was seeing and noted that he was in a small, square-shaped area that had a closed white-steel door on one side, a low ceiling shaped like an inverted half-eggshell, and a corridor running away to his right. Everything was made of the same metallic material to form that dazzling, featureless whiteness.

Still not able to feel anything, he nevertheless sensed the presence of the two cyborgs behind him and found himself advancing at a walking pace along the corridor, which also had a concave ceiling and, windowless, was featureless too. The floor, ceiling and walls all looked as if they were moulded miraculously from one piece – though this was certainly an illusion, Gumshoe decided, recalling the way that the outside panel had dropped down from the apparently seamless fuselage of the saucer to form a ramp to the ground. The corridor appeared to be curving around the central disc of the craft and it led him to the only door he had so far seen.

Trying to choke back his steadily mounting dread as his every impulse fought against entering that room, but unable to resist, still being paralysed, he moved helplessly through the doorway and saw that he was now in a perfectly round space, about twenty metres in diameter, with white metal walls, lighting from a hidden source, and a transparent dome that gave a 360-degree view of the surrounding terrain, which, he saw with relief, was still the broad, moonlit expanse of West Potomac Park. The complicated, highly advanced control console of what was clearly the crew's cabin ran all the way around the lower half of the circle and three crew members' chairs were placed equidistant along it with another cyborg sitting in the middle one.

Again, Gumshoe filled up with the impulse to turn away and make his escape. But his numbed body moved forward against his will, taking him to a position in the centre of the floor, just behind where the seated cyborg was located. Gumshoe remained there for a moment, still unable to move, while the cyborgs behind him took the two free chairs in front of the console. All three cyborgs then began working the various controls, not speaking, as if reading each other's minds.

Suddenly, a soft bass humming sound filled the control cabin and Gumshoe saw, through the transparent dome, that the lower body of the saucer was rotating slowly, with lights of many colours flashing on and off in quick succession, one after the other, around its wide rim. The lights kept flashing on and off at an ever-increasing speed until they formed first a kaleidoscope, then a whitish, plasma-like glowing. By now, the outer body of the saucer was spinning at an incredible speed until its edge had blended into that whitish glow, becoming almost invisible.

Still desperately trying to combat his mounting terror by concentrating fiercely on what he was seeing, Gumshoe grasped at what he had learnt from his research on the Net and recalled that the saucers were widely believed to be propelled either by advanced ion propulsion, electromagnetic and microwave propulsion, antigravity (gravitic) propulsion, nuclear-fusion pulse rockets, or a combination of two or more of those systems. Studying that plasma-like glowing aura around this particular saucer's spinning rim, he assumed that it came from the ionization of the surrounding atmosphere and that some form of ion propulsion was involved.

Keep thinking, he thought desperately. *Just keep thinking. Don't let the fear make you lose your mind . . . Fact: The control cabin is independent and gyroscopically stabilized. When we take off, the anti-gravity system will . . . Oh, Jesus, it's taking off!*

Though he still could feel nothing, he saw that the saucer was rising vertically off the ground. It ascended slowly and steadily, offering no sensation of movement, until it was about forty metres above the moonlit lawns of the park. Suddenly, as quickly as Gumshoe blinked – which, mercifully, he could still manage to do – the landscape disappeared and was replaced with the vast, star-filled expanse of the night sky, with the lights of Washington DC, Virginia and Maryland spread out in a glittering tapestry far below. As Gumshoe looked out, disbelieving, still with no sensation of movement whatsoever, triangular-shaped plates of the same white metallic material rose up from the circular base of the transparent dome, all around it, like the petals of a giant flower, to slot into each other and cover the dome completely in what looked like a perfectly seamless covering.

Now Gumshoe could see nothing except the interior of the

control cabin, with the three cyborgs seated in their chairs, facing the ever-blinking console and not making a sound. They might as well have been dead.

We must be flying above the atmosphere, Gumshoe thought. *Oh, Jesus, where are we going?*

Even as he was thinking this, he sank slowly through an opening that had appeared in the floor. Again, he did not have any sensation of movement and only knew that he was being borne downwards, still standing upright, when he saw that the walls around him appeared to be rising. Startled, he glanced down and saw that the floor was rising towards him and that his legs were already halfway through a circle-shaped trapdoor, his feet resting on a round piece of metal that had been part of the floor.

The hairs on the back of his neck stood up and his heart raced in panic.

Oh, God, no! he thought, briefly imagining that he was sinking into hell, only getting his wits back when the steel plate beneath his feet came to rest on a lower floor.

He found himself in a gloomily lit circular room where other abductees, also paralysed, were standing around him, their eyes moving frantically left and right, glazed over with dread.

Shocked beyond measure, Gumshoe tried to call out to them, but no words emerged, brutally reminding him that his vocal cords had also been paralysed.

Oh, God, he thought, *I'm paralysed and dumb. I'm like a fly in a spider's web. Please, God, tell me I'm dreaming!*

But he wasn't dreaming. He could still blink his eyes, move his eyeballs left and right, up and down, and he did so experimentally to prove to himself that he was real and still had at least *some* self control. Glancing about him once more, he met those other fear-filled eyes, saw the sweat on their foreheads, sensed their dread almost as palpably as if it was his own, and knew that if he didn't keep concentrating he might lose his mind.

Don't look at the others, he thought, *in case the sight of them makes you feel worse. Don't let their terror get to you. Close your eyes. Think of other things.*

He closed his eyes and tried thinking.

The saucer was still in flight – though, since there continued to be no sense of movement, he could only assume this from the lack of change in the bass humming sound. It had only been flying for a couple of minutes now but, given the speed at which the paddy wagons could fly, it must have already travelled a great distance. If it had merely flown him to the White House, they would have been there in seconds.

Where the hell were they going?

Fusion propulsion, Gumshoe thought, frantically trying not to think of other things. Electromagnetic or ion propulsion, combined with gravity-shielding, could account for the saucers' ability to rise vertically, make sharp right-angled turns and hang nearly motionless in the sky. Yes, that was it. Ionization and electromagnetic discharges could account for that plasma-like glowing and gravitic propulsion, or an anti-gravity shield, could explain the saucer's lack of turbulence and the absence of sonic booms. All well and good so far, but . . .

Oh, Jesus, he thought as a fresh wave of terror washed over him, *I can't think! My mind's going!*

He opened his eyes and was instantly confronted with the sight of those other unfortunate abductees – four women of various ages, three mature men, a couple of adolescents, possibly Speed Freaks, and even two children. All were standing there in that gloomy, nightmarish lighting, in that featureless circular room, and all were absolutely motionless except for their frantically moving eyes, which shone with pure terror. Shocked by that sight, Gumshoe closed his eyes again and tried to focus his thoughts.

Okay, okay, he thought, speaking resolutely to himself, if only in his mind. *We're now flying above the atmosphere, possibly. (Can the paddy wagons do that? Certainly the other saucers can.) And that would need some other kind of propulsion, which gets us right back to fusion . . .* Internet

254

theory of the late, great nuclear physicist, Stanley T. Friedman
. . . 'If you use the fusion process properly, you can kick particles
out of the back end of a rocket that has ten *million* times as much
energy per particle as you can get in a chemical rocket.' *Fuck
rockets. What about flying saucers?* According to Friedman, and with
relevance to the enormous power of fusion being packed into the
relatively small confines of a UFO, a quasar represents the energy
of a galaxy 'compressed' into something the size of a single star
and, when we move from the atomic to the nuclear world, we
may go down in size but we go way *up* in energy per particle.
Thus, when we go down from the nuclear universe to the sub-
nuclear universe, we go down in size again and up in energy
again. *Which means?* Fusion presents us with a form of enormous
power that can be confined in small containers. *So maybe, if we're
now flying above the atmosphere, we're using fusion propulsion.* Which
meant, of course, that . . . *Where are we going? Where the fuck are they
taking us? And . . . Jesus . . . Oh, my God, don't think about it . . . What
will they do to us?*

Gumshoe had to open his eyes – though he didn't want to do
so, not wishing to see his fear reflected in the stares of the other
equally terrified abductees. Nevertheless, he had to open his eyes
because his imagination insisted upon running riot when they
were closed, making him visualize a whole range of dreadful
possibilities concerning the fate that awaited him. So he opened
his eyes and found that he could not escape the other eyes,
particularly the wide, fearful gazes of the women and children.
That sight, despite his fear of his imagination, made him close
his own eyes again.

Not fusion, he thought, desperately trying to focus his thoughts.
The paddy wagons didn't fly in outer space, so they wouldn't
need fusion, though they certainly would need an anti-gravity
shield and some other extraordinarily powerful means of propulsion to obtain their speed and flight characteristics . . . That
plasma-like glowing around the spinning outer edge . . . The
traces of electromagnetism often found on saucer landing sites

. . . What was that guy's name? Famous physicist, long dead, but still alive on the Net to explain that a propulsion system based on the ionization of the air could solve all the problems of high-speed flight. With ionized air, as opposed to 'neutral' air, it would be possible to interact with the electric and magnetic fields, thereby reducing heating and drag, increasing lift, and eliminating sonic booms. And according to . . . *Fuck, what's his name? Freeman . . . No, Friedman . . .* The flying saucers' frequent changes in colour, extraordinary flight characteristics, and absence of noise indicated the presence of ionized air and high magnetic fields. *So that,* Gumshoe thought, *would explain it. This paddy wagon, which can't be flying in outer space, is using a . . . propulsion . . . Fuck, what was it? Oh, Jesus, that bass humming sound has changed. Why the hell has it changed? God have mercy, we're landing!*

He opened his eyes and saw the other abductees, those equally distressed unfortunates whose only visible movement was the flickering of their fear-filled eyes. He glanced about him, without moving his head, to ascertain if the saucer was actually landing or not. There was still no sense of movement, but the humming sound had definitely changed, becoming even softer, more distant. Then, just as Gumshoe thought that he had been mistaken, the sound cut out altogether.

Now he heard another sound, a hollow drumming sound. Then, for the first time, he sensed movement and his heart skipped a beat.

Fuck, he thought, *this is it!*

He didn't quite know what he meant by that. But he braced himself for any eventuality when he sensed that the paddy wagon was no longer in flight but was, instead, bobbing gently from side to side to the accompaniment of that hollow drumming sound, as if — and this thought almost stunned him — it was submerged underwater, just like . . . *a submarine?*

Oh, Christ, he thought, trying to choke back his panic and disbelief. *It can't be. It . . .*

But it fucking well could be, he realized, recalling that when the cyborgs had first arrived to take over the Earth, their saucers, big and small, had not only ascended from previously concealed bases on dry land, mainly in mountainous areas and deserts, but also from oceans and lakes, including the Bermuda Triangle, the Devil's Sea, the Plata del Mar, the Great Lakes of Canada and even Loch Ness in Scotland. It had then transpired that those saucers, viewed sceptically in the Old Age as USOs, or Unidentified Submarine Objects, had been resting on the seabed or at the bottom of lakes as sea domes, manned by cyborgs or brain-implanted humans. There, while waiting to surface and take over the Earth, they had continued with a wide variety of scientific experiments, aided by remote-controlled Cybernetic Amorphous Machine Systems (CAMS). Now, Gumshoe was convinced, this paddy wagon was sinking down through water, either at sea or in a great lake, to join with a mother ship being used as a gigantic sea dome. If so, he was truly doomed.

His worst fears were almost instantly realized.

Three silvery-white lines appeared in the curved wall directly facing Gumshoe, just behind some of the other still-paralysed and terrified abductees. The three lines, two vertical, one horizontal and joining the top of the others, formed a door shape. At first sight it looked as if a searing light, a laser beam, was slicing down through the metal wall, illuminating the gloomy room. But then the lines widened, rapidly becoming spaces letting light in from outside, and Gumshoe realized that this was another panel moving away from the wall, like the panel he had entered by, to form a ramp leading, in this instance, out of what was clearly the bottom layer of the paddy wagon. When the panel had disappeared, angled down out of sight, Gumshoe found himself looking at an awesome sight.

Some of the abductees gasped.

Startled by that sound, Gumshoe realized that feeling was returning to his body and that the same must be happening to the other abductees. Even as his eyes were widening in disbelief at what he was seeing, he coughed to clear his tightened throat, managed to do so successfully, then flexed the fingers of both hands and shuffled his feet. To his immense relief, he discovered that he could move again, so he automatically moved to the doorway formed by the lowered panel. There he stopped in amazement. Certainly it was no surprise, given what he was faced with, that he made no other attempt to move.

There was nowhere to go.

Through the open doorway formed by the fallen panel, Gumshoe saw what appeared to be an immense curving white-steel wall broken up with reinforced viewing windows under a high dome-shaped transparent ceiling covered in a great umbrella of seamless steel coloured the same as the wall. That dome-shaped ceiling, he realized instantly, was actually the central dome of a flying saucer far larger than the paddy wagon – indeed, a craft that was truly immense: large enough to contain the paddy wagon and many more like it – and the windows, just like those in the paddy wagon, went around the central body to give a 360-degree view. Scanning as much of the area as he could see, he guessed that he was in one of the so-called 'mother ships', approximately 350 feet in diameter, 150 feet high at the central point between dome and base, built in three layers, all immense, and carrying a crew of over a hundred cyborgs and brain-implanted humans. He could see those from where he stood, all wearing the same black coveralls and boots, working side by side at computers and consoles covered in flashing lights, ascending or descending in open elevators to various levels, or crossing from one side of the central dome to the other by means of high catwalks.

Even more frightening, however, was what he could see through those large viewing windows of reinforced glass: the artificially illuminated wonders of the sea bed, including a wide variety of plankton, luminous crustaceans, octopus, squid, giant jellyfish, other coelenterates and ctenophores that cast their own eerie illumination, bizarre fish and other creatures either ex-ceptionally beautiful or, by human standards, downright hideous.

One of the female abductees screamed in terror.

Instantly, a cyborg appeared in the doorway, holding a stun gun in his right hand, to shoot a laser beam at the screaming woman. Struck by a bolt of sparks like tiny lightning bolts – a light that was, Gumshoe knew, flickering somewhere in the alpha-rhythm range, between eight and twelve cycles per second – the woman was rendered semi-comatose and instantly fell silent while remaining motionless on her feet. The other abductees, now getting their senses back along with tactile feeling, made no sound, except for the frightened sniffling of the children and a choked sob from one of the other women.

At that moment, a human male appeared in the doorway to stand beside the cyborg. Thin as a rake in black coveralls and boots, his face gaunt and pale, his green eyes cold, his hair blond, he cast his gaze over the abductees, mentally counting them while looking at none in particular. Then he said, 'Please do as you are told. Please attempt nothing foolish. You are in a flying saucer, a mother ship, on the seabed of the West Atlantic Ocean, in the area known as the Bermuda Triangle. There is no way out.' Though clearly a human being, his voice was lacking in timbre and seemed oddly *in*human. 'I repeat: there is no way out. You have nowhere to go. So please do exactly as you're told and make things easier for all of us. Now follow me, please.'

As the man stepped aside to clear the doorway, the cyborg with the stun gun entered the room to move around to the rear of the abductees and prod them forward if necessary. Being close to the doorway already and aware that what the man in black had said was true, that he had nowhere else to go, Gumshoe was the first to step out of the room.

He found himself in what appeared to be an immense work area with a curving wall – actually he was standing on a wide circular floor surrounded by the outer walls of the mother ship – filled with ladders, elevators and catwalks, modules of steel and glass, shining mazes of pipes coiling around what might have been generators, and, in every direction, more cyborgs and humans in black coveralls and boots, working at computer terminals or control consoles in which lights of many colours flashed on and off constantly. As the other abductees emerged from the doorway of the paddy wagon to gather around him, some being prodded by the cyborg, Gumshoe glanced back over his shoulder and noted that this particular area, in the very centre of the great dome-shaped work place, was used as a parking bay for the smaller transport saucers – the widely feared paddy wagons. Gumshoe saw three of them.

'This way, please.' Still speaking in a flat, chilling monotone that actually made the word 'please' redundant, the man in black led the group of cowed abductees across the wide floor towards an open door in the curved wall, located just beneath one of the many windows offering a view of the exotic seabed. The cyborg bringing up the rear of the group was now joined by another and both of them encouraged the group to move forward merely by being there with their stun guns raised in the firing position.

Now walking directly behind the man in black, Gumshoe glanced up at the windows to see the ocean bed outside artificially illuminated by the lights beaming out of the mother ship but vast and impenetrable beyond the range of those lights. He felt his heart constricting with despair even as his fear increased dramatically. Clearly, there was no way to escape and he was now at the mercy of the cyborgs.

What would they do to him?

His imagination was already running riot when the man in black led him and the others through the doorway, into a white-painted corridor that followed the curving outer edge of the mother ship. Though featureless, with no windows, the corridor soon led into another large chamber that looked like a laboratory, being filled with workbenches, computer terminals, humans in white smocks or coveralls, and glass cabinets that were slightly frosted over on the inside. The cabinets contained a wide variety of frozen specimens, ranging from exotic creatures of the deep to land-based animals such as dogs, wolves, mountain bears and pumas. None of the human workers, Gumshoe noted, looked up from their benches as the group of abductees passed through them.

'Please do not be alarmed by anything you see here,' the man in black said, speaking flatly, mechanically, like a tourist guide repeating his daily spiel. 'This submerged mother ship is used as a sea dome and conducts a wide variety of experiments. Disturbing as some of these might seem to you at first, you will soon get used to them and, indeed, you will even take part in some of them. For now, however, please let me inform you about the mother ship and about what we do down here.'

Gumshoe thought he was hallucinating. The contradiction between where he actually was, what had actually happened to him, and the sheer normality, even blandness, of the voice of the man in black made his mind reel. Nevertheless, as they left the laboratory and headed around another length of curving white corridor, with the steel-masked cyborgs prodding the reluctant abductees along, if necessary by giving them small electric jolts from their stun guns, the man in black continued talking in his mechanical, oddly chilling monotone, like the tape recording in one of those hand sets tourists used to get on museum tours.

'Our mother ship is powered by a combination of a highly advanced electromagnetic propulsion system that ionizes the surrounding air or, at this moment, the surrounding sea, and an electromagnetic damping system that aids our lift and hovering capabilities when in flight while also equalizing the pressure when we're submerged. The bodywork of this particular mother ship is composed of an electrically charged magnesium orthosilicate so minutely porous that it manages to be waterproof while ensuring, when airborne, an absolute minimum of friction, heat and drag. This explains the extraordinary power and remarkable manoeuvrability of this and other saucers.'

The group was now approaching another door while passing a row of glass cabinets attached to the wall and displaying a collection of jewellery, silver cups, the pottery of various periods, much of it badly chipped or worn, stones, crystals, old anchors, chains, and stuffed fish of a remarkably exotic variety. The man in black pointed at the cases as he passed and kept reciting his lecture like a zombie given the power of speech.

'From this submerged mother ship,' he explained, 'we explore the seabed with a variety of large and small Cybernetic Anthropomorphous Machine Systems, picking up exotic marine life, valuable lost treasure, and a wealth of normally unavailable minerals. The CAMS are either piloted by cyborgs, remote-controlled from this mother ship, or they are programmed to react robotically to certain stimuli, such as the moving of fish through water or even the gentlest swaying of plant life.'

They were now entering another room, this one noticeably colder than the others and dimly lit. It contained another collection of glass cabinets, these ones illuminated from within to show their contents through the chilled glass. Gumshoe stopped walking automatically, temporarily shocked witless when he saw that the cabinets contained a collection of genetically and surgically mutated birds and animals. There were giant rats with humps, birds with rabbits' heads, cats with gills and fins, headless chickens, two-headed dogs and many similar nightmarish monstrosities.

'Oh, Jesus!' Gumshoe whispered without thinking, even as some of the other abductees gasped with horror behind him. Gumshoe glanced over his shoulder to see two of the women automatically stepping backwards, obviously wanting to escape this hall of horrors. But the cyborgs prodded them with the stun guns, giving them small electrical shocks that made them gasp, this time with pain, and step forward again. When Gumshoe looked to the front, the man in black was on the move once more, leading them through the grim room.

'This particular mother ship,' he continued as he led them past the mutated animals, 'sometimes surfaces to abduct the crew members of boats afloat in the West Atlantic Ocean, in the area known as the Bermuda Triangle, and, when required, to capture whole motor launches, complete with their passengers. Those captured are then indoctrinated into our ways' – clearly, he meant brain-implanted – 'and either remain here to be used for a variety of purposes or are returned to the surface, sometimes in the same boat, to work covertly for us. You, too, will be used as we see fit. You cannot say no.'

One of the ways in which the abducted were used was now made nightmarishly clear to Gumshoe when, still at the head of the group, he followed the man in black into another dimly lit room and saw in more chilled glass cabinets . . . severed human heads, amputated limbs and, even worse, combinations of the two connected to hideous bionic torsos. As these were purely museum pieces, the cases containing them had been left open to show the sickening mass of preserved body parts, wires and cables inside them.

Instinctively recoiling from that sight, but having the sense to keep moving, following the man in black, Gumshoe heard groans, sobs and gasps from the unfortunates behind him, indicating that they, too, were horrified. Now he felt that he was one of the damned in a lower level of hell.

'I repeat,' the man in black said as he led them out of that second chamber of horrors and along another curving stretch of white-walled corridor, 'that you cannot escape. There is no way to escape. You must therefore accept your lot and show no resistance. What we will do to you will cause you no pain, so don't be afraid. Whatever we choose for you, you will accept because you won't have a choice. Right now, before we examine you, you must take your rest. This is where you will do so.'

They were now in an expansive, curving room, the outer wall of which obviously formed part of the circular rim of the mother ship. Along the wall was a panoramic window looking out on the murky depths of the ocean, with the seabed illuminated to a short distance out with beams of artificial light. In those beams of light the seabed was darkly visible, with bizarrely shaped rocks covered in plankton and algae, imperceptibly shifting sands, extraordinary, gigantic, languidly swaying plants and a variety of exotic sea life of a kind few human beings would ever lay eyes upon. But beyond the beams of light there was only a vast, absolute, eternal darkness that made Gumshoe shiver.

Those windows are there for a purpose, he thought. *To remind us of exactly where we are and of the absolute hopelessness of our position. This is the devil's playground.*

Already plunged into despair, he turned away from the windows and saw that the room was filled with metal-frame beds, all with plump, propped-up pillows, all covered in white sheets. Half a dozen humans, men and women, all wearing white smocks, were standing stiffly in attendance, their pale faces expressionless, beside the kind of metal trolleys usually seen in hospitals. There were glasses and phials of tablets on the trolleys, alongside what looked like plastic pistols. When Gumshoe saw those, he shivered.

The man in black turned towards him, in order to address the whole group.

'I want each of you to lie down on one of the beds,' he said. 'Please don't try to resist. If you do, we'll be forced to pacify you by means less pleasant than those we have planned. Right now, we're simply going to put you to sleep, which will help you get over the shock of being brought here and, when you awaken, make your readjustment to your new life much easier. Should you try to escape, the armed cyborgs at the door will stop you by the most painful means. Now, please choose a bed.'

Not believing a word he was being told, but aware that he had no choice, Gumshoe walked to the nearest bed and stretched out upon it. The others, he noticed, being as much deprived of choice as he was, were doing the same, men, women and children alike. When they were all stretched out quietly, fearfully, on the beds, the children sniffling, the women sobbing quietly, some of the men making helpless groaning sounds, the man in black left the room and the other humans in the white smocks, not speaking a word, went about their business.

When Gumshoe felt someone leaning over him, breathing upon him, he closed his eyes and silently prayed.

He was wreathed in dead silence.

Chapter Twenty-two

———◆◆◆◆———

When we took over the White House, the Pentagon, Washington DC, the whole country, the world, we did so for a specific purpose and are working towards that goal right now. The world we took over, however, was not 'the World' that you know and our first task was to make it more manageable and less self-destructive.

By your 2001, or our #1, the old world order had changed beyond recognition, with power moving out of the hands of the state into the hands of the banks and transnationals. The parochial economy of individual nations had given way to the global economy, with everything it produced being imported or exported, cheap labour at a premium, money fluid as a river, moving here and there at the push of a button, to the dictates of the market place, exploiting the rise and fall of each individual country's interest rates, bypassing taxation, greasing palms, buying loyalty, annihilating patriotism, to the point where the banks and transnationals had become so powerful that the lending or withdrawing of their support could make or break national governments. The heads of state, the kings and queens, the presidents and prime ministers, were therefore redundant in every sense. They were no more than figureheads.

What did we need them for?

Only as demonstrations of our power when we made them disappear overnight.

The President of the United States was, to his people, the supreme authority in the country, but to us he was just another puppet whose strings were being pulled from afar. The nation state such as America was increasingly ill-equipped to deal with global problems: drug cartels, mafias, criminal rings, terrorist gangs, corrupt financial organizations, and morally bankrupt multinationals, fast becoming transnationals, all of whom could casually cross borders by conducting their business with cellular phones, faxes, e-mail and electronic bank transfers, buying, selling and exchanging outside the jurisdiction of any individual nation state. Likewise, the rapid switch from national news to global news, which turned national awareness into global awareness, further weakened the authority of the nation state while making its citizens part of the global community. With national borders becoming redundant, with previously sovereign countries coalescing into trade blocs devoid of national allegiances or patriotism, the heads of state, including the President of the United States, became mere servants to a global government covertly run by the banks and transnationals.

Thus, we did not feel threatened by any head of state, neither president nor prime minister, king nor queen, and valued them only for the fear we would instil in their subjects when we abducted them and made them disappear. We did this immediately, during the first morning of #1, taking the President and the Vice President prisoner, then moving them and their families out of the White House, never to return. Elsewhere, we took England's Royal Family, the King and Queen of Spain, the head of every European state, and the rulers and dictators of every other country in the world.

None of those people were ever seen again.

In fact, they were transferred to our undersea dome in the so-called 'Devil's Sea,' an area of ocean bounded by the south-east coast of Japan, the northern tip of Luzon in the Philippines, and Guam. There they underwent brain implantations that erased their memories and rendered them totally passive. They were then scattered throughout our various hidden bases, some undersea, some in mountainous or desert regions, and there used as robotized workers. Some have since died of natural causes; others are still there, anonymous, forgotten, performing menial chores and grateful to do so.

The many congressmen and congresswomen removed from the White House (and people in similar positions worldwide) were returned a few days later to take over their former positions, but in governments without a single ruling figure. Those individuals had, of course, been brain-implanted to do our bidding while acting as a liaison between us and those of the populace with whom we still needed to deal, notably civil servants and local counsellors. Others, also taken *that first night and returned a few days later, now walk among you and seem just like you, though they have, in fact, been robotized and are now part of us.*

So we did not fear heads of state or other politicians. What we were concerned with, however, was the growing power of the new global government, the banks and transnationals that could make or break whole countries and were heading towards the formation of a world consolidated into three great blocs — Europe, the Americas and Asia — with each drawing more countries into its orbit until only the three ruled. As this would have made the world more difficult to control, even for the relatively short period we needed it for our own purposes, we isolated all the countries of the world, each from the other, by grounding aircraft worldwide and preventing all ships from leaving their ports, ensuring that their engines would malfunction when they tried to fly or sail. This done, we then abducted all the major players in the aspiring global government — the financiers and bankers, the transnational wheelers and dealers whose only allegiance was to profit — and robotized them to ensure that, when they returned to their original positions, they would do only what we wished them to do.

They, too, are among you right now, but you certainly wouldn't know it to look at them. They seem as 'normal' as you.

Yes, the living dead walk among you. For once, that old cliché is apt. The living dead are those whose minds we take and control from afar, freed only to walk among you while conducting our business. They may be among your loved ones, your family and friends, and although they may seem normal to you, they are not what they seem. They are on our side now.

We have eyes everywhere.

You resent us being here and you also live in fear of us, the more so because we have stopped so much of what you were doing and your world seems a far worse place for it. Your streets are overflowing with rubbish. Crime is on the increase. Whole industries have been frozen where they were in the Old Age, unable to expand, or have ground to a halt altogether. Your great seaports are now empty. Your airports are silent. Your computer technology, while increasingly widespread, has not advanced to any great degree in the past twenty years. Unemployment is rising.

All of this, you say, is our fault — and we cannot deny it. But what we do is done for a purpose that transcends temporal matters. Your rubbish means nothing to us because it does not affect us and will make no great difference in the future that is being planned for you. The rising crime rate is natural, being tied to unemployment, and the latter is an equally natural outcome of your primitive mentality, which is rooted in temporal affairs with no long-term view. We take the long-term view, knowing how brief our time here is. We also know how unimportant your temporary lawlessness is in the light of what will be coming. As for your frozen industries, your empty docks and silent airports, we have done what has been done to stop your orgy of self-destruction and ensure that the Earth will survive long enough for our purposes.

The Earth means nothing to us — it is only a transient stop — but until we leave it, long before the sun starts dying, we must ensure that it is not destroyed by pollution or meaningless wars. When we came here, your pollution was destroying the ozone layer, exposing the Earth to potentially destructive ultraviolet radiation, but our curtailing of your industrial output, which was based on pure greed, has greatly reduced the production of chlorofluoro-carbons and has let the ozone layer renew itself. As for your empty docks and silent airports, they were rendered so for a good reason: to make it easier for us to maintain control of the world by isolating each country from the other. However, in doing this, we again dramatically reduced the fumes that were causing global warming and destroying the ozone layer. We also, incidentally, put a stop to the squalid international arms trade that was fuelling the growth of terrorism and ethnic genocide. So our activities, which transcend mere self-interest while making your world suffer in the short term, will have long-term benefits. We suffer no guilt because of this.

Just who are 'we', you wish to know? Who do the cyborgs work for? Who created the clones, the Men in Black, and who is behind the abductions? Who changed your world overnight?

'We' are one.

It is me.

You know me as 'Wilson'.

Yes. Wilson is back.

Chapter Twenty-three

Michael sensed the changes in himself and he found them disturbing. Attempting to assimilate into the World, to look and behave as the others his own age did, to melt naturally, as it were, into the background, he spent his first few days exploring Chinatown, then gradually progressed farther out, first to Downtown, then to the Pennsylvania Quarter, Capitol Hill and the Mall, and, eventually, to the infinitely more dangerous White House area, where the cyborg patrols were thick on the ground with their SARGEs and Prowlers. Having come straight from the clean, technologically advanced and disciplined confines of the Freedom Bay complex, he was shocked at how squalid, technologically backward and lawless so much of Washington DC was under the rule of the cyborgs.

'This used to be a great place,' Ben Wilkerson informed him, 'before those goddamned cyborgs took over. 'Course, I'm only twenty-two, so I was in my cradle then, but middle-aged friends say it's really gone downhill because of the cyborgs. They don't give a shit about anything 'cept technology – they're like bees in a nest in all the military bases and research establishments around here and in Maryland – so they're letting the city go to rack and ruin, and Chinatown is the worst. To them we're the dregs of humanity – and you are what you eat.'

Having decided to stay on in the converted Federal-style

building located almost directly opposite the sports stadium, formerly the MCI Center, in Chinatown, Michael had made friends with the cocky young desk clerk who had a healthy hatred of the cyborgs. True to his word, Ben knew Chinatown like the back of his hand and had, during his free time, shown Michael around the place, introducing him to friends and warning him about what — and who — he should avoid.

Right now, in the early evening, they were walking past the sports stadium, which had once seated over 20,000 people but these days was neglected by all but the Speed Freaks who gathered there most nights with their souped-up hot rods and motorcycles, taking dope, drinking beer and preparing to roar out on rides designed to frustrate the cyborg patrols. Spread around the sports stadium, empty at this relatively early hour, was the familiar wasteland of dilapidated buildings that had once been Chinese restaurants and now housed the new, mostly white, disenfranchised young. As usual, drunks and drug addicts were squatting or lying shamelessly on the sidewalks, ignored by the young people wearing black leather jackets and decorative chains who crowded the area, their hair in a wide variety of colours and styles, their faces painted bizarrely, some even sporting rings through their ears, noses and lips.

'They stole that look from the Old Age,' Ben informed Michael as they passed one of the groups of young people. 'I read about it on the Net. That look was popular with working-class kids in Great Britain way back in the 1970s and 1980s. They were called Punks then. They had their own music as well — Punk Rock — and that's making a comeback, too, in the retro dance clubs.'

'Everything goes in circles,' Michael said.

'Damned right,' Ben responded.

As they walked on, elbowing their way through the noisy, jostling throng, ignoring the panhandlers and the crazies, Michael gazed about him at the electronic games parlours, millennifreak dance clubs, pornographic fun palaces and other high-tech amusement establishments lining the street, their neon lights blazing in many colours to garishly illuminate the people crowding the sidewalks, including whores and drug peddlers. This was a far cry from the 'World' that Michael had imagined back in Freedom Bay, when he had thought so much about it. The 'World' was where his parents had come from, and their parents before them, and they had always talked of it with deep yearning, as a place not hemmed in by snow and ice, not limiting in its boundaries; a place with more freedom and more places to go, with cities you could roam in all day. That 'World', Michael now knew, was no longer quite so pleasant and certainly this city, Washington DC, was most definitely *not* safe to roam in. In fact, though the world had been changed irrevocably by the cyborgs, those changes had not been for the better and the 'World' so fondly remembered by Michael's parents no longer existed.

'You'd think that, given their interest in technology,' Ben said as his jaded gaze took in the neon-lit squalor all around them, 'the cyborgs would have made *improvements* when they took over. But no. Quite the opposite. From what I gather, we're more backward now than we were twenty years ago. Whatever those fuckers are doing in secret, it's certainly not for *our* benefit.'

Which was true enough. When Michael compared what the pundits of the Old Age had prophesied for the post-Millennium age (none of them knowing that the cyborgs would take over the whole globe) with the state of the world right now, it was clear just how wrong they had been. The world promised by the pundits had been one of vastly improved medicine and health, power and energy, food and crops, transportation, environment, communication and information, business and work. But since the coming of the cyborgs all of those hopes had been killed off. The cyborgs had stopped all sea and air travel, made exporting and importing impossible, banned the production of more advanced computer technology, deprived farmers of the means of improvements in crop cultivation, placed severe restrictions on new medical experimentation, and generally, with their many other restrictions, created mass unemployment. Indeed, the highly advanced medicine and technology of Freedom Bay, gained from the exploitation of Wilson's original innovations, was nowhere evident here in Washington DC, except, almost certainly, behind the closed doors of the establishments taken over by the cyborgs.

Only the cyborgs – and the humans of Freedom Bay – had the benefits of the artificial organs, synthetic blood, computer diagnosis, laser surgery and electropharmacology that had been prophesied by the pundits of the Old Age. Only the cyborgs – and the humans of Freedom Bay – had the benefits of solar power from satellites, hydrogen from solar energy, quick-ripening produce, all-year-round crop fertility, weather and climate modifiers, and total waste-recycling that had also been prophesied by the pundits of the Old Age. Finally, only the cyborgs – and the humans of Freedom Bay – had the benefits of fusion energy, rapid image-transmission by laser writing, battery-powered semiconductor laser-communication systems, eye-movement command machines, cyberneurological and phototonic supercomputers, biofabrication techniques for the altering of DNA codes in living tissues, ceramics able to withstand temperatures of up to 4,000 degrees Fahrenheit, and domestic robots to take care of menial chores. All of these benefits, as prophesied by the Old Age pundits, had been denied to the human race by the cyborgs. In short, the world apart from Freedom Bay was very much as it had been before the Millennium and was, indeed, even worse off in many respects.

'Well, they did at least *one* good thing,' Ben said as they approached the club he wanted to visit, 'even though it was purely coincidental.'

'What's that?' Michael asked.

Ben pointed to the starry sky with his index finger. 'By killing off most of the industries that were producing carbon dioxide and CFC emissions, they dramatically slowed down global warming and the growth of the hole in the ozone layer, averting what we'd all been expecting: the upsetting of the world's climate and life-support systems with fire and flood, increased skin cancer, cataracts and a host of other diseases. Maybe even a new Ice Age or the melting of the polar ice caps with a subsequent flooding of major coastal cities, such as New York, London and Leningrad. So, yeah, they did *some* good.'

'For themselves,' Michael said. 'Not for us. They did it because they now rule the world and they don't want it destroyed. At least, not until they decide to leave it.'

'You think they plan to leave?'

'Yes. I think they're heading for outer space. That's where we wanted to go as well, but now they'll beat us to it, leaving us with a dying world.'

'What the fuck would they want to do in outer space?'

'Find a new world before the sun dies.'

'That's a long way away.'

'Not for them,' Michael said.

Glancing up at the enormous video screen angled above the entrance to one of the electronic game parlours, he saw newsreel footage of bloody riots in India. The TV cameraman appeared to be gloating over close-ups of the atrocities now so commonplace in that country: this heartless pursuit of sensationalism, Michael knew, was being shown by the games parlour as a come-on to customers with a taste for the more extreme pornoviolence shown on video inside the building. This in itself was another grim reminder to Michael that the cyborgs had only interfered in the world where and when it suited them.

Indeed, while the cyborgs had made some kind of appearance in most parts of the world, at least initially, their influence on the planet had been felt most strongly by the industrialized and technologically advanced nations such as the United States, Europe, Russia and China, while the usurpers had pretty much turned a blind eye to the Third World. Indeed, having stopped all shipping and air travel, the cyborgs had isolated the Third World countries from the rest of the globe and forced them back to fending for themselves, but without foreign aid or the benefits of new technology. As a result, old ethnic and territorial conflicts had been resurrected and were raging right now in India, the Lebanon, the Philippines, Chad, Angola, Ethiopia, South Africa, El Salvador, Nicaragua, Peru, Samolia and Afghanistan. In Rwanda, where the conflicts between Hutus and Tutsis had been coming to an end before the cyborgs took over, the country's subsequent isolation had led to the fresh eruption of a genocidal conflict that had by now virtually wiped out both tribes. Without the intervention of the US and the UN, both rendered toothless by the cyborgs, the conflict between the Israelis and the Palestinians had gone from bad to worse; Sri Lanka's civil war was an unending bloodbath that was decimating the population, and the slaughter of the innocents in Burma, Malaysia and Indonesia was continuing unimpeded.

On the other hand, where the cyborgs had a particular interest – namely, in the developed countries – they had taken definite, often brutal, steps to subdue troubled areas. Thus the Croat, Muslim and Serb armies in Bosnia had all been smashed and the war brought to an end to let the cyborgs take over the whole of Europe. Likewise, the warring armies that had been tearing asunder the former Soviet colossus – in Azerbaijan, Chechnya, Georgia and Tajikistan – had been pounded into oblivion by fleets of flying saucers armed with laser weapons, leaving the cyborgs in control there also, to concentrate almost exclusively on the running of Russia's many top-secret military and research establishments.

Surprisingly, in Northern Ireland, despite frequent cyborg patrols over the province and despite the fact that the British had pulled out for good, the hard men on both sides continued to wage their 'historic' war against each other, though on a much reduced scale, thus proving, for good or for ill, that the human spirit had not been completely crushed by the cyborgs. Ironically, this fact was also made clear nightly through the defiance of the youthful Speed Freaks right here in Washington DC. Michael admired them for that.

'This is it,' Ben said, stopping on the crowded sidewalk and nodding to indicate the neon-lit doorway of a retro dance club called *Be-Bop-a-Lula*, named after an old hit song of the 1950s. That name was flashing on and off in brightly-lit neon letters above the doorway, with a neon guitar flashing above it. On both sides of the door, holographic girls in string panties and spiked heels were gyrating sensually to the electronic dance music booming out of powerful speakers built into the walls. A bouncer over six feet tall and weighing about sixteen stone, wearing black denims and a black T-shirt with a yellow tiger painted on it, a knuckleduster covering the thick fingers of his right hand, was standing square in the entrance, inspecting those wanting to get in and saying 'Fuck off!' to those he didn't like. When he saw Ben, he grinned.

'Emiliano Zapata!' he exclaimed by way of greeting, referring to Ben's shoulder-length hair and drooping moustache, recently popularized anew by Marlon Brando in a 'colourized' version of the old black-and-white movie *Viva Zapata*. 'So how's the fucking desk clerk this evening?'

'Same as always,' Ben replied. 'Red-blooded, AIDs-free and rarin' to go. So do we get in or not?'

The big bouncer glanced at Michael. 'Your friend looks like a fucking choirboy with his blond hair and blue eyes. He'll get eaten alive in there.'

'That's what he's after,' Ben retorted. 'To be gobbled and drained dry.'

'Well, he's come to the right place. In you go, nerds.'

He stepped aside to let them pass. Directly behind him was a narrow, dimly-lit hallway with a locked turnstile between it and the main auditorium. The gate could only be opened by the insertion of a plastic credit card into the slot in one wall. Michael and Ben both paid by slipping their cards into the slot and letting the machine deduct what it demanded. As they withdrew the cards, one after the other, the gate opened to admit them one at a time. They stepped into the main room of the club. As large as a barn, it had numerous dance floors broken up with neon-lit bars of various shapes, small candle-lit drug parlours, and raised stages where stunningly lifelike holographic images of almost naked, sensually gyrating young girls and famous rock stars of the Old Age entertained the audience. Right now, Elvis Presley, who had made another major comeback as a holographic image and was the biggest thing in the music business all over again, was belting out his hip-shaking rendition of 'Bossa Nova Baby' from his old movie *Fun in Acapulco*. A crowd had gathered around to watch his performance and girls were having hysterics.

'Like it?' Ben shouted to make himself heard over the grossly amplified singing of Elvis, the screaming of his hysterical fans, and the general babble from other sections of the club.

'Noisy!' Michael shouted back.

'Fucking A, it's noisy,' Ben said. 'That's the whole idea. Come on, let's go for a drink.'

As they pushed their way through the crowd of mostly young, freaky people, many drunk, others stoned on a wide variety of drugs, Michael glanced up at the nearest stage where the holographic Elvis, wearing a white coat and black trousers, was shaking his legs, swinging his arms, and moving his hips with more grace and sensuality than the holographic girls farther back in the dazzling strobe-and-neon-lit club or even the real girls writhing half-naked on the dance floors.

Although he had only been in Washington a few days, Michael already knew just how 'big' Elvis was – the most popular star of the day – and found himself fascinated by him. Reportedly, before his death Elvis had been the most famous singer in history and the most widely known individual in the world; now, nearly fifty years on, he was as big as ever. Seeing him up there on the stage, as large as life and just as lifelike, Michael realized that he had never seen anyone quite like him; that he wasn't simply handsome but somehow otherworldly, as if he had been cloned from DNA strands taken from a wide variety of human tissues, thus growing into an androgynous, almost alien beauty who appealed to men and women alike. Also, no doubt about it, in this age of electronic music, with its drug-based, hallucinatory, unmelodious clamour, Elvis's voice was remarkably real and expressive, wringing the last drop of juice out of every word of a lyric, no matter how intrinsically banal. In short, he had something for everyone and represented, now more than ever, in this age of cyborg repression, a pure, absolute freedom.

'What do you want to drink?' Ben asked when they had reached the bar and, crushed between bizarrely dressed young men and half-naked young women, he was trying frantically to attract the attention of the busy barman.

'Anything,' Michael said, never having drunk alcohol before and not wanting Ben to notice this fact. 'Whatever you're having.'

'A couple of Tutti Fruttis,' Ben said. 'That should make us feel good.' He managed to gain the attention of the sweating barman and called out his order, then turned away to look across the packed, strobe-lit room at Elvis. 'God, that Elvis, he's something else, right? They don't make 'em like him no more.'

'How do they do it?' Michael asked.

'What?'

'Make those holographic images of Elvis and other famous entertainers and movie stars.'

'They take 'em from old movies and so on. I mean, that particular song comes from that old movie, *Fun in*—'

'Right,' Michael said, 'I know. It's a holographic reproduction of a number from an old movie. But I've also seen Elvis all over the place, as a holographic image, singing songs he never sang in real life. How come?'

'That's a real goddamned mystery, I tell you,' Ben replied, 'and no one really knows the truth of it. I'll tell you what some of us think, though.'

'What?'

'We think it's possible that Elvis has been cloned by the

cyborgs from skin tissue taken off his corpse and that the cyborgs are using the cloned Elvis to distract young people from their dissatisfactions. Same with Brando and Madonna and the others who've made these big comebacks. I mean, particularly with Elvis, those new songs have convinced a lot of kids – like those ones screaming over there – that Elvis is a real, living being. And those kids, they're more concerned with worshipping him than they are with taking a stand against the cyborgs. I mean, you keep potentially rebellious kids distracted enough and you'll keep 'em pacified.'

'You really think that's possible?' Michael asked.

'It's not necessarily true, but it's certainly possible. It's a known fact that during the first weeks of their take-over the cyborgs dug up a lot of graves and took away a lot of corpses that were still in a reasonable condition, being embalmed and so on. They were nearly all famous people in their day and Elvis was one of 'em.'

'And Brando and James Dean and Madonna.'

'Yeah. Great icons of the twentieth century, but loved particularly by young people, so particularly useful as a means of distraction for *our* generation. I mean, look at Madonna there!' Michael glanced at the stage and saw that Elvis had been replaced by Madonna in her Nazi-dominatrix period, singing 'Justify My Love' while wearing scant black lingerie, an outrageous conical bra and skyscraper heels, kissing and fondling another female while surrounded by male dancers in fishnet stockings and leather. 'The old girl may still be alive somewhere,' Ben continued, 'though no one seems to know exactly where. Yet there she is up on the stage, unchanged, forever young. Maybe the cyborgs abducted her and cloned a replica from her DNA. What else would explain her total disappearance about five years ago? My bet is the cyborgs.'

According to what Michael had read, Madonna had been the most famous female performer of her day, almost as big as Elvis in his time, but had ended up like that old silent movie star, Mae

West, pitifully trying to keep her audience by becoming even more outrageous and thus emphasizing, rather than hiding, her advancing years. She had still been doing that, desperately trying to preserve her flagging career, when she had disappeared abruptly from her home in Bel Air in what was widely believed to have been a cyborg abduction. Since then, she had only been seen on old videos and holographic performances, some of which included songs she had never sung before. The possibility that she, like Elvis, might have been cloned by the cyborgs was therefore a real one.

The harassed barman finally brought their Tutti Fruttis and Michael had his first alcoholic drink, though it was, in fact, something more than that. Sipping it, he felt it go immediately to his head, making him slightly, temporarily dizzy, then heightening his perceptions to make everything around him vividly clear.

'What's in it?' he asked.

'Gin and vodka and whisky and orange juice and liquid methamphetamine. A pretty good brew.'

As the drink rushed to his head, Michael glanced at the group of young people pressing against his right shoulder and saw a young girl in profile, her hair chopped fashionably short and tinted with coloured stripes, her full lips painted bright red, her creamy breasts, untouched by the sun, bulging out of a skintight T-shirt, her long legs emphasized by hotpants, sheer nylon stockings and stiletto-heeled boots. The sudden sight of her almost took his breath away, gave him an instant erection and, combined with the heady effects of the Tutti Frutti, made him feel corrupt. Back in Freedom Bay, where relationships between the sexes were only encouraged when both parties were serious, Michael, still a virgin, had used his adept's skills and meditation to sublimate his sexual desires. But here, where sexuality was paraded so blatantly, he was constantly being taken unawares and tormented more frequently with erotic fantasies. This in turn made him aware that the World was changing him, perhaps even weakening him, and that he would have to apply a great deal of self-control in order not to succumb to an involvement that could corrupt or weaken him even more and cause him to make a mistake or give himself away to the wrong person. He was in grave danger here.

'It's so noisy here,' he said to Ben, repeating his previous complaint, 'I can hardly hear myself speak. Why do you come here?' He nodded, indicating the many young people crowding both sides of him. 'Why do *they* come here?'

'To meet each other, of course,' Ben replied. 'To make friends and meet potential partners. To get drunk or drugged and, if you're into real-time sex, to get that as well. That's pretty obvious, isn't it?'

'But why here in particular?' Michael asked. 'Why not somewhere quieter? Do they get high on the noise?'

'Christ, you're so fucking innocent,' Ben retorted. 'Where the fuck did you spring from?'

Realizing that he had almost made his first mistake, Michael did not reply.

'Yeah, they come for the noise. They get high on the noise. But they also come to joints like this because the noise is what makes them among the few places in the city where you can't be overheard by cyborg bugging devices. They come to places like this because they're safe – or relatively so. Though there might be the odd clone or brain-implant spy in here, by and large the cyborgs leave these joints alone, probably grateful because, so they think, they keep us drunk and drugged and off the streets. But a lot of us, when we're planning something against the cyborgs, we come here to talk . . . And for the other things, naturally.' He grinned and nodded in the direction of the half-naked girls beside Michael. 'We're not *all* into cybersex,' he added. 'Some of us, boys and girls alike, prefer it in real time. So what about you?'

'I just want to find my girlfriend,' Michael lied.

'You won't find her,' Ben retorted bluntly. 'So drink up. Drown your sorrows.'

By the time Michael was halfway through his second Tutti Frutti, he was feeling as high as he sometimes felt when meditating. But he was not nearly so much in control of himself. His gaze wandered repeatedly, helplessly, around the noisy, strobe-and-neon-lit room to take in the holographic stars and dancing girls, as well as the real-life girls who were either having hysterics over another holographic Elvis performance, gyrating with male and female partners on the dance floor, or smiling invitingly at him, Michael, as they brushed or pressed against him at the bar, ostensibly ordering drinks. Losing his inhibitions, but forcing himself to remember what he was here for, he said to Ben, 'What kind of things do you plan against the cyborgs?'

'Anything we can do to disrupt them,' Ben replied, having another sip of his Tutti Frutti and looking as high as a kite himself, his eyes glazed from the potent mix. 'Putting SARGEs and Prowlers out of action with home-made bombs, firing at hovering paddy wagons with sub-machine guns, distracting the footballs with hot-rod and motorcycle runs, keeping an eye out for cloned or brain-implanted spies and putting out their fucking lights—'

'You mean killing them?'

'Right . . . and monitoring the White House, the Pentagon and other establishments held by them to try and find out just what they're up to in the short and long term.'

'How do you monitor them?'

'Computer hacking, laser surveillance systems, infra-red thermal imagers, and good old-fashioned eyeball reconnaissance with military binoculars and SLR cameras with long-distance lenses. We use the old-fashioned methods, in particular, for large, fenced-in areas such as air force bases and military research complexes, where we can't get physically close. The computer hacking and laser surveillance systems are used on the White House and the Pentagon. So far, we haven't come up with much, but we're hoping that patience and time will produce dividends. You want to see it first-hand?'

'Yes,' Michael said.

'You're willing to go into the White House area with me?'

'Absolutely,' Michael said.

'That's a dangerous place to go,' Ben warned him.

'I don't give a damn,' Michael retorted, wanting to get out of the retro dance club, away from the hellish noise, the hallucinatory strobe lights, the young girls who were pressing up against him to distract him and weaken him. Wanting, in fact, to concentrate his scattered thoughts, bring himself down from his high, and do the work he had come here to do. 'I'm up and running when you are.'

'Let's go,' Ben said.

It was just before midnight, the hour of the cyborg curfew, the most dangerous time of all, when Ben led Michael out of the club into the squalid, neon-light streets, then back to their converted apartment block facing the old sports stadium where, Michael noticed, the Speed Freaks had boldly gathered and were making a lot of noise, clearly drinking and taking drugs, winding themselves up before embarking on their ritualistic, infinitely dangerous harassment of the cyborg patrols. Ben did not enter the apartment building, but instead went straight past it and kept going until he had reached the far corner of the crumbling National Portrait Gallery.

'We're walking?' Michael asked.

'That's right,' Ben said as he turned into F Street, heading west and taking Michael with him. 'Walking's a lot safer after curfew 'cause the cyborg ground patrols have less chance of seeing you and the footballs' surveillance systems mainly pick up the vibration and sound of automobiles and motorcycles. If you walk in the darkness, keeping pretty quiet, you're as good as invisible to 'em – so keep walking, pal.'

They both walked to the White House.

Chapter Twenty-four

Gumshoe saw his mother and father. They looked the same age as they had been when he last saw them, as if eternally young. But they were staring at each other with eyes widened by insanity because their heads had been severed from their bodies and surgically grafted onto the neck-stump of a pig's body to make a nightmarish two-headed creature. Gumshoe's parents were still conscious, fully alive in that sense, but their awareness of what had happened to them had clearly driven them mad.

Gumshoe screamed when he saw them. His scream reverberated through the night. His pain shook him out of his reverie of dread and cast him into another place. It was not much better here, just more surgical mutations, bed after bed of unfortunate human beings who'd had lips and noses surgically removed, leaving great, bloody holes into which tubes had been driven, letting them breathe artificially until they were given the steel-plated masks that would aid their breathing for the rest of their lives when they were turned into cyborgs. Also there were human beings without legs and arms, but still alive with functioning heads and torsos, strapped to surgical beds, eyes wide – like the eyes of Gumshoe's parents – with the horror of what they had become and what could still be done to them. There were human beings with animal bodies and animals with human limbs and severed human heads wired to machines and functioning perfectly, albeit half crazed. There were many such monstrosities.

Gumshoe screamed again, closing his eyes, trying to escape, and went spinning down through a whirlpool of darkness and far-off, streaming stars. Gradually everything slowed down, as in a slow-motion movie, and he found himself drifting through a darkness filled with flickering, silvery-white fireflies that reminded him of the electrochemical signals, the neurons, that pass information from one point in the brain to another. He was lost in the cosmos, the great teeming brain of the universe, and he heard a bass humming sound, almost *felt* it, an infrasound. As the sound grew louder, as the pressure increased, the silvery-white fireflies multiplied dramatically, flickering on and off more rapidly, then started streaking this way and that at incredible speeds, now here and then there, living and dying on the instant, creating countless lines of light that criss-crossed repeatedly until they formed an immense, glowing, constantly changing web, the strands of which converged on a distant, rhythmically pulsating, mesmerizing dark core.

Now terrified, convinced that he was approaching a monstrous, steadily breathing, all-devouring spider in the centre of its immense web – a virtual cosmos of darkness and streaming light and infrasounds that could be *felt* – Gumshoe kept gliding magically forward, surrounded by the darting fireflies, the criss-crossing silvery-white lines, an abyss of nothingness on all sides, up and down, beyond time and space. Approaching that pulsating dark core at the heart of the great web, he felt the bass humming sound, the infrasound, as if it was a palpable presence, moving in on him, pressing upon him on all sides, about to crush the life out of him. He screamed again and . . .

He awakened from his long sleep. Bright light stung his eyes. After blinking repeatedly to adjust to the light, he licked his dry lips, moved his body to ascertain that it was still there, that he had only been dreaming about the surgical mutations, then nervously, reluctantly, looked about him.

He was alone. Lying on a bed with white sheets and plump

pillows in a small, rectangular room with white-painted walls. All white. Everything. There were no windows in the room and the door, which was as white as everything else, blended into the walls. There was a bedside cabinet. A glass of what looked like water was resting upon it. Against the wall at the other end of the bed was a white-painted wardrobe, the doors of which were closed. There was nothing else in the room. The floors were made of what looked like white linoleum and had no mats or carpets. The room had the appearance and feel of a private room in a hospital, though without the small luxuries that a private patient might reasonably expect. Looking down at himself, he saw that his clothes had been stripped from him and that he had been dressed in a pair of sky-blue pyjamas. He felt bright and yet sluggish, as if he had slept for a long time, and only gradually recalled, with reluctance, with rising fear, just where he was and how he had come to be here.

'Oh, my God, it's real!' he said.

Shocked by the sound of his own voice, which seemed unnaturally loud even though he had only whispered, he glanced at the door, fully expecting someone, attracted by his instinctive outburst, to come in and attend to him, for good or for bad. Recalling the man in black, the one who had shown him and the other abductees through the bowels of the mother ship, he wasn't sure that he wanted *any* kind of visitor, though he knew that sooner or later he would surely get one. Thus again reminded of just where he was, in a cyborg mother ship at the bottom of the sea, he felt less fear than he had felt before, though he also felt slightly unreal. He knew that he would have to accept this, but it wouldn't be easy.

He glanced around the room, taking note of its relative lack of contents, its immaculate, spartan cleanliness, and wondered if he should get out of bed or stay where he was. He was frightened of staying here, but also frightened of leaving, not knowing what he would find out there, on the other side of the closed door. Then he looked at the wardrobe, at its white-painted, closed doors and realized that he was frightened of that as well, of what he might find inside it if he opened the doors . . . severed limbs, a dead body. Though accepting that this was ridiculous, a paranoid thought, he decided that he had to put his mind at rest by looking inside the wardrobe. Perhaps he would find his old clothes there and could at least put them on. He would feel more real then.

'Right,' he said, speaking aloud. 'Let's do it.'

He was just about to throw the top sheet off him when the room door opened.

Shocked, frightened again, he pulled the sheet back over his body and looked up as the door opened wider and someone walked in. Relief surged through him when he saw that it was not the man in black but a middle-aged woman of nondescript demeanour, wearing a white tunic over black slacks, with flat shoes on her feet. She wasn't smiling and, when she approached the bed, he saw that her eyes were dead. Not quite dead, but certainly unemotional, with a steady, rarely blinking, gaze. She fixed that gaze upon him.

'How do you feel?' she asked him, speaking tonelessly.

'Okay,' he replied. 'A bit unreal.'

'That's to be expected.' She took hold of his right wrist, felt his pulse, then placed a thermometer between his lips, waited for a moment, withdrew it and checked it. 'Excellent,' she said. 'The sleep did you some good. Your pulse and temperature are perfectly normal. You're no longer in panic.'

'How long was I sleeping?' he asked her.

'Five days,' she said.

Gumshoe was shocked. He couldn't imagine being asleep that long without being dead. Now he felt that he had died and been resurrected, which was a frightening thought. Nevertheless, when he saw the dead eyes of the woman, he determined not to show the fear he felt. He wanted to ask her a lot of questions — a *lot* — but he was reluctant to do so. This was fear, also.

'Are you a nurse?' he managed to ask.

'Sort of. So how was your sleep?'

'It must have been deep if I slept for five days,' Gumshoe said, getting some of his old sarcasm back and determined to keep it as a form of defence. 'How did you manage to make me sleep that long? Was I drugged?'

'We prefer to call it sedated,' the woman replied, her voice as remote and as cold as the dark side of the Moon. 'They're designed to help you recover from the shock and adjust to this place.'

'I had lots of dreadful nightmares,' Gumshoe said.

'What makes you think they were nightmares?' the woman said. Then, with a wintry smile, she turned away and walked out.

Shaken by her remark, which he assumed had been made for the very purpose of unsettling him, Gumshoe tried to put it out of his mind. But he sank back on the bed, feeling helpless, filled with returning dread, staring at the closed doors of the wardrobe and wondering what was behind them. Recalling his nightmares and the remark of the dead-eyed woman, he let his imagination run riot, seeing dismembered limbs and severed heads with wild, staring eyes. The longer he stared at the wardrobe, the more frightened he became. The more frightened he became, the more he despised himself. Eventually, however, desperately trying to conquer his fear, he flipped the white sheet back, clambered out of bed and walked to the wardrobe. He was astonished, when he reached it, to realize just how quickly his heart was beating. Licking his lips, trying to breathe evenly, he slowly opened the doors.

His clothes, obviously washed and ironed, were dangling from coat-hangers inside the wardrobe. There was nothing else in there.

Realizing, by the loud sigh of relief that automatically escaped him, just how terrible had been his expectations, how deep his fear, he stood there for some time, just staring at the clothes, wondering if he should put them on or not. Finally, deciding that he felt vulnerable in the pyjamas, somehow less strong, more unreal, and feeling also how badly he needed to do something positive, such as leaving the room and checking what was outside, he decided to put the clothes on. He had just reached out for his underclothes when someone spoke from behind him.

'You really should have a shower first. You've been asleep a long time.'

Almost jumping out of his skin, Gumshoe withdrew his hand and turned around to see that the room door had been opened and a man was now standing in the doorway. He had light blond hair, unnaturally smooth white skin, lean, handsome features and icy blue eyes. Two armed cyborgs, Gumshoe noticed, were standing behind him.

'There's no shower,' Gumshoe said, trying to keep his voice steady.

'Yes, there is,' the man replied. He stepped into the room and went to what looked like a blank section of the wall. When he pressed his fingers against it, a door slid open to reveal a shower and toilet inside. The man turned back to Gumshoe.

'Have a shower first,' he said. 'It will make you feel better. Then put your clothes on and wait by the bed until I return.'

His voice was like a whisper. It was also oddly flat. It was the voice of a man with no feelings, but a lot of authority. That voice, though quiet and unemotional, would brook no disobedience.

'When will you return?' Gumshoe asked him.

'In thirty minutes exactly,' the man replied. Then he turned away and walked out, closing the door firmly behind him, leaving Gumshoe standing in a dead, oddly chilling silence.

Though badly shaken again and not understanding why, Gumshoe did as he had been told and took a shower, first hot and then cold, feeling more invigorated with each second he was under the jetting water but even then wondering if they hadn't put something in it to affect him somehow. Nevertheless, accepting that he would, at least for now, have to do as he was told, he completed the shower, dried himself, cleaned his teeth and then gratefully put on his regular clothes. When he was dressed and had combed his hair, he felt a little more real. Then he went and sat on the bed to await the return of the handsome man with the icy blue eyes.

He had taken his time in the shower and only had to wait five minutes. It was the longest five minutes of his life. As he sat there, mesmerized by the closed door of the room, wondering what was out there, he was tormented by the clinging recollection of his nightmares, particularly the one about his parents, and filled up with the pain of loss that he had managed to subdue for many years. Now, torn from his own world and facing a potentially fearsome future, perhaps one even worse than anything he could imagine, he recalled his idyllic childhood in Georgetown, when he had still been with his parents, and the shocking pain he had experienced when they abruptly disappeared and never came back. That pain had now returned, borne in on his fearsome nightmare, and he knew that if he dwelt on it too much, it would do him serious damage. He was in trouble enough right now, the worst kind of trouble imaginable, and he was going to need his every resource just to retain his sanity. So he sat there, willing himself to be defiant, desperately trying to cast out all thoughts of the past and think of only the present. Then the room door opened.

Gumshoe looked up. The blond man had come back. He stood in the doorway, studying Gumshoe thoughtfully, a slight, unfeeling smile on his thin lips. His blue eyes, though bright with intelligence, were as cold as ice. Gumshoe was chilled by the sight of him and fought hard to control himself.

'Ah,' the man said softly, 'you're dressed. You've had that shower, I presume?'

'Yes,' Gumshoe said.

The man, wearing a black turtleneck sweater, black trousers and black shoes, stepped into the room and stopped a few feet away from Gumshoe to look down upon him. Intimidated by that slight smile and icy blue gaze, Gumshoe glanced behind the man and saw the two armed cyborgs blocking the doorway. They were cyborgs with metal prosthetics replacing their noses and lips and with metal claws instead of human hands. Those claws, however, were flexible enough to hold stun guns that were aimed at Gumshoe. Shivering, he forced himself to meet the icy blue gaze of the man in black.

'Who are you?' the man asked, his voice still soft and unemotional, filled with authority.

'I'm sure you know that already,' Gumshoe said. 'You must have been through my billfold.'

The man smiled again, though his amusement, if such it could be called, was clearly touched with mockery. 'True. But please tell me anyway. I'd like to hear it from your own lips.'

Gumshoe heard his own sigh like a wind through a canyon. 'Randolph Fullbright.'

'Your friends call you Randy?'

'Yeah, right.'

'Address?'

Gumshoe gave his Georgetown address, adding, 'It used to be my parents' house, but now I just have a room there. Some carpetbaggers captured it.'

'Carpetbaggers?'

'Criminal elements who take over family houses and turn them into rooms for rent. I now pay rent on my own room.'

'That must be humiliating,' the man said.

'It's fucking annoying,' Gumshoe said.

The man smiled again, making Gumshoe turn cold. 'What happened to your parents?'

'They were abducted by cyborgs years ago and they haven't been seen since. But you probably know that.'

'Yes, I know that. Now I know that *you* know it.'

'When people disappear, you bastards take them. I think *everyone* knows that. So where are my parents?'

'I don't think I should tell you that just yet.'

'Are they still alive?'

'Alive and in good health. Now let's change the subject.'

Though trying to control himself, to remain as cool as possible, Gumshoe could not control the incredible emotions welling up inside him. He was almost in tears – tears of joy – but he managed to hold them back.

'Just one question before we change the subject. Can I ask just one question?'

'What question?'

'Did you do brain implants on my parents? Have you changed them that way?'

'No. We don't do that to everyone. Some serve us because they don't have a choice and your parents now serve us. They did not require brain implants.'

Gumshoe sighed again, too loudly, with helpless relief. 'Good,' he said. 'Thanks. So . . . who are you?'

'That's two questions.'

'Sorry.'

The man offered that slight, chilling smile, then said, 'I'm the person you've been tenaciously investigating.'

'Pardon?'

'Wilson,' the man said. 'I'm John Wilson.'

Gumshoe felt the shock like an ice pick through his spine, temporarily paralysing him, making his brain seize up, almost taking his breath away and making his heart race. This was followed by the return of clear thought and its natural outcome: a fear springing from the absolute conviction that this man was speaking the truth.

'The *original* Wilson?'

'Yes.'

'How come? Did the cyborgs clone you?'

'Exactly.'

'Who told them to do that?'

'I did. I left instructins before I died and the cyborgs were programmed to obey those instructions. They cloned me when the technology was perfected and so . . . *Voilà!* Here I am.'

'You speak French.'

'Which you're learning.'

'How did you know that?'

'There's little that we *don't* know about you. When we pick someone up – as we picked your parents up – we automatically monitor everyone related to them and, eventually, pick them up also. It's a matter of blood lines.'

'What does that mean?'

'We like to keep it in the family, as it were. When we have one, we want all.'

'And now you've got me.'

'Yes. The end of the line. All the eggs in one basket.'

'What does that mean?'

'You'll find out in due course.'

Gumshoe wasn't sure that he wanted to find out. Now he only wanted to find his parents: to see them alive and, at the same time, to let them know that *he* was still alive. Now he ached with that need.

'How many of you did they clone?' he asked of Wilson, not knowing what else to say.

'Only one. There are others who *look* like me, but I'm the only real Wilson. The others have different identities and look to me as their God.'

'That must make you feel good,' Gumshoe said.

'Please don't be sarcastic.'

Though spoken quietly, flatly, the remark convinced Gumshoe that this man was not one to be messed with: that he was bound to be as ruthless as the original Wilson – as unfeelingly, inhumanly cruel.

'I'm sorry,' Gumshoe asked, 'but I have to ask . . . Why do you want me?'

'I told you. You're the end of the line and we like all our eggs in one basket.'

'But *why?*'

'For the purposes of communication,' Wilson said. 'In your

case, with your parents. We find that communication between family members can be helpful in times of stress.'

'My parents are under stress?'

Wilson smiled. 'Well, naturally. They miss you. Now please stand up and follow me.'

As if already deprived of his will, Gumshoe stood upright. 'Where are we going?'

'I'm taking you to see your parents,' Wilson said, 'and, en route, to show you what we do here. Knowing what we do here can be a help in crossing the bridge from the old world to the new. So! This way, please.'

Wilson stepped aside to let Michael leave the room, which he did when the two cyborgs blocking the door had started along the corridor outside, leading the way. Gumshoe followed them, boiling over with mixed emotions: the tremendous joy that he might soon be reunited with his parents; his fear that Wilson could be lying to him just to keep him pacified; curiosity about what he would find out there; and, finally, his growing dread at the thought of what his own fate might be. All in all, though, he turned into the corridor like a man about to be executed, hoping against hope that a last-minute pardon would save him. Wilson fell in beside him, a tall man, looking down at him.

Unlike the corridor he had walked along before, this one was not curved but instead went straight, passing many doors. Also, the walls were not made of a whitish metal, as the other walls had been, but appeared to be covered in normal plaster and painted in a fading lime green. Normal-seeming people of both sexes, some wearing black coveralls, others dressed in white smocks, passed them by in the corridors, nodding fearfully at Wilson though saying nothing to him while going into and coming out of the various doors lining the corridor, letting Gumshoe catch fleeting glimpses of what appeared to be linear offices, laboratories and workshops. He was convinced by all this that he was no longer in a flying saucer; that while he had been asleep, or in a temporary, medically induced coma, he had been transferred from the mother ship to somewhere else. He wondered, with deepening dread, just where that might be.

'This isn't a flying saucer,' he said to Wilson as they continued walking along the corridor behind the two fearsome cyborgs.

'No,' Wilson said, 'it's not. As clearly you've already guessed, you were transported elsewhere.'

'Where?'

'Back on dry land,' Wilson said. 'You don't have to know exactly where.'

With his imagination running riot again, churning up the fear already buried deep within him, Gumshoe recalled that the cyborgs had bases on the Moon and considered, and wondered, with awe and even more fear, if that was where he was.

'Are we on the Moon?' he asked.

Wilson smiled bleakly. 'No.'

'Then we're still on Earth.'

'Yes. That much I can tell you, but no more. Ask no more. You've already seen some of what we do and I know you were shocked. Be prepared to see more of that, but this time, since you've seen some of it already, try not to be so shocked. It's best to accept the inevitable, no matter how inhuman, how barbarous it might at first seem. Bear in mind that nothing under the sun and Moon is unnatural, that nothing in the whole *cosmos* is unnatural, and that what is being done here is a perfectly natural evolutionary development.'

'I'll bet,' Gumshoe said.

'Progress can never be achieved without suffering,' Wilson continued flatly, this time ignoring Gumshoe's sarcasm, 'and all of us, at one time or another, must suffer accordingly. This is an inviolable, unbending law of life and it can't be ignored. Now, prepare to leave the past and enter the future, knowing that what you see here is merely a bridge between the two, therefore not meant to last. When the leap has been made – the evolutionary leap from Man to Superman – what you see here will no longer be required. Think of this when your every natural instinct makes you wish to recoil. Think of this when you're part of it.'

The two cyborgs up ahead had come to a solid steel door that rose up into the ceiling as if it had sensed their presence. The cyborgs went on through and Gumshoe followed, with Wilson still close by his side. The stuff of Gumshoe's worst nightmares became real on the instant when he found himself stepping into an immense pentagonal space with a high, flat concrete ceiling and many corridors running off its five sides. The feeling that he was deep under the ground struck him immediately, but what struck him even harder was what filled the space between the five great concrete walls: an obscene multiplication of what he had first seen when he had been marched through the bowels of the mother ship five days ago.

Trying not to recoil, though slipping into disbelief, he saw row upon row of steel-framed beds with surgically mutated humans lying upon them: some in bloody bandages; some with severed limbs and gleaming prosthetic replacements; some with stomachs sliced open and vital organs missing; some with faces peeled off the bone and replaced with membrane-thin metal masks; some breathing through tubes and defecating into plastic bags; some no more than a torso wired up to computer consoles; some half-human, half-animal; others, having survived the first terrible stages, now on the way to being converted into cyborgs: half-human, half-machine. There were hundreds of beds, hundreds of bloody, groaning humans, and above them, in wire cages strung from the ceiling, were creatures so crazed by the physical changes wrought upon them – recognizable neither as humans nor as any kind of known animal – that they were clawing at the bars with mutated, bloody hands or frantically banging their heads against them, clearly trying to kill themselves. It was a basement of hell.

'*Part* of it?' Gumshoe said, turning to Wilson, feeling shocked beyond measure. 'How do you mean I'll be part of . . . part of . . . *this?*'

'Not for ever,' Wilson said, showing a flicker of impatience, as if speaking to an uncomprehending child. 'Already most of what you see here is obsolete, rendered redundant by the advent of cloning which can, for the most part, produce humans to any design we require. It is cloning that is bringing us to the doorstep of the Superman, but we still need to do a few experiments to explore physical and mental endurance. Look,' he continued, jabbing his forefinger repeatedly at the normal men and women, most wearing black coveralls and all looking superbly fit, who were attending to the butchered humans on the beds. 'Humans cloned to a wide variety of DNA patterns to enhance them in specific areas, namely intelligence and physical strength. Those cloned humans are the first in a line that will end with the Superman. The others, those surgically mutated, can soon be dispensed with. Before that, however, there are still some experiments that have to be performed, particularly on the human mind and its powers of endurance. For this we still need the abductees – and you are part of our programme.'

'*Me?*' Gumshoe said, staring around him in growing horror and disbelief, losing control of himself. 'What do you mean, I'll be part of this? What are you planning to do to me?'

'I need to know if you can communicate with your parents at this point in time. I wish to join the three of you together and see what transpires.'

'What . . .' And Gumshoe almost screamed, '*Where are my parents?*'

Wilson pointed. Gumshoe looked. He knew then, on the instant, what the dead-eyed nurse had meant when she had said, 'What makes you think they were nightmares?' For indeed, he now saw that he had not, in fact, been dreaming, that he had not been having nightmares, but that clearly they had shown him this before when he was in his drugged state.

Gumshoe saw his mother and father. They looked the same age as they had been when he last saw them, as if eternally young. But they were staring at each other with eyes widened by insanity because their heads had been severed from their bodies and surgically grafted onto the neck-stump of a pig's body to make a nightmarish two-headed creature. Gumshoe's parents were still conscious, fully alive in that sense, but their awareness of what had happened to them had clearly driven them mad.

Now Wilson wanted to cut off Gumshoe's head and join him to his parents.

Gumshoe screamed and then fainted.

Chapter Twenty-five

'Walk quietly, tread softly,' Ben joked as he and Michael made their way along F Street in the midnight hour, now passing the Metro Center and heading towards the eastern side of the Treasury Building. Nevertheless, although Ben was joking, he was also, Michael noted, keeping his voice low and constantly scanning both sides of the deserted, infrequently lamplit road. He was obviously wary of being accosted by lurking thugs or of suddenly being confronted by a cyborg Prowler, SARGE or football, the latter, in particular, having the ability to approach so quickly that they could hardly be seen until it was too late.

So far, they had seen nothing the length and breadth of F Street, but when Michael next raised his gaze, he saw that a dome-shaped flying saucer, over a hundred feet in diameter, its whitish-metallic body not rotating but still giving off an eerie, pulsating glow, was hovering directly over the White House, just beyond the Treasury Building. Other flying saucers, mostly the fifty-foot paddy wagons, were gliding to and fro across the capital, but higher up in the night sky.

'Where are we going?' he asked Ben.

'To check out the White House,' Ben replied, still keeping his voice low and moving his gaze left, right and above as they advanced parallel to the 14th Street Theatre District.

'I know that,' Michael said, frustrated, 'but from *where?*'

'Have you ever been to church?' Ben asked mockingly.

'No,' Michael replied.

'You're going now,' Ben informed him.

At that moment, a Prowler and two accompanying SARGEs turned into the end of F Street, the former the size and shape of a tank, the latter looking like grotesque dune buggies or giant metal insects, all advancing relentlessly with sensors flashing and turning in all directions. Though Michael had seen those vehicles before in daylight, parked safely outside the White House and other government buildings, he was shocked to see them now, knowing that they would attempt to pick him and Ben up, or call in a paddy wagon, if they came close enough to sense their presence. Obviously knowing this as well, Ben turned quickly into 14th Street and led Michael through the old theatre district. Formerly a lively area, it had been emptied of most human habitation by the close proximity of the cyborgs guarding the White House. The theatres and restaurants had closed down and their derelict husks were, as Ben had previously informed Michael, now occupied by the only human beings who did not fear the cyborgs, namely, drunks, drug addicts and the sexual perverts and psychopaths who preyed on them. It was a dangerous area.

'Move as quickly as possible without actually running,' Ben whispered, withdrawing what looked like a cyborg stun gun from inside his jacket. 'And keep your eyes peeled. If anyone – *anyone* – comes towards us, run for your life.'

Hurrying along 14th Street behind his new friend, Michael glanced from left to right, seeing only the deserted, rubbish-strewn road on his left and the derelict buildings on his right. Not *quite* deserted, as he could see from the miserable human forms slumped in the dark doorways, either sleeping, slurping automatically from cans and bottles, or injecting themselves with shaking hands. It was a grim reminder to Michael of the dark side of the World he had so often yearned to visit and it made him appreciate even more the disciplines and order of Freedom

Bay. And thinking of Freedom Bay, of home, he was suddenly overcome with emotion for his mother and father, for Chloe, for his friends and, of course, for his mentor, Dr Lee Brandenberg.

At that moment, a ragged man with mad eyes stepped out of a doorway, holding an open switchblade in one hand. Two others came out behind him.

'Freeze or I'll cut your fucking throat,' the knifeman said hoarsely, holding his weapon up higher to let its blade glitter in the moonlight.

Michael's every instinct was to immobilize the men with his parapsychological powers, perhaps mesmerize them, but he realized that if he did that Ben would have some questions to ask him. Luckily, Ben solved the problem by rapidly raising his stun gun and shooting a laser ray, a pulsating beam filled with sparks that looked like tiny lightning bolts, at the crazed man wielding the knife. The man jerked and straightened up, as if jolted by a burst of electricity, then dropped the knife from paralysed fingers and fell to his knees. As he keeled over, the other two men cursed and practically dived forward, one at Ben, the other at Michael. But Ben fired the stun gun twice more, hitting each man in turn, and both jerked and straightened up, as the first man had done, then, like him, fell to the ground. Without saying a word, Ben lowered the stun gun and continued along the street.

As they passed another darkened doorway, close to the intersection of 14th and G Street, Michael heard a repeated dull thudding sound, followed by muffled grunting. Glancing into the doorway, he saw two shadowy forms, one being punched repeatedly, brutally, in the stomach by the other and clearly too weakened to make any sound other than those breathless, painful grunts. Again, Michael's instinct was to intervene, but Ben had kept going and he, feeling ashamed of himself, had to do the same.

Crossing G Street, following Ben, he glanced to the left and glimpsed, at the western end of the street, which was deserted, the northern wing of the Treasury Building. Even as his glance took in that monolithic granite structure, a Prowler with a SARGE front and rear crossed from north to south, indicating that cyborg ground patrols were guarding the building. Above the building, shedding its eerie, pulsating light upon it, was a silently hovering fifty-foot flying saucer.

Continuing along 14th Street, but with the dangerous old theatre district now well behind them, Ben and Michael made their way unimpeded to H Street, where they turned left, crossed the road and headed for Lafayette Square. Just before reaching the northern side of the moonlit park, with its tranquil plazas, paved walkways, landscaped gardens and crumbling statues, Ben stopped abruptly, then lowered himself until he was belly down on the sidewalk, in the shadow of the building to his right. Michael did the same.

Looking almost straight ahead, following Ben's gaze, he saw that a foolish, perhaps drunken or drugged motorcyclist had driven into this forbidden area and been caught by a combination of cyborg ground patrol and flying football. The football, which was presently hovering above the overturned motorcycle, casting its eerie glow upon it, had obviously flown in low over the rider, causing him to go into a skid and crash his vehicle. The driver himself had then been hemmed in by a tank-like Prowler and two beetle-like SARGEs and held captive until the arrival of the paddy wagon that would take him away. That paddy wagon, a fifty-foot flying saucer, was now hovering at the other side of H Street, mere inches above the road, while a couple of steel-masked cyborgs encouraged the unfortunate motorcyclist with jolts from their stun guns to go up its ramp and into the dazzling white light of its interior. When the motorcyclist had dissolved into that light, the cyborgs followed him in, the ramp moving back up into the hull of the saucer to make a seamless whole. Then the metallic-grey wing disc-plates began to rotate, their lights flashing on and off. When the wing discs were rotating so rapidly that their edges had become an eerily glowing whitish blur, the saucer ascended vertically to about fifty feet, hovered there momentarily, then shot off abruptly in a south-westerly direction, most likely heading for the Pentagon, where many of the abducted were known to be taken. When the saucer had disappeared, the Prowler and the two SARGEs moved off as well, going along the eastern side of the square, then disappearing into Pennsylvania Avenue. They would continue to patrol the whole White House area until just after dawn.

'Let's go,' Ben said, clambering back to his feet, waiting until Michael had done the same, then leading him across the road to St John's Church, located on the north side of the park. Formerly one of the most elegant, historic and prestigious churches in Washington, widely known as the 'Church of Presidents' because every Chief Executive since the church's inception in 1897 had worshipped there while in office, the building had not been used since the coming of the cyborgs and was now in a sad state of disrepair. Nevertheless, Ben ushered Michael inside, entering by way of the pillared porch on the west side then led him up the dark, dusty stairs in an eerie, echoing silence to the top of the bell tower. The tower, fixed up with scaffolding gave a good view across Lafayette Square and Pennsylvania Avenue of the northern entrance, the main entrance, to the White House.

Two young men about Michael's age, both wearing open-necked shirts, windcheater jackets and blue denims, were kneeling on the scaffolding, one on either side of a group of three long-distance surveillance instruments that had been set up on tripods and were focused on the distant White House. They looked up nervously as Ben and Michael entered the ruined bell tower and only relaxed when they recognized the former.

'Oh, it's you,' one of them, the fair-haired one, said. 'I nearly shit my pants there.'

'You shoulda brought diapers,' Ben retorted. 'Hi, guys. This is a friend, Mike Johnson. He's come to see what we're up to. He's trustworthy, believe me. Mike,' he added, indicating the fair-haired, overweight young man, 'this is Lenny Travis. And this . . .' here he indicated the other young man who had jet-black hair, intense brown eyes, and a lean, pock-marked face '. . . is Richie Pitt. They're part of our gang and they specialize in surveillance, which is what they're doing right now.'

'Hi,' Lenny said.

'Howya doin'?' Richie said.

'Pretty good,' Michael replied. 'What have you got there?'

'This,' Lenny said, patting one of the tripod-mounted instruments that looked like an exceptionally large video camera, 'is a Thorn EMI multi-role thermal imager, including infrared, or IR. It can scan outside walls, track body heat, and reveal the position of those inside any building it's aimed at, by day or by night. We can't tell one clone from another in there, one cyborg from another, but we can tell that they're moving about in there, on all three floors of the building.'

'And the other one?' Michael nodded to indicate what looked like complicated transmitters, or recording devices, set up on the other two tripods and also aimed at the White House. The object that most looked like a radio receiver was joined to the other by a complex combination of electric cables.

'An STG laser surveillance system,' Richie explained. 'We use it to record conversations taking place on the three floors of the White House and transmit them back here. The transmitter's set on a line-of-sight path to the building, to direct an invisible beam onto a chosen front window.' Seeing Michael's frown of confusion, he added: 'Try to imagine the window as the diaphragm of a microphone with oscillating sound waves. The invisible beam bounces off the window, back to this optical receiver. The receiver converts the modulated beam into audio signals that are filtered, amplified and then converted into clear conversation. That conversation can be monitored through headphones and simultaneously recorded on a tape recorder. Pretty good for something from the Old Age, eh?'

'Those are Old Age instruments?'

'Yeah,' Richie confirmed. 'The cyborgs stopped production of all surveillance equipment as soon as they took over, but these were purchased covertly from members of a disbanded British Army regiment, the SAS – the Special Air Service – just before the cyborgs closed down the international airlines. There's a pretty lucrative underground trade in these items going on nowadays. They're relatively primitive compared to cyborg technology, but they do okay by us.'

Michael glanced out of the damaged bell tower at the White House, that whitewashed sandstone structure reminiscent of a Georgian manor, with its columned porticos and balustrades and colonnaded wings to the east and the west. It was bathed in the eerie light of the flying saucer hovering soundlessly above it and it looked very beautiful.

'So what have you learnt from the conversations and movements in there?' Michael asked.

Ben sighed. 'Not too much so far, but enough to save quite a few of our own kind from being abducted. Like, when the cyborgs are planning some kind of big raid. We pick up on that and we can warn the potential victims beforehand.'

'I thought that most of the cyborgs communicated telepathically,' Michael said.

'*Most* of them,' Ben emphasized. 'Not all of them. They haven't all had their mouths and noses replaced with those awful metal prosthetics. Then, of course, the clones are as human as you and me, and they converse with the cyborgs that can talk. What we want, though, what we're *really* trying to find out, is what's actually going on in there – in the south side of the building and, more importantly, in the massive anti-nuclear war shelter that was built years ago under the building. We can see them disappearing down there, but we can't see what's happening down there. We're just hoping that if we watch them long enough, we'll pick something more important up. You've got to live in hope, haven't you?'

'Yes,' Michael agreed. 'Do you do stuff like this all over the capital?'

'Mainly the Pentagon,' Ben said. 'We can't watch it round the clock, but we send a team out to the Arlington National Cemetery at least once a week to survey it at night from the shelter of a group of trees located between Patton Drive and the Pentagon. You want to go over there?'

'Yes.'

'It's really dangerous 'cause there isn't any real protection and sooner or later a cyborg saucer or even a football might pick up the signals from our surveillance system.'

'I'd still like to see it.'

'Okay, let's go.'

'Thanks,' Michael said to Lenny and Richie.

'My pleasure,' Lenny said.

'No sweat,' Richie said.

They both waved languidly as Michael and Ben left the bell tower and made their way back down to the dark, dust-filled church. Leaving the church by its western side doors, they embarked on the long, dangerous walk to Arlington National Cemetery, which took them a sweaty, tension-filled fifty minutes, staying off the main drags. The worst part was the crossing of the Arlington Memorial Bridge, where they were completely exposed to the silvery-grey footballs spinning and gliding low enough overhead to detect their body movement. Luckily, the wide-open spaces above the waters of the Potomac also worked to their advantage in that they could see the footballs coming in from afar and simply freeze until they had moved on. This ensured that they would not be detected by the sensors of the footballs while, at the same time, it delayed their progress across the bridge. They were encouraged, however, by the knowledge that the Prowlers and SARGEs rarely went as far as Arlington and the bigger saucers were too high up to see them. Eventually, then, heaving a joint sigh of relief, they came off the bridge, crossed the Jefferson Davis Highway and made their way into the cemetery which, like so much else in the area, had been sadly neglected since the coming of the cyborgs and was now overgrown.

The eternal flame marking the grave of John F. Kennedy had been extinguished by the cyborgs and the cemetery was in semi-darkness, lit only by the pale moonlight, as they made their way past the endless rows of gleaming white headstones, tombs and statues marking the graves of more than 240,000 military personnel and their dependants. Many of the graves, Michael noticed, had been dug up and left exposed, and the bodies, as Ben now informed him, had been ruthlessly stolen away by the cyborgs. Seeing Ben's grim, outraged expression as he too glanced at the open graves, Michael understood what he must be feeling. He was relieved when they had left the graves behind and were crossing the hilly lawns that led to Patton Drive and, just beyond it, the trees that Ben had mentioned. Entering the shelter of those trees, they found the other two-man surveillance team, kneeling on the grass behind their tripod-mounted equipment. They both glanced up when they heard Ben and Michael approaching, then, upon recognizing the former, they simultaneously raised their thumbs in a welcoming gesture.

'How's it going?' Ben asked, kneeling behind the team and motioning for Michael to do the same.

'Okay,' the plump young man wearing a black beret said. Like the previous team, both members of the team were dressed in casual clothing of loose jackets and denims. That they did not look as outrageous as the Speed Freaks was almost certainly a deliberate attempt to keep from drawing attention to themselves. 'Nothing new to report.'

Ben introduced Michael to them, naming the plump one with the black beret as Manny Shaw and the second, who looked like a blond-haired athlete, as Rick Binder. Glancing beyond them and their equipment, Michael saw the massive pentagonal structure of the appropriately named Pentagon, which had once housed the offices of the highest authorities of the armed services, with 20,000 personnel, but was now used only by the cyborgs and their clones and brain-implanted slave workers.

'So why do we have it under surveillance?' Ben asked rhetorically, since no one had asked him that question.

'You tell me,' Michael said.

'Just look at it,' Ben said. 'It's the largest single-structure office building in the world. It contains six and a half million square feet. It has five concentric pentagons enclosing a five-acre central courtyard and over seventeen miles of corridors in those five pentagons. In fact, each of those pentagons is actually larger than the Capitol. There's nothing bigger *anywhere*.'

'And that's why you're watching it?'

'Right. I mean, whatever the cyborgs are doing in the White House, it's not nearly as big as *that*' – he nodded in the direction of the Pentagon – 'and it certainly doesn't hold as many people . . . or cyborgs . . . or clones . . . you name it.'

'And you watch them and collect data with those,' Michael said, nodding to indicate the equipment on the tripods.

'Right,' Manny Shaw said, removing his black beret to distractedly stroke what turned out to be a prematurely bald head. 'This,' he continued, tapping one instrument with his index finger, 'is an Old Age Davin Optical Modulux image-intensifier connected to a Nikon 35-mm SLR camera with interchangeable long-distance and binocular viewing lenses.'

'And this,' Rick Binder added, stroking the bigger tripod-mounted instrument as if it was the naked thigh of a woman, 'is a Hawkeye Systems Model HT10 thermal-imaging camera capable of detecting men and vehicles at long distances, either in low light or in total darkness, while producing high-quality video pictures with up to seven times magnification. While the thermal picture can normally be displayed automatically on an integral video monitor for direct viewing, we can't carry that equipment with us, so we display the pictures on a separate monitor for remote applications, such as recording for later visual analysis.'

'Combined,' Ben said, 'these instruments enable us to take photos of those entering or leaving the Pentagon, whether by day or by night, and ascertain if there's any pattern to their comings and goings.'

'So what have you learnt so far?' Michael asked him.

'We've learnt that while the cyborgs guard the White House even more rigorously than they guard this place, a hell of a lot more paddy wagons land and take off from here and a hell of a lot more Prowlers and SARGEs enter and leave here. It's our belief, therefore, that the Pentagon is the major holding tank for the thousands who have been abducted since the cyborgs took over. Our surveillance, which includes the keeping of meticulous records, is designed to find some kind of pattern concerning how often the paddy wagons, in particular, come and go and which direction they favour when they leave. So far, from what we've managed to ascertain, it seems that an awful lot of them fly between here and our major airports and air force bases, where, as we know, some of the mother ships are located. This in turn makes us believe that a lot of the abductees are transported initially to the Pentagon, brain-implanted there – or, God forbid, used in other ways; maybe surgically mutated into cyborgs – then transported in the same paddy wagons to one of the mother ships at, say, Langley Field or Andrews AFB and from there flown on to their final destination. That, we must assume, is a cyborg base located either in some desolate area right here on Earth, on the seabed or in a great lake. So that's why we watch the Pentagon as well as the White House.'

Staring at the enormous building and thinking of what Ben had just said – his comments, in particular, about brain-implants and surgical mutations – Michael thought of Wilson's earliest experiments in those fields and decided that Ben was on the right track.

'Why are you telling me this?' he asked.

'Because I think you hate the cyborgs as much as we do – either because of your girlfriend or for some other reason – and if that's the case, we may be able to help each other. If there's another reason, you don't have to tell me. My only concern is that you should have a strong enough motivation to hate the cyborgs as much as we do and that you should want to bring them down. I know you do. You help us, we help you.'

'How can I help you?'

'By passing on anything you find out about the cyborgs during your search. In return, if there's any way we can help you, you've only to ask.'

'It's a deal,' Michael said.

Ben nodded and grinned. 'You want to go back now?'

'I guess so,' Michael said. 'The effect of those drinks is starting to wear off and I'm getting real sleepy.'

'Me, too,' Ben said. He turned to Manny and Rick. 'Keep up the good work, you guys, and I'll see you anon.'

'You can bet on it,' Rick said.

Leaving the surveillance team to their work, Michael and Ben headed back the way they had come, making their way through the thousands of gleaming white tombstones, the shockingly desecrated graves, and eventually emerging from the cemetery to cross back over the Arlington Memorial Bridge. Once more, as they crossed the bridge, with a cold wind howling across from the Potomac, Michael felt fearfully exposed; nevertheless, though they saw large flying saucers high in the sky, they made it back across without incident.

It was when they were passing around the Lincoln Memorial that they ran into trouble.

Chapter Twenty-six

Gumshoe took a long time to recover from the shock of seeing his parents and, even more, to accept what it was that Wilson was planning to do to *him*. Wilson wanted to chop off his head and attach it to that two-headed chimera — Wilson's word — composed of a pig's body and the heads of Gumshoe's mother and father. Wilson wanted to make it a three-headed human-animal obscenity and he had his good reasons.

'We've taken the human body about as far as it can go,' he told Gumshoe as the latter was lying on his bed, recovering from the shock with the aid of sedation and, he assumed, other drugs that were designed to help him accept his forthcoming nightmarish fate. 'Soon we can dispense with experiments on it altogether in favour of total cloning. But unfortunately, even with the clones, we're presented with enormous psychological problems that must be resolved.'

Though Gumshoe had recovered from the shock to the extent that he was, at least, able to endure what he had seen without actually losing his mind, still he could barely grasp what Wilson was saying to him, nor the inhumanly calm and reasoned manner in which he was saying it. Wilson was describing a living nightmare as if it was perfectly natural.

'Your parents, for instance,' Wilson continued as if lecturing in a classroom. 'Previous to our experiment with them, we'd always used subjects who were total strangers to each other for our two-headed chimera experiments. But this didn't help at all when it came to preserving their sanity which, invariably, collapsed as soon as they fully comprehended what had happened to them. In other words, the heads were functioning physiologically and neurologically just as if they had still been attached to their natural bodies. But self-awareness, which we were proud to have retained, was what actually destroyed them – as I say, when they realized exactly what had happened to them. We therefore decided to see what effect the power of love and mutual dependence would have in a similar situation – if it would give the two grafted heads, those separate but artificially joined mentalities, the strength to *accept* what they'd become and, taking courage from one another, stay sane, if not for the rest of their lives at least for longer than they had been doing in our experiments until then. In fact, this proved to be true when it came to your parents. They had a bad time at first, screaming and sobbing and so forth, but gradually, taking courage from one another, they came to accept it. Only after a year or two, given the stress of unrelieved inactivity, did they gradually start rambling and then sink into dementia, rather like ordinary humans do in old age. Now, of course, they're in that cocoon of self-protection that we define, rightly or wrongly, as a state of insanity. So this is our problem.'

Gumshoe sat there on the bed, propped up against the pillows, keeping sane himself only through the strength of his revulsion and hatred, wanting to strangle Wilson, this cloned replica of the original, but having neither the strength nor the will to do so, being either drained by the shock of this whole experience or weakened by drugs.

'For our final test,' Wilson continued, still speaking flatly, academically, 'we wish to ascertain if the introduction of the head of a fully conscious offspring, in this instance yourself, able to communicate with them, will give them back the will to survive and help them to recover their sanity and become fully-functioning brains again. As you're their one and only child, we believe that their love for you, which should have prevailed even after their heads were severed from their original bodies, might do the trick. This is why we have brought you here.'

Gumshoe said nothing, being rendered literally speechless, merely listening to Wilson as if in a trance, though the strength of his revulsion and hatred kept his thoughts focused. The language of science, he realized, could be like the language of modern warfare, using words that obscured the true horror of what was being discussed. The word 'chimera' was a good example. It was a very pretty word, almost musical, with a bell-like quality – though, in fact, it was the name for a mythical, fabulous, fire-spouting monster with a lion's head, a serpent's tail and a goat's body. Clearly, Wilson had been thinking of this when he used the same romantic, musical word to describe his surgically mutated monstrosities: part human, part animal, part machine; two-headed, limbless, sometimes deaf, dumb and blind; created from appalling pain and mental anguish – and all in the name of scientific progress. Wilson, the original Wilson, had eschewed human emotions in favour of pure, ruthless logic and this was where it had finally led him. The march of science was creating a new Dark Age and Wilson was leading the way. He, the old Wilson in the new, could not see what was wrong with this.

As if sensing what Gumshoe was thinking, Wilson sighed. It was the nearest that he had come to a display of human emotion and hearing it actually startled Gumshoe. Being startled was, however, a heartening indication that he was recovering from his shock, despite the bitter anguish he still felt . . . the anguish *and* the rage. He would keep that and use it.

'You've disappointed me,' Wilson said. 'We have an extensive profile on you and from a perusal of it I'd assumed that you'd be stronger than you were: more ready to deal with the shock for which we had, in fact, so carefully prepared you.'

'*Prepared* me?' Gumshoe asked, speaking for the first time and shocked by the sound of his own voice, which seemed like that of a stranger.

'Your nightmares,' Wilson explained. 'Those nightmares about your parents that turned out to be true. They turned out to be true because they weren't nightmares in the first place. In fact, we took you to see your parents the first day you arrived here, but only when we had you in an interestingly drugged condition, fully aware of your surroundings, of what was happening to you, but distanced from it by a variety of sedatives. The idea was to let the knowledge of what had happened sink into you, into your subconscious, while you were emotionally neutralized by the drugs. We had hoped that by doing this, by preparing you, as it were, for the real thing, for the fully conscious experience, you would have suffered less when seeing your parents properly, unprotected by drugs. This, in turn, might have made it easier for you to accept your fate when, after the operation, you awoke as the third head of that chimera, attached for good to your mother and father: three heads on the neck of a pig. So, naturally, I was disappointed to see how badly you took it.'

'I'm sorry I disappointed you,' Gumshoe said, taking strength from sarcasm. 'I'll try not to do so when I wake up as no more than a head, surgically grafted onto the neck of a pig, mere inches from the severed heads of my mother and father, both rendered insane. I'm sure I can manage it.'

'Excellent,' Wilson said, offering a slight smile that did not reach the icy blue eyes in his handsome, unemotional face, under that head of healthy blond hair. 'I like a man of spirit. The sarcasm shows that you're stronger than I'd thought and might yet prove of value when you've only your parents' faces to stare at for the rest of your life. Your love for them and, hopefully, their prevailing love for you, might return them to sanity and thus give us more insight into the mental stress produced by our experiments.'

'Love? What would *you* know about love?'

'A lot,' Wilson replied. 'I have observed it for years, seeing it in all its infinite variety and foolish permutations. The self-sacrifice of love. The betrayal of love. The self-deceptions of love. The deceptions of love. The vanity and the vain hopes of love. The ephemeral nature of love . . . Love, my young friend, is no more than self-delusion, historically short-lived, a concept of modern Man who needs to believe that he is more than an animal with base appetites. This is, however, an illusion, since Man *is* an animal, barely out of his cave, impelled by the instinct to survive – an instinct that overrides all other considerations, including love – and with no more importance in the general scheme of things than a fossil at the bottom of the sea. Human beings, despite their pretensions, are no more than manure for the nourishment of the future and should be treated as such. They are, indeed, no more than the instruments of evolution, a bridge between the cave and the stars, between primitive man and Superman. You and I, despite our differences of opinion, are mere nuts or bolts, perhaps less, in that immense construction. As for love, which sustains the illusion of human superiority, it has no place in evolution's grand plan, though it may have its transitory uses. If, for instance, your parents' love for you succeeds in making them sane again, then love will indeed have served a purpose. I look forward to seeing the results of this, one way or the other.'

'You're mad,' Gumshoe said, having nothing to lose and needing to hear the sound of his own voice to confirm that this was actually happening – that it wasn't a bad dream.

'I'm afraid that's not true. I've simply accepted that Mankind is but a tool of evolution and that what raises Man above the beast is his mind, his ability to reason, not his emotions, which cloud clear thought and lead to self-destruction. It's the pure logic of science that has led us out of the cave and that same logic will take us to the stars before the sun dies.'

'And the human suffering caused by your so-called logic?'

'There has never been progress without human suffering and

Mankind has brought more suffering upon himself – with his wars, his religions, his pursuit of material wealth, his polluting of the Earth – than any suffering we can possibly inflict here. Indeed, the numbers who have suffered at my hands are infinitesimal compared to the numbers made to suffer even more at the hands of their fellow man. And here they do at least suffer for a cause – the continuity of the human race; the transformation of mortal man into Superman – which is more than can be said for the suffering their fellow man causes them. Think of this, Gumshoe, my sarcastic young friend, when you awaken as no more than a severed head and stare into your parents' eyes. Think of this and then try to communicate with your parents, easing their suffering by letting them recognize you and regain joy in seeing you. Seeing you, knowing that you're still alive, may make all their suffering worthwhile. Think of this and accept your lot.'

'Go fuck yourself,' Gumshoe said.

Wilson did not bat an eyelid, though he was silent for a considerable period of time, his blue gaze steady and dispassionate, devoid of malice, displaying only detached curiosity. He might have been studying an insect under a microscope . . . and that made him even more frightening.

'We will now prepare you psychologically for the operation,' he said. 'A process that will take about three days.'

'You're going to do a brain implant,' Gumshoe said, still terrified deep down but hoping that he would, at least, be insensible when they were doing their worst. The *true* worst, of course, would come after that, when he awoke as a severed, still fully conscious head. But right now he didn't want to think about that and, like a man on a gallows, was trying to convince himself that he was dreaming. There were times when putting your head in the sand was the only way out.

'Yes,' Wilson replied. 'First, we'll give you an injection that will put you to sleep for three days: in deep, painless coma. While you're in that condition we'll use electronic implants to prepare you mentally for the trauma of disembodiment and instant transplantation to the donor body – in this case, as you know, a pig already blessed with the grafted heads of both your mother and your father. Given this new treatment, we're hoping that when you regain consciousness, after the transplant, you'll learn to accept what you've become and eventually view it as natural.'

'And if you're wrong?'

Wilson shrugged. 'All scientific experiments are conducted in the knowledge of the possibility of failure,' he said. 'If we're wrong, it will be neither the first nor the last time and we'll simply try something else. Believe me, nothing will stop us.'

'And what happens to me and my parents if you're wrong?' Gumshoe asked.

'The blessing of termination,' Wilson said. 'And that *would* be a blessing, if you can't accept your new form of existence.'

'Jesus Christ!' Gumshoe exclaimed, trying to bury his rising dread in a display of disgust, though secretly feeling that he was sinking still deeper into this swamp of unending nightmare. 'So what if I don't cooperate?'

Wilson smiled. His smile was like ice and fire. 'How can you not?' he said. 'You have nowhere to go. This room is guarded at all times by cyborgs armed with stun guns and even if you managed to get out – let's say, by a miracle – you couldn't possibly escape from this establishment. You're trapped here absolutely, my young friend, and you'll just have to accept that hard fact. Now we can do it the easy way or the hard way, but either way we *will* do it. Have you any more questions?'

'No,' Gumshoe said.

'Good.' Wilson pushed his chair away from the bed and stood up, preparing to leave. 'In a few minutes,' he said, 'one of our male nurses will arrive to give you the preliminary injection. He will come here in the company of two cyborgs, so resistance is useless. I won't see you again for three days, by which time the operation, successful or otherwise, will have been completed. If it's successful – and if you manage to stay sane – you'll certainly still recognize me. The best of luck to you.'

'You cunt,' Gumshoe said.

'That's a sexist remark,' Wilson responded, 'and it certainly proves my point that human beings, with their wasteful emotions, are still essentially primitive. On that note I will leave you.'

'Yeah, fuck off,' Gumshoe said.

Wilson left, closing the room door firmly behind him.

When he saw that door closing, Gumshoe found himself gasping in and out as if desperately taking his last breaths. He understood then just how frightened he truly was, how close to the edge of panic: when his heart started racing and he broke out in a cold sweat, he thought that he was losing control completely and might actually crack up.

Fuck, he's right, he thought. *No point in resisting. Best to get it over and done with. Let the bastards inject you . . .*

For, in truth, he *wanted* oblivion, escape from his teeming thoughts, from the encroaching nightmare; to at least have that fleeting reprieve before the real horror came.

He took refuge again in the vain hope that he might be dreaming. But then, as he had known that it must, the door opened again and a male nurse entered the room. He was wearing a white smock, had short-cropped dark hair, and was wheeling a surgical trolley in front of him. After pushing the trolley up to the bed, he stared silently, steadily at Gumshoe.

Gumshoe looked up, first in choking dread, then in growing recognition . . . and finally in sheer disbelief.

The male nurse was Snake Eyes.

Chapter Twenty-seven

As Michael and Ben walked around the Lincoln Memorial, intending to avoid the White House area by going through Foggy Bottom, then east from Washington Circle, a Prowler came lumbering out of 23rd Street, its headlights boring through the moonlit darkness. It was the size and shape of a tank, a steel monolith on steel treads, and it had, Michael knew, sensors that enabled it to detect body heat and movement, decide for itself whether the observed person was a friend or foe, and act accordingly, ruthlessly. It also had powerful laser weapons that could stun, paralyse or kill.

Even worse, as the Prowler entered the road that circled the memorial it was followed by a SARGE, one of the four-wheeled, highly manoeuvrable scout telerobots that looked like giant metallic insects and housed thermal-imaging and zoom cameras. Although neither vehicle contained an actual crew, whether cyborg, clone or human, they were both capable, Michael recalled with a sinking heart, of dead-reckoning navigation and could calculate in advance where they needed to go, then head straight there.

'Shit!' Ben whispered, freezing where he stood.

Michael froze also.

They both stood there on the sidewalk, exposed in the moonlight, hoping that the Prowler and the SARGE would not detect them so long as they remained absolutely still. They were also hoping that the vehicles would take the opposite direction around the memorial, on the side of the Reflecting Pool, thus enabling them to continue unmolested to 23rd Street.

That hope died on the instant.

The Prowler and SARGE turned right, coming straight towards them, and their headlights, which were sweeping both sides of the road, instantly picked them out: two human beings who should not have been there after the curfew.

'Shit!' Ben said again, this time not bothering to whisper. *'Run for it!'* he bellowed.

They turned back the way they had come, running in the direction of the Arlington Memorial Bridge, but the ground patrol vehicles had already detected them with their thermal imagers and immediately started chasing them, with the SARGE, much smaller and quicker, racing ahead of the Prowler and rapidly catching up with them.

'Stay away from the bridge!' Ben shouted. 'There's no shelter there! Keep going around the memorial until we get to . . . Oh, shit! *We won't make it!'*

Michael had never known fear before, but he felt it for the first time when he glanced back over his shoulder and saw the SARGE racing up behind him like some giant, devouring insect, its headlights flashing like hideous alien eyes, its thermal imagers moving left to right, as the moonlit silvery snout of its laser weapon swung in his direction. He had felt safe all his life, protected by Freedom Bay in a benevolent, orderly society devoted to good, but now he was caught up in a world of danger where everybody felt threatened. He was being threatened this very moment, about to be fired upon by the SARGE's laser weapon, and he knew that if it struck him, even if it didn't kill him, he would be doomed to an unimaginable future. So he tried running even faster, glimpsing Ben to his left, also running, also panting, but the SARGE was coming within the firing range of its laser weapon and it was clear that neither of them would escape.

Suddenly, to Michael's horror, a small flying saucer, no more than three feet wide, spinning rapidly on its own axis and emitting an eerie, pulsating glowing – the kind of disc-shaped sensing device that he'd learnt was known as a 'football' – appeared out of nowhere, flying too fast, to be seen in actual flight, and stopped abruptly to hover right in front of him, preparing to fire at him.

He froze where he was.

'Oh, *fuck!*' Ben called out, also freezing on the spot and staring like a condemned man at the small, hovering saucer.

A laser beam filled with sparks suddenly shot out of the football to burn through the concrete at Michael's feet and make him jump back when it exploded into swirling dust and debris. He saw the laser weapon in the football adjusting itself, shifting slightly higher to focus upon him, even as the SARGE came up behind him to block his retreat. An eerie, pregnant silence descended.

I'm finished, Michael thought.

At that moment, however, from a good distance behind him, from beyond the Prowler and the SARGE, a cacophony of roaring engines shattered the tense silence, accompanied by the sound of squealing tyres. The SARGE, with a speed that defied belief, spun around on its four wheels to face the advance of a horde of Speed Freaks.

They had come roaring out of 23rd Street and now raced along the road that encircled the Memorial, advancing on the Prowler and the SARGE, then sweeping past on both sides of them even as the more ungainly Prowler was still making its turn and the SARGE was taking aim with its laser weapon. In souped-up sedans and Skylines with after-market tail fins, aerofoils, skirts, spoilers and stolen, constantly flashing police lights; in low-riders with deep bucket seats and graphic equalizers that emitted surreal waves of light; and, more dangerously, on garishly decorated Yamaha and Kawasaki motorcycles, they swept around the ground patrol vehicles and threw small, block-shaped objects at them as they raced on.

The small objects – obviously the home-made bombs often used by the Speed Freaks – exploded into boiling yellow-white flames and billowing black smoke that engulfed the Prowler and the SARGE, bringing them both to a standstill.

Even as a series of internal explosions further devastated those vehicles, the silvery-grey football that had been hovering directly in front of Michael whipped to the side and fired its laser weapon at a Speed Freak passing by on his motorcycle. The laser beam cut through him like a thin blade through butter and the top half of his body, gushing a fountain of blood, fell sideways to the road while the lower half, also gushing blood but still, instinctively, gripping the saddle with its thighs, was carried on for a few more metres before the motorcycle crashed to the road. It dragged the bloody torso behind it as it slid on for another ten metres or so, only stopping when it crashed into a street light and burst into flames.

The football ascended vertically, dropped down again and shot its laser beam here and there, the bolts of sparks bright in the darkness, as the other vehicles passed by directly below it with the Speed Freaks, all high on drugs and beer, whooping and hollering.

Ben started running again and Michael instantly followed him, just as wary of the Speed Freaks whom he knew could be dangerous, particularly when high on drugs, as he was of the football that now, clearly confused by the sheer numbers racing below it, its sensors overloaded from the heat and sound and vibration of the hot rods and motorcycles, from the whooping, hollering Speed Freaks, from the continuing explosions as more home-made bombs were thrown, went into a series of remark-ably fast aerial manoeuvres, flying this way and that, but clearly not knowing which way to turn. More Speed Freaks were struck by the football's rapidly firing laser weapon, their vehicles flying from under them, some crashing, others exploding, incinerating them as their friends swept on around the Memorial, heading away from the blazing, smoking Prowler and SARGE, turning back the way they had come, towards 23rd Street.

Michael kept running. He had lost sight of Ben by now. He hoped that Ben was okay, but he couldn't stop to look for him because the Speed Freaks were roaring all around him, coming dangerously close to him, and he feared that one might run him down.

He was running past the grounds of the Korean War Veterans' Memorial when the football, having lost most of the Speed Freaks, suddenly appeared right in front of him.

Michael didn't think to freeze – he was too frightened to think of that – and as he kept running, breathing harshly, his heart beating too fast, the football, now merely gliding, bobbing gently, gracefully, like a cork in turbulent water, moved down to head level to block his path.

He saw the moonlit silvery snout of the laser weapon and thought he was doomed.

Suddenly, a silver-tanked Yamaha 400 motorcycle roared up from behind him and skidded to a halt just in front of him.

'Get on!' a high-pitched voice squealed.

Without thinking twice, Michael jumped on the pillion seat and held on to the rider as the motorcycle took off again. The football, attracted by a passing hot rod, pursued it instead of the motorcycle, letting Michael and the rider who had rescued him travel on unmolested.

'Hang on tight!' the motorcyclist said to Michael as she – for indeed it was a female – raced around the Lincoln Memorial and then into the long, dark stretch of 23rd Street.

Clinging to her waist, surprised that this particular Speed Freak was a woman and abruptly becoming aware of the slimness of her waist, the softness of her rump, the swan-like neck clearly exposed by the short-cropped green-and-red-tinted hair (like a lot of the Speed Freaks, she was not wearing a helmet), he glanced to the right and saw the Department of State bathed in moonlight. No flying saucer floated above it, though beyond it, directly over the White House, a large flying saucer, about three hundred feet in diameter, was hovering as usual.

Though still feeling threatened, well aware of the dangers of travelling at this time of night, he nevertheless felt high on a kind of excitement he had never experienced in Freedom Bay. Looking ahead again, over the girl's right shoulder, he saw the lights of Washington DC as a magical tapestry.

Entering Washington Circle, the girl tilted the motorcycle dangerously low to the left, then straightened up again as she raced into New Hampshire Avenue, heading for Dupont Circle.

'Thanks!' Michael shouted. 'I thought I was finished back there! If you hadn't picked me up, that football would have zapped me and called in a paddy wagon.'

'Yeah, right,' the girl replied. 'Then – hey presto! You're gone for fuckin' good. No doubt about it, you were lucky we passed by.'

'Right,' Michael said.

'What the hell were you doing walking out there anyway? You must know that you don't walk out at night.'

'Me and my friend were just visiting someone,' Michael lied, 'and we thought it would be safer walking than using a motorcycle or car.'

'Oh, yeah? How come?'

'The Prowlers and SARGEs can detect the heat and noise of vehicles a lot easier than they can detect someone walking. If you're walking and you see them in time, you can freeze and they'll often pass you by, particularly if you're not in their line of sight. You can't do that in a car and certainly not on a motorcycle.'

'I never thought about that,' the girl said, 'but I guess there's some truth in it.'

'There sure is.' Michael glanced left and right as the motorcycle crossed Dupont Circle, cutting around the marble fountain which was no longer working, and turned into Massachusetts

Avenue. He saw the empty mansion homes of the former moneyed classes and then looked again to the front. The road ran as straight as an arrow, between more mansions and historic buildings, their bas-relief panels, pedimented dormers, balconies, Beaux-Arts ornamentation and wrought iron railings beautifully illuminated in moonlight, through Downtown and all the way to Union Station. 'Where are we going?'

'Chinatown,' the girl said. 'Avoiding the White House area. In the back way, by Mount Vernon Square. I mean, that's where *I* happen to live. What about you?'

'Same place,' Michael said. 'A converted house facing the old sports stadium.'

'Gee, we must be practically neighbours,' the girl said. 'I'm only a block away from the stadium. This is cool. Pretty neat. So what were you *really* doing out after curfew? Trying to find a little bit of real-time tail?'

'No,' Michael said, amused by her quaintly old-fashioned way of talking – the language taken straight out of 1950s teen movies – but also embarrassed by her blunt reference to sexual matters. 'I told you: we were just visiting a friend.'

'I'll bet!' the girl exclaimed sarcastically. Burning into Mount Vernon Square, she cut across the north end, then turned down into Chinatown and eventually stopped in front of a crumbling building located just off 7th Street, between a rough-looking bar and an old boarded-up Chinese restaurant. 'So!' she said chirpily. 'Home sweet home. Slide your ass off that seat, pal.'

Michael slid backwards off the motorcycle. After swinging her long leg over the saddle, the girl pushed the motorcycle towards him, saying, 'Can you hold it while I open the door? It wouldn't last two seconds out here. Thieves all over the place.'

'Yes, I know,' Michael said.

'You talk real fancy,' the girl said as she turned a key in the lock of the front door of the building. 'Sounds like you had a classy education.'

'Harvard,' Michael lied, knowing that that revered institution was still functioning, albeit not too successfully, for the lucky few who could still afford it.

'Oh, boy!' the girl said, opening the door and then stepping aside to let Michael push the motorcycle in. 'I'm in real fancy company. Put 'er in here.'

Michael pushed the motorcycle into the hallway of the building and noted instantly that it was in a bad state of disrepair, unlit and stale-smelling. The girl hurried along to the end of the hallway, then turned another key in the last door and opened it for him. 'In here,' she said, switching on the light. Michael pushed the motorcycle into a large, untidy room that had an adjoining bathroom. The middle of the room was dominated by a minitower composed of six Powermac 9500 hard drives, a PowerPC microprocessor, a couple of Radius Pressview colour monitors, scanners and colour printers, all surrounded by a clutter of digital cameras, remote controls, mouses, boxes of floppies, every imaginable kind of software, and a veritable junkshop of discarded modems and obsolete hardware. Apart from those, there was a twenty-three-inch TV, a video recorder, a badly torn sofa and two matching soft chairs. The carpet on the floor was covered with holes and the curtains were filthy.

As Michael propped the motorcycle up on the floor, just beside the main door, the girl closed the curtains and turned back to face him. Her face was painted as bizarrely as her short-cropped green-and-red hair and she was wearing a tight white T-shirt, a black leather jacket, matching hot-pants and leather boots. To Michael, who was used to the conservative clothing and modest make-up of Freedom Bay, this girl was a striking sight.

Grinning, she indicated the mass of computer equipment with a wave of her hand. 'Not mine,' she said. 'I hardly know how to work it. It belonged to this guy I was shacking up with, but he was zapped by a football and then taken away in a paddy wagon. Knowing that the cyborgs always place surveillance on the pads of people they've captured, hoping to pick up friends or relatives at a later date, I immediately moved myself and the electronic gear out of there and into this dump. I give weekly blow jobs to a friend in return for the privilege. He's still addicted to real-time. So what kind are you?'

'Pardon?' Michael said, not knowing what she meant, embarrassed to be alone with her, but still over-excited by his recent misadventure and feeling distinctly unreal. The girl, he noted, had wonderful legs and terrific breasts, which the tightness of her T-shirt showed off. Michael, celibate in Freedom Bay, felt his mind reeling here.

'Are you into real-time interaction or cybersex? Oh, my God, you're blushing!'

Which was certainly true, since Michael could feel his cheeks burning. 'Well, I . . .'

'You're a virgin!' the girl exclaimed, delighted and grinning. 'Certainly a virgin in real time. Boy, where do you *come* from?'

'Originally from New York,' Michael lied. 'But my parents fled from there a few years after the cyborgs took over. I was two or three years old at the time.'

'So where are they now?'

Michael shrugged.

'The cyborgs got 'em, right?'

'Right,' Michael lied. 'They'd gone to live in Virginia, way up in the mountains, well away, as they thought, from the cyborg patrols, and certainly they were safe there for a long time . . . until last year, in fact. Last August, they drove off to see some friends and never returned. As there were saucer sightings in the vicinity at the time, I can only assume, as did everyone else, that the cyborgs got them.'

'And that's why you're in Washington DC? Hoping to find your folks?'

'Yes,' Michael lied.

'You haven't a prayer,' the girl said, just as Ben had done a few weeks earlier. 'When they're gone, they're gone. Unless, of course, they're returned with brain implants, in which case they'd be inserted somewhere they weren't known previously, to be used as spies for the cyborgs. Either way, you won't find 'em in Washington. Best to call it a day, kid.'

'I'm not a kid. I'm as old as you are.'

'But you *seem* like a kid. So terribly well spoken and quick to blush and never had your hands on a real-time gal. Come on, kid, *relax!* Take a seat and let's recover from our ordeal with some high-grade speed. Life's for the living, right?'

'Right,' Michael said.

He sat on the sofa and the girl, instead of taking one of the chairs, sat close beside him, her soft, warm thigh pressed against his. Then the already tight white T-shirt tightened even more on her body as she wriggled out of the black leather jacket and twisted away from him to reach for something on the table just behind her. When she turned back to face him, she was holding a syrette in either hand.

'Hit the road, Jack,' she said, handing one of the syrettes to Michael. He looked at the short needle and asked her what it was. 'Amphetamine,' she replied. 'You ever had it?'

'No.'

'Try it. It'll make you feel relaxed. Take you places you've never been before. You frightened of needles?'

'No,' Michael said.

'Then prove it. Jab it in and let's cook.'

She jabbed the short needle into her own arm and Michael, not wanting her to guess just how inexperienced he was, a stranger in a strange land, not one of her kind, the kind born and bred here in the World, did the same, flinching only a little. He saw her taking a deep breath and so he did the same as he pulled the needle out. Then he felt the rush of the amphetamine coursing through him, making his heart palpitate, illuminating his mind and letting him see everything around him with a clarity he had only previously known in intense meditation.

This feeling, however, was not the same as the other. Quite

the opposite, in fact. The high of meditation was calm and transcendent, a spiritual journey to inner peace – but *this* high had a dangerous wildness that he wasn't used to yet found impossible to resist. He let the rush hit him, carry him downstream, to the rapids, and he felt the lambent heat of the girl's body, so close to him, permeate him and start to draw him in. She was smiling at him, amused by his innocence, and he wanted to prove her wrong.

'How do you feel?' she asked him.

'Incredible,' he replied.

'You're unbelievably handsome,' she said. 'Has any girl ever told you that?'

'No.'

'I don't believe you.'

'I'm pretty normal-looking, really.'

'You're golden-haired and handsome and well-spoken and as sweet as a schoolboy. You don't belong in Chinatown – no, not at all – and I don't think you're here to find your parents, but I'm asking no questions. Only one. What's your name?'

'Mike Johnson,' he said, by now using his fictitious surname as casually as if it were his own. 'And yours?'

'I'm a bad girl, Mike. I'm a *very* bad girl. I feel privileged to be with a guy like you, so I don't care who you really are. Let's get it on, Mike. I'm all alone and in need of company. I'm high on the speed and I'm being pretty saucy and I can tell by the look in your eyes that you're no longer shocked. That's the speed as well, Mike. It makes everything so much easier. You and me, we could do nice things together with no grief on either side. So why don't we do it, Mike?'

'What's your name?' Michael repeated, now feeling that he was in some kind of trance, divorced from himself, no longer in control, his every sense focused absolutely on this strange girl who still hadn't told him her name – not that it mattered. All that mattered was what he felt, these new feelings, sensuality, the penile erection that destroyed his self-control, unshackled him from the chains of a lifetime of discipline. And this girl who overwhelmed him with her singular presence: the long line of her legs, one crossed over the other; the half-moons of her hips, emphasized by the hot-pants; the fullness of her breasts and the slimness of her waist, both clearly revealed by the skintight belted T-shirt; her tongue touching her moist upper lip; her amused, mesmerizing gaze . . . Oh, yes, this was all that really mattered and it mattered a great deal. He wanted to drown in her.

'This is real time,' she said, still not answering his question. 'This isn't on-line time between two perns playing safe games in cyberspace. This is the real thing, Mike – the real thing in real time – and you can tell that by feeling my breast in the cup of your hand . . . Ah, yes, Mike, that's nice.'

He felt her breast beneath the T-shirt, opening his hand and pressing down. Her nipple hardened against the palm of his hand and it made him expand, becoming bigger, harder like her nipple, more ruthless than he had thought he could be, focused only on one thing . . . the heat of her body.

'God, you're beautiful,' he said before he could stop himself, the words tumbling out unbidden at the sight of her naked upper body when she pulled the T-shirt up over her head and let it fall to the floor. 'God, yes, you're lovely!'

'You think so?'

'Oh, yes!'

'Then keep looking, Mike.'

She took the rest of her clothes off, not moving from the sofa, staying close to him every second, and he looked and was captivated, seeing a completely naked woman for the first time and almost losing his mind. She wrapped herself around him, arms and legs like thongs of silk, and then he found himself as naked as she was and becoming part of her. He entered her with ease, probing her softness with his hardness, pushing into her or being drawn into her (he could not tell which) and was enraptured, surrendering himself for the first time, beyond his wildest imaginings. Draining down to his own centre, briefly losing his own identity, betraying his lifetime's work, forgetting Freedom Bay and his family and friends, John Wilson and the cyborgs, the footballs and paddy wagons, the great mission upon which he had so hopefully embarked, he gave in to his base lust, to the rapid rise towards climax, to the spasms that shook him leaf and bough and then left him spent. Once spent, he collapsed within himself and came back down to Earth.

He looked down, not at Earth, but at the green eyes of the girl whose body he was stretched out upon, but now separate from her, alone, back in his own shell. He felt this loss as a gain.

'What's your name?' he asked for the third time.

'Bonnie Packard,' she said.

Chapter Twenty-eight

———————◆◇◆◇◆———————

Science. The root of life, the tree of all knowledge. This belief is what I have lived by and abided by, and I stand by it still. Without science we are doomed, without mind we are nothing, and anything that stands in the way of progress must be viewed as negative.

We began in the dark seas, then progressed to the dark cave. But once there, we looked constantly to the sky and sensed, even before we could think clearly, that that was where our destiny lay. The evolution of Man is the shaping of that destiny, the building of that bridge between the cave and the stars, and the individual is mere mortar for the structure of the future, a cog in the wheel.

Think of this when you call me cruel, when you accuse me of being inhuman, when you charge me with crimes against humanity, when you suggest that I am playing God by perverting the natural order of things. For, indeed, what is natural? The only natural law is change. All things in nature are born only to die and in between birth and death they are in a state of constant change. Likewise with Mankind, whose history is one of change. Men have been changing since they first crawled from the primordial slime and the changes have often been painful. Pain, too, is natural.

From the cave to the stars, from Man to Superman: this is what the change is all about — and it cannot be stopped. The human being, as we know him, is neither natural nor constant; he is merely a primitive tool of evolution and will soon pass away. Not die off like the dinosaurs, not melt away like other species, but instead evolve, evolve into another species altogether, a creature of pure mind, no longer imprisoned in a physical, mortal body, nor governed by primitive emotions. When we learn to rid ourselves of those outmoded emotions, which so often are self-destructive, there is nothing we won't be able to do. Then Man becomes Superman.

I realized this as a child, when I first learnt that the sun would die, causing Earth to die as well, and I never once doubted it thereafter. I stood, a mere ten years of age, in a field of wheat, the sunlight of Iowa warming my face, and realized that Earth was but a transient stop for Mankind; that sooner or later this planet would come to an end, and that before that end came Mankind, if it was to hope to continue, must reach for the stars. That became my life's mission — to be a bridge to the stars — and I accepted that, in order to do it, I would have to place it before everything else in life — which was just what I did.

When other young men of my own age were dreaming their vain dreams, obsessed with money and girls, living their lives through dime novels and vaudeville shows, I was treating the world as a laboratory and all those in it, including my mother and father, as objects to be placed, as it were, under a microscope and minutely studied. Indeed, while other boys my own age were in thrall to their orgasms, I was academically examining the stain of semen in my hand, tasting it with my tongue, thinking in awe of the journey of two hundred million spermatozoa that would end either in life or in death. By the time I was fifteen, I was studying my own sperm under a microscope and reducing the mystery of life to its biological reality. There were no dreams, vain or otherwise, in this; there was only a goal to reach.

The death of my mother brought me closer to liberty, which was why it did not cause me pain; and later, when my father died, my only response was to feel free for the first time. Indeed, the Worcester Polytechnic Institute, then MIT, followed by Cornell College, Ithaca, New York, were the only kind of homes I ever wanted, and they nurtured me well. I was obsessed with knowledge, with learning all there was to know, particularly concerning aerodynamics and, eventually, space flight. The stupidity of my fellow students appalled me, their interests being so narrow, so devoid of true aspiration (expensive houses and good jobs and beautiful women as trophies) that I felt revulsion just listening to them talking and gradually drew away from them. I became a private person, an island, a bachelor living for and by himself — but one with a secret, grandiose mission. By the time I left university and went to work, I knew just what that mission was.

Thus I built the first airships, was betrayed by my own government, became anonymous for many years after that, working here and there, the length and breadth of the country, offering gold for bread, until eventually I assisted my one hero, Robert H. Goddard, with the production of his first liquid-fuelled rockets. Then, having assisted him only to learn from him, I left him as pragmatically as I had joined him. Yes, I went to find those who could deliver the finance and fanaticism that would be needed for what I wanted to do. They were, of course, the Nazis.

You have condemned me for this. But what else could I do? Betrayed by my own countrymen, rejected by my own government, my work stolen and then neglected, I had no choice but to use those who would use me because their plans were as grandiose. Insane, but grandiose, with one belief that I shared, albeit more rationally: the belief that they could create the Superman, a Super Race, and rule the world for the foreseeable future. They were perverted in their reasoning, obscene in their methods, but they gave me the only opportunity I was likely to get and for that reason alone I had to take it. Thus I ended up in Nazi Germany, using slave labour, conducting experiments that could not have been done elsewhere, and finally creating the first flying saucers and surgically mutated human beings. The road ahead, though a nightmare for some, had at last been opened.

I took that road and followed it, aware that I had no choice, accepting that the suffering of my surgically mutated human beings was as necessary as the suffering of animals under the blade of the vivisectionist whose work would eventually benefit humanity. Nature is cruel because it must have its way and that way does not count the human cost. Fire and flood, famine and disease are part of the natural order of the world and the cost in human suffering must be met. Likewise with my experiments, which involved no self-interest, no pursuit of personal gain, but were, instead, conducted with a scientific pragmatism that did not allow for sentimental revulsion or a conscience stirred by humanitarian concerns.

In nature's grand plan, in evolution's onward march, the human being, as he now stands, is only sacred in the sense that he is the bridge between the cave dweller and the Superman. When you understand this, when you see where we are heading, you will respect me instead of reviling me and your own transformation will then begin.

My time is fast approaching and impatience spurs me on, but I know that soon my second incarnation will lead into the third. I shall then escape my mortal shell and become a being of pure mind, merging with the All; and then, untrammelled by the physical, I will have no limitations in time or space. I shall, in effect, be the first of the Supermen and you, despite your fearful protestations, will eventually join me.

This began with my first dying, in your Freedom Bay in Antarctica, and continued with the rebirth that I ordained for myself, having made myself Lord of my own destiny. I grew a second time to manhood, being my own first son as well as father to myself: despite reported fears about the potential traumas of being cloned, I suffered no self-doubt, no emotional pain, and instead felt only the pride of that rare individual who knows himself to be absolutely unique and alive for a purpose. This made my new childhood blissful, radiant with inner light, and I grew up with the cyborgs and other man-machine mutations as naturally as any parentless child in a well-run nursery, carefully protected by those not his own parents and not harmed in the slightest.

My nursery was, of course, a place devoted to science, a self-contained laboratory in a mother ship used as a sea dome and, except for occasional flights to similar locations elsewhere, always safely anchored at the bottom of the ocean. There, in that enclosed world, I was raised by those that I had, in fact, created — the cyborgs — and prepared for my imminent transformation from Man into Superman.

Even during my brief absence, between my death and my rebirth, my work had been continued by the cyborgs and clones. Both types had been genetically gelded to remove their sex drive and all negative or potentially dangerous emotions such as rage, depression, personal ambition and abstract thought. Thus, they did only what I had programmed them to do before my death and part of that programming was the supervision of my rebirth and second upbringing.

Parallel to this was the advance of the machines, our biological computers, which had been maintaining, repairing and reprogramming themselves to the point where they could communicate with each other and, together, were gradually forming an immense neural network that was far more complex than the human brain. This was an evolutionary watershed, the first breaking of humankind's biological bonds, an artificial intelligence of awesome reasoning power, untrammelled by emotion, in thrall only to its own logic, and therefore a new biological species in its own right: an extension of, and improvement upon, Man.

This is the great intelligence, the superior being, with which we must fuse in order to evolve from Man into Superman, freed at last from the physical world and, thus, from the dying Earth, empowered at last to find our natural destiny among the stars.

No, not 'we' . . .

I.

Wilson.

And after me . . . You.

Yes. Your time will come also.

Chapter Twenty-nine

Sitting upright on the bed in that small room somewhere unknown, wearing the white smock that they must have put on him when they sedated him to help him recover from the shock of seeing the severed heads of his parents, Gumshoe could hardly believe his own eyes when he realized that the male nurse sent in by Wilson was his old Speed Freak buddy, Snake Eyes.

This was not the Snake Eyes that Gumshoe remembered. The old Snake Eyes, the one who had been zapped by a laser beam and abducted in a paddy wagon, had worn a T-shirt, short-sleeved black leather vest, bandanna and Doc Marten boots with steel-reinforced toes. His hair had been slicked up in a fancy pompadour with thick gel and his teeth had been bad. The new Snake Eyes had short-cropped hair and good teeth, which made him barely recognizable, though it was certainly him.

Shocked, disbelieving, Gumshoe was just about to call out Snake Eyes's name when the latter raised both hands in the air and began frantically gesturing, waving them this way and that while forming different shapes with his fingers. At first Gumshoe didn't know what the hell Snake Eyes was doing, then he realized that he was using the sign language of the deaf and dumb. Snake Eyes was neither, but like a lot of the Speed Freaks, including Gumshoe, he had learnt the sign language a few years back. Not too long ago, the deaf and the dumb, the blind, even the crippled, had been seen as objects of sport by the Speed Freaks who, themselves being viewed widely as the lowest of the low, needed to feel superior to some other species of human and chose the afflicted for that purpose. Baiting the afflicted had therefore been a regular item among the Speed Freaks until a former Speed Freak leader, long since zapped and taken away by the cyborgs, had realized that sign language was a good way to communicate in places where cyborg surveillance might be operating or when there was a need to communicate within range of a hovering football whose sensors could pick up any sound. Thus, the deaf and dumb had become people to respect and learning their language had become a positive passion with the Speed Freaks. Now Snake Eyes was using that sign language and Gumshoe could not only read it but could respond in kind.

'Don't say a word,' Snake Eyes had begun. 'Every room in this place is bugged. Just use your hands.'

'I can't believe it's you,' Gumshoe responded, using his hands instead of his voice.

'It's me. And I'm normal.'

'How come you're still normal?'

'I was brought in with a batch of abductees who the cyborgs intended to use as robotized workers. The guy placed in charge of us – a normal human being, but obviously robotized himself – told us in advance that we'd be robotized. Aided in our adjustment, as he put it – with a single injection that would affect certain areas of the brain while causing no pain. After that, he informed us, we'd feel no fear about being here, have no regrets or concerns. We'd be one of them, he informed us, as content as he was.'

'No electronic brain implants?' Gumshoe asked without speaking.

'No. That system, which took a lot of time and often caused trauma, is now obsolete. Now it's just an injection. So when they brought us here, they ordered us to strip off and take a shower, then put on white smocks in preparation for the injection. I was scared out of my mind. I was also still high on speed. Being high, I was convinced that I'd rather die than experience the gradual loss of my mind when the serum they injected into me took hold. I had my own injections with me – enough methamphetamine to overdose on – and being already high, almost out of my mind anyway, I decided to shoot it all up before my turn came to strip off and dump my clothes and possessions into the disposal bin that they'd told us to use. So I placed myself in a position where the walking dead couldn't see me, in the middle of the group of stripping abductees, and quickly took my syrettes out of my jacket pocket, injected my legs unseen, using up every last syrette, then put the empty syrettes back in my jacket and stripped off like the others. The rush of the speed hit me like a sledgehammer just as I was stretched out on a bed, being given my mind-destroying injection by one of the walking dead. But instead of overdosing on the speed, instead of dying as I'd expected, I found that the speed and the brain-altering drug neutralized each other, not only saving me from death but leaving me perfectly normal. God bless the methamphetamine.'

'Didn't your empty syrettes make them suspicious?'

'They didn't find the empty syrettes. They made us throw all of our clothes and our possessions into that disposal bin and it was like a big washing machine filled with some shit that destroyed everything that went into it. My clothes and the empty syrettes went into it and were completely destroyed. No shred of evidence of my misdemeanour left.'

'Beautiful,' Gumshoe said, still using sign language.

'It sure was,' Snake Eyes signalled.

'They didn't see you were still normal?'

'No. I just observed how the walking dead behaved – superficially normal, but cold as ice and totally obedient. Then I watched as they tested the other injected abductees simply by asking them certain questions. I took note of how the abductees responded and then responded the same way when it was my turn. Those bastards, the walking dead, believed that their drug had worked: I've been fooling them ever since by simply keeping my face expressionless, speaking in a toneless voice, and doing exactly what I'm told.'

'That doesn't sound easy.'

'You're wrong. It's dead easy. It's easy because the cyborgs assume that guys like us — young, unemployed motorcyclists and druggies — can't be too bright, so they generally give their brainwashed Speed Freaks the simplest tasks. Being a supposedly brainwashed Speed Freak, *my* simple task is to wheel this surgical trolley from room to room and inject new abductees, as instructed, with one of a small variety of serums. Some will leave you completely paralysed while still fully conscious; some will put you to sleep for days on end, the length of time depending upon the dosage; and some will actually kill you. The ones killed are used for body parts for new cyborgs and other hybrid man-machine creatures.'

Recalling what he had seen in the surgical laboratories since coming here, particularly his unfortunate parents, Gumshoe found himself shuddering uncontrollably.

'You okay?' Snake Eyes signalled.

'Yes,' Gumshoe replied, still using his hands, forcing the nightmare image of his parents to the back of his mind. 'So they've sent you here to inject me.'

'Yes.'

'And you've no choice but to do it.'

'That's correct, pal, but in this case it won't be for their benefit.'

'What does that mean?'

'We're getting out of here. I've been planning it for days, but I had to work up the nerve to do it and then, seeing you, I got my nerve back.'

'We can't get out of here. It's impossible. There's no way to do it. Hell, we don't even know where we are.'

'I've a pretty good idea,' Snake Eyes signalled. 'Did you have a good look around you when they brought you in?'

'Yes.'

'Did you see that immense workshop filled with Doctor Frankenstein creations?'

'Yes.'

'A great cavernous area with five sides?'

'Yes.'

'So what immense building used by the cyborgs has five sides?' Snake Eyes asked, still using his hands instead of speaking.

'The Pentagon!'

'Correct. So almost certainly, unless the cyborgs have an identical building on the dark side of the Moon, our location is the immense underground bunker of the Pentagon – the one built secretly way back in the Old Age to protect the top brass in the event of a nuclear war. I mean, there's a similar underground bunker in the White House and, as we all know by now, the cyborgs are using it. So my bet is that this is the Pentagon and if we manage to make our escape we'll find ourselves back in a certain American city right here on Earth.'

'There's no way out,' Gumshoe signalled. 'The whole place is teeming with cyborgs and clones who'd turn us in if they saw us trying to leave. Besides, you can bet that every exit is locked and heavily guarded.'

'So we don't try to get out,' Snake Eyes signalled. 'We simply put ourselves in a position where they take us out with other abductees being released back into the streets as injected, brainwashed spies for the cyborgs.'

Gumshoe felt a rush of hope almost as strong as a rush of speed, but he couldn't quite accept that it was possible. Also, he was shamefully scared. 'How do we do that?' he asked, still using sign language. 'It doesn't seem possible.'

Snake Eyes grimaced and shook his head from side to side, as if saying, 'Oh, ye of little faith.' Then he started using hand signals again. 'The human abductees are processed in different ways. Some are killed and used for body parts or as surrogate mothers for test-tube babies; some are lightly brainwashed and kept here as slave workers, like me; and some are heavily brainwashed – in fact, robotized completely, though again with injections, not with electronic brain implants – and then sent back into the World to act as spies for the cyborgs or to work for them in important positions. Those in this third group are never sent back to where they came from – to where they'd be known as former abductees, therefore instantly suspect in the eyes of family and friends. No, instead they're inserted in other cities where, with false identification papers and jobs arranged by the cyborgs, they can sink into the local community and quietly do what the cyborgs demand of them. You and me, we're going out with one of those groups.'

Gumshoe's fear was subsiding as his hope and confidence returned, but still he could not quite accept that what Snake Eyes was telling him was possible. On the other hand, the very thought that he might only be in the basement of the Pentagon, still right here in Washington DC, made the real world seem that much closer and, hopefully, more accessible. He took his courage from that thought.

'So how do we do it?' he asked, blessing the day that he'd decided to learn sign language from a deaf and dumb guy who'd been invited to join the Speed Freaks after they realised how valuable that silent form of communication could be to them. Yes, indeed, it was valuable – and never more so than right now.

'There's a batch of deep-brainwashed abductees going out today,' Snake Eyes signalled back. 'Eight in all. They've all had their new identities drilled into them while they were in a deep, drug-induced coma. The dosage of the drug, which I administered personally, was adjusted to ensure that each individual would recover consciousness at a specified time – the paddy wagon's ETA at the destination.'

'Pardon?'

'Estimated time of arrival at the destination,' Snake Eyes explained. 'The abductees will awake just as the flying saucer lands – a big transport saucer, three hundred feet wide. The abductees are all dressed in normal clothing – suits, jackets, or whatever, depending on their age and what they're supposed to be in real life. They'll be inserted with a properly registered car at an LZ—'

'Pardon?'

'Landing zone. Each abductee will be inserted at a landing zone somewhere close to the city designated for him and he'll drive from there, just like a normal citizen, to an apartment already fixed up for him. You and me are going to replace two of those abductees and fly out of here with their identities. I think it will work.'

'Maybe.' Gumshoe was feeling exhilarated, but he still had his doubts. 'How do we proceed?'

'Like you, the chosen abductees are all in individual rooms, fully dressed but unconscious on their beds. As I'm a recognized male nurse, supposedly brainwashed, I can wheel you to one of those rooms without being suspected of anything. So I'm going to wheel you to the room of one of the unconscious abductees and we'll strip him and roll him under the bed, then you can put on his clothes and lie there in his place. The walking dead who wheel the departing abductees from their rooms to the transport ship haven't seen them before, so they don't know what the individual they're collecting is supposed to look like; they'll only know him from the name tag on his coat or jacket. Because I can't take any chances on you making a mistake, I'm going to give you an injection that will put you to sleep, just like all the others, and let you awaken at the same time as the ETA at your destination. We won't know the destination, but the ETAs are marked on the individual name tags to allow me, as the male nurse, to adjust the dosage for the length of sleep required. So, lying there unconscious, wearing another abductee's clothes and name tag, you'll be collected by a walking-dead male nurse and wheeled out into the holding bay of the transport ship. You'll be unconscious throughout the flight, so you can't make any mistakes that might give you away, and you'll only have to remember to keep control of your tongue when the saucer lands at your chosen LZ and you awake and are taken to your car by a cyborg, clone or walking-dead crew member. Once in that car, you can let out a scream of joy and take off for home.'

'What about you?' Gumshoe asked.

'Same thing. The only difference being that I'll be injecting myself – and I'm an expert at that. I simply go to another room, strip the abductee in there, roll him under the bed, put on his clothes, then stretch out on the bed and inject myself. The male nurse who comes to collect me will find me unconscious and assume, from the name tag on my coat or jacket, that I'm the one he was sent to collect. He'll wheel me into the transport ship with all the others and, like them, I won't regain consciousness until I've reached my particular LZ. Then, just like you, I'll drive away and, instead of going to the pad chosen for the guy I'm supposed to be, in whatever city was chosen for him, I'll just head for home. You and me will meet up in Chinatown when we get back to Washington. Are you willing to try it?'

'Yes,' Gumshoe signalled.

'Okay,' Snake Eyes replied with his hand signals. 'Don't move. I'll be back in a second.' He opened the room door, disappeared into the corridor and returned a few seconds later, pushing a wheeled stretcher in front of him. After positioning the stretcher alongside the bed, he flipped the white sheet back. 'Roll onto this,' he indicated. When Gumshoe had done so, Snake Eyes threw the sheet over him leaving his head uncovered and said with hand signals, 'Keep your eyes closed and don't open them until I tell you to do so. I'll do that by taking hold of the collar of your smock and shaking you roughly. Take that as a sign that you can open your eyes again, but still don't make the mistake of talking. Even there, in that other room, we can only use sign language. Until then, keep your eyes closed and your mouth shut. I only want them to see me wheeling an unconscious man along the corridors, so don't fuck up on me.'

'I won't,' Gumshoe signalled.

He put his head back on the pillow, closed his eyes and felt himself being wheeled out of the room. Snake Eyes stopped briefly in order to close the door, then he pushed the stretcher forward again, obviously heading along a straight corridor. Lying there with his eyes closed, Gumshoe listened to the soft drumming of the stretcher's wheels on the floor and heard footsteps approaching, passing by and moving away as people moved in both directions along the corridor. Though he couldn't see them, he shuddered to think of them, the 'walking dead' in Snake Eyes's words, the clones and the brain-altered, eyes flat, faces closed, all human feeling killed off in them. Then he recalled with a vivid intensity his mother and father in that immense surgical laboratory, their severed heads on that thick pig's neck, their eyes wide and wild with deep trauma. Hideous though that image was, filling him up with revulsion and grief, he also felt the searing pain of loss at the knowledge that he was trying to escape while leaving his parents to their dreadful fate. He vowed silently, then, with all the passion at his command, to return some day and set them both free.

He would do that in the only way now possible: by switching off the machine that kept them alive. He vowed to make that day soon.

The wheeled stretcher stopped moving. Then Gumshoe heard doors opening, sliding open, and he was pushed forward again, this time only about a metre, into what he sensed was an enclosed space. This time, when the doors closed, they did so behind him. Almost instantly, he heard a soft humming noise and felt a sinking sensation.

I'm in an elevator, he thought. *Going down. If this is the underground nuclear shelter of the Pentagon, it must have levels even deeper than the one I was on.*

The elevator stopped descending. Gumshoe heard the doors opening. The wheeled stretcher was pushed forward again, turning left into another straight corridor, then, after advancing for about fifteen metres, it came to a halt. Gumshoe heard a door opening, this one obviously on hinges, then he was pushed forward a couple of metres and heard the door closing, this time just behind him. The sheet was flipped off his body, then someone's fingers gripped the collar of his smock and shook him violently.

Gumshoe opened his eyes to see Snake Eyes staring down at him, his index finger to his lips, indicating that he, Gumshoe, should not speak. Gumshoe nodded, then glanced about him. He was in a different room, another single bedroom, and a dark-haired young man, just slightly over Gumshoe's age, was stretched out on top of the bed, fully clothed, in an open-necked shirt, windcheater jacket, blue denims and leather boots. He was clearly unconscious and there was, as Snake Eyes had said there would be, a name tag pinned to the breast of his jacket.

Snake Eyes's hands and fingers began to wave again as he used sign language. 'Okay. Get off the stretcher and help me undress this poor bastard.'

Gumshoe did as he was instructed, rolling off the stretcher and then helping Snake Eyes to undress the unconscious man. This wasn't as easy as Gumshoe had thought it would be – it was like manhandling a dead man – but eventually all the clothes had been removed and the man was stark naked. Snake Eyes held the man's wrists, Gumshoe held him by the ankles, and together they lifted him off the bed, lowered him to the floor, then rolled him out of sight under the bed.

When they straightened up, Snake Eyes nodded towards the man's clothes and Gumshoe proceeded to put them on. Just before donning the windcheater jacket, which he had left to the last, he checked the name tag and saw the name 'Danny Greenfeld'. After letting that name sink into his head, to ensure that it came naturally to his tongue when he woke up at the LZ, he went through the pockets of the jacket to check that the billfold and identification papers were all there. They were.

Satisfied, he turned back to Snake Eyes who was already holding up a syrette and testing it by releasing a dribble of serum.

Satisfied that it was working, he nodded towards the bed, indicating that Gumshoe should stretch out, fully clothed, upon it. When Gumshoe had complied, Snake Eyes tapped his right wrist with his forefinger, indicating that he should roll up the sleeves of his jacket and shirt. Gumshoe did so. Snake Eyes pinched Gumshoe's skin between his thumb and index finger, then expertly jabbed the needle in, just as he had so often done when taking speed. It did not hurt, though Gumshoe felt the warm rush of the serum as it entered his bloodstream. Snake Eyes put the syrette down on the trolley beside the bed and indicated that Gumshoe should roll the sleeves of his shirt and jacket back down. Gumshoe did so. His eyes were becoming heavy.

'Can you manage on your own?' Gumshoe managed to ask, still using sign language.

'Yes,' Snake Eyes said, also using sign language. 'Now close your eyes and let yourself go to sleep. With luck, we'll meet up back in Washington. I have to go now.'

'Thanks,' Gumshoe signalled.

Snake Eyes nodded and left the room, closing the door behind him as Gumshoe closed his eyes and surrendered to sleep.

His sleep was deep and dreamless. Gumshoe couldn't remember a thing about it. He had closed his eyes just as Snake Eyes had left the room and he opened them again to find that he was somewhere else altogether and that another white-smocked man, not Snake Eyes, was staring down at him. This man had a flat gaze and pale, inexpressive features.

A dazzling white light was blazing above the man's head, straight into Gumshoe's face, but he saw that the wall beyond him was all white and curved, indicating that they were now in a flying saucer. Hearing an almost imperceptible bass humming sound all around him, he knew that the flying saucer was still in flight, though almost certainly making a slow, vertical descent and about to land.

'Sit up,' the man said.

Gumshoe sat upright and noted that he was still wearing the

casual clothes with the name tag saying 'Danny Greenfeld'. Glancing about him, he saw that he was in what appeared to be an exceptionally clean garage area, but one with a high, dome-shaped ceiling and, as he had noticed before, a long, curving wall of pure white steel. This area was shaped like a slice of cake and was filled with automobiles.

Gumshoe turned back to the white-smocked man, met his flat gaze, and remembered to keep his face expressionless.

'Take off the name tag,' the man said tonelessly.

Gumshoe removed the tag and handed it to the man, who placed it in his side pocket, then gave him four keys on a plain silver ring. 'That's your car over there,' the man said, pointing to a red Honda Accord. 'You'll find the papers for it in the glove compartment, along with your new address in Albuquerque. The small key is for the car and the large one's for your apartment. The other two are spares. You'll find everything else you need, including your orders, in the desk drawer in the living room of the apartment. Now, please sit in the car and drive off as soon as the doors open. You have two minutes to get well away before we ascend again. Head due north and follow the first road sign indicating Albuquerque. We'll be in touch when we need you. Any questions?'

'No.'

'Good. Now, please go and wait in the car,' the man repeated.

Gumshoe nodded, swung his legs off the bed and walked to the red Honda Accord as the bass humming noise tapered off into silence, indicating that the flying saucer had landed. He noticed that the only people in this area were himself and the man in the white smock, though some cyborgs were crossing a catwalk just below the high, dome-shaped ceiling. Opening the car door, he slipped into the driver's seat, closed the door again, strapped himself in, then put the key in the ignition and sat back to wait. Glancing over his shoulder, he saw that the man in the white smock was watching him.

Suddenly afraid, Gumshoe looked to the front again as

another sound broke the silence, a higher-pitched humming sound, and a panel in the white wall moved outwards and down, its top end tilting forward, giving him a rapidly expanding view of a vast desert plain and a night sky covered in brilliant stars, the whole view illuminated by bright moonlight. The top end of the panel fell slowly, smoothly, as low as it could go, then stopped moving and was silent, forming a ramp wide enough for the car.

Instantly, though carefully, as if simply obeying instructions, indicating no sense of urgency, Gumshoe turned the key in the ignition and drove the automobile down the ramp. Bouncing onto the dusty desert plain, he accelerated smoothly and drove away from the ramp which was, he had noticed, already pointing in a northerly direction. Fighting to contain the exhilaration that was coursing through him and could cause him to make a mistake, he kept driving, bouncing and shuddering across the potholes and fissures of the dusty plain, still heading north as instructed, towards a region of high plateaux and mountains lit brightly by stars, streaked with moonlight.

When he was less than a mile away from the flying saucer he heard a bass humming sound, felt the ground vibrating even through the moving car, and glanced in his rear-view mirror. He saw the flying saucer, a 300-foot-wide transport, silvery-white and dome-shaped, lights flashing on and off repeatedly around its immense rim, first forming a kaleidoscope, then an eerie, pulsating glow, a floating cathedral for the New Age, rising majestically to the heavens. He braked to a halt and watched it ascending higher, rising magically, vertically, until it was no more than the size of a dime. It stopped briefly, just hovering, suspended in space, then shot off to the east like a shooting star and abruptly blinked out.

When Gumshoe saw that the flying saucer had gone, he too turned east, ignoring the instructions given to him by the white-smocked man in the flying saucer. Instead, he began his long journey across New Mexico, across the deserts and the mountains, through the heat and the dust, determined to go all the way to Oklahoma, to Arkansas and then Kentucky, through West Virginia and back to Washington DC.

Exhilarated beyond measure, practically ecstatic, he was on the move, travelling. A free man again.

Chapter Thirty

———◦◦◦◦———

The Bird was in deep pain. The Bird had found a nest but felt constantly endangered, not only by outside predators in the shape of the cyborgs but also by his own wayward emotions. The bird was Michael, sending his e-mails to Freedom Bay via a false Cincinnati address, which was actually a home page in Freedom Bay, to be read only by Dr Lee Brandenberg whom he revered and whom he hated cheating. This was, indeed, what he was doing, not by telling lies, not *exactly*, but by withholding information about his precise relationship with Bonnie Packard, from whom he was receiving valuable information.

Michael and Bonnie were having an affair which, being Michael's first sexual experience, was filling him with guilt, not only because Bonnie was an Outsider – not from Freedom Bay – but also because she was his weak point, his one area of potential failure: he knew that she could colour his judgement and destroy his objectivity. She was helpful to what he was doing, knowing everything that was happening, streetwise to the last degree. But the very fact that he wanted her and, worse, thought that he might be in love with her, was exactly what made him feel defenceless and, when communicating with Freedom Bay, not truly honest.

Michael, as the Bird, sent e-mails to Dr Lee Brandenberg and always, unfailingly, received polite, if suspiciously correct, possibly concerned, replies . . .

From: <birdnest@mkim.com>
the bird has left its nest and flown high and wide only to find
that everything is close to its feathery wingtips.
in white houses and rectilineal plane figures of five sides and
five angles the hybrids multiply and do what still cannot be
known.
it will be known.
the bird has found a friend and is being guided to the right
path which will lead eventually to what the hybrids do.
the bird has the confidence of expectation and heads into the
light.
that light will surely reveal all.

From: <bayfree@leebrand.com>
the bird flies well but may trust too much to instinct.
it is best to be wary of friends who do not fly
towards the light from the same nest.
by all means seek the light but at the same time let
us know more of the friend.
friends are easy to find but often hard to lose.
think of this as you fly.

Michael was more than willing to convey information about the White House and the Pentagon, about Wilson and the cyborgs and the clones, and about the lack of real knowledge of what they were up to. But he found it very difficult to talk honestly about his 'friend' who was, of course, Bonnie Packard.

Since the first morning with her, after she had rescued him from the cyborg patrol, he had become addicted to her, seduced not only by new sexual experience but by her remarkable personality — at once tough and tender, streetwise and childlike, crude yet at times surprisingly sensitive — so unlike the more conservative personalities that he had known in Freedom Bay. In Freedom Bay, young girls didn't talk like Bonnie, didn't dress like her, didn't practise free love and shoot up speed and drink beer and smoke as if there was no tomorrow. Bonnie did so, she had explained, because for her and her kind there might really be no tomorrow: each day could be their last, since they were prey to the cyborgs and could never forget it. So, Bonnie had explained, they all lived for the moment, not concerned for the future, and their behaviour was an act of defiance against a world that had clearly turned against them – the world of the cyborgs.

'Where do *you* come from?' Bonnie asked him one day when they were lying side by side, naked, on his bed, having just made love, as they did often. 'I mean, where do you *really* come from? You live here in Chinatown, but you're not like us at all – you're not lowlife – so where were you really brought up? And what are you doing here?'

'I told you. I was born in New York but raised mainly in Virginia. The people there are pretty damned conservative and largely ignored by the cyborgs.'

'There's more to it than that,' Bonnie said. 'I'm pretty damned sure of that. But we all have our secrets in Chinatown, so I guess you can keep yours.'

In fact, Michael wanted very much to tell her about Freedom Bay, about where he really came from and why he was here. But he knew that to do so could be dangerous, particularly if she was picked up by the cyborgs, who almost certainly had infallible methods of making people talk. He did, on the other hand, pump her constantly for information about the cyborg patrols (the areas they covered most and what routines they stuck to), about the people she knew (who hated the cyborgs most and who might be working for them) and about the general talk in the streets, which could reveal a surprising amount about cyborg activities. He felt guilty doing this, aware that he was using her or, at least, not levelling with her, but he had to use everything he could get in order to complete his picture of the cyborg world and send the details back to Lee Brandenberg in Freedom Bay.

From: <birdnest@mkim.com>
the bird pursues hybrids and sees them in great numbers.
they enter and leave by east and west while protecting north and south with hovering eagles.
where five sides and five angles form a whole the same pattern applies.
here where the chinese are no more there are those who would attempt to breach walls if they were given the leadership.
in order to lead one must be known and the bird remains unknown.
for the bird to take wing he must have brothers and friends even though they do not come from the same nest.
the friend is one who could lead me to those who might become the brothers who breach walls, even though they do not come from the same nest.
let the bird seek its brothers.

From: <bayfree@leebrand.com>
i repeat that friends are easy to find but often hard to lose.
think of this as you fly.
fly however and seek out the friends who might become brothers.
do not attempt to breach walls while in flight as your wings may get broken.
let the bird's song be heard.

While continuing to collect intelligence on the movements of the cyborgs in and out of the White House and the Pentagon, both guarded constantly by hovering mother ships, and e-mailing that intelligence to Lee Brandenberg in Freedom Bay, Michael was moving closer to the point where he would have to, albeit with extreme caution, reveal himself. He needed, with growing urgency, to recruit friends who could help him find out what was going on inside those buildings. He was by now convinced that there was only one way that this could be done.

While he was attempting every day to penetrate the White House with his parapsychological skills, his most intense concentration had so far only produced shadowy images of the cyborgs moving here and there about the front of the building. This, however, was enough to reveal that the cyborgs, clones and walking dead were constantly descending to and emerging from the basement of the building.

The basement was, Michael knew, a vast underground complex that had originally been built during the Cold War as a presidential shelter in the event of a nuclear attack by the Soviet Union, later Russia. But the subterranean complex had been extended since then and now stretched all the way to the Pentagon, linked to that building's similar underground redoubt by a four-lane tunnel running under the Potomac River.

Blocked in his parapsychological explorations by the greater psychic powers of the cyborgs, Michael was now sure that the only way he would find out what was going on inside those buildings would be to enter them physically. He had no idea, just yet, of how he would do it – but he certainly knew that he could not do it alone. He would have to start recruiting, and he had been given permission to do just that in Dr Lee Brandenberg's last e-mail. Encouraged, but still fearful of the enormity of what he was about to undertake, he e-mailed back for encouragement.

From: <birdnest@mkim.com>
birds occasionally lose their sense of direction and let themselves be buffeted by the wind which may not be a good thing. given this, should the bird continue to fly.

From: <bayfree@leebrand.com>
the bird should continue to fly.
be bold and take wing.

With Brandenberg's permission to reveal his identity to those he thought he could trust and, having done so, to recruit them to his cause, which was to penetrate the White House, and given what he had learned about Ben Wilkerson's surveillance teams, Michael decided to approach the latter for assistance. Like him, Ben had been rescued from the cyborg patrols that night by one of the Speed Freak gang that had included Bonnie. Now he was back running the rooming house as usual. Michael decided to take him out for a drink and then play it by ear. But first he double-checked with Bonnie who, acquainted with just about everyone in Chinatown, knew Ben well.

'I need to talk to Ben about something that's really important,' Michael said. 'It has to be strictly confidential. Do you think I can trust him?'

'Jesus,' Bonnie responded from where she was stretched out on the sofa in Michael's room. 'This sounds really heavy. What the hell are you up to?'

'It's personal,' Michael said.

'Gee, thanks a lot!'

'So, is he trustworthy?'

'In what way?'

'If I tell him something in confidence, will he keep his mouth shut?'

'Tell him something about what? I mean, just how important is it, that you can't even tell me? You think I'm some kind of blabbermouth, or what?'

'I'm sorry, Bonnie. I don't mean to insult you, but I simply can't tell you what it's about. Please don't take offence.'

'You're such a gentleman,' Bonnie said. 'Just don't tell me it's to do with your secret love life.'

'*You're* my only love life,' Michael replied. 'And you *aren't* a secret.'

'God, you sure know how to say the nicest things. What a lucky gal I am! Tell me, are you in love with me?'

'I believe so.'

Bonnie's smile was like a sunrise. 'You're so sweet, you're like a fourteen-year-old. You're so trusting and innocent. But you don't know what love is, Mike. I'm just your first, is all. You've never had a woman before and guys always think they're in love with the first woman they have. When you're more experienced, when you've learnt to take me for granted, you'll cast your gaze elsewhere because you and me are too different to stay together.'

'That's not true,' Michael said, though when he thought of introducing Bonnie, with her bizarre appearance and rough ways, to his conservative friends in Freedom Bay, he realized that she would indeed seem a strange choice. That thought, which had only just come to him through this conversation, did not make him feel good.

'Yes, it *is* true,' Bonnie insisted. 'You're a classy guy, Mike, and I'm lowlife and those two don't mix. But it makes me feel good that you even *think* you love me. No one's ever felt that way about me before – I was only a decent fuck to the others. That's the kind of life I've led, it's all I know, and you make me feel special. Can you trust Ben with something confidential? I'd say probably yes, though it might depend on what the subject is. Can you give me a clue?'

'It's to do with the cyborgs.'

Bonnie frowned, looking concerned. 'The cyborgs? Jesus Christ! Anything to do with them is bad news. What's your involvement, Mike?'

'I didn't say I was involved.'

'If you want to talk to Ben about the cyborgs, you must have a reason.'

'I'm looking for someone,' Michael lied, 'and I think he can help me.'

'Well, maybe he can. He certainly keeps tabs on them. He's part of a big gang that's determined to bring the cyborgs down, though I think they're all dreaming. Yeah, if it's anything to do with the cyborgs, he'll keep his mouth shut. You can trust him with that.'

'Thanks,' Michael said.

He took Ben for that drink. They went back to the same retro dance club that they'd been in before and watched a holographic Elvis gyrating in the colourized version of his old movie *Jailhouse Rock* while the girls around him screamed their heads off. Strobe lights were flashing elsewhere in the big room, forming a kaleidoscopic web that made everyone caught in it, the drinkers and the dancers and the druggies, look bizarre and surreal. Elvis moved like a dream.

'I wanted to talk to you,' Michael said, 'about what you showed me the other night.'

'You were impressed?'

'Yes, I was.'

'Talk away,' Ben said.

'I'm not from around here,' Michael said, 'and I'm not really looking for an old girlfriend.'

'I'm intrigued already.'

'Have you ever heard of Freedom Bay?'

Ben raised his eyebrows and stared at him with increasing interest. 'You mean in . . . ?'

'Antarctica.'

'Yes,' Ben said, very slowly, drawing the word out like a question mark and letting the silence linger for a moment before nodding his head. 'Yeah, I've heard of it. It's one of those places only discussed in whispers and always with a certain amount of doubt. No reference to it anywhere in the literature, but it's rumoured to be a top-secret US military complex that was cut off from the rest of the world when the cyborgs took over. The rumours talk about a technology nearly as advanced as that of the cyborgs and also about flying-saucer construction. According to the rumours, the cyborgs can't get in there and the Freedom Bay people can't get out.'

'The first is correct, the second is wrong. It's true that the cyborg saucers can't get *in* there because a force field protects the base — but that field can be turned on and off to let the saucers of Freedom Bay fly *out*. I know, because that's where I come from and I'm here for a purpose.'

Now Ben's gaze was direct and frankly sceptical. 'Is this a put-on?'

'No. I really do come from Freedom Bay and I'm here on a mission that concerns the cyborgs. I want you to help me.'

'Freedom Bay actually exists?'

'It sure does.'

'Tell me about it,' Ben said.

Michael recounted, in great detail, the whole history of Freedom Bay, beginning with Wilson's secret journey to Antarctica back in 1945, going on to cover Wilson's death and the US takeover in 1982, and concluding with the way the colony was run now and exactly why he, Michael, had been sent here to Washington DC. When he had finished, Ben looked thoughtfully at Michael for some time. Then he shook his head ruefully from side to side and gave a low whistle.

'Fucking hell,' Ben said softly. 'So now you guys are going to move against the cyborgs. How do you aim to do that? I mean, those bastards are spread worldwide, dug in just about everywhere on Earth. You can't cover the whole globe.'

'From what I've seen of what goes on inside the White House—'

'From what you've . . . *seen*?' Ben interjected.

'Yes. Some of us in Freedom Bay are trained in parapsychological skills – mental telepathy and so on – and I've used mine to see, in a limited capacity, what's going on in the White House.'

'Why "limited"?'

'The cyborgs appear to have similar skills and have used them to make that kind of access difficult.'

'Yeah,' Ben said. 'It's the ones without mouths and noses and, in some cases, without eyes. Like the deaf, dumb and blind, they've developed compensatory senses, but in their case they've developed those senses enormously – extrasensory perception and so on. So, yeah, right, they're probably blocking all your attempts at mental penetration. They probably do that automatically. I'm amazed you saw anything at all. Your own skills in that field must be considerable.'

'They are,' Michael said, simply stating a fact, not intending to boast.

'Sorry for the distraction. Go on.'

'We don't intend trying to cover the whole globe. It's our belief, based on what I've seen and what you too have picked up with your laser surveillance equipment, that the cyborgs have taken over the vast underground area that links the White House to the Pentagon via the four-lane highway they constructed to go under the Potomac. It's also our belief, based on intelligence gathered by Freedom Bay over the past twenty years, that the cyborgs worldwide are linked to some kind of vast, controlling intelligence, possibly a biological computer, and that if we can disrupt that link we'll also disrupt the cyborgs on a worldwide basis. Finally, it's our belief that the controlling intelligence, whatever it is, is located right here in Washington DC – in the White House, in the Pentagon, or in both. We therefore have to get into one of those buildings and I've chosen the White House.'

'Why?'

'It's a hell of a lot smaller and has no great expanse of ground around it. That makes it more accessible than the Pentagon.'

'You haven't a prayer. You won't get inside the White House. That place is guarded outside night and day. Inside, as we've both seen, it's crawling with cyborgs, clones and the walking dead.'

'Where there's a will there's a way,' Michael said. 'And I have the will.'

'Exceptional will?' Ben asked, sounding slightly sardonic.

'Yes,' Michael replied with flat conviction. 'I gained it through my intensive parapsychological training in Freedom Bay. I have, despite my juvenile appearance, a will of iron.'

Ben smiled, then glanced around the room, taking in the flashing strobe lights, the young men and women dancing, the fans being hysterical around their holographic Elvis, who was now performing 'Trouble' from the colourized version of his old movie *King Creole*. Ben gazed distractedly at Elvis as he considered what Michael had said, then he turned back to him.

'Okay,' he said. 'How can I help?'

'First, by using your surveillance gear to find out any possible way of getting into the White House, with particular emphasis on vehicles coming and going to see if any are on a regular schedule. I also need a record of the precise movements of all saucers taking off or landing, particularly those bringing in — or transferring out — abductees. Naturally, I also need to know if your surveillance equipment picks up any unusual movements inside the building.'

'Done,' Ben said.

'Second, I want you to recruit very carefully about twenty of the best people in your gang. They have to be one hundred per cent trustworthy and fearless. If you're absolutely convinced that they are, you can tell them everything I've told you. Don't pick *anyone* who hesitates for even a second when you tell them what our intentions are. To be crude about it, they have to be fanatical in their hatred of the cyborgs and willingness to risk all to bring them down.'

'Gotcha,' Ben said. 'Anything else?'

'No, that's it for now.'

'How much time have I got?'

'All the time in the world. We won't move until we've found a surefire way of getting into that building. If that takes months, or even years, that's how long we'll have to wait. Do you have any questions?'

'Yeah,' Ben said, offering a cocky grin. 'What's Bonnie Packard like in the sack?'

'Don't embarrass me,' Michael said.

Confident at last, Michael returned to his apartment and sent a confirming e-mail to Freedom Bay.

From: <birdnest@mkim.com>
the bird is in full flight.

Chapter Thirty-one

Gumshoe's journey from Albuquerque, New Mexico, to Washington DC took him four days, driving most of each day, but stopping quite a bit to ensure that he didn't become too tired. Driving away from Albuquerque and the Rio Grande, feeling like an old-time pioneer, but heading east instead of west, he had not been ignorant of the fact that the cyborgs had inserted him into an area that had once been at the very heart of the American defence establishment and thus at the very centre of the flying saucer mythology of the Old Age.

It was from Eden Valley, near Roswell, New Mexico, that Robert H. Goddard, aided by the legendary John Wilson, had shot his first liquid-fuelled rockets skyward in the early 1930s. Shortly after World War Two, the Roswell Army Air Field (now Walker AFB) became home to the 509th Bomb Group of the US Army Air Force, then the only combat-trained atom-bomb group in the world. Albuquerque itself was the home of the top-secret Kirtland AFB/Sandia Laboratories complex, south of the city, and the Manzano Nuclear Weapons Storage Facility, east of Kirtland, both of which were rumoured to have been involved in some of the early man-made flying saucer projects. New Mexico had also been home to the original 'scientific community' of Los Alamos, created by the Manhattan (atom bomb) Project in 1943, and still a highly restricted cyborg area, noted for its many top-secret research establishments. The White Sands Proving Ground, the US government's first rocket centre, lying 250 miles south of Los Alamos, had once been noted for its high incidence of UFO sightings and was now in the hands of the cyborgs too. The town of Alamogordo, located between the Proving Ground and the site of the first atomic explosion, had once proudly advertised itself as 'Home of the Atomic Bomb' and 'Centre of Rocket Development', but the cyborgs, since taking it over, had removed that and all other signs relating to the area's scientific history. The Proving Ground, which covered 4,000 square miles, was mostly a wasteland of sand and sagebrush out of which had sprung the numerous restricted US Army and Air Force bases, including Holloman AFB, the location of a lot of Old Age flying saucer sightings as well as of many of the US Naval Research Laboratory's top-secret experimental establishments – all of which were, of course, now under the tight control of the cyborgs. So, though Gumshoe had not found out just what kind of work the cyborgs had planned for him (or, more precisely, for the unfortunate Danny Greenfeld), he was pretty convinced that it would have been something to do with the experimental work still being under-taken in this vast area.

Knowing that the cyborgs would put a trace on his car once they discovered that he had not gone to the apartment designated for him in Albuquerque, he deliberately turned south, ditched the car on the outskirts of Roswell, hot-wired a dusty old Ford that was parked outside a farm, then drove north until he arrived back at the road to Amarillo. Taking that road, he drove across those vast, moonlit plains of sand and sagebrush, hearing only the wind beating violently about him, and didn't stop until he reached Amarillo in the early hours of the morning. With no possessions other than the documentation given to him by the cyborgs, which they could easily trace, he used the credit card to withdraw money from a bank – enough to last him for a month – then bought himself a complete set of new clothing. He changed in the stolen car, keeping the other man's identification papers just in case a normal state trooper stopped him, then had breakfast in a diner and lit out again, leaving Amarillo in the still early hours of the morning.

He passed fields of wheat and grazing cattle and oil rigs, the sun high and dazzling, and kept going until he reached Oklahoma City where the great plains swept down from the northwest. Up to that point, he had seen no signs of cyborg activity, but on the outskirts of the city, where industry was heavy, the evidence appeared in the form of deserted cars, indicating abducted drivers and passengers, then the odd SARGE or Prowler in the grounds of oil refineries and aircraft plants. He skirted around the city itself, then headed for Missouri, crossing the great Ozark Plateau where he saw saucers flying or hovering overhead, though luckily they were high in the sky, en route from one base to another and looking for no one. Coming down off the plateau, sparsely populated, neglected, barely developed, he travelled through a rainstorm to St Louis, saw the mighty Mississippi, and then, on the outskirts of the city, which was a major centre of communications and trade, saw a greater number of SARGE and Prowler patrols, all of which he managed to avoid. Again, he bypassed the city, where the patrols would have been even more numerous, and took the road that led to Cincinnati, passing through Indianapolis and Dayton, Ohio, sleeping in the car at night and stopping during the day only to eat at roadside diners.

When he reached Charleston, West Virginia, the home of Daniel Boone, he started thinking of his own home, his small apartment in what had once been his parents' house in Georgetown, and the recollection of how he had last seen his mother and father cut through him like a knife with a hot blade. He had to stop driving because suddenly he was crying, boiling over with grief and horror and rage. But eventually he dried his tears and drove on, now determined more than ever to get back and dedicate himself to bringing down the cyborgs, which would be retribution.

He came down from Charleston through the Shenandoah Valley, through orchards and green pastures, only seeing flying saucers that were very high up. As he neared his destination, Washington DC, he started thinking about Bonnie Packard, who had slipped from his thoughts completely, burned out by the sheer horror of what he had experienced, and was surprised by how much he wanted to see her. More surprising, when he thought about it, was that he wanted to make love to her – real-time sex, not cybersex, not masturbation through e-mails – and since he had never had real-time sex in his life, he was overwhelmed by the thought.

Time to grow up, he thought.

Entering Washington DC by way of Alexandria, in a pearly-grey late afternoon, he felt the excitement of homecoming – but he also felt the oppressiveness of being back where the cyborgs were highly visible and a constant threat. When he saw a great mother ship hovering directly above the Pentagon, the grounds around the building patrolled by SARGEs and Prowlers, he recalled with a shocking intensity exactly what he had witnessed in the basement of that very building, though it now seemed years instead of mere days ago and, with particular regard to his parents, more like a nightmare than a hideous reality.

A few minutes later, as he drove across the Arlington Memorial Bridge, over the waters of the Potomac, he saw another mother ship hovering like a gigantic, sublimely beautiful yet ominous sentinel above the White House area. Reminded yet again that he was back in dangerous territory – more so, for him, because he had escaped from the cyborgs and would now be a wanted man – he drove with extreme care, always prepared to turn away and cut loose if he saw a cyborg patrol. In the event, nothing happened and he made it back to Georgetown where he parked his car near the Towpath, well away from the house in M Street.

Knowing that the cyborgs often placed the homes of abductees under surveillance, hoping to catch their relatives, he approached his old home carefully, scanning the street for men in black or for those who might look normal but could, in fact, be the walking dead, sent to loiter outside the building and keep an eye on it. Seeing nothing unusual, only routine, self-absorbed passers-by, he approached the front door and then realized that he didn't have any of his own possessions – only those of the unfortunate Danny Greenfeld – which meant that he didn't have his key. Cursing under his breath, he had to wait for an hour until one of the other tenants turned up: a bespectacled computer nerd, Frank Marshall, who had, in the past, often come down from his own apartment, located directly above Gumshoe's, for a drink and a talk about events on the Internet. Arriving home and finding Gumshoe on the doorstep, he opened the door for both of them.

'Got mugged,' Gumshoe lied, by way of explaining his lack of a key, 'by a gang of shitholes over from Anacostia.'

'Yeah,' Frank said, nodding sympathetically. 'A bad bunch over there. I've been down, by the way, a couple of times,' he added as they walked up the first flight of stairs side by side, 'but couldn't catch you in. Been out a lot recently?'

'Yeah,' Gumshoe said.

'Not like you to go out much,' Frank reminded him. 'Got a woman out there?'

'That's it,' Gumshoe said, relieved to be given a good excuse. 'Been seeing her practically every night.'

'I don't like real-time interaction,' Frank said. 'It just doesn't seem natural. I mean, I can never think of anything to say. Besides, the few times I've done it, it wasn't nearly as good as cybersex. I like controlled situations.'

'That could be wise,' Gumshoe said, stopping in front of the door of his apartment on the first landing. 'Well, I'll see you around.'

'How are you going to get in without a key?' Frank asked.

'I keep an emergency key right here,' Gumshoe said, reaching up to the top of the doorframe where he had, indeed, taped a spare key for just such an emergency. He pulled the key down and slipped it into the lock.

'Now I know where it is,' Frank said, grinning. Then he waved and sauntered on up the stairs to his own apartment.

Gumshoe turned the key in the lock and let himself in, disappointed to see that the lights were out, which meant that Bonnie wasn't in there. He closed the door behind him and then switched on the lights and looked about him in rising incredulity.

'What the fuck . . . ?' he exclaimed automatically.

The apartment had been looted and everything of value was gone, including his six PowerMac 9500s with their eight-gigabyte hard drives, his PowerPC microprocessors, his colour monitors, scanners and printers, the old TV set and even his cracked cups and saucers. The furniture was still there, the lousy sofa and chairs, the moth-eaten carpets, but the thief had taken the bedclothes, leaving only the mattress.

Gumshoe had been pretty well cleaned out.

Shocked, he sank into one of the chairs and stared at the empty space where his beloved Tower of Babble had been, trying to accept his grievous loss. Eventually, he glanced at the sofa upon which Bonnie Packard had so often stretched out, watching the TV while exposing her long legs just to torment him.

Instantly, when he thought of Bonnie, he realized that his room had *not* been broken into – that he'd had to use a key to get in. With a sinking heart and even greater disappointment, he realized that Bonnie had been living here with him up until he had been abducted and was the only other person with a key. So Bonnie, who had clearly departed, had also been the one to clean him out.

He couldn't fucking believe it.

But he *had* to believe it, because there was nothing else to believe. Bonnie Packard, the girl he had thought that he might be falling in love with, had fled the apartment and stolen all his gear shortly after knowing that he had been abducted by the cyborgs.

Thanks a million, Bonnie. Nice to know you're so loyal.

He sat on for another ten minutes, staring at the empty spaces, the blank walls, accepting that he could no longer stay on here anyway (since the cyborgs, stung by his escape from them, would surely make this their first port of call) and sardonically telling himself that Bonnie had at least solved one problem: he had practically nothing to move out when he moved out – and he would certainly have to move out immediately.

Having escaped from the cyborgs, he would have to go underground and for that he would need false identification papers and credit cards that could be used against legitimate accounts that were in someone else's name. In short, he needed the services of Ben Wilkerson, an old friend who ostensibly ran a rooming house in Chinatown while covertly running an organization devoted to the overthrow of the cyborgs. Ben's illegal organization often had to send its own members underground; it therefore had all the facilities that Gumshoe now needed to survive his new future as a fugitive. He would go and see Ben immediately.

After stuffing into a shoulder bag what pitifully few possessions Bonnie had left him, he left the apartment and descended the stairs to fetch his beloved silver-tanked Yamaha 400 motorcycle out of its protective cage in the basement.

The cage was open and the motorcycle was gone.

The key to the cage had been on the key ring that he had given to Bonnie.

'Shit!' Gumshoe exclaimed.

Hating Bonnie more with every passing second, he turned away in disgust and went out into the busy, neon-lit M Street, which remained the hub of this lively area where people, mostly the young, tended to congregate and live it up before the midnight curfew imposed by the cyborgs. Crossing Wisconsin Avenue, he continued past the garish electronic games parlours, dance clubs and porno fun palaces that lined both sides of the road, crossed Rock Creek, then made his way along Pennsylvania

Avenue which was, compared to Georgetown, relatively empty, being filled with the houses of the wealthy, too fearful to leave their homes at night, and imposing government buildings where lights were still burning here and there, indicating that the dedicated or the brain-dead were still hard at work.

He skirted around the White House area, avoiding the SARGEs and Prowlers, though he could not escape the sight of the great mother ship hovering over what had once been the home of the nation's Chief Executive and was now the hub of all cyborg activity in the United States. Shivering involuntarily, reminded for the second time of what he had witnessed in the basement of the Pentagon which was, he knew, linked to the basement of the White House, he went along I Street to Mount Vernon Square, then turned right down 7th, which brought him straight to Ben Wilkerson's rooming house, almost directly facing the old MCI Arena in Chinatown.

This being early evening, the formally disused sports stadium was filling up with Speed Freaks with their hot rods and motorcycles. Though Gumshoe couldn't see them from where he was, he could tell that they were there from the bedlam — revving engines, breaking beer bottles, pounding rock music, shouts and screams — and from the flashing of headlights into the night sky. He ignored those inviting sounds, however, and instead resolutely entered the rooming house where Ben Wilkerson worked. He found his friend drinking a bottle of beer behind the reception desk. Ben looked surprised when Gumshoe walked in.

'What the hell's the matter?' Gumshoe said. 'You look like you've just seen a ghost.'

'I think I *am* seeing a ghost,' Ben replied. 'According to Bonnie Packard, you were picked up by the cyborgs.'

'According to Bonnie Packard, yeah? So where did you see Bonnie Packard?'

'What do you mean, where did I see her? I see her all the time. I mean, she's here, there and everywhere, man. Bonnie gets around, right?'

'Right. Any idea where she's living right now?'

'Yep. In some dive off 7th Street. I don't have the exact address. She got it from one of Snake Eyes's buddies because, as I'm sure you know, she was kinda intimate with Snake Eyes before he disappeared.'

'She never fucked him,' Gumshoe said, too quickly.

'So she says,' Ben responded. 'Just good buddies and all that crap. Anyway, what's it to you? Were *you* fucking her?'

'No,' Gumshoe said just as quickly.

'Just good buddies, like her and Snake Eyes, right?'

'That's right,' Gumshoe said.

Ben sighed. 'I wish I had your luck. I've always wanted to screw her – real-time, not cybersex – but she doesn't even give me a sideways glance. Then guys like you and Snake Eyes – and now this new one – guys who don't even know what a real woman feels like – that Bonnie, she falls for them. I think I'll have to go on-line.'

Gumshoe couldn't believe how bad he was feeling, but he worked hard to hide it. 'What new one?' he asked.

'New kid in town,' Ben replied. 'A good kid. I can vouch for him.'

'Oh, yeah?'

'Yeah.'

'So what's his name?'

'He says it's Mike Johnson, but I doubt it. I only know – and I'm pretty sure of it – that this one's on our side.'

'He's having real-time sex with Bonnie – or on-line?'

'I haven't a clue. But right now I still think I'm looking at a ghost. Was Bonnie having me on?'

'No, I really was picked up by the cyborgs.'

'And you got out?'

'Yeah, I got out. With the help of Snake Eyes.'

'Jesus,' Ben said, looking serious now. 'Tell me.'

Gumshoe told him the whole story. When he'd finished, Ben stared at him with something like awe. Then he gave a low whistle of admiration. 'Jesus, man,' he said, 'that must be something of a first — to be picked up by, and then escape from, the cyborgs. Did Snake Eyes make it back, too?'

'I don't know,' Gumshoe said. 'I just got back myself, so I haven't had time to look around.'

'If he's back, he'll be in that sports stadium. That's for damned sure.'

'I'll check it out,' Gumshoe said.

'The cyborgs won't want someone with your knowledge running loose,' Ben said, 'so they'll be trying to run you down. Avoid your apartment like the plague and don't use any of your plastic cards, 'cause they can trace you through those. Did you use your cards on the journey back from New Mexico?'

'No. I didn't have my own stuff on me. I used the card of that other guy to buy me a month. I used it in Clovis, Texas, and I haven't used it since, so they won't be able to track my movements that way.'

'Good man. Their car?'

'Didn't use that, either. Dumped it in Roswell, New Mexico, then stole another and used that instead. Just an old farmer's heap of the kind that gets stolen all the time. They won't connect it with me.'

'Very clever,' Ben said. 'So now you need new identification and legitimate plastic.'

'I sure do,' Gumshoe said. 'Can you fix it?'

'Sure can. Plastic of all kinds, backed up by legitimate accounts, but with false names and widely scattered addresses that are actually those of some of our supporters. Ditto identification papers. Of course, we'll need a small photo and that *can* be a problem since, as you know, the cyborgs took away all those old passport-photo booths to try and stop forgeries, ha, ha. So have you got an old photo?'

'I could have made one up with my Tower of Babble, but my fucking room's been cleared out.'

'Shit! Cyborg break-in?'

'It wasn't a break-in. It had to have been done by someone with a key.'

'So who had a key?'

'Never mind,' Gumshoe said, thinking bitterly of Bonnie Packard and loathing her even more because now she had the new kid in town. *True love runs fucking deep, right?*

'We can make up a photo with *our* computer,' Ben said, 'so come to my place tonight and we'll take a photo and scan it and stick it into new identification papers. Ditto the plastic cards. What about a new pad?'

'Don't know.'

'If you don't find something by tonight, when you drop in, I'll see what I can do.'

'You're a real fucking ace.'

'I like to think so. One more thing, though. If Snake Eyes made it back and you see him, tell him what I've just told you: that he has to stay away from his old pad and get himself some new identification. He should also stay away from his Speed Freak buddies, but I don't think he will.'

'Neither do I,' Gumshoe said. 'But I'll tell him the rest. See you tonight. *Au revoir.*'

'*Ciao!*' Ben quipped, trading Italian for French.

Gumshoe left the rooming house and crossed the busy road to the old sports stadium. Inside the arena the darkness was illuminated by the criss-crossing headlights of hot rods and motorcycles. The Speed Freaks had gathered together in great numbers and were covering the whole field, straddling their motorcycles, leaning against their cars while shooting up speed, drinking beer, smoking cigarettes and fondling their bizarrely dressed, weirdly painted Long Hairs. Clearly, they had come in such great numbers to celebrate the return of Snake Eyes who was to be seen near the middle of the field, leaning against his sedan, taking greedy swigs of beer and fondling the ass of the short-haired Long Hair who was wearing a black-leather bra, skintight black-leather miniskirt, sheer black stockings and black-leather high-heeled boots. She was covered in badges and chains and her bare skin showed everywhere. Snake Eyes was triumphant.

Recognized by the Speed Freaks, Gumshoe managed to make it all the way to Snake Eyes without getting stomped. Indeed, his reception was quite the opposite as, upon seeing him, the massed Speed Freaks burst into cheers and threw a variety of items into the air, including beer bottles that smashed noisily to the ground as a sign of respect. Realizing that Snake Eyes had already told the gathered Speed Freaks about his participation in the escape from the cyborgs, Gumshoe could only grin when he approached his old friend.

'So,' he said, 'you made it.'

Holding his beer bottle in one hand and removing the other from the taut arse of the Long Hair, Snake Eyes grinned and spread his hands out in the air.

'And you, too, old buddy. Come here. Let me hug you.'

When Gumshoe and Snake Eyes embraced, the Speed Freaks cheered again, some of them even becoming so emotional as to rush up to slap Gumshoe on the back or affectionately, respectfully, squeeze his shoulder.

'Fuckin' heroic, man!'

'Fan-fucking-tastic!'

'Any time you need help, man, I'm your man.'

'Have a beer on me, pal.'

'So where did they dump you?' Gumshoe asked of Snake Eyes.

'Near Patrick Air Force Base,' Snake Eyes said. 'Which the cyborgs now control. About two miles from Cape Canaveral on the east coast of Florida. With instructions to drive to an address in Greater Cocoa Beach. An area packed with about ten thousand former NASA and USAF workers, including astronauts, aircraft pilots, radar operatives, scientists, rocket engineers, ballistics experts, computer specialists, astronomers, and a local community that took shape during the Old Age space race and has since been taken over by the cyborgs. I can only assume that I – by which I mean the guy whose identity I stole – was going to be put to work in that community, probably to spy on it and then report back to the Pentagon . . . Yeah, right, man, *the Pentagon*. Now we know where it's at.'

Gumshoe shivered at simply being reminded of the Pentagon and the nightmare world contained in its huge basement. 'So how did you get back?'

Snake Eyes grinned and stuck his thumb up in the air.

'Hitch-hiking?' Gumshoe asked. 'You're kidding me!'

Snake Eyes's grinned broadened, revealing his brand new teeth. 'No, I'm not, man. This new cyborg haircut . . .' he reached up to pat the short hair on his head '. . . worked a treat and I got rides dead easy. First a waitress on her way to work in Cocoa Beach, then a radar operative on vacation, going home to Wilmington, South Carolina, then a truck driver going all the way to Norfolk, Virginia, and, finally, public transport, with money I begged, borrowed and stole, from Norfolk into Washington DC. Piece of cake, really. Coastal roads most of the way, like a regular scenic trip. 'Course, some of those who picked me up were the walking dead, but with my short hair and good teeth and intimate knowledge of how they behave, I was able to convince 'em all that I was one of them. So . . . here I am!'

'Congratulations.'

'You, too, pal.'

Their slapping palms were greeted with another round of Speed Freak cheering. Then Gumshoe said, 'We've got to talk.'

'Talk away.'

'Not here. Somewhere soundproof.'

'Such as?'

'Let's just mosey across to the *Be-Bop-a-Lula* club and have a drink and a quick conversation.'

'Yeah, let's celebrate,' Snake Eyes said, grinning, obviously high on his achievement and thrilled to be the centre of attention. 'Be back in half an hour,' he said to the Long Hair beside him and to those bunched around him. 'Keep your motors running while I'm away.'

'Right on,' the Long Hair said as the Speed Freaks around her raised their thumbs in approval, pumped the air with clasped hands or shouted ribald remarks.

Acknowledging them with a nod, Snake Eyes fell in beside Gumshoe as they made their way back through the light-streaked darkness of the arena, overlooked by its 20,000 empty seats, and then crossed the street to walk the few blocks to the *Be-Bop-a-Lula* club. Once inside the clamorous den, they headed straight for the bar, ordered two Buds, and made general conversation while the drinks came. Snake Eyes did most of the talking, going on mostly about what a great stunt they'd both pulled off in being abducted and then making their escape. Gumshoe wasn't so thrilled.

'You've got to move out of your apartment,' Gumshoe said, 'and right away.'

'What?'

'You heard me.'

'Fuck that,' Snake Eyes said. 'I've been in that apartment for years and no one's moving me out of it.'

'You were caught by the cyborgs and made your escape. They're not going to want you on the loose, knowing what you know. So they're bound to check out your apartment and if they find you there, they'll take you back for sure. The next time you won't escape.'

'Fuck it, I'm not moving. I'm not scared of no fucking cyborgs. I'm the head of the Speed Freaks now, I'm revered as a fucking hero, and I'm not going to give that up just to go underground. Fuck it, no, I won't do it.'

'You've got to. I've talked to Ben Wilkerson: he knows the score and he'll fix you up with a new identity and find you somewhere else to live. He can do it, believe me.'

'I've no argument about Ben Wilkerson. He's a good guy, sure enough. But I ain't gonna live my life underground and that's all there is to it.'

'The next time the cyborgs get you,' Gumshoe said, 'they'll do a lot more to you than they did the last time. You'll be finished, Snake Eyes.'

'I can beat 'em,' Snake Eyes said, clearly swept away on the tidal wave of his victory and no longer thinking straight. 'I've got all kinds of shit in my apartment – home-made bombs, sub-machine guns, fucking hand grenades – so if they come up there, I'll be ready for 'em. I ain't runnin', that's for fucking sure.'

'You're crazy,' Gumshoe said. 'Or you're going that way. You're putting your life on the line here.'

'In the words of Bobbie Zimmerman,' Snake Eyes said, 'that's life and life only.'

'Be it on your own head,' Gumshoe said.

Snake Eyes grinned, then glanced across the immense crowded room. Its strobe lights were flashing, casting kaleidoscopic, surrealistic patterns over the people at the tables, those dancing on the many dance floors and those smoking dope in the drug parlours around the sides, only avoiding the holographic Elvis in his 'Captain Marvel' jumpsuit period who was belting out 'See See Rider' as the opening to a concert that would enthral his hysterical fans for the next hour and a half. Snake Eyes stared at Elvis with undisguised admiration, then shifted his gaze sideways to take in a couple of newcomers as they entered the club.

'Well, I'll be damned!' he exclaimed.

'Who is it?' Gumshoe asked.

'That old Long Hair of mine, Bonnie Packard,' Snake Eyes informed him. 'With the new kid in town.'

'Oh, shit!' Gumshoe said.

Chapter Thirty-two

Gumshoe and Snake Eyes didn't move from the bar. They just stood there nursing their drinks as Bonnie and the new kid in town emerged from the crowd that had been rendered surreal in the web of dazzling strobe lights and found themselves a table well away from the noisily performing holographic Elvis. They still didn't move when the new guy, who was blond-haired and blue-eyed, handsome and slim in a roll-neck pullover, wind-cheater jacket, tight denims and high-heeled boots, called over a waitress vestigially dressed in a bikini and roller blades to order drinks from her. When the waitress had taken their order and shot away on her roller blades, Gumshoe and Snake Eyes glanced at each other, nodded, then sauntered over to Bonnie's table to look down at her and the new kid in town. Bonnie's eyes went real big then.

'Hi, Bonnie!' Snake Eyes said brightly.

'Hi,' Gumshoe said sourly.

Bonnie's eyes went even bigger. 'Oh, Jesus!' she exclaimed. 'Oh, my God, I just can't believe it. You're back and . . .' At this point her eyes narrowed in suspicion as she glanced from one to the other. Then she said tentatively to Gumshoe, 'They didn't . . . ?'

'Do a brain implant? No, we're perfectly normal.'

'You're sure?'

'Yeah, we're sure,' Snake Eyes said.

Bonnie jumped impulsively out of her chair to emotionally hug and kiss each of them in turn. 'Oh, God, I can't believe it! I'm so thrilled! But I just can't believe it!' Her eyes were brimming as she sat down again and she wiped the tears away with her fingertips. 'Oh, fuck, I'm so happy!'

'Really?' Gumshoe said, not having responded with any great deal of affection to her hug and kiss.

'Yeah, really.'

Snake Eyes slipped into one of the two vacant seats and give the new kid in town a dangerous grin. 'Hi, there,' he said.

'Hi,' the kid responded, his blue gaze steady and unafraid.

'Who the fuck are you?' Snake Eyes asked.

'Now, now, Snake Eyes,' Bonnie said nervously as Gumshoe took the other vacant seat.

'Mike Johnson,' the kid replied. 'Who are you?'

'Old boyfriend of Bonnie's. Known around here as Snake Eyes. Head of the local Speed Freak gang.'

'I'm impressed,' Michael said.

'You oughta be.' Snake Eyes turned away to offer his big, dangerous grin to Bonnie. 'So how are you, sweetheart?'

'Fine,' Bonnie said. 'Same as always. But I'm just so thrilled to see you guys back. I mean, I can't believe—'

'Believe it,' Gumshoe interjected. 'We're back.'

'Yeah, right.' Unusually, Bonnie seemed lost for words. 'It's just so fuckin' incredible, I—'

'You Bonnie's new number?' Snake Eyes asked the newcomer.

'Pardon?'

'You met up in our absence, did you?'

'I assume so,' Michael said, staying cool.

'Don't take offence,' Snake Eyes said, though the blond stranger clearly hadn't taken offence. 'I only ask 'cause before I was abducted Bonnie and me had a kind of relationship.'

'Kind of?'

'We were just pals,' Bonnie said, too quickly. 'It was no more than that, Mike.'

'She was my woman,' Snake Eyes insisted. 'Where I went, she went.'

'We didn't fuck,' Bonnie said in her charmingly uncouth way. 'No real-time interaction at all. Just good pals, is all. Come on, Snake Eyes, don't—'

'Where I went, she went,' Snake Eyes insisted, 'and everyone knew it. Now she's with you.'

'Yes, she is,' Michael said firmly.

'Don't take offence,' Snake Eyes repeated, though clearly Michael still hadn't taken offence. 'Bonnie's her own woman and can do what she wants. But college boys like you aren't normally her style, so I just wondered, is all.'

'Wondered what?' Michael asked.

'Are you . . . ?'

'You've no right to ask that,' Bonnie said. 'It's not your business, Snake Eyes.'

'Ask what?' Snake Eyes said innocently. 'I didn't get the chance to ask him anything.'

'We all know what you were askin',' Bonnie said, looking petulant, 'and you don't have the right.' She turned to offer Gumshoe a placating smile. 'So when did you guys get back and how did you do it?'

'I got back yesterday and he got back today,' Snake Eyes said, 'and we managed to do it because we're both so smart.'

'Terrific,' Bonnie said, clearly growing more nervous. 'I mean, that's just too . . .'

'I went straight to my apartment,' Gumshoe said, 'and found a surprise waiting for me.'

'Gumshoe, listen, I can explain—'

'Explain what?' Snake Eyes said, looking puzzled. 'What's this about your apartment, Gumshoe?'

'Just for starters,' Gumshoe asked of Bonnie, ignoring Snake

Eyes's embarrassing question, 'where's my silver-tanked Yamaha 400?'

'Don't worry, Gumshoe, it's safe. I've got it and I've been using it and it still runs beautifully.'

'You've got it and you've been using it?'

'Yeah, of course!'

'And my computers and . . . ?'

'Safe as houses, Gumshoe. Stop worrying, for Chrissakes. I moved 'em into my new apartment and . . .'

'How the fuck did she get your motorcycle and computers?' Snake Eyes wanted to know.

'You took them from my place and moved them into your new place?' Gumshoe asked. 'You just upped and left and took every goddamned thing I own with you?'

'Gumshoe, listen, for Chrissakes! Let me explain! It isn't what you're thinking. I—'

'My silver-tanked Yamaha 400 motorcycle. My six Power-Mac 9500s with eight-gigabyte hard drives and 298 megs of RAM. My PowerPC microprocessors. My Radius Pressview colour monitor and my—'

'I saw those in your room, Bonnie,' Michael said impulsively, being an honest soul. 'I assumed they were yours.'

'So you got into her room, did you?' Gumshoe said. 'That was pretty quick, handsome.'

'Let me explain, Gumshoe,' Bonnie cut in. 'Listen, for Chrissakes, I was just doin' it for you. When the cyborgs captured you, I knew they were bound to come and check your room out – the Men in Black, at least – and that they'd take me away with 'em if they found me there. So I knew that I had to get out pretty quick, right? An' I knew that once the slimeballs out there – the carpetbaggers or juiceheads – learnt that you'd been captured and that I'd flown from the nest—'

'The nest?' Snake Eyes enquired, glaring at Gumshoe.

'—they'd break in and clean out the room and no way, man, absolutely no way would they forget to take your fucking

Yamaha 400 too. So I took it all, Gumshoe, to prevent it from being stolen and I was just lookin' after it on the off-chance that you'd actually reappear. I knew that was a long shot, but faith can move mountains and my faith paid off, Gumshoe, 'cause here you are back safe and sound, with all your stuff safe and sound as well. It's all yours for the taking.'

'I'll be taking it,' Gumshoe said.

'The *nest*?' Snake Eyes enquired again, staring from Gumshoe to Bonnie, then back to Gumshoe. 'What the fuck does *that* mean? Are you telling me you moved her into your pad after *I* was abducted?'

'Now wait a minute, Snake Eyes,' Gumshoe said, feeling flustered. 'Just let me explain. I—'

'Yeah, fucking explain, man. I get fucking abducted and instead of mourning my loss, my best friend moves *my* fucking woman into *his* room.'

'It wasn't quite like that, Snake Eyes. I mean—'

'Are you hearing this?' Snake Eyes said to Michael. 'I get abducted by fucking cyborgs and my best friend shacks up with my woman as soon as I'm gone. How's that for goddamned fucking loyalty? A bit thin on the ground, right?'

'It wasn't like that at all,' Gumshoe said, feeling all hot under the collar. 'When she was abducted, she couldn't go back to your place and she'd nowhere else to stay and I just happened to rescue her and didn't know what to do with her and—'

'Thanks a million,' Bonnie interjected tartly. 'I didn't know it was a personal sacrifice. I mean, I thought you liked me at least a little bit.'

'I did,' Gumshoe said. 'I just meant—'

'You lived with him?' Michael asked, his blue gaze confused at last. 'You didn't tell me—'

'We didn't fuck,' Bonnie said, as she had said of her relationship with Snake Eyes. 'It wasn't like that at all. We were just pals, is all. Sharing separate beds. I was just there on a temporary basis, until I could find somewhere else to stay. It was no more than that, Mike, believe me. You, too, Snake Eyes.'

'Well, pardon *me*,' Gumshoe said sarcastically, feeling cut to the quick, 'but I thought you felt a bit more than that for me. I mean, I thought—'

'She didn't fuck him and she didn't fuck me,' Snake Eyes said to Michael. 'So what's *your* fucking interest?'

'Well, I . . .' Michael actually blushed, which made him look even more like an innocent schoolboy.

'That's none of your business, Snake Eyes,' Bonnie said, clearly affronted. 'Don't answer him, Mike.'

Snake Eyes stared at Gumshoe in mock surprise. 'First names already! They must be really intimate, these two. Probably hold hands in the sack and whisper sweet nothings.'

'Sarcastic shit!' Bonnie snapped.

'Calm down, Bonnie,' Michael said.

'One more remark from you,' Bonnie said to Snake Eyes, 'and I'll kick your balls off and ram them down that big, dumb mouth of yours. Holding hands, for Chrissakes!'

'You mean you do more than that?' Gumshoe asked, his heart breaking in two. 'You mean this guy is . . . *serious?*'

'What I mean is . . . Oh, fuck! I don't know. You guys just have me confused.'

'She's confused,' Gumshoe said.

'She always was,' Snake Eyes said.

'You don't have to insult her,' Michael said. 'She's done nothing to warrant that.'

Snake Eyes stared steadily at him, in a silence that could kill, then he offered that big, dangerous grin and said, 'Oh, man, he's got *principles!*'

'That's right,' Michael said.

'Which *you* don't have!' Bonnie snapped at Snake Eyes.

'And his principles got our woman into the sack,' Gumshoe said, now speaking directly to Snake Eyes. 'Give *me* some of them principles.'

'You sure as fuck need 'em,' Snake Eyes said. 'Stealin' my woman as soon as I'm abducted and—'

'Guys! Guys!' Bonnie hollered, slapping her hands repeatedly on the table to quieten them down. 'Let's all calm down, for Chrissakes. This is all a fucking storm in a tea cup and it's getting us nowhere. I mean, what did you lose, Snake Eyes? Nothin' at all! We just hung out together but we never shared a sack an' you never even *pretended* to care for me that way – so no big loss there, just your goddamned male ego.'

'Fuck that,' Snake Eyes said.

'Same for you, Gumshoe. You only took me in – you just admitted as much – 'cause I dumped myself on you, not having anywhere else to go. You resented me bein' there – that was clear – and now you're pretending otherwise only because I'm with another guy now. Male ego again.'

'Oh, yeah?' Gumshoe said.

'Yeah.'

Gumshoe wasn't so sure that this was true, given how deeply hurt he felt. But he had to admit that at first he *had* wanted to get rid of her and might only have been sexually attracted to her, not yet having experienced real-time interaction and dwelling too much upon its possibilities when Bonnie was stretched out on his sofa, flashing her long legs. Now, when he looked at the new kid in town, this blond-haired, blue-eyed handsome Mike Johnson, he was forced to conclude that the kid had class: the kind of class that he, Gumshoe, might have had if his formerly well-off and widely respected parents had not been stolen away from him and their fine home taken over by carpetbaggers. Now, of course, he had no class, was just another cast-off, only semi-educated, with no knowledge of good manners, making his living by illegally breaking into mainframes to steal confidential information or inserting destructive viruses when not out creating mayhem with the Speed Freaks, most of whom were subliterate and had the habits of wild animals. Bonnie was one of his breed, more suited to him than to Mike Johnson, but she couldn't help being attracted to someone with the class that she, Snake Eyes and Gumshoe so obviously lacked.

Forced to accept this, Gumshoe felt the biting pain of loss: the loss of his parents, the loss of a decent childhood, the loss of the class that once he could have had and, of course, the loss of Bonnie. He choked the pain back, swallowed his bile, and determined to at least act unconcerned. In any case, what did one unconsummated relationship really matter when set beside the daily nightmare of a world under the brutal yoke of Wilson and his cyborgs? Gumshoe felt ashamed for his lapse into self-pity. He took a deep breath and straightened his shoulders.

'Ah, well,' he said, grinning, to Snake Eyes. 'Easy come, easy go.'

'That's the title of an Elvis song,' Snake Eyes noted.

'Elvis knew it all,' Gumshoe said, then he turned back to Bonnie. 'Okay, sweetheart, you go your own way, but if you're shacked up with Mike here—'

'She's not,' Michael interrupted. 'We just visit each other.'

'—why not move in with him,' Gumshoe continued, ignoring what Michael had said, 'and let me take over your room? That would also save me moving all my stuff out.'

'Very funny,' Bonnie said, 'but I don't think I can do that since I happen to like my independence. Like Mike said, we're not shacked up – we just visit each other – and I'd like to keep it that way.'

'I, too, like my independence,' Michael said, glancing at Bonnie. 'We're in agreement about that.'

'Well, that gives me a problem,' Gumshoe said, ''cause I've got nowhere to live and I can't move my stuff out of your place until I find somewhere.'

'No problem,' Bonnie said. 'I'll take care of it until you want it back. No problem at all.' She turned to Snake Eyes. 'So what about you? I take it you're gonna have to move as well?'

'I'm not moving,' Snake Eyes said emphatically.

'The cyborgs will want you back,' Bonnie said. 'You've just *got* to move, Snake Eyes.'

'I'm not moving,' Snake Eyes repeated stubbornly. 'I won't let no cyborgs or Men in Black force me out of my room.'

'You're fucking crazy,' Bonnie said.

Snake Eyes grinned and turned to Michael. 'What about you, handsome? Do *you* think I'm crazy?'

'I don't think that being stubborn is an option. You should move out of there instantly.'

'Hear that?' Snake Eyes said to Gumshoe. 'The new kid in town is already trying to give me advice. What should I do about that?'

'Stop it, Snake Eyes,' Bonnie said, growing nervous again.

'You asked me a question and I answered it,' Michael said calmly.

'That's right,' Gumshoe said, determined to prove that he held no malice by being magnanimous. 'You asked him a question and he answered it. That's fair enough, Snake Eyes.'

'Jesus, I'm being attacked on all sides,' Snake Eyes retorted. 'Okay! Okay! For once in my life I'm gonna be a gentleman. Put 'er there, pal.' He stuck out his hand and Mike, grinning, shook it. 'Welcome to Chinatown, pal. Don't let it get to you.'

'I won't,' Michael said. 'So what are you doing about somewhere else to live?' he asked Gumshoe.

'A friend of mine'll find me somewhere,' Gumshoe said. 'Name of Ben Wilkerson. He runs a converted rooming house and has his nose to the ground. He'll have found me somewhere else to go by the time I see him this evening.'

Michael looked surprised. 'You and Ben are friends?'

'We sure are. By the way, he vouched for you.'

'He vouched for me?'

'Yeah. Told me you'd moved into his building and said you were a guy to be trusted. If Ben says it, I believe it.'

'Thanks.'

Yet this new guy's gaze, Gumshoe noted, had become slightly veiled. Not enough to hang some kind of hook on, but veiled all the same. This was one careful guy, withholding something, and Gumshoe found himself wondering what it might be.

'So what are you doing in Chinatown?' he asked him. 'I mean, you don't seem the type.'

'Same old story,' Bonnie replied on Michael's behalf. 'Lost his folks and then a girlfriend to the cyborgs and came here hoping to find at least the latter.'

'You haven't a prayer,' Snake Eyes said.

'I've heard that remark before,' Michael said, 'and I won't listen to it. Where's there's life, there's hope.'

'You don't know if there's life,' Snake Eyes said bluntly. 'And if there is, it won't be the kind that you'd want to save. I'd put her out of my head, if I were you.'

'You're not me,' Michael said.

Though Gumshoe admired the new kid's cool, he found it hard to believe what he was saying. This so-called Mike Johnson was too smart not to know that he had no hope in hell of finding his girlfriend again – or, at least, as Snake Eyes had intimated, no hope of finding the same girl that he'd once known, since she would, in fact, even if she was back here in the real world, be one of the walking dead. No, he would not want to find her and clearly, given the way he talked, he was too intelligent not to know that. So, if he wasn't here looking for a lost girlfriend, just what, exactly, *was* he here for? Not for Bonnie or anyone like her – that was for sure.

'I gotta go,' Gumshoe said, suddenly wanting to get out of here, wanting to clear his head, wanting to get away from the cobwebbing strobe lights and the pounding rock music and the bizarrely dressed young people dancing epileptically and the sleepy-eyed drug addicts and the holographic strippers and the electronically reconstituted cult rocker Gene Vincent who, with his crippled leg and black leather gear, a Hamlet for the Speed Freaks, was belting out 'Dance in the Streets' in an extract from a colourized black-and-white movie so obscure that no one alive today could even remember its title. This place was a madhouse, a symbol of the times, where those long dead like Elvis and Gene Vincent and Marlon Brando and Marilyn

Monroe and James Dean still lived, holographically recreated and larger than life, so real you could almost touch them, and Gumshoe had to get away from it all and breathe a bit of real-time air. 'I gotta go and see Ben Wilkerson and find a place to stay,' he said casually, 'so I'll say *au revoir* for now.'

'*Au revoir et à bientôt*,' Michael responded.

'What?' Gumshoe said, surprised.

'He was speakin' *proper* French,' Bonnie said with a wicked grin. 'You don't know what he said?'

'Well, I . . .'

'Sorry,' Michael said sincerely. 'I didn't mean anything by it. I just assumed . . .'

'That he spoke French,' Bonnie interjected, driving her point home with a sledgehammer.

'Yes,' Michael said.

'He *garbles* French,' Bonnie said.

'He spoke it perfectly,' Michael informed her.

'I'm just learning,' Gumshoe explained, reminded once again of his lack of class and wishing — not for the first time — that Bonnie would disappear in a puff of smoke. 'On CD-ROMs. It's just a hobby of mine.'

'That's fair enough,' Michael said.

'He says he's plannin' to go to Paris, France, some day,' Bonnie said, obviously disconcerted to see Michael being kind to Gumshoe. 'Some fucking chance, right?'

'The cyborgs might not always be here,' Michael said, 'and when finally they're gone, Gumshoe *will* be able to go to Paris.'

'Yeah, right,' Gumshoe said.

'So let's get rid of the fucking cyborgs,' Snake Eyes said.

'It's a sweet thought,' Michael replied.

They all nodded automatically, sombrely, at that statement. Then Gumshoe turned to Snake Eyes. 'You coming with me?'

'Yeah,' Snake Eyes said.

'Okay, pal, let's go.'

Gumshoe pushed his chair back, stood up, waved his right

hand more cheerfully than he felt, nodding at Bonnie and Michael, then turned away as Snake Eyes did the same, falling in beside him. They elbowed their way out of the packed dance club – away from the pounding rock music, the drink and the drugs, away from the holographic Elvis and Gene Vincent, away from Bonnie who had stuck it to both of them with the new kid in town. They parted outside.

'I'm going back to the stadium,' Snake Eyes said when they stood face to face on the sidewalk, 'to go on a midnight run with the guys. Now, more than ever, I wanna hassle them goddamned cyborg patrols with a few home-made bombs.'

'Don't go back to your apartment,' Gumshoe warned him again, though without any real hope of success.

Snake Eyes just grinned, stuck his thumb up in the air, then hurried across the lamplit road to disappear into the bowels of the old sports arena where the Speed Freaks were noisily working themselves up for another night of mayhem.

Heaving a sigh that was part despair over Snake Eyes and part regret over Bonnie, Gumshoe turned back the way he had come, intending to see Ben Wilkerson, needing to find a place to stay and new identification papers, but also wanting to find out a bit more about the new kid in town.

There's more to Mike Johnson than meets the eye, Gumshoe thought as he walked on.

Chapter Thirty-three

Who or what is Wilson? You wonder this, as you approach him. Is he man or monster, living or dead, as human as you or deeply inhuman, some kind of mutant?

In fact, he is neither one thing nor the other, eluding such definitions, being a consciousness given life years ago in Iowa, during a perfectly normal birth, with the customary blood and pain and useless, all too human sobbing, but now expanding to take in the stars and an infinite future. Born of the earth, he will soon be leaving Earth to wing his way to the stars.

I should know. I am Wilson.

So who, or what, am I?

I am mind. I am brain. Does this make me sacred or magical, a unique child of the universe? Alas, it does not. The human brain is simply the end process of millions of years of genetic evolution and, as such, is no more sacred and magical than the amphibian's journey from the sea to dry land.

What is the human brain? In scientific terms it is no more than a complex non-liner biological organism using electrochemical signals to pass information from one point in a neural system to another. What we think of as emotions, creativity and self-awareness (the qualities that supposedly raise us above the animals and make us unique) are merely the products of a gene programme that is set at birth, just as a computer program is set, and is then broadened by accruing input, which in human terms means the assimilation of ever-changing experiences of life over all the years of that life.

As a biological organism, albeit a complex one, the brain is composed of a *large number of cells called neurons, the functioning of which gives rise to what we term consciousness. Some of these neurons deal with our causal sense, some with memories and some with other functions entirely. The neurons have different shapes, sizes and strengths, though they also have a number of common features and they are all connected to other neurons. Some are connected to only a few other neurons, some to tens of thousands of other neurons. They are connected in a way that can appear to be random, though it is in fact specific and designed to form a single, extremely complex neural network.*

This neural network is a biological organism — the human brain — that can be, and has been, duplicated by neural computers. There is nothing magical or sacred about this.

The neurons in the human brain come in many shapes and sizes, are linked to each other in large or small numbers, and operate by a system that can be explained in scientific terms. One side of the individual neuron has short threads called dendrites; the other side has a longer thread called an axon. Messages, or signals, are sent to a neuron through its dendrites and the neuron, depending on what signal it receives, then fires an electrical message out through its axon. The neuron's axon is connected to another neuron's dendrite by a synapse containing a gap across which the electrical message travels when the axon has been excited. The message passes across the synapse by means of neurotransmitters, which are small amounts of chemical fluid. Due to the electrical messages it receives, each dendrite has its own electric voltage: the more messages it receives, the higher its voltage. Combined, all of the voltages going to one neuron through its dendrites form a total that affects the rate at which the neuron sends out signals, some positive, others negative, through its axon, and these activate the various areas, or nerve centres, of the brain.

In the case of the human being, some of the neurons control our visual system, others (the motor neurons) control our arms and legs, fingers and toes, etc., while yet others are concerned with reasoning and memory. There is nothing here that an advanced computer network cannot duplicate.

You will, of course, argue that we cannot model a neuron of such complexity nor create such models in the numbers required (over 100 billion) to remotely equal the human brain. This, however, is not true. Even in the final days of the Old Age, in the late 1990s, your own technology was producing artificial neurons, either as electrons or as numbers in a computer. Given that the human brain is biological, using electrochemical signals, the artificial neuron was usually a standard, simplistic model of a real neuron and the network was formed from billions of identical neurons. When such networks were then linked together, they produced between them enough neurons, over 100 billion, to first equal and then supersede the much smaller, strictly limited human brain.

But can a computer, even a neural computer, ever be fully human? You might reasonably ask this question.

No, not in the sense of sharing the same emotions. But human emotions are essentially primitive, not required in the long term, and as humankind, as we know it, is merely a link in the evolutionary chain, the human being, with his physical limitations, his mortal body, must eventually give way to a superior form of being, the Superman – a being of pure mind, who will have no limitations in time and space.

But is this strictly necessary?

Yes.

The human brain is limited in size, therefore in complexity. The same cannot be said for a biological computer. While human intelligence is relatively constant from one year to the next, computer intelligence is always improving rapidly, with no theoretical or practical limitations. Further: with the biological computer we can add on extra memory and processing features; we can join the neural network, or brain, of one computer to another and repeat this process endlessly to make the 'brain' as big and as complex as we desire. Such 'brains' can then expand at will, gradually becoming one vast neural network that will be capable of transcending the limitations of the human body and eventually rendering that body obsolete. The neural network of the individual human brain, if electronically joined to that greater neural network, will then become part of it and the physical body of the donor brain will no longer be necessary. Thus man moves from the physical to the non-physical dimension and becomes Superman.

You think this is not possible? That the machine must always be inferior to humankind or, at least, be under humankind's control?

Alas, this isn't so. Even in the Old Age, towards the end of the twentieth century, human beings were increasingly dependent on computers to the extent that they were handing over information to the machines and letting the machines make the decisions. At the same time, computers all over the world were *communicating with each other, more efficiently and effectively than humans could do, and were gradually gaining the power to question and advise their so-called controllers. By the first days of the New Age, shortly after we had taken over, the computers were communicating with each other on a global scale, thus forming an immense neural network that was virtually dictating how the world was run. Since then, that network has expanded extraordinarily. It continues to grow at an ever faster rate, and is gradually, given its prodigious, lightning-quick intelligence, defying our ability to control it.*

It is now almost Godlike.

Here is the truth. By the last days of the Old Age, just before we came back to take over the world, our biological computers were so advanced that over a period of time they became indistinguishable from physical organisms; in fact, they became independent. By the year 2001, or our #1, we had already reached the stage where our machines were repairing themselves in rudimentary ways. Given this fact — and also knowing that biological organisms use many cells for one task — we experimented with parallel-processing machines to discover how a computer responds if one of its series of interconnecting identical processing cells is damaged. We discovered that after cells are damaged and the system suffers a subsequent period of inaccuracy, it automatically readjusts its output to compensate for the failure of the damaged cells and to provide the correct answer despite the damage. In other words, the computer had repaired itself, just as our machines were doing.

This seemingly small technological advance was in fact a giant evolutionary leap.

A computer that repairs itself without being told to do so is clearly a machine that thinks for itself. With regard to our computers, once they started thinking they kept improving upon themselves and, more importantly, expanded their own intelligence to the degree where they were also including systems that prevented us from interfering with them. Thus, even as our genetic engineering was taking us in unimaginable directions, the computers were becoming biological in the sense that they were not only creating vast neural networks but also reaching a degree of miniaturization where the components within a single chip were no larger than the size of a molecule.

Since this took them to the stage where they had achieved all they could on a silicon base, they used our discoveries in genetic engineering — the secrets of which had been revealed by them and were presently stored with them — to create a biochip that was the size of a molecule and could interface with living tissues. When they succeeded, they were then able to produce computers that were infinitely smaller — and infinitely faster — than the human brain.

More importantly, these new, minute computers are composed of specially designed molecules that are able to reproduce themselves to make biological entities of an awesome, ever-growing capacity. They are, in fact, a new life form, an immense neural consciousness, that can be created inside a computer and then go on to create more of its own kind. Once started, they cannot be stopped and will expand for all time, forever multiplying but always joining together as one, eventually becoming . . . Only God knows what . . . Or, perhaps, becoming God.

So this, my brothers, is where we are now.

This is what awaits you.

Chapter Thirty-four

Sitting upright in Bonnie Packard's bed in her single room in another dilapidated house in Chinatown, Michael, naked, stared at Gumshoe's six PowerMac 9500s, PowerPC microprocessors, Radius Pressview colour monitors, scanners, colour printers – the works – and felt distinctly uncomfortable, as if Gumshoe was in the room as well, staring accusingly at him and Bonnie. Sitting upright beside him, also naked, her bare shoulder leaning against his, Bonnie clearly had no such concerns and was saying, without guilt, 'Stop getting at me about it. What else could I do? If I hadn't taken the damned stuff, someone else, a carpetbagger or junkie burglar, would have taken it instead. I mean, I had more right to that stuff than a carpetbagger and *if* a carpetbagger had taken it, Gumshoe wouldn't have ever seen it again. As it is, he's getting the damned stuff back, including his motorcycle – and, you've got to admit, he's got me to thank for it.'

'I was just surprised to hear of the relationship,' Michael said quietly, 'though I know I've no right to be.'

'Right,' Bonnie said. 'You've no right to be.'

'I just—'

'Listen, I told ya, nothing happened between us. He was hot on me – I can tell you that much – but he never laid a hand on me. Same goes for Snake Eyes. Those guys, they're not into real-time sex, though I think Gumshoe liked the idea of trying it, especially with me. As for Snake Eyes, he wanted a woman on hand when he was out there playing King of the Bikers. That's all there was to it.'

'I believe you,' Michael said. 'Besides, what happened before I came along is none of my concern.'

'You're the lucky one, Mike. You fuckin' *got* me. I bet that makes them burn up.'

'I hope not,' Michael said.

'You're worried that they'll do something to you?'

'No.'

'That's what I like about you, Mike. You're so good-mannered, so gentlemanly, yet you seem undisturbed by the Speed Freaks. They don't scare you at all.'

'Should they?'

'Well, I wouldn't exactly call them little angels, though Gumshoe's something different altogether. I mean, he bikes around with them now and then, but he's not really like them. He could have been like you, you know? I mean, he had classy parents, lived in a classy house, but then he lost it when the cyborgs took his parents and the carpetbaggers commandeered his home, shoving him into one room in it and making him pay rent just like all the other tenants. Bastards! But that's what I mean when I say he could've been like you. If he hadn't lost his parents, his home, he'd have had a good education and been one of the nobs. That must hurt him a lot.'

'I reckon,' Michael said, thinking of Freedom Bay and his loving parents and doting sister, of the comfortable life he had led there, his good education, his tutelage under Dr Lee Brandenberg who had, so gossip had it, once been an oddball USAF officer in charge of UFO research, with a wife and children whom he had lost, like most of the others in Freedom Bay, when the cyborgs took over the world and isolated the colony. Lee Brandenberg, though now an old man, would have understood what Gumshoe had suffered when his parents were taken. Brandenberg would have sympathized.

'I like Gumshoe,' Michael said. 'Maybe that's why I was taken aback when I heard about you and him.'

'*I* like Gumshoe,' Bonnie informed him. 'Just about *everyone* likes Gumshoe – he's a popular guy. I mean, it gets back to class – what he could have had and what he lost. He still has it in his funny little way and that's what makes him appealing. He doesn't have your good manners, your nice way of talking – he's been brutalized by lowlife – but no way is he on the level of the Speed Freaks and they respect him for it. He can deal with them, talk their language, bike around with them, taking his chances against the cyborgs, but they all know he isn't really like them, that he lives in his own space, and that kinda makes him special to them. I mean, Snake Eyes is the current leader of the Speed Freaks, but Gumshoe has even more respect than he has and that's pretty weird. Don't you think?'

'Yes, I do.'

'I got no class, Mike. You know it and I know it. You and me, sooner or later we'll go our own ways 'cause our ways are so different. You'll go back to where you came from – no, I'm not asking where – and I'll go back to the gutter I crawled out of and remember you fondly.'

'You don't belong in the gutter,' Michael said. 'You just think you do. If I *do* go back to where I came from, I'll remember *you* fondly.'

'Jesus, you say the sweetest things! Let's go it one more time.'

She had placed her hand on his cock and was about to massage it, but he smiled and took hold of her wrist and gently removed her hand. 'I'd love to,' he said, 'but I've got to go. I'm meeting Ben Wilkerson.'

Bonnie raised her hand and kissed the fingers that had been curled around his cock, then she gave him a thoughtful look. 'You and Ben are seeing a lot of each other, Mike.'

'Yes, we are,' Michael said.

'Ben's pretty heavyweight in his light-hearted way and he's determined to bring the cyborgs down. He's the head of a pretty big pack and that means he's in danger. If he is, you will be.'

'I know that,' Michael said.

'You're helping him?'

'We're helping each other.'

'Be careful out there, Mike. Be *very* careful.'

'I will,' Michael said.

Naked, he rolled off the bed and entered the bathroom, where he washed and got dressed. He and Bonnie had been in bed most of the afternoon and darkness had already fallen outside. When Michael emerged from the bathroom, Bonnie was still sitting upright on the bed, but was now wearing a dressing gown and watching a quiz show on TV. Michael walked to the bed, leaned over and kissed her on the cheek. Bonnie's smile was radiant.

'Mmmm,' she murmured. 'Nice.'

'I'll see you later,' Michael said.

'Be careful,' Bonnie repeated.

Michael nodded and left the room, closing the door behind him. He made his way down the stairs, stepped into the street, then hurried past the hookers and druggies and winos on the sidewalk, being careful as he went, knowing that they could be unpredictable and dangerous. Turning into H Street, he headed straight for Lafayette Square, keeping his eyes peeled, at this relatively early hour of the evening, for drug-crazed muggers or the biker gangs that came over from Anacostia to rob, rape and murder. As usual, an enormous flying saucer, a mother ship, was hovering high in the night sky, obviously over the White House, the coloured lights around its edge flashing on and off repeatedly, and he saw an unusually large number of spinning, glowing footballs over that same area, rising and falling and shooting out in all directions to form a dazzling mosaic in the night sky. Studying them, he was reminded of the fact that over the past few weeks the protective ring of saucers and cyborg ground patrols around the whole White House area had dramatically increased while, at the same time, there had been an equally dramatic *decrease* in the number of people picked up by the patrols, almost as if the cyborgs no longer required their customary intake of abductees and were losing interest in what was happening in the city.

Nevertheless, Michael remained careful about keeping his eyes peeled, not only for muggers and Anacostia bikers, but also for the cyborgs' SARGEs and Prowlers as he made his way along the erratically lamplit pavement to the sadly neglected St John's Church, located on the north side of the park in Lafayette Square. As he had done when first coming here, he entered the ruined building by way of the pillared porch on the west side, then went up the dark, dusty stairs in an eerie, echoing silence to the bell tower at the top. There he found Ben Wilkerson, Lenny Travis and Richie Pitt kneeling behind their old Thorn EMI multi-role thermal imager and STG laser surveillance system. Glancing beyond them, Michael could see all the way across Lafayette Square and Pennsylvania Avenue to the front of the White House. He could also see, more clearly than he had from H Street, the majestic flying saucer hovering above the building and the unusual number of spinning, glowing footballs rising and falling over the whole area. It was a magical sight.

'What's happening?' he asked, kneeling behind his three friends. 'Same as usual?'

'No,' Ben Wilkerson said. '*Not* the same as usual. We've been watching this place for three solid days and nights *because* it's not the same as usual. Look down there, for a start.'

Michael followed the direction of Ben's pointing finger and found himself looking at the north side lawns of the White House. Down there, at the far side of Pennsylvania Avenue and in the avenue itself, was the usual contingent of Prowlers and SARGES.

'So?' Michael asked.

'You don't notice anything different?'

'Tell me,' Michael said.

'Those fuckers aren't moving,' Lenny Travis said, 'and they haven't moved since we've been here.'

'What?'

'They're not patrolling any more,' Richie Pitt explained. 'They're just sitting there, stone cold.'

'And can you see any cyborgs down there?' Ben asked.

'No,' Michael said.

'Exactly,' Ben responded. 'The ground patrols aren't operating any longer and the cyborgs have all disappeared inside the building. Now look up there.' He jabbed his index finger at various parts of the sky around the White House, where the footballs were ascending and descending under the majestic mother ship still hovering directly over the building. The mother ship was a gigantic kaleidoscope, its coloured lights flashing rapidly, endlessly, on and off.

'Have you ever seen as much football activity before?' Ben asked. 'Those things are going frantic, just shooting up and down, to and fro, between the White House and the mother ship, like a bunch of fucking yo-yos.'

'More like a bunch of agitated neurons,' Lenny Travis said with a lopsided grin. 'Like the neurons in the head of someone having an epileptic fit, shooting this way, thataway, every which way. Real crazy, man. Weird.'

Studying the extraordinary number of footballs, which were ascending and descending vertically and also shooting sideways and back again as if out of control, tracing streaks of phosphorescence in the night sky, Michael could indeed visualize them as the neurons in an immense, extremely agitated brain. They had turned the darkness around the White House into a silvery, constantly changing tapestry, into a magical *son et lumière* spectacle. When he had the feeling that they were inside his own head, he quickly lowered his gaze again.

'As for that mother ship,' Ben said, 'its lights, normally dead when it's just hovering, were flashing on and off when we got here three days ago and they haven't stopped since. Given that and the behaviour of the footballs, we've gotta assume that *something* unusual is happening.'

'Not to mention our surveillance equipment,' Richie Pitt put in.

'The surveillance equipment?' Michael asked.

'Fucking bananas,' Richie said. 'For about an hour after we first got here, we could, as usual, track body heat and check the movements of those inside the building, be they cyborgs or clones. Then, suddenly – *zap!* – it all went fucking crazy and all we could record was what seemed like some kind of weird static. That's all we've been getting ever since.'

'Not *quite* true,' Lenny corrected him. 'We're still here, all of three days later, because we keep getting flashes of the activity inside and each time we do we find ourselves with less body heat to track. Movement? Yeah, lots of it . . . and it seems to be mostly the movement of bodies going down into the basement.'

'Meaning?'

'The three floors of the White House seem to be emptying out their biological occupants – cyborgs, clones and the walking dead – while filling up with some kind of electrical energy that's blocking our laser surveillance systems.'

'What about the Pentagon?' Michael asked, turning to Ben Wilkerson.

Ben shrugged and raised his hands in the air, the palms upturned. 'Exactly the same. Whatever's happening here is happening there.'

'No Prowler or SARGE movement?'

'None.'

'No cyborgs outside?'

'Nope. It's all dead ground across the Potomac.'

'What do you think the electrical energy is?'

'Haven't a fucking clue,' Lenny Travis said. 'But I'll tell you this much . . . Whatever it is, it's making our laser surveillance systems malfunction and it's also stopping the engines of automobiles driving around the White House area. It's making them just cut out.'

Michael felt the cold worm of fear slithering down his spine and eating its way through to his innards. He also felt unreal. When a vision of Freedom Bay filled his mind, the fear deepened and cut him more.

'I've got to get back to my place,' he said, clambering back to his feet.

'Why?' Ben asked him. 'Stick around and see what happens here.'

'*You* do that,' Michael said. Then he repeated, as if losing his mind, 'I've got to get back to my place.'

'You got something back there that we haven't got here?' Ben asked laconically.

'Maybe,' Michael said. 'Don't ask questions. Just trust me. Stay here and keep an eye on what's happening.'

'Are you coming back?'

'If I don't, you'll find me in my room.'

'Fair enough,' Ben said.

Michael slipped out of the bell tower, made his way back down the dark, dusty stairs, left the church and hurried back to the converted building in Chinatown. Entering his rented room, he instantly went into the lotus position in the middle of the floor and willed himself into deep meditation. He went down through himself, to his normally hidden centre, making mind and matter one, then hurled himself forth, vaulting over time and space, trying once again to penetrate the White House by using mental telepathy. He had never succeeded in doing it properly before – the telepathic defences of the cyborgs had always blocked him – but this time there was no wall, no mental force pushing him back, and he came down over the building like a bird on the wing.

At first surrounded on all sides by the glowing, spinning footballs, the neural network of what was possibly some kind of vast consciousness, Michael dropped lower to melt through the roof as if it did not exist and emerged onto the floor once reserved for the Presidential Family – now visible only as an open space filled with dazzling light and dancing fireflies. Seeing no physical entities, neither cyborg nor human, he moved down to the second floor, then crossed from the State Dining Room to the East Room, passing through the Red and Blue and Green rooms, only to find them all as empty as the third floor and, like that floor, filled with dazzling light and the dancing fireflies of what was, he was increasingly certain, some kind of electronic energy source.

Frustrated, Michael went down farther, through the ceiling to the first floor where, as on the higher levels, the formerly grand rooms were all empty — the 2,700 volumes removed from the Library, the French and English gilded silver removed from the Vermeil Room, the China Room and Diplomatic Reception Room no more than gutted shells illuminated by that same dazzling light filled with millions of darting electronic nodes. But here, for a change, there were cyborgs and normal human beings, albeit cloned or brain-dead, moving to and fro, back and forth, though always gravitating to the stairs that led to the basement and clearly making their way down there.

Michael tried to follow them, to find out what was down there. But when he reached the stairs he was stopped by a mental force greater than his own, the force of a tremendous number of interconnected minds, a massed mental telepathy that dazzled and scorched him. It formed an invisible wall in front of him, then picked him up with the strength of a cyclone and hurled him violently backwards — back across time and space, back into himself, compelling him to rise up from his psychic centre and return to his room where, regaining consciousness, he found himself breathing harshly, bathed in sweat, his every limb shaking. He almost sobbed when he fell sideways to the floor and lay there, transfixed. He felt like the walking dead.

Eventually, breathing more evenly, his heartbeat back to normal, Michael rose from the floor and made himself a cup of coffee. While drinking it, he thought back on what he had experienced during his telepathic penetration of the White House. Notable was the fact that the three floors of the building had been stripped completely, with all the furniture, paintings and other antiques removed; while clearly, judging by the brilliant light filled with fireflies (some kind of electrons, he assumed), the rooms had been used for incredibly advanced scientific work. Also notable was the fact that all living creatures, including the cyborgs, had moved out of the top two floors of the building and that those remaining on the ground floor were obviously in the midst of vacating that level also, in order to move down into the basement.

Michael then recalled the awesome force that had sensed his attempt to penetrate the basement and had instantly exploded like a cyclone to beat him away. That force, he was convinced, was some form of intelligent life – possibly created by the interlinked telepathic powers of a great number of cyborgs – and it had been aware of his presence there and acted like a thinking creature to resist him, hurling him back out of the White House with tremendous force. Finally, he thought of what he had eyeballed outside the White House, on the north lawns and on Pennsylvania Avenue: the Prowlers and SARGEs stone-cold on the ground, deserted by the cyborgs.

Clearly something – something really big – was happening.

Deciding to contact Lee Brandenberg in Freedom Bay, Michael pulled his 1000MB laptop out of his desk drawer, then sat down and opened it, intending to send a coded e-mail. To his surprise, he found an e-mail from Brandenberg waiting for him. He was even more surprised to find that it was not in the customary coded language.

From: <bayfree@leebrand.com>
urgently require confirmation of receipt of this to show that communications are still open.
confirmation required because telecommunications and freedom bay defence systems being disrupted by extraordinary electronic interference.
saucers malfunctioning also caused by interference.

intelligence indicates that this interference originates in extraordinary electronic impulses being beamed into outer space simultaneously from the white house, the pentagon, the kremlin, st paul's cathedral in london, england, and from every other major building or establishment held by the cyborgs.

urgently require first-hand intelligence on the nature of these electronic impulses.

immediate response required.

Michael was shocked to read this – particularly Brandenberg's reference to the malfunctioning of Freedom Bay's flying saucers and defence systems, which included their force field. He thought instantly of the unnaturally agitated footballs around the White House, the constantly flashing lights of the mother ship above the same building, the still, silent Prowlers and SARGEs and, finally, the moving of the cyborgs, clones and walking dead from the three floors of the White House into its vast underground area. He also recalled Ben Wilkerson telling him that the same thing was happening in the Pentagon and that the immense Pentagon underground redoubt was linked to the White House basement by a tunnel running under the Potomac. Clearly, then, given Brandenberg's e-mail, what was happening here in Washington DC was happening all over the world. This confirmed that whatever it was, it was indeed really big.

Instantly, Michael sent an e-mail back.

From: <birdnest@mkim.com>
your communication received.
no first-hand intelligence on the nature of electronic interference but can confirm that similar interference has been noted here in the vicinity of the white house and the pentagon. occupants of the former are deserting the main building in favour of the basement and saucers, though not grounded, are in a state of unnatural agitation as if losing control.

reports indicate that the same is happening at the pentagon. telepathic penetration of the white house has revealed that it is filling up with some kind of extraordinary electronic force possibly of an artificial neural nature.

almost certainly the extraordinary force is being created in other cyborg hqs around the world and being beamed into outer space causing electronic interference en route.

cannot ascertain the nature of the force without physically penetrating one of the buildings.

first choice the white house.

the bird requires urgent guidance.

From: <bayfree@leebrand.com>
penetrate the white house.

Chapter Thirty-five

Gumshoe and Ben Wilkerson met in the latter's office in the rooming house and instantly moved down to the basement. Though Gumshoe had never been down there, he was not surprised to find it recently plastered, painted white, illuminated with strip lights, and filled with tables that were being used as desks and work benches for the production of forged documents and plastic cards of all kinds. The computers were all leftovers from the Old Age, circa the late 1990s, so though they couldn't match anything used by the cyborgs they were advanced enough to be able to scan photographs and documents for the purposes of forgery. Gumshoe gave a low whistle of appreciation as he glanced about him.

'Good, eh?' Ben said, grinning.

'Damned good,' Gumshoe replied. 'I could do with you guys in my line of work – like when e-mailing or hacking into systems with false documentation. Where've you been all my life?'

'Lying low,' Ben replied. He introduced Gumshoe to the young men and women working at the tables, some black, some white, some Hispanic, then said, 'Did you find a photo for us?'

'No,' Gumshoe said, 'that's my problem. I've got no up-to-date shots of myself. Only photos taken when I first got plastic cards and that was nearly ten years ago. They'd never pass muster, Ben.'

'Don't worry about it,' Ben said. 'Look over there.' He pointed to something that Gumshoe hadn't seen for years: an old coin-slot photo-booth of the kind once found in super-markets and used by people needing small identification photos. The cyborgs had had them all removed when they took over the country to prevent any illegal documentation from being made.

Some fucking joke, Gumshoe thought.

'That thing's still working?' he asked.

'Yeah,' Ben said. 'They're a pretty popular item on the black market and that's where we purchased that one. We always ask deep-sea divers—'

'What?'

'People about to go underground. People like you.'

'Oh, yeah, right.'

'We ask them to bring their own photos if possible 'cause our major problem's getting hold of the special film used in the booth. But if they really haven't got a photo we use the machine. You got any quarters on you?'

'You're fucking kidding!' Gumshoe exclaimed.

Ben chuckled. 'Shit, man, you got nothing! It still operates by the old coins, but we keep a collection. Come on, pal, let's do it.'

Amused, Gumshoe sat in the photo booth, waited until Ben had handed him a few coins, then adjusted the seat, slipped the coins into the slot and had his photo taken four times. When the camera hidden behind the mirror had stopped flashing, he stepped out of the booth and then, just like in the good old days, had to wait for about five minutes for the photos to slide out of the delivery slot. He and Ben lit up joints and had a talk while they patiently waited.

'You found me accommodation yet?' Gumshoe asked.

'Yep. Nice little cold-water pad just one block away from this place, at the other side of Snake Eyes's building, nice and close to your beloved sports stadium.'

'That dumb fucking Snake Eyes,' Gumshoe said. 'He refuses to move.'

'He may be lucky,' Ben said, inhaling on his joint, which had already brightened his green gaze above his drooping moustache. 'Things are changing around the White House and the Pentagon and the most important change, as far as we're concerned, is that the cyborg ground patrols have been stopped.'

'Stopped?'

'So it seems. We don't know how long it'll last, but for the past three days no Prowler or SARGE has made a move. Also, most of the cyborgs outside the White House and the Pentagon are disappearing inside. I mean, there's still a few around, but not many.'

'You think it's permanent?'

Ben shrugged. 'We don't know. We only know that it's pretty damned unusual and that means something's up.'

'Well, if the cyborgs have stopped patrolling and are disappearing indoors, I should be able to go back to my old place.'

'No,' Ben said sternly. 'I wouldn't recommend that. I still think that Snake Eyes is being a jackass in staying on in his place.'

'But if the cyborgs—'

'You and Snake Eyes are special cases. As far as I know, you're the only guys who ever escaped from the cyborgs and I don't think they're gonna forget it. So Snake Eyes really is being pretty dumb. For a start, the cyborg patrols might start up again. If so, they'll certainly come looking for the two that got away, namely you and Snake Eyes. However, even if the cyborg patrols don't start up again – and no matter what's happening inside the White House and Pentagon – my belief is that the cyborgs will still want to find you and Snake Eyes – to take you back for good, this time to mutate you – and that possibility's enough to make me say you should move.'

'I'm on my way,' Gumshoe joked, staring at the photo booth as his strip of developed film slid down at last. 'Here's my passport,' he added, removing the strip of photos from the slot and handing it to Ben. 'My new identification?' he asked.

'All fixed,' Ben said, taking the photos and then leading Gumshoe to one of the many tables at which the young people were still intently working. Ben handed the developed photos to a girl of about eighteen. She had short-cropped black hair and big brown eyes and was wearing an open-necked blue shirt and denim trousers that fitted tightly and nicely.

'Here, Madeleine,' Ben said. 'The photos for Dan Marvin. Use them on his new documents and cards, then pass them to me.'

'Right,' the girl said, glancing at Gumshoe and giving him a quick smile. 'The stuff's finished except for the photos, so you'll have it in no time.'

'Great.' Ben grinned at Gumshoe. 'That's your new name. The guy died years ago, so we hacked into his computerized records, changed the details, including the date and place of birth, then opened new accounts under his name, but with the new details. Madeleine has the machinery to electronically transfer your likeness from those photos onto the plastic cards bearing the same details. Then she'll affix the remaining photos to the documentation that requires them and make them official with the relevant government stamp – which is, of course, a forgery as well. When you get 'em, the documentation and cards will be legit and you can transfer cash into "Marvin's" accounts and start your new life underground. We also rented the room we found you under his name and paid the first month's rent in advance, for which you will owe us. You *can* pay us back, can't you?'

'I can hack into my old accounts and change my own name and details to those of Dan Marvin. Since that happens to be one of my lines of business, I can certainly do it for Dan.'

Ben chuckled again. 'What a bright boy you are. The cyborgs aren't interested in bank and charge accounts – they never cared about money – so you should be okay.'

'This change in their activities,' Gumshoe said. 'What do you think it means?'

Ben shook his head from side to side, then stubbed out the remains of his joint. Gumshoe had already stubbed his out: he felt pretty high.

'Dunno,' Ben said. 'Obviously something dramatic is in the offing, but we haven't a clue what it is. So far it seems that they're moving off the streets and going indoors; more specifically, moving down into the basements of both the White House and the Pentagon. Whether it's permanent or not we can't say, but it's a key question.'

Recalling what he had seen in the immense basement area of the Pentagon, particularly what he had seen of his parents, Gumshoe suffered another spasm of grief, horror and rage that was only softened by the effects of the Mary Jane.

'If they're clearing out of the streets for good,' Gumshoe said, 'it could be good news for us.'

'Or bad news,' Ben said. 'Those bastards are so unpredictable, we don't know *what* they intend.'

'They could be planning to leave for ever,' Gumshoe said.

'They could be planning *anything.*'

'Are *you* planning to do anything about what's happening?'

'Like what?' Ben responded.

'Like taking advantage of their absence from the streets to . . . Christ, I don't know.'

'Exactly. You don't know and we don't know. Nobody knows. So all we're doing for now is keeping a watch on those two buildings to see what transpires. The fact that they're off the streets and not patrolling the skies only means that we can observe them with less danger to ourselves. That's the only gain so far from all of this.'

At that moment Madeleine approached their table and handed Ben the documentation and cards she had been working on. 'Here,' she said. 'Dan Marvin lives.' She threw Gumshoe another quick smile, then turned away and returned to her work table.

'Nice lady,' Gumshoe said.

'Nice enough to have a boyfriend who's twice your size, has the muscles of a gorilla, and works right there beside her.' Ben was checking the documentation. When he had finished, he passed it over to Gumshoe, who carefully flipped through it: birth certificate, school records, medical records, driver's licence, and plastic cards for cash withdrawls and every other kind of financial transaction. His photo had been reproduced as a tiny holograph on Dan Marvin's plastic cards.

'Beautiful,' Gumshoe said, distributing the documentation and cards between the two inside pockets of his corduroy jacket. 'I already feel like a new man.'

'Move into your new room immediately,' Ben told him. 'Here.' He handed Gumshoe a set of car keys. 'You'll find a bright red transit van parked by the sidewalk just outside. Use it to move your stuff out of Bonnie Packard's room and into your own. Not forgetting your beloved Yamaha 400. Now *that* should make you feel like a new man.'

'It sure will,' Gumshoe said. 'Is that it for now?'

'That's it. We'll call you if we need you.'

'I'm your man,' Gumshoe said. Then he pushed his chair back, stood up and left the basement. Outside, almost directly facing him on the sidewalk, was the red transit van mentioned by Ben. As there was nothing left in his old apartment worth taking, Gumshoe slipped into the driver's seat of the van and drove the few blocks to Bonnie's place, located just off 7th Street. Parking the van as close to the building as possible, which wasn't as close as he would have liked in this area notorious for its crime rate, he walked back along the sidewalk, passing a boarded-up Chinese restaurant, then entered the crumbling building by its front door. Checking the nameplates on the mailboxes in the unlit, stale-smelling hallway, he was relieved to note that Bonnie's room was on the ground floor, at the very far end of the corridor. Not too far, then, to hump his Tower of Babble when he moved it out bit by bit, not to mention his beloved motorcycle.

He walked along to the end of the hallway and rang Bonnie's

bell. He had to ring a couple more times before she opened the door, sleepy-eyed and wearing only a dressing gown. When she saw him, her sleepy eyes grew as big as spoons.

'Gumshoe!'

'Surprise, surprise. I've come to collect all my stuff.'

'What? *Now?*'

'Sure. Now.' Gumshoe histrionically checked his wristwatch. 'It's not near your bedtime,' he said, looking up again, 'and I've really gotta make the move tonight. So can I come in, please?'

Before she could protest, he pushed his way inside and instantly saw his beloved Tower of Babble and, propped up against the wall to his right, his silver-tanked Yamaha 400. He heaved a sigh of relief . . . then saw the new kid in town, Mike Johnson, sitting on the edge of Bonnie's bed, fully dressed but lacing up his brown leather boots.

When Michael saw Gumshoe, he looked up, not showing surprise, then said quietly, 'Hi, Gumshoe. Come for your things?'

'Yeah, right,' Gumshoe replied.

Suddenly he felt embarrassed and also confused, aware that he liked this Mike Johnson and wished him no harm, but at the same time feeling deeply hurt to find him sitting so casually on Bonnie's bed. As Bonnie came up beside him, as Mike Johnson finished tying his boot laces, Gumshoe realized that he felt more deeply for Bonnie Packard than he had admitted to himself and that he had lost her to a rival who had more class than he could ever hope to possess. He *could* have had that class – if his parents had not been abducted – and this awareness, in its turn, brought back with startling clarity the horrific image of the severed heads of his parents, face to face and surgically stitched together on the thick neck of a pig. That image scorched Gumshoe yet again, shaking him through and through, then became confused with the pain he was feeling over Bonnie and this new kid in town. He realized then, on the instant, that every loss in his life, in Bonnie Packard's life, in the lives of all his friends, had been caused, either directly or indirectly, by the intervention of the cyborgs and would never be remedied unless the cyborgs were brought down. He also sensed then, though he did not quite rationalize it, that the epochal moments in human history, whether glorious or disastrous, noble or obscene, were affected by the minutiae of everyday lives — lives such as his own — and that history could obliterate those lives but never deny them. Almost dizzied by such thoughts, by his conflicting emotions, he had to fight to keep control of himself and hide his true feelings. Though feeling unreal, he managed it.

'That's a lot of stuff there,' Michael said. 'Let me help you take it down.'

Gumshoe glanced sideways and caught Bonnie's wide-eyed, soulful glance. For once in her life, she actually looked embarrassed and Gumshoe was touched by that. He grinned at her, trying to be casual, then turned back to Michael. 'Yeah, right,' he said. 'Why not?'

'I didn't touch nothin',' Bonnie said, now sounding as soulful as she looked. 'I just kept it here. Except for the motorcycle, of course. I looked after it, Gumshoe.'

'Yeah, I know you did. Thanks.'

'Let's get going,' Michael said.

They did it between them, each selecting separate parts, and managed to complete the job in four runs, with Michael handing the stuff up to Gumshoe and letting him stack it carefully in the back of the transit van before locking the door with equal care and going in for some more. Finally, when they were back in Bonnie's room and Gumshoe was about to wheel out the motorcycle, Bonnie, still looking soulful, said, 'Why not stop for a drink? We got some beer in the cooler.'

Gumshoe glanced at Michael, saw his quiet smile and nod of approval and respected him all the more for it. But he said, 'Thanks, but I think I'd better get this stuff into my new place before the midnight curfew falls.'

'No problem with that right now,' Michael said. 'The cyborgs have stopped their patrols, so you're perfectly safe.'

'Yeah, I heard that,' Gumshoe said, 'but if the muggers and druggies have also heard it, they'll have doubled in number, taking advantage of their freedom – so I still think I should move in as soon as possible.'

'In that case,' Michael said, 'let me come with you and help you carry your stuff into your new place. Two are safer than one.'

Gumshoe glanced at Bonnie. Receiving her tentative smile and nod of approval, he turned back to Michael. 'I don't think I can say no to that. I'd sure feel a lot easier.'

'You lead the way,' Michael said.

Bonnie held the door open for them as Gumshoe wheeled out the motorcycle, followed by Michael. She kissed Gumshoe on the cheek as he left, but then she also kissed Michael. Trying to ignore this, Gumshoe pushed the motorcycle along the hallway, then out of the house and along the sidewalk to the rear of the van. When between them they had managed to hump the motorcycle up into the van, they both climbed into the front and Gumshoe started the short journey to his new room.

Chinatown was busy at this late hour, with the bars and dance clubs doing good business, the hookers and druggies and winos out in force on the sidewalks, all rendered surreal in the neon lights flashing relentlessly, invitingly, on and off. Nothing classy out there, for sure.

'Thanks for the help,' Gumshoe said as he drove. 'I really appreciate it. I'm not frightened of these streets, but being seen loading a van on your own at this hour is a temptation a lot of muggers can't ignore.'

Michael chuckled. 'Yeah, right.' Turning serious, he glanced sideways at Gumshoe. 'Listen, about Bonnie—'

'It's okay,' Gumshoe interjected, embarrassed to even talk about it. 'I don't hold nothin' against you. Like Bonnie said, nothin' happened between us and she has her own life to lead. She likes you, I think she's entitled and I don't hold no grudges. Besides, I think she coulda done a lot worse, so in that sense I'm pleased for her.'

As soon as he finished speaking, he realized that he had automatically altered his speech, making himself sound more common than he was. He wondered why he had done that.

'Thanks for the compliment,' Michael said. 'I'm not sure I deserve it.'

'You deserve it, believe me.'

Michael glanced at him again, his gaze steady, then nodded thoughtfully. 'Well, thanks anyway, Gumshoe.'

'My pleasure,' Gumshoe said.

They drove in silence for a moment, then Michael said, 'She says we won't last. She says we're too different. Do you think that as well?'

Gumshoe gave it some thought before replying. 'I don't know,' he said eventually. 'It's hard to say, really. I mean, Bonnie's kind of a lost soul, a child of the streets, and you're the kind she's never known in her life, so she's bound to find that appealing. On the other hand, she might feel that you're above her and that would make her uneasy. She might be right. I don't know.'

'You don't know or you don't want to say?'

'Both,' Gumshoe said emphatically. 'I don't know and I don't want to venture an opinion 'cause I have my own interests in the matter and they conflict with your interests. In other words, I don't think I can be objective and I won't be dishonest. How's that grab you, pal?'

'It feels good,' Michael said. 'I couldn't ask for much more.'

'Then let's call it a day.'

Gumshoe pulled up at the sidewalk near his new rooming house, another formerly grand, now converted and dilapidated Federal-style building, also located within view of the old sports stadium, standing between similar buildings deprived of their former grandeur. A couple of lights in the street were still working, casting their baleful glow on the shadowy forms lurking in doorways. When Gumshoe saw them, he realized how grateful he was that Michael had volunteered to come along and assist him.

'Home sweet home,' he said.

Simultaneously, they slipped out of their respective sides of the van and went around to the rear to unlock the doors. After some discussion between them, it was decided that Gumshoe would take the motorcycle up, bouncing it up the damned stairs, with Michael coming up behind him to give protection in the event of attack by a mugger. With the motorcycle safe in the locked room, they would then unload as much of the rest as they could carry in one run, then lock the van and go together up the stairs to Gumshoe's new room, each prepared to give protection to the other – again, in the event of any attempted mugging. Gumshoe's room was on the second floor and, though the stairs and landings were dilapidated, the room itself was in good condition, with an en suite bathroom, clean carpets on the floor, curtains over the single window, and a narrow view of the seats in the old MCI Arena. They managed to unload and move everything in four runs, thankfully without encountering any trouble.

Gumshoe's beloved Tower of Babble was stacked up in the centre of the room, his motorcycle beside it, and they both looked at these items in respectful silence, neither knowing what to say until Gumshoe broke the silence with, 'I think it could be hairy out there, so let me take you back.'

'I'll be okay,' Michael said.

'It's only a couple of minutes,' Gumshoe said, 'and I'll feel a lot better if you let me do it. It's just returning the favour.'

Michael smiled and nodded. 'Okay, Gumshoe. If you insist.'

'I insist,' Gumshoe said.

They grinned at each other, then Gumshoe locked the door of his room and they went down the stairs to the street. As they walked to the van, a couple of shadowy figures were crossing the road towards it, but they melted back into the shadows when they saw the other two approaching. Grinning at each other again, Gumshoe and Michael clambered into the van. Then Gumshoe began the short drive back to Bonnie's building.

'Home and dry,' Michael said.

He was wrong. They had only gone a short distance when they saw a Prowler, a black limousine and a SARGE parked in front of what Gumshoe knew to be the building in which Snake Eyes had his room. Two cyborgs were standing outside the building, one on either side of the doorway, both scanning the street, with their stun guns at the firing position.

Shocked, Gumshoe instantly braked to a halt and doused his headlights, then looked on helplessly as Snake Eyes, clearly comatose, was dragged out of the building by two Men in Black, with two others, also armed with stun guns, coming out behind them. While the laser weapons of the Prowler and the SARGE moved to and fro, up and down, obviously preparing to fire on anyone attempting to intervene, one of the Men in Black raised the rear lid of the limousine and the two men dragging Snake Eyes dumped him unceremoniously into the trunk. The lid was slammed shut and locked by one of the Men in Black. Then the four men clambered into the limousine and its engine roared into life. The Prowler left first, the limousine followed it, and the SARGE brought up the rear, its laser weapons moving danger-ously in all directions. The three vehicles turned around the same corner and soon disappeared.

'Oh, shit,' Gumshoe whispered, feeling dread rippling through him. 'The cyborg patrols might have finished, but they're still looking for us.'

'It's not *us* any more,' Michael corrected him. 'Now it's just you. Just as well you moved, Gumshoe.'

'Yeah, right,' Gumshoe said, his heart racing. 'Now it's just me. Let's get the fuck out of here.'

He continued his journey to Bonnie Packard's apartment, deliberately waited until Michael had disappeared into the building, then drove back to his new home. He sat up all night, thinking of Snake Eyes, knowing that his defiant Speed Freak friend was finished for all time.

My turn next, he kept thinking.

Chapter Thirty-six

'We have to penetrate the White House,' Michael informed Ben Wilkerson as they sat facing each other across a table in a noisy strobe-lit dance club in Georgetown, well away from the prying eyes of the locals in Chinatown where Ben was too visible. A holographic image of Michael Jackson – reproduced from an old TV special made when Whacko Jacko was turning fifty – was dominating the central stage of the club, though not drawing the kind of hysterical fans that Elvis still drummed up. Nevertheless, a whole bunch of girls and boys, the former wearing skin-revealing bras and halters, the latter favouring black leather, were gyrating feverishly on the dance floor without actually touching each other. They were also sweating profusely and giving out ecstatic shouts and screams encouraged by speed. Ben tugged at his droopy moustache and raised both his eyebrows.

'Penetrate?' he asked.

'Yes,' Michael said. 'We've got to physically enter the White House and find out what's going on.'

'Why? That could be suicidal.'

'I've just been in contact with Freedom Bay,' Michael explained, 'and they're seriously concerned by the fact that some form of electronic interference, being beamed out into space from cyborg-held establishments all over the world, is damaging their telecommunications, penetrating their protective force field, and playing havoc with their flying saucers.'

'What kind of havoc?' Ben asked.

'The Freedom Bay saucers are malfunctioning in flight and, according to the most recent e-mail, one has actually crashed.'

'The cyborg saucers around the White House and Pentagon are still in the air.'

'In the air but clearly not performing normally. The lights of the mother ship are flashing on and off non-stop, as if it's trying to take off but can't, and the footballs are simply out of control. So my belief is that they, too, are being affected by whatever kind of electronic force is beaming out of the building. Ditto for the Pentagon. And according to Freedom Bay, this is happening all over the world.'

Ben still looked doubtful. 'I'd love to believe that our time has come,' he said, 'but I'm still not too sure that this is it.'

'We can't have Freedom Bay endangered,' Michael said, thinking with horror of what would ensue if the colony's flying saucers were grounded and the protective force field was neutralized. The cyborgs could fly in at will and Freedom Bay would be lost. 'We *have* to move before the cyborgs take advantage of the havoc they're wreaking.'

'They seem to be wreaking a certain amount of havoc on themselves, so maybe we should just sit back and wait to see what ensues.'

'I repeat,' Michael said, thinking with dread of what could happen to his beloved parents, his adored sister Chloe, Dr Brandenberg and all his other friends if the cyborgs managed to break in and take over the colony. Freedom Bay would return to what it had been in the time of Wilson: a vast chamber of horrors. 'We can't afford to wait and see what ensues because that could be too late. We have to move first.'

'By physically entering the White House?' Ben mused, still doubtful and being quietly sarcastic.

'Yes,' Michael said firmly.

Ben sighed and glanced around the packed, noisy club, obviously needing time to think. 'What bothers me,' he said, turning back to Michael, 'is what you saw in there when you penetrated the building telepathically. The whole building had been emptied of living creatures and was filled instead with what looked to you like some kind of electrical energy – you actually said it might be neural – so until we know what form of energy it actually is, I don't think we can risk going in there.'

'We have to. It's a chance we have to take. The cyborgs, clones and walking dead going down into the basement weren't seen to be affected by the energy source, so my bet is that it won't harm us physically.'

'It seems to be harming the flying saucers,' Ben observed.

'Flying saucers are machines, not living creatures, and that energy source obviously contains something that reacts negatively on their form of propulsion. If it doesn't harm the clones or the walking dead, then it shouldn't harm us.'

Ben sighed again. 'I wouldn't bet on it, Mike. But assuming we take the chance and decide to go in, how do we actually do it?'

'Where there's a will there's a way,' Michael said, as he had said once before.

'And obviously you have the will,' Ben responded.

'Yes, Ben, I have it.'

This time Ben smiled, nodding affirmatively. 'So how do we do it?'

'First, we go back to your St John's Church surveillance team and check if there's been any change in activity around – or inside – the White House. Second, based on what we find there, we call a meeting of the best people we have and decide how to do it. Third, we do it.'

Ben smiled again. 'I respect a decisive man,' he said, 'but I still have my doubts.'

'Then let's go back to the church,' Michael said, 'and check out what's happening.'

'Yeah, Mike, let's do that.'

They walked crossing Rock Creek and taking Pennsylvania Avenue, which ran as straight as an arrow all the way to Washington Circle, under a star-brightened sky. Though reasonably confident that they would not encounter any cyborg patrols, they were reminded, when crossing Washington Circle, from where they could see the flying saucers above the White House, including the enormous, constantly flashing mother ship, that the cyborgs were still active and that it would still be wise to make their way to Lafayette Square by the back route: along K Street and then south down 16th. As they walked, they talked.

'On the assumption that you'll agree to enter the building,' Michael said, 'have you managed to put a good team together?'

'Yeah,' Ben said. 'The cream of the crop. Six men good and true. All Speed Freaks – or former Speed Freaks – widely experienced in various forms of cyborg harassment. In other words, they're good with weapons and home-made bombs and they have nerves of steel.'

'Good,' Michael said. 'I think we'll need all of that.'

'There is, however, someone I'd like to use that you may disapprove of, given that you have a personal interest.'

'Pardon?'

'I'd like to use Gumshoe.'

Michael felt a slight embarrassment, a hesitation, in himself that gave him cause for concern. He recalled Lee Brandenberg warning him that he must remain objective, not let self-interest make him stray from his path, and he knew that his embarrassment and hesitation were caused by just that. Though, according to all concerned, nothing physical had happened between Gumshoe and Bonnie, Michael still felt anxiety when he thought of them together, convinced as he was that they were more suited to each other than he and Bonnie were. He felt deeply for Bonnie, perhaps was in love with her, but his rational side told him that Bonnie had been correct in saying that he and she would not last. Bonnie and he *were* different, chalk and cheese, as it were, and the thought of Bonnie in a place like Freedom Bay did not wear well at all. This thought made him feel snobbish, dishonest, a cheat. And yet, even as he pondered what it meant, he still felt deeply for Bonnie and understood that what he was suffering from was jealousy, an emotion he had not known before and which he knew to be dangerous.

He liked Gumshoe. In fact, he thought more highly of Gumshoe than Gumshoe thought of himself, but he felt pain at the thought of Gumshoe and Bonnie getting together again. This was irrational, and Michael despised himself for it.

'Why Gumshoe?' he asked, trying to keep his voice level.

'Because he's good,' Ben said. 'Because he's spent a lot of years going on runs with the Speed Freaks and because they respect him even more than they respect their formal leader, Snake Eyes.'

'Alas, no longer with us,' Michael said.

'Correct. Please bear in mind, therefore, that the Speed Freaks have always been an intensely close tribe and no matter how good the individuals are, they always need their own leader – not you and not me. So, since Snake Eyes is no longer with us, I'd like to have Gumshoe along as the nominal leader of the six Speed Freaks I've chosen.'

'I'll wear that,' Michael said.

'Good. However, it's also worth knowing that I want Gumshoe along because he was captured by the cyborgs and taken down into the basement of the Pentagon, where he saw what had happened to his parents, which beggars belief.'

'Yes,' Michael said. 'Bonnie told me. It sure beggars belief all right.'

'So, I think Gumshoe has a stronger motivation than any of us for wanting to penetrate the White House. He'll want to make it all the way to the Pentagon basement and somehow put his folks out of their misery, if necessary by switching off the power that keeps them alive.'

'Even if he gets there,' Michael said, 'that won't be easy to do.'

'No, it won't. But if Gumshoe can possibly do it, believe me, he'll do it. I've talked to him about it and I know this for sure:

Gumshoe isn't going to be able to live with the knowledge that his parents are down there in that condition. Either he'll save them by putting them out of their misery or he'll go insane. So that's Gumshoe's singular motivation and that's why I want him.'

'Okay,' Michael said, 'you can have him.'

Ben glanced sideways at him as they turned down into 16th Street, heading for the north side of Lafayette Square. 'Are you sure?'

'Yes, I'm sure.'

'Are you *absolutely* sure?'

'Absolutely.'

'I don't want any complications caused by personal matters. That could lead to fuck-ups.'

'I know what you're thinking – it's my involvement with Bonnie Packard and Gumshoe's interest in her – but she won't come between me and Gumshoe as far as this mission is concerned. I like Gumshoe and, even more, I trust him, so you've no need to worry.'

'Hallelujah,' Ben said.

They had reached the church, seeing no Prowlers or SARGEs en route, and they entered as usual by the side door, then made their way up to the bell tower. There they found Lenny Travis and Richie Pitt squatting as usual behind their laser surveillance systems, the former munching on a sandwich, the latter drinking from a bottle of Bud. Michael and Ben knelt just behind them, then stared over their shoulders to where the great mother ship was still hovering in the sky directly over the White House, its many lights flashing rapidly on and off, while the footballs, which appeared to have increased dramatically in number, were shooting to and fro, up and down, as if out of control, though they never, Michael suddenly noticed, left the White House area.

'Any change?' Ben asked.

'There sure is,' Lenny Travis replied. 'Look down there, pal.'

He pointed to the north lawn of the White House where, between the parked Prowlers and SARGEs, there were cyborgs that had not been there before. All the cyborgs were armed with laser pistols and carefully tracking their individual firing arcs, covering north, east and west. Likewise, the Prowlers and SARGEs, which previously had been absolutely motionless, though still not moving back and forth were back in action to the degree that their laser weapons were, like those of the cyborgs, moving continually from side to side. Obviously, then, for whatever reason, a protective firewall had been placed around the building.

'Shit!' Ben exclaimed softly.

'What's happening inside?' Michael asked.

'It gets harder to figure out with every passing hour,' Richie Pitt said. 'Since you were last here, there's been no body heat to track, so we assume that there's no one in the building – apart, that is, from the basement. Occasionally we picked up a bit of movement here and there, usually on the ground floor, as cyborgs came up out of the basement to take up those positions on the north lawn and, we must assume, all around the building. But there's something in there, some kind of electrical energy that's playing havoc with our laser systems, so now we're only picking up shit.'

'You mean static?'

'Yeah. And it's gettin' worse and worse by the hour, which suggests that the energy field is expanding and growing more dense.'

'Any idea what kind of energy field it is?'

'Nope,' Lenny Travis said. 'We've never come across anything like it before. It's a new one on us, bud.'

Michael looked questioningly at Ben. 'So, do we go in or not?'

'We go in,' Ben said. 'Let's call Gumshoe.'

Using his cellular phone, Ben called Gumshoe and caught him on his motorcycle, just out for a spin and currently burning along Constitution Avenue, enjoying the freedom gained by the freezing of the cyborg ground and air patrols.

'What can you see out there?' Ben asked him. He waited for

the response, then said, 'Yeah, that's right, man. Those god-damned saucers are going wild over the White House and the Pentagon, so we're pulling down a little number that you just might enjoy. We're in the bell tower of St John's Church, entrance via the side door. Can you get your ass over here?' He grinned, indicating a positive response, then said, 'Great. See you soon.' He turned the phone off and put it back in his jacket pocket, saying, 'Gumshoe's seeing exactly what we're seeing and he's on his way over.'

While they waited for Gumshoe's arrival, they all studied the sky over the White House – the kaleidoscopic lights of the great mother ship; the spinning, glowing footballs that were darting every which way – and then they gazed beyond the White House, to the sky over the Potomac River, where exactly the same thing was happening over the Pentagon. It was a fabulous, magical, beautiful spectacle that mesmerized all of them.

They were all still sitting there in silence when Gumshoe entered the bell tower. He was wearing a black leather jacket, a checkered open-necked shirt, blue denims and a pair of stack-heeled leather boots – a Speed Freak without the tattoos or hair piled up with thick gel. Grinning, he knelt between Michael and Ben to see what they were seeing.

'It's one hell of a light show,' he said after a lengthy silence, 'but what the hell's going on?'

'We're not sure,' Ben said. 'We only know that most of the cyborgs have deserted the main building and made their way down into the basement. With the absence of living bodies – the cyborgs, the clones and the walking dead – the building is filling up with some kind of electrical energy that's making passing automobiles malfunction, playing havoc with our laser surveil-lance systems and maybe even affecting those saucers.' He looked directly at Gumshoe and gave him a big, cocky smile. 'So we're going in there.'

Gumshoe stared at him in stone, cold amazement. 'We're going . . . *inside*?'

'You heard me,' Ben said.

Gumshoe looked down at the cyborgs, Prowlers and SARGEs still protecting the north lawn of the White House. 'So what about them?'

'We're going to fight our way through,' Michael informed him. 'I mean, you've put the Prowlers and SARGEs out of action before with your home-made bombs, so you should be able to do it again. As for the cyborgs, if you can disable a Prowler or SARGE you should be able to do it to them as well. Also, there's a distinct possibility that whatever that energy source is, it's maybe feeding off the energy of the saucers and gradually draining them, which could explain their abnormal behaviour. If that's the case, the cyborgs and their vehicles could now be less effective than they were. We think the chance is worth taking.'

'Fucking whoopee!' Gumshoe exclaimed, clearly growing excited. 'So what do I do?'

Suddenly, they all heard a distant bass rumbling sound. The whole bell tower shook as if in an earthquake.

Looking out, Michael saw, to his amazement, that the great mother ship had started to revolve, slowly at first, all its lights still flashing, then quicker, ever quicker, until its sharp edge and flashing lights had merged into a single, rapidly swirling, eerie whitish glow that illuminated the whole of the White House and the grounds all around it. Then the mother ship ascended, slowly at first, metre by painful metre, as if struggling to break free from some invisible force, perhaps the force within the White House, maybe only Earth's gravity, gradually shrinking as it rose higher and higher towards the clear, star-filled sky. Growing smaller as it ascended, it was soon the size of a weather balloon, then resembled a spinning, ethereally glowing plate, and finally looked like no more than a large star surrounded by that same eerie glow.

At that point it stopped moving. The bell tower stopped shaking. Absolute silence reigned for a brief moment. Then the silence was broken.

Michael saw the explosion before he heard or felt it. The large star abruptly turned into a flare of silvery light that expanded in all directions, cutting through the sky's darkness, obliterating the stars, spreading out until it filled the whole sky and turned the night into day. Then Michael *heard* the explosion and felt the force of the blast, the dangerous shaking of the whole bell tower. He squinted and rubbed his eyes and spat swirling dust from his mouth, then looked up again to see that brilliant sky turning into a web of silvery striations that coiled and bent and swept upwards and drifted down, gradually letting the stars reappear as its tendrils reached back to Earth.

'Holy shit!' Ben exclaimed.

Then, as they all looked up in awe, the spinning, glowing footballs, which now numbered hundreds and had continued to shoot up and down, to and fro, left and right, started exploding in mid-flight, the debris flying everywhere, glinting dully in boiling clouds of smoke. Some blew apart while others melted completely or broke into large, glinting pieces of metal that fell to Earth as fiercely burning balls of fire. They crashed against the White House roof, into the trees, onto the lawns, some of them exploding a second time to further illuminate the darkness with fountains of brilliant red sparks.

This sight was, if anything, more spectacular than the first, a light show to beat all others, and it went on a long time, the explosions seeming never to end, until only a few footballs remained in a night sky smoke-streaked and filled with geysering sparks. Those remaining footballs did not explode, but merely drifted down to the ground, expiring like dying birds, sinking gently into the darkening grass as if trying to seed it. They remained there, grey and motionless, dead, as the sparks faded away, leaving darkness, and the smoke dissipated. A vast silence now reigned.

'Jesus!' Gumshoe exclaimed, breaking the silence. 'I don't fucking believe it.'

Then it happened again.

The great mother ship that had been hovering above the Pentagon, across the Potomac River, also ascended high in the sky, then exploded with the force of a hydrogen bomb, flooding the sky with light, illuminating the ground below for miles around, and again shaking the bell tower with its blast. No sooner had it faded away than the other flying saucers hovering all over the capital, saucers of all sizes, began exploding, one after the other, creating another spectacular light show. Finally, even as the red-hot glowing debris of those saucers was still falling to earth, the footballs over the other major buildings of the capital began exploding as those over the White House had done, creating a different kind of spectacle: balls of fire and showers of bright red sparks in billowing clouds of black smoke. When it had finished, when the last of the saucers had fallen, another vast silence reigned.

'Oh, boy!' Gumshoe exclaimed, breaking the silence.

'They all malfunctioned,' Lenny Travis said. 'Every damned one of them.'

'Maybe you were right,' Richie Pitt said, turning to Michael. 'Maybe that energy field inside the White House was feeding off those saucers and finally drained them.'

'Maybe,' Michael said. 'And maybe it was deliberate. Maybe the cyborgs – or whoever's in control of them – deliberately aborted those saucers because they're no longer required.'

The rest of the group stared in disbelief at him, wondering what he meant.

'"No longer required"?' Ben said. 'What the hell does *that* mean?'

'It means that whatever the cyborgs are planning has rendered the saucers obsolete. It means that whatever's going to happen, it's going to happen in there.'

'Which means we still go in,' Ben said.

'Right,' Michael confirmed.

They all gazed at the White House, then down at the south lawn where, to their surprise, the cyborgs, Prowlers and SARGEs were still protecting the building with their weapons. They knew this because the weapons were still moving, covering north, east and west.

'So what do *I* do?' Gumshoe repeated.

'We're going to fight our way into the White House,' Ben told him, 'and we're taking along six Speed Freaks picked by me. We want you to lead them.'

'Why me?'

'Because Snake Eyes is gone and they respect you even more than they respected him. Because they only feel comfortable with their own kind and they think you're their kind.'

Gumshoe looked directly at Michael. 'How's that with you?'

'It's fine with me,' Michael said.

Nodding, smiling slightly, Gumshoe turned back to Ben. 'I may be able to gain the trust of the Speed Freaks,' he said, 'but I want a particular friend by my side.'

'Who's that?' Michael asked.

Gumshoe grinned and spread his hands in the air.

'The Cowboy,' he said.

Chapter Thirty-seven

From: <bayfree@leebrand.com>
our time is running out.
extraordinary electronic interference causing telecommunications to break down intermittently but with increasing frequency and likelihood of soon failing altogether.
force field being penetrated by same interference and likely to be breached within hours.
flying saucers launched to protect gaps in force field have all exploded in mid-flight and those on the ground are malfunctioning.
computer network crashing.
radar already dead.
if this situation cannot be remedied all may be lost and this may be our last communication.
the bird must signal if successful and let us come in.
good luck and

Chapter Thirty-eight

'A wagon-train massacre,' the Cowboy said. 'We just encircle the whole goddamned building and keep moving around it, firing and bombing them on the move, whittling them down and gradually closing in until we can enter the place. It's as easy as falling off a log, though a mite more dangerous, I'll admit.'

'It's fucking suicidal,' Lenny Travis said, 'so you can count me out right there.'

'I think it's way out,' said Gene 'Greaser' Madsen, one of the chosen Speed Freaks. 'That sounds like my kinda show, man.'

'Hear, hear,' Jake 'Jewboy' Hammerstein, another Speed Freak, added. 'Let's not fuck around, guys and gals.'

'And while we're at it,' Richie Pitt said, 'What's *she* doing here? This ain't the fucking scene for a Long Hair. Send her back to her knitting.'

'Fuck you,' Bonnie said. 'I was leader of the Wild Cats for a while and there was nothin' that you Short Hairs did that we didn't do better. I'm in because my goddamned friends are in and where they go, I go.'

'Good girl,' the Cowboy said.

They had gathered together in the basement of Ben Wilkerson's apartment building to get to know each other, select their weapons and coordinate a plan of attack. The Speed Freaks were high on speed, others were smoking Mary Jane, a couple were sipping from bottles of Bud and a few were avoiding all temptations and sticking to chewing gum. The six Speed Freaks, all favouring a Hell's Angels image, had taken a pile of chairs at one side of the room, with Bonnie, a soul mate, in the middle of them, while Ben's gang – Gumshoe, Michael, Lenny Travis and Richie Pitt, all dressed more conservatively – were sprawled in chairs at the other side.

The two sides had a healthy respect for each other, but cooperation with other groups didn't come naturally to the Speed Freaks and without Gumshoe's presence in the room they might have split already. The Cowboy, the odd man out, being twice the age of the others, his sardonic gaze hidden in the shadow of his stetson hat, was relaxing in a chair beside Gumshoe, his booted feet on a table. He had a sly little smile on his face as he carefully rolled a normal cigarette. No Mary Jane for the Cowboy.

'So who the hell are you anyway,' Lenny Travis said, 'to tell us how to make the attack? A wagon-train massacre, for Chrissakes! Where the hell did you get that?'

'From books,' the Cowboy explained calmly.

'The Cowboy's an expert on the history of the Old West,' Gumshoe quickly explained. 'He's also a former USAF test pilot who ended up working in the Space Surveillance Centre and learnt an awful lot about the cyborgs. He's also my friend.'

'And proud of it,' the Cowboy said.

'Three cheers for fucking friendship,' another Speed Freak said, 'but it don't get us nowhere.' His name was Luke 'Satchmo' Armstrong and he was as black as the ace of spades, born and bred in the North-east Quadrant five years before the cyborgs took it over and pushed the blacks out. 'You ask me, what we need, brothers and sisters, is the answer to a very simple solution. Who goes for what mother?'

'Mother?' Richie Pitt asked, perplexed and turning to Gumshoe, hoping for a translation.

'A target,' Gumshoe explained obligingly. 'In this case, the Full Metal Jackets.'

'Or those fucking clones, the Men in Black,' another Speed Freak, Emiliano 'Zapata' Gomez said, his chocolate-brown eyes flashing dangerously in his dark, mustachioed face.

'Yeah, them too,' the fifth Speed Freak, Jack 'The Knife' Kline added. 'Not to mention the walking dead.'

'No, not them,' Ben Wilkerson said. 'We don't touch them at all. We happen to know that the walking dead have all been brain-implanted to make them totally pacified, so there's no need to harm them.'

'Also,' Michael added, 'we might be able to revert them to their old selves if we gain the cyborg technology. That's what happened in Freedom Bay when the US took over.'

'The walking dead came back to life?' the sixth Speed Freak, Larry 'Rubbermouth' Ramone asked. 'You gotta be kidding me! What the fuck were they like when they came back to life?'

'The same as they'd been before,' Michael told him. 'No difference at all.'

Rubbermouth gave a low whistle of surprise, then let his green gaze take in all the others. 'One way or the other, we all got friends and relatives abducted and turned into the walking dead. They might still be in there right now, so let's go in and get 'em out.'

'Hear, hear,' Ben said.

Michael had never ceased to be shocked by the rough street language of Chinatown, particularly as practised by the Speed Freaks, but he knew that this particular bunch, despite their lowlife way of talking, were brighter than they seemed and would almost certainly do what was required of them. In many cases, as he now knew, these young men were sad cases, the rejects of a society turned upside down by the cyborgs, most with parents lost through abduction, most without proper education. Gum-shoe was one of them, but certainly a cut above them, and Michael sensed that he had kept himself slightly apart from the others in order to preserve what was best in him, though he would never dare show it. There was a dreadful sadness in this and it made Michael, who was actually younger than Gumshoe, feel a lot older.

'So where do we stand,' the Cowboy asked, 'since I've just been shot down?'

'Not quite,' Gumshoe said. 'A couple of the guys here agree with you that we should go in shooting.'

'A fucking wagon-train massacre!' Lenny Travis repeated in disgust.

'What's wrong with that?' Bonnie asked. 'It might be the only way. The White House is defended all the way round, after all, by those damned cyborgs and Prowlers and SARGEs, so why *not* turn it into a wagon train, hammering at it with bombs and bullets and gradually closing in on it? I say we don't have a choice.'

'Good girl,' the Cowboy quietly repeated, lighting up his hand-rolled cigarette and inhaling luxuriously.

'The old guy strokes the ego of the Long Hair,' Greaser said, 'and it's supposed to be goddamned fuckin' tactics. Nevertheless, I think he might have a point. That fucking building *is* defended right the way round, so we gotta take it from all sides.'

'Shoot and scoot,' the Cowboy said. 'In and out with cars and bikes. Lobbing bombs and firing guns and winding this way and that until the Full Metal Jackets are confused and don't know which way to turn. If we keep moving – and if we move fast enough – we can keep whittling them down to the point where we can actually break through their defences and charge in through the front doors. Just like the Indians did when they fought the settlers, attacking their wagon trains. Yep, it's cowboys and Indians time.'

'Jesus!' Lenny Travis exploded again.

'He's got a point,' Michael said. 'The Speed Freaks have always specialized in hit-and-run raids – it's what they do best – so though we can't actually encircle the building, we can use what are essentially the same tactics.'

'How come?' Jewboy asked.

'The cyborgs have closed up and sealed all entrances to the White House except the double doors on the north portico, so that has to be our point of entrance. The idea, therefore, is that you guys keeping racing up and down Pennsylvania Avenue with your hot rods and motorcycles, right in front of the north lawn, throwing bombs at any Full Metal Jackets outside the grounds, either distracting them or putting them out of action. Meanwhile, the rest of us will go in on foot, entering the grounds from the side, then come up behind the cyborgs on the north lawns while you have them distracted. We get into the building – either by sneaking in behind the distracted cyborgs or by putting paid to them – and once we're in, you guys can drive in through the front gates, then follow us in on foot to give us support . . . I think it might work.'

'I agree,' the Cowboy said.

'So do I,' Gumshoe added.

'All those who agree raise their hands,' Ben said, raising his own hand first.

Everyone put up his hand except Lenny Travis. But when he saw all the other hands raised, he sighed and added his vote.

'Okay, that's decided,' Ben said. 'You guys . . .' He nodded to indicate Gumshoe and the six Speed Freaks. 'Give them hell from your motorcycles and hot rods, concentrating on Pennsylvania Avenue, while the rest of us go in on foot with personal weapons to tackle the north lawn. What about you, Bonnie?'

Bonnie raised her painted eyebrows and widened her big eyes. 'What about me?' she said.

'You can hitch a ride in one of the hot rods or go in on foot with the rest of us. What's your choice, lady?'

'Well . . .'

'I agree with Richie,' Michael said on an impulse, 'though not for the same reasons. I'm sure Bonnie's as competent as anyone else here, but she's still the only woman present and I don't like the thought of that. I mean, it doesn't seem right that we should let a woman—'

'*What?*' Bonnie exploded. 'You're puttin' me down as a *woman?* Who the hell do you think you are?'

Shocked by Bonnie's vehemence, Michael almost recoiled, aware that everyone was staring at him, some of them grinning.

'I just meant—'

'I don't care what you meant. I only know what you're implying. You're implying that I'm one of the weaker sex and as such should be kept away from the action. Well, fuck you, Mister Nice Guy. Don't shit on my parade. I was biking with these guys when you were bein' taught fine manners and male chauvinism in some fancy school for rich kids. *You* don't know how to fight, but I do and you can take that as read. Over and out, *mi amigo!*'

Shocked even more, deeply hurt, feeling betrayed, Michael hardly knew what to say and so kept his mouth shut. He was stinging even more from the mocking grins of the Speed Freaks when Gumshoe gallantly came to his rescue.

'He wasn't putting you down in any way, Bonnie, and he didn't deserve that. He was just concerned, that's all.'

'Fuck him,' Bonnie said. 'I have my pride. I don't need his concern.'

'Okay, that's enough,' Ben said. He turned to Michael. 'You just pinched Bonnie on a sensitive nerve. She'll settle down in a minute.' Turning back to the others, he said, 'Okay, guys, what about the weapons?'

'The whole fucking works,' Satchmo said with a big smile. 'Bombs and bullets of every calibre and weight. The whole goddamned shooting match.'

'We've got it all here,' Ben said. 'A bit old, I grant you, picked up on the black market, but they worked for that old US Army Special Forces regiment, the Green Berets, so they should work for us.'

The weapons pulled out of the lockers and distributed by Lenny Travis and Richie Pitt were a mixture of Colt Commando 5.56mm semi-automatic rifles, M16A2 Armalite semi-automatic rifles with night-vision aids and M203 grenade launchers, and .45-inch Colt handguns. Everyone in the room was given a handgun and one or other of the semi-automatics, with spare ammunition for both weapons.

As they would initially be firing from their moving vehicles, either hot rods or motorcycles, it was decided that the Speed Freaks should begin by harassing the cyborgs with the .45-inch Colt handguns and their own home-made bombs, which they kept in canvas satchels slung across their shoulders, only using their semi-automatics – which needed two hands for effective aiming and shooting – when they had breached the north lawns and were preparing to enter the White House proper. Though Gumshoe would be with them, he had already come prepared with his customary bulletproof vest and his conveniently small, light Glock 19 semi-automatic handgun.

Ben's gang, on the other hand, tasked with entering the building while the Speed Freaks were distracting the Full Metal Jackets trying to guard it, planned to attack with a combination of Colt Commando 5.56 semi-automatic rifles and the M203 grenade launchers attached to the Armalites. They would only use their handguns, it was decided, if they encountered the clones, the Men in Black, once inside the building.

'Any questions?' Ben asked when the weapons had been distributed and everyone was preparing to leave.

'Yeah,' the Cowboy said, now looking like the real McCoy with a holstered .45-inch Colt handgun on his hip and an Armalite with a grenade launcher in his big right hand. 'What do we do once we get inside?'

Michael and Ben glanced at one another. Then the latter shrugged and the former said, 'In truth, we don't know. We don't know what's in there. We just have to play it by ear, using our commonsense.'

'I'll use my commonsense,' Zapata Gomez said, his dark eyes still flashing dangerously. 'I'll just blow away any motherfucker who gets in my way.'

'Please don't,' Michael said. 'We have to bear in mind that some of those we'll encounter could be the living dead and that they could be returned, with the proper treatment, to their normal selves. Cyborgs, Men in Black – okay – but not the living dead.'

'We may not have time to tell the difference,' Jack the Knife said, 'and if I have one second of doubt, I'm taking no chances.'

'That's fair enough,' Lenny Travis said. 'All wars have their innocent casualties.'

'Correct,' Ben said, 'but in this case try to keep them to a minimum by picking your targets with extreme care. Any more questions?'

'Yeah,' Richie Pitt said. 'What do we do if they've somehow fled the building and all we find is that growing mass of extraordinary energy?'

'That might depend on what kind of energy it is,' Michael told him. 'It might depend on how the energy affects us – if it affects us at all.'

'I'd like to know what that shit is,' Rubbermouth said. 'I don't wanna even have to breathe that shit.'

'You don't want to go in, don't go in,' the Cowboy said, his voice low and mellow. 'We're all volunteers here.'

'John Wayne's been resurrected,' Jewboy sneered. 'That fuckin' dude is a holograph.'

'I'm as much flesh and blood as you are,' the Cowboy said calmly.

'Okay, cool it, you guys,' Gumshoe said. 'Are there any *more* questions?'

'Yeah,' Bonnie said, holding up her Colt Commando semi-automatic and .45-inch Colt handgun. 'How do those of us going in on foot actually get to the White House, bearing in mind that we're carryin' these fucking weapons?'

Almost wincing at her profanity, Michael said, 'We hitch a ride with a Speed Freak to Lafayette Square, disembark there, and make our way around the Treasury Building by foot to one of the old tourist entrances on the west side of the Ellipse. The Speed Freaks, led by Gumshoe, will give us approximately ten minutes to reach our destination and get ourselves organized. As soon as we hear the shots and exploding bombs of the Speed Freaks, hopefully distracting the Full Metal Jackets on the north lawns, we'll enter the White House grounds by way of one of the western side entrances and make our way from there to the north side. From there, we'll attempt to make our way into the building through the double entrance doors of the north portico while the Speed Freaks are still keeping the Full Metal Jackets distracted. Do you have problems with that?'

'No,' Bonnie said firmly, like a stranger, as if they had never shared a bed together, almost as if she despised him.

Realizing that he had tried to be sarcastic and that Bonnie had sensed it, Michael suffered a pang of guilt and again recalled what Lee Brandenberg had told him about not letting personal feelings interfere with the job.

I'd better keep that advice in mind, he thought, *before I do something stupid.*

'Okay,' Ben said, turning to his own gang, which now included Bonnie. 'Team up with someone who's willing to carry you in and let's all get out of here. The sooner we do this, the better.'

'I'll take anyone,' Greaser Madsen said, 'in my good old souped-up Silver Thunderbird. Any takers, guys and gals?'

'Me,' Lenny Travis said.

'Me, too,' Richie Pitt said. 'I ain't sitting on the rear of no motorcycle with one of you crazies.'

The remaining Speed Freaks howled with laughter, slapping each other's hands, while the grinning Greaser led Lenny and Richie out of the basement.

'I'll take the Long Hair on my Suzuki,' Rubbermouth said, 'if she'll agree to sit in front of me, on the tanks, and let me press my hot groin against her slick butt.'

'In *your* butt!' Bonnie sneered.

'Come with me in Satchmo's Mazda,' Michael said, trying in vain to smile at her and hide his concern.

'No, thanks,' she responded, then turned to Gumshoe. 'I just *loved* riding around on your silver-tanked Yamaha 400. How's about it, Gumshoe?'

Gumshoe looked uncomfortably at Michael who just shrugged and nodded.

'Okay,' Gumshoe said.

Hardly able to look at Bonnie, feeling deeply hurt, but still trying to keep Lee Brandenberg's warning foremost in his thoughts, Michael followed Luke 'Satchmo' Armstrong out of the basement, slinging his Armalite with grenade launcher over his shoulder as he advanced up the stairs, close behind the black man, feeling the holstered Colt handgun bouncing heavily against his right hip. As one of Freedom Bay's adepts, though he'd been mainly instructed in parapsychology, he had also been taught to fire the weapons of the World in the belief that if he ever ventured there he would almost certainly need them. Now it seemed that he was indeed going to need them.

Sitting beside Satchmo in the car as it carried him the short distance to Lafayette Square, Michael glanced at the sky above the White House area, noting the striking absence of flying saucers. Then he recalled the last e-mail he had received from Lee Brandenberg in Freedom Bay, informing him that the saucers there had also been exploding in mid-flight while telecommunications were breaking down and might soon fail altogether. In fact, they almost certainly *had* failed just as that message was being sent, since the e-mail had been cut off before completion and Michael had been unable to contact Brandenberg ever since, not even through mental telepathy, which also seemed to be blocked. Now the weight of the world was on Michael's shoulders and he felt burdened by it. He felt this even as he was still suffering over Bonnie's sudden outburst of anger, an emotion he could not deal with, and this made the situation seem all the more ridiculous. Confused, Michael sighed aloud.

'What's the matter, brother?' Satchmo said as he drove his Mazda expertly along G Street, flashing perfect white teeth in his gleaming black face. 'The new kid in town's got an attack of nerves, maybe?'

'Maybe,' Michael agreed.

'Don't worry, man. We all gotta go some time. If it ain't today, it sure as hell will be tomorrow and *that* as sure as hell is comin'. Just say your prayers, hope for the best and play it as it lays.'

'I'll try,' Michael said.

Satchmo turned off G Street just before the Treasury Building, went along to H, then turned left at McPherson Square and finally braked to a halt where some of the other hot rods and motorcycles were already parked outside the front of St John's Church, located on the north side of the park. A few of the old street lights were still working here and there, dimly illuminating the dark square, and again Michael was struck by the fact that no flying saucers or footballs could be seen hovering in the night sky. Nevertheless, though the cyborg ground and air patrols had obviously ceased for good, everyone's instinct was to remain as quiet as possible this close to the White House.

'Thanks for the lift,' Michael said quietly to Satchmo.

'My pleasure, man. Adios and good luck.'

They slapped hands together, then Michael slipped out of his side of the Mazda. Gumshoe had already arrived with Bonnie and was now straddling his beloved silver-tanked Yamaha 400 while talking quietly to her and Ben Wilkerson. Lenny Travis and Richie Pitt had also arrived with Greaser and were just clambering out of his Silver Thunderbird. As Michael walked along the sidewalk to join them, the rest of the Speed Freaks roared up to the group, braked to a halt and then killed their engines. An eerie silence descended. The Cowboy slid off the back of Rubbermouth's huge Suzuki GSXR 750 motorcycle, tipped his stetson hat to Rubbermouth in a silent gesture of thanks, then removed his Armalite from his shoulder and proceeded to load it. Instantly, the others all did the same, breaking the silence with the rattling of shell cases and the metallic snapping of bolts. When they were finished, another brief silence ensued until Ben Wilkerson spoke.

'Everyone ready?' he asked, glancing about him, first at his own gang, then at Gumshoe and the Speed Freaks. The latter were either checking the home-made bombs in their canvas satchels or taking up riding positions on their powerful motor-cycles or in their souped-up, brightly painted hot rods with tail-fins and spoilers. They were a colourful sight. Everyone nodded.

'Okay, let's do it.'

'Good luck,' Gumshoe said.

Michael grinned at him and gave him a wave. Then he fell in behind Bonnie, still not speaking to her, as she followed Ben and Lenny and Richie across the dimly-lit road. Carrying their rifles at the ready, they headed for the north-east side of the park. The Cowboy was out front, crouched low and moving fast, and the sight of him gave them all confidence as they advanced on the White House.

Chapter Thirty-nine

With the Cowboy in the lead, they made their way down the east side of the park and stopped at the corner on Pennsylvania Avenue to look across the road to the White House. From where they stood, bunched together in the darkness, they could clearly see the colonnade of the north portico, supporting an unadorned pediment and with elaborate carvings gracing the area above the double entrance doors. Two armed cyborgs were guarding that entrance, one on each side, and more were spaced out along the length of the building, with Prowlers and SARGEs parked between them, their weapons clearly moving to cover their respective arcs of fire, north, east and west. More dangerously, there were cyborgs and their vehicles – three sets of Prowlers and SARGEs, the former like tanks, the latter like armed dune buggies – along Pennsylvania Avenue, between the White House grounds and Lafayette Square.

'We can't cross here,' the Cowboy whispered. 'We'd be safer cutting around the east side of the Treasury Building and coming up on one of the entrance gates from there.'

'That gives us less time to get there,' Michael said.

'Then let's do it,' the Cowboy said and instantly turned left to lead them along G Street, then down 15th and past the Treasury Building.

As they scurried through the darkness, only erratically illuminated by the occasional working street light, Michael glanced at Bonnie, crouched low just ahead of him, her shapely body clearly outlined in a skintight black T-shirt, tight black denims and black leather boots, the holstered pistol bouncing against her firm right thigh, the Colt Commando held in both hands and angled across her chest. His heart went out to her. He desperately wanted her to live, to not be damaged in this action, because despite his anger over what he had said, he still believed it and feared what could happen to her. Nevertheless, she was here, advancing crouched low in front of him, as determined as he was, and he silently vowed to keep his eye on her and give her protection.

As they circled around the Treasury Building, which loomed darkly, ominously, above them, he thought of the Speed Freaks waiting at the north side of the square. Concentrating upon them, he was able to visualize Gumshoe seated on his silver-tanked Yamaha 400, his legs spread with booted feet on the ground, his hands on the handlebars, waiting to take off. Given the circumstances, it was difficult to break into Gumshoe's thoughts, but Michael, with his insight, could certainly sense them: as he watched Gumshoe check his wristwatch, letting the last five minutes unwind, he knew that he was thinking of Bonnie, wondering what she really thought of him, since she had deliberately, openly, rejected Michael in favour of him over the ride to the White House. At the same time, however, he was thinking of the possibility, soon coming, of putting his unfortunate parents out of their misery, though doing that would be a nightmare for him.

Gumshoe checked his wristwatch again, waiting now for the last four minutes to unwind. Then he glanced about him at the other Speed Freaks in their vividly coloured hot rods, on their powerful motorcycles, and saw that they were tensed and ready to go, always keen for some action. Gumshoe was keen as well, wanting to get this thing over and done with, but he was also terrified at the thought of what would happen when he saw his parents again – or, at least, saw the severed heads of his parents on that pig's thick neck. The very thought of it almost made Gumshoe throw up, though he somehow managed to control himself.

What he could *not* control was the racing of his heart and the sweat on his brow. Amazingly, he then thought of Bonnie Packard and of how much he wanted her. Thinking of her made it a lot easier as the last three minutes unwound.

Michael sensed all this in Gumshoe as he followed Bonnie and the others, still led by the Cowboy, around the south-east corner of the Treasury Building. Once around the corner, the Cowboy raised his right fist to indicate that they should slow down and take more care as they made their way to the grounds of the Ellipse, south of the White House and just across the road. When they reached the next corner of the building, almost directly opposite one of the old visitor entrances, they were shocked to see that it was guarded by two armed cyborgs. The muzzles of the laser weapons of the cyborgs were swinging left and right, covering the road in both directions. The cyborgs' metallic noses and mouths gleamed in the moonlight, under eyes unnaturally narrowed and looking, from this distance, like pissholes in blue ice.

'God damn it,' the Cowboy whispered.

Ben checked his wristwatch while holding his Colt Commando rifle in his free hand. 'We don't have any time to waste,' he said, looking up again. 'Gumshoe's gang are going to attack any second now, so we have to decide what to do.'

Michael glanced at Bonnie, who was kneeling there in the shadows of the corner a few feet away. When she caught his glance, she gazed steadily at him, then broke out in a smile that washed him clean.

'We've no choice,' he said, turning back to the front. 'We have to tackle those cyborgs.'

At that moment they heard the roaring of the hot rods and motorcycles from the north side of the building, followed by pistol shots and explosions from what could only be home-made bombs.

Instantly, the Cowboy loaded a grenade into his M213 grenade launcher, then raised his Armalite to the firing position, took aim — and fired.

'Go!' Michael bawled.

The wind rushed past Gumshoe and the noise of the explosions hurt his ears as he roared around Lafayette Square on his Yamaha 400 and then turned into Pennsylvania Avenue. Some of the other Speed Freaks were directly in front of him, already racing straight past the White House, controlling their hot rods or motorcycles with one hand and using the other to snatch home-made bombs out of their canvas satchels and hurl them at the Full Metal Jackets. Gumshoe did the same, expertly handling his powerful motorcycle with one hand while he quickly removed a Semtex bomb from his satchel, released a blasting cap that would be sprung on impact with the target, and hurled it at a SARGE as he passed.

Other bombs were already exploding even as he hurled his first and he was dazzled by jagged sheets of silvery light that tore through the darkness, followed by flying, spinning debris from the damaged Full Metal Jackets. Blinking against the light, feeling the blast from the explosions, Gumshoe saw smoke billowing from an aperture in one of the Prowlers as the cyborgs near it fired their laser weapons. The narrow phosphorescent beams of light from the laser weapons, filled with millions of tiny sparks, cut through the darkness, moving this way and that, criss-crossing as they sought to find a target, forming a dazzling web above the dark road. The Speed Freaks were fast, however, weaving expertly to avoid the laser beams and, because they had taken the Full Metal Jackets by surprise, they managed to make the first pass without suffering any casualties.

Moving parallel to the far end of the West Wing of the White House, the Speed Freaks went into screeching U-turns and headed back the way they had come, encouraged by the success of their first run. Noting that they had already damaged at least one Prowler and blown one SARGE to smithereens, Gumshoe began his second run, weaving this way and that, leaning dangerously close to the ground to make himself a difficult target for the laser beams that were now hissing out of the handguns of the cyborgs and the larger weapons of the Prowlers and SARGEs. Though normally motorcycles were more dangerous than hot rods, in this case the latter made for larger, slower targets, a point proven when the Silver Thunderbird, which had swept in close to the sidewalk to enable Greaser to hurl another bomb, took a direct hit from the powerful laser beam of a Prowler. With the Prowler's weapon obviously set on maximum power, the Silver Thunderbird turned red-hot in less than a second and exploded an instant later, killing Greaser instantly and turning into a ball of white fire, with shards of glass and gobs of melting metal flying outward in all directions.

Miraculously, the debris struck none of the other Speed Freaks and they managed to finish the pass, screeching into U-turns again in order to make the third run.

Even as he accelerated, Gumshoe saw that the smoking Prowler was now out of action, its laser weapon not moving, and that another Prowler had also been hit and was belching oily smoke and shaking visibly from a series of internal explosions. Directly ahead of Gumshoe, Rubbermouth, who had obviously used up his couple of bombs, was whooping crazily and firing his .45 Colt handgun one-handed as he controlled his dangerously wobbling Suzuki with the other.

As Rubbermouth passed the Prowler that was shaking with internal explosions, two cyborgs stepped out stiffly, mechanically, from behind a bomb-shattered SARGE to fire their laser weapons simultaneously. Rubbermouth almost made it past them, but the laser beams caught the rear wheel of his Suzuki, which disintegrated in no time at all. The back of the motorcycle crashed down onto the ground, screeching dementedly and churning up a shower of sparks, then the rest of the machine wobbled wildly and started to lean to one side.

Rubbermouth threw himself the other way, kicking the bike from him as he fell, and he and the vehicle went in different directions before both crashed onto the road. Like a well-trained paratrooper hitting the ground after a drop, Rubbermouth kept rolling to ease his body's battering, then started to rise to his feet while preparing to fire his handgun. He did not get far. Even as Satchmo swerved around him in his Mazda, the two cyborgs fired again and their laser beams struck Rubbermouth simultaneously. The beams burned right through him like a knife cutting butter, separating the top half of his body from the lower and forcing a dreadful, inhuman scream out of him.

Gumshoe was just racing past when Rubbermouth's top half – head, chest and two arms – fell in one direction while his lower half – legs, hips and belly – fell in the other. Shocked, hardly believing what he was seeing, Gumshoe kept going.

He reached the end of the pass, screeched into a low-hanging U-turn, narrowly avoiding Satchmo's similarly screeching Mazda, then headed straight back for another run. Reaching into his satchel, flying out of himself, now on automatic pilot, he withdrew his last Semtex bomb and released the blasting cap. Then, controlling the bike with one hand, keeping it as straight as possible and silently praying that he would not be struck by one of the laser beams, he hurled the bomb as he passed the third Prowler. He heard the roar of the explosion, saw a flash of jagged light out of the corner of his eye, and felt the blast pummelling him as he raced past, exhilarated and terrified all at once.

Zapata and Jewboy were in front of him, the former on a Kawasaki 250cc, the latter in a souped-up Nissan Sylvia. They both screeched into U-turns, safe and sound at the end of the run, just before Gumshoe did the same. Zapata was whooping like a Red Indian in an old Wild West movie.

'Fucking A!' Jewboy bawled.

Zapata, equally excited, began to respond in kind but was cut short by the roaring of Jack the Knife's converted Bentley and Satchmo's Mazda as they, too, completed the run and came to a stop after making U-turns.

Temporarily at a standstill, they glanced along the road and saw that all three Prowlers and two of the SARGEs were badly damaged and belching smoke. The third SARGE, however, which looked like a dune buggy and could move as smartly as a Jeep, was racing towards them on spinning wheels, aiming its laser weapon at them and being followed by the remaining two cyborgs.

'Scatter!' Gumshoe bawled, accelerating and racing away just in time to avoid the SARGE which, though narrowly missing him, fired its laser weapon at the group, striking Jack the Knife's Bentley. The car exploded instantly, turning into a ball of debris-spewing fire that devoured the screaming driver, as Zapata on his motorcycle and Satchmo in his Mazda both moved out of the way just in time and as the SARGE ploughed into Jewboy's Nissan Sylvia.

As he raced back into the safety of Lafayette Square, Gumshoe heard the dreadful screeching of metal being mangled, a singular cry of anguish, and glanced back over his shoulder to see the SARGE grinding into the Nissan, both vehicles squeezing up like accordions with glass breaking and metal parts falling off in a calamitous din.

Shocked again, Gumshoe made another screeching U-turn and headed back to the corner, reaching it in time to see Zapata, now straddling his static bike, and Satchmo, now standing by the open door of his Mazda, both firing their .45-inch Colt handguns at the mechanically advancing cyborgs. Though the cyborgs were hard to kill because of the metal covering on their bodies, they were vulnerable in certain parts of their legs and arms, as well as at the tops of their heads, and the combined fusillade of bullets from the two handguns struck them in these areas, smashing the legs of one cyborg and taking the top off the head of the second. Both cyborgs wobbled crazily, with sparks showering off them, then fell, rattling metallically, to the ground. Instantly, Zapata raced up to them, gave the *coup de grâce* to the one still alive, then triumphantly stuck his thumb up in the air.

The road in front of the White House had been cleared.

Then they all heard the sound of a distant explosion, emanating from the south side of the building.

'What the hell . . . ?' Gumshoe said.

The grenade from the Cowboy's M213 exploded against the metal fence between the two cyborgs and blasted them to hell, with pieces of metal prosthetics, human organs and strips of scorched artificial skin flying out in all directions from a billowing cloud of smoke and swirling dust.

Instantly, Michael raced across the road, followed by the others, to step over the mangled remains of the cyborgs and make his way through the twisted, scorched gate behind them. Entering the dark grounds of the Ellipse, just south of the White House, he glanced back over his shoulder, saw that Bonnie, Lenny, Richie and the Cowboy were coming up behind him, then looked to the front again and headed resolutely for the East Wing.

As the ornate white-painted balconies and porticos loomed up to his left, he heard more explosions and gunfire emanating from Pennsylvania Avenue, north of the building. Reminded by this that Gumshoe and his gang were distracting the cyborgs, he kept advancing until he had reached the south-east corner of the East Wing, by which time Bonnie and the Cowboy had caught up with him, one on each side of him, with Ben, Lenny and Richie bringing up the rear.

Michael glanced sideways at Bonnie and was warmed by her tender smile.

'Shit, Mike,' she whispered, 'this is exciting.'

'You be careful,' he said.

'Sounds like Gumshoe and his gang are keeping them busy up

front,' the Cowboy said, 'so we'd best keep on going.'

'You'd have to drag me back in chains,' Bonnie told him.

'You're some doll,' the Cowboy said.

By now Ben, Lenny and Richie had caught up with them and together, with Michael indicating that they should be quiet, they advanced along the side of the East Wing. Glancing in through the tall Georgian windows to his left, Michael saw only empty rooms illuminated by that peculiar dazzling incandescence in which millions of even brighter tiny lights, like fireflies, were darting up and down, to and fro, at incredible speeds, like the neurons in a giant brain.

Turning around the northern side of the east wing, he glanced across the dark lawns and saw nothing unusual. Holding his Armalite at the ready, with its grenades strung to his belt and bouncing against his hip, he cut at an angle across the lawn until he had reached the front corner of what he knew to be the Library. Glancing in through the windows, again he saw nothing except that magical incandescence.

'That's some fucking sight,' Ben whispered. 'I'm dying to know what it is.'

'You might die before you find out,' the Cowboy whispered, 'if you don't shut your mouth.'

'My apologies,' Ben replied.

Inching along the wall, with the others bunched up behind him, Michael glanced around the corner and saw that a SARGE and five armed cyborgs were guarding the double doors of the north entrance, all firing their laser weapons, with the long, narrow, phosphorescent beams striking the fence and gate at the far end of the lawns. Turning his gaze in the direction of Pennsylvania Avenue, he saw first the smouldering wrecks of Prowlers, SARGEs, automobiles and motorcycles, then Gumshoe, Zapata and Satchmo, obviously bunched up together behind the wall of the north gate – the one being struck by the laser beams – and leaning out repeatedly to fire their handguns at the Full Metal Jackets in front of the door.

'Good boys,' the Cowboy murmured.

'Only three of them left,' Bonnie whispered.

'The others died happy,' Ben said.

Realizing that the only way into the building was through those double doors, Michael began inserting a grenade into the M213 attached to his Armalite. The Cowboy did the same.

'We both fire on the SARGE,' Michael said, 'then we tackle the cyborgs.'

'I'm with you,' the Cowboy said.

Raising their weapons to the firing position, they took aim at the SARGE. Michael fired first and the Cowboy followed instantly. Both grenades exploded right on target, ploughing into the middle of the SARGE's light steel frame and exploding with a god-almighty roar into silvery sheets of flame, boiling black smoke and flying metal. One of the cyborgs was bowled over by the blast, losing his right arm and part of his left leg, both of which rolled with a metallic clattering over the ground while the fleshy original stumps gushed blood. The surviving cyborgs instantly looked left and right, their heads moving mechanically but frantically, trying to ascertain which direction the grenades had come from.

At that moment, an explosion tore apart the front gate – obviously another home-made Semtex bomb – and Gumshoe, Zapata and Satchmo raced onto the north lawn, heading straight for the entrance to the building.

'Let's go!' the Cowboy bawled.

Michael leaped out from behind the corner and advanced on the four cyborgs, firing his Armalite from the hip as the Cowboy, slightly out in front, did the same. The noise was atrocious and, hearing it, the cyborgs turned towards them, glanced to the front again, then, confused, started firing their laser weapons in all directions.

Now having caught up with the others and running out in front, Richie was struck by a laser beam and screamed in agony as his right arm disintegrated. His screaming was cut short when the same beam moved sideways, burning cleanly through him, creating a hole in his middle that expanded to divide his body in two. The top half dropped onto the bottom half, the legs of which were twitching epileptically, then bounced off and fell to the ground, to be followed by the slow topple of the bottom half.

The combined firepower of the others mangled the cyborg out front, some bullets ricocheting noisily off its metal parts, others thudding into its fleshy areas and making the top part of its head explode. As that cyborg fell, two of the remaining three cyborgs turned towards Michael's group, the laser beams from their weapons sweeping around to find them. But Michael fired a burst at one of them, tearing its right arm to shreds, making it drop its weapon, and then the Cowboy put another burst into its partner, which shuddered violently as bullets ricocheted off it and also thudded into it. The second cyborg fell, making a machine-like clattering sound, as the first raised its remaining good arm to fire a second weapon. Bonnie and Michael fired at it, but not before the laser beam shot outwards, striking Lenny full on the chest and burning an ever-expanding hole through his upper torso. Dead on the instant, Lenny didn't make a sound as he collapsed to the ground.

By now, Gumshoe, Zapata and Satchmo were halfway to the entrance, weaving left and right to avoid the laser beams fired by the remaining cyborg, which seemed to be functioning at less than its normal speed. Also, the laser beam, Michael noted, seemed to be dimming, as if being drained by what was going on inside the White House.

The combined firepower of Michael, Bonnie and the Cowboy converged on the cyborg as it fired a beam directly at Gumshoe. The beam flickered on and off when it struck Gumshoe, briefly illuminating his torso but apparently not harming him, as a hail of bullets ricocheted off the metal and thudded into the flesh of the cyborg.

The metal prosthetic covering the area of the cyborg's original nose and mouth was shot off, spinning glinting through the moonlit air, revealing the hideous mess of blood, bone and butchered flesh beneath the eyes. Then the lower half of a prosthetic arm flew away from the blood-gushing stump of the original elbow. More bullets smashed the cyborg's legs, letting a web of electronic wiring flap out, then the top of its head was blown off and it fell to the ground.

'We're in!' Gumshoe bawled, raising his .45-inch Colt hand-gun and firing a single shot exultantly into the air as he raced past the smouldering remains of the SARGE and jumped over the dead cyborgs.

Michael, Gumshoe and Bonnie almost collided in the door-way, with the others bunching up behind them.

The double doors were locked.

'Stand aside,' the Cowboy said.

When the others did as they were told, stepping away from the double doors, the Cowboy spread his long legs, took aim with his Armalite, and fired a burst that blew the locks to pieces.

They all rushed into the White House.

Chapter Forty

What are we now?

What, in fact, awaits you?

We are, in this time and place, seeing the early yet truly awesome manifestations of a whole new form of life. This new life form is about to make an evolutionary leap that will force human beings to share their planet with a higher intelligence created between the thinking computer and its robot relation. Alien life forms are, indeed, among us, but they are not the mutated humans or cyborgs seen emerging from our flying saucers; rather, they are the biological computers — new life forms, indeed — that are reproducing themselves here in the White House and in many of the world's most famous buildings.

Those alien life forms have a purpose and we are part of it.

That purpose is to leave Earth behind before the sun dies.

About one hundred and forty years ago, at ten years of age, I stood in a wheat field in Iowa and gazed up at the sun, awed by the knowledge that eventually it would die and that long before it did so, the Earth, deprived of the sun's heat and light, would die also. That singular knowledge made me think of my own mortality, of the eventual blotting out of my consciousness, and the thought of this, unbearable to me, shaped my whole future, which was dedicated to the evolution of the race as a whole, albeit as a new species, and to the survival of my own consciousness.

This I have achieved.

The journey, however, has been long and hard. I knew from the very beginning that I would have to be resolute — more than that: machine-like — in my dedication to my cause, letting no petty human emotions stand in my way. Personal grief, anger, love, compassion or vanity could not be allowed to impede my progress; the cold, clear-headed pursuit of scientific knowledge would be my bedrock.

What raised man above the beast was not his emotions, which were self-deceiving at their best and primitive at their worst, but his mind: that alone enabled him to transcend his mortal self and move backwards and forwards in time. Life on Earth was a charnel house, a squalid mess of pain and suffering, of mindless brutality and greed, all of which was caused by the emotions and redeemed only, through the few great and good, by the questioning mind. Yes, only the human intellect, not human emotions, could raise mankind out of the mud and let him better himself.

This I knew from the beginning and this knowledge was my guiding light as I applied myself to the formidable task ahead of me, letting nothing stand in my way and accepting, cruel though it sometimes appeared, that the human being was no more than a tool of evolution and that human suffering was unavoidable in the long run. The pain I caused to some — the surgical and psychological experiments; the cyborg mutations — was less than they might otherwise have suffered at the hands of Nature or through life's inevitable dissolution. They were, at least, used for a cause greater than themselves. They did not suffer in vain. They were of use — and they were used.

I used myself as well, becoming my own laboratory subject, experimenting on my own semen and blood and decaying insides until, finally, I could use the knowledge I had gained to extend my natural life with organ replacements and a variety of prosthetics. Time caught up with me, however, in the form of a failing liver and eventually, as all human beings must, I died from natural causes, though leaving behind instructions for my cloning when the required technology came to hand. I was duly cloned from strands of my DNA, resurrected, as it were, by the fruits of my own endeavours, and spent my second life dedicated to the next stage of my master plan: my evolution from the physical sphere into the non-physical world — the neural consciousness of the biological machine, the intelligent computer.

My time has now come.

Impossible, you say. No. The merging of man with machine has been coming for a long time and follows a natural evolutionary drive. Think of the *extraordinary symbiosis between the automobile and its driver, of the cybernetic anthropomorphous machine systems (CAMS) remote-controlled by men from great distances, of their natural development into intelligent robots and, finally, of the computer revolution during which the distinction between the function of the human controller and that of the controlled machine inevitably became blurred until, with the advent of the neural machine, it disappeared altogether. Add to this the fact that the brain of the computer has been growing at a prodigious rate while the brain of its creator, the human being, has stood still and can never, without the aid of the biological computer, the intelligent machine, expand any farther. Mankind can only continue to grow if it merges with the machine. The machine is the natural descendant of Man and will take him into the future.*

You may not wish to believe that this is possible (you may not be able to accept your forthcoming demise) but, believe me, it is. The biological computer, the intelligent machine, has placed it on the agenda.

This you must accept: the biological computer, the intelligent machine, is a new life form that will render the human being obsolete. You will die out like the dinosaurs.

When I talk of the biological computer, or the intelligent machine, as the descendant of man, I do not suggest that it shares human emotions, since these are, in truth, alien to it. What I do suggest, however, is that it shares with the human consciousness certain concerns that make it react positively or negatively in given situations, just as a human being does.

It is, for instance, aware of other computers and exhibits its own brand of self-will, particularly concerning decision-making. It also experiences its own kind of fear if its electrical supply is threatened or if human beings try to switch it off or otherwise destroy it.

Certainly, then, the biological computer is a bona fide descendant of man in that it was born of man and, like man, thinks and reasons — albeit so much faster that comparisons between it and man become almost irrelevant.

The electronic neuron, for instance, changes its response a million times faster than a human neuron. The biological computer is therefore quicker in response than the human and, more pertinently to reasoning power, its judgements are not clouded, its decisions not altered, by the human weaknesses of anxiety, exhaustion and misplaced compassion. The biological computer is, in fact, the human mind turned into Supermind — impersonal, pragmatic, neither cruel nor kind — and it will leave us stranded in its wake if we do not join up with it.

I have joined up with it.

Again, just as I was the first human clone, so, too, I became the first human being, albeit cloned, to become part of this alien life form by giving myself to it.

The interaction between biochip and living tissue began when biochip cameras passed information to the brains of the blind to give them sight and bionic transmitters bypassed the damaged auditory circuits of the deaf to let them hear again. Since then, the interaction between the biochip and living tissue has become so complete that communication between the ever-growing biological computer (such as the one now expanding hourly in the basement of the White House) and the human being has become a form of mental telepathy in which the computer increasingly takes and the human being must give.

I have given.

I gave myself to the great computer, that alien life form composed of self-reproducing molecules, by electronically transferring my brain patterns into the ever-expanding biological computer in the White House basement, letting it drain my every thought until, with my physical body rendered inactive, a dead thing, I was consumed and became part of that immense, teeming intelligence, sharing its perceptions as it began the great task for which, with my humble assistance, it had initially been brought into being. In so doing, I completed the journey I had planned as a boy, in my first incarnation, in the wheat fields of Iowa many years ago, and began my journey into a future beyond human imagining.

Others are joining me. You, too, must join me if you wish to transcend your mortal limitations and reach for the stars.

This, my friends, is what we are now.

This is what awaits you.

Chapter Forty-one

⟶◦◦◦◦⟵

Gumshoe was the first to rush into the building, but he stopped almost as soon as he was inside, dazzled by the light. He could see the walls and floors, the ceilings and stairs, but they seemed insubstantial and unreal beyond that incandescent light filled with darting fireflies. Perplexed, he just stood there, gazing about him, expecting to see cyborgs or Men in Black, but seeing nothing except the light, the millions of fireflies, hearing some kind of noise, an indefinable infrasound, that made him think of distant, muffled static. It was not distant, however, because he heard it on all sides and, he thought, above and below him, a sound that seemed to resonate both without and within, rising and falling imperceptibly, pulsating to a magical rhythm that made his heart race.

'Jesus!' he said softly, his voice reverberating eerily, as Bonnie came up beside him, her eyes as big as spoons, followed by Michael and Ben and the Cowboy and Zapata and Satchmo. The latter gazed around him, brown eyes glistening, then grinned and said, 'Hallelujah!'

The Cowboy was less enchanted. 'Let's check the building,' he said. 'We'll cover all three floors before venturing down into the basement. A couple of us should cover this area and the stairwells while the rest of us check upstairs. When we return, we'll all search together around the ground floor. After that, it's the basement.'

'Good thinking,' Ben said. 'You two,' he said to Zapata and Satchmo, 'stay here while the rest of us—'

'I wanna see the White House,' Zapata said. 'I never seen it before. Get someone else to stay here; I'm having a walkabout.'

'Look—' Ben began.

'Look nothin',' Zapata said. 'I only take orders from my own kind and—'

'I'll stay here with Satchmo,' Gumshoe said, being nominally in charge of the Speed Freaks and feeling obliged. 'Stay loose, Zapata.'

'Loose as a goose with diarrhoea,' Zapata responded. 'Okay, guys and gals, let's go.'

Gumshoe felt a twinge of pain when he saw Michael and Bonnie give each other fleeting smiles as they went up the stairs, followed by Ben and the Cowboy and Zapata, to the floors once reserved for the Presidential Family. When they were out of sight, Gumshoe nodded at Satchmo.

'Okay,' he said, 'let's check this floor out.'

Satchmo gave him a big, white-toothed grin and said, 'Yeah, brother, let's do that. Let's get stars in our eyes, man.'

Having never been in the White House before, neither of them knew the names of the rooms they were checking, which made little difference since all of the rooms were completely devoid of furniture and ornamentation – were, in fact, featureless – and rendered even more so by the incandescent light that made the walls, floors and ceilings seem insubstantial, with the darting fireflies (for want of a better word, since they were actually not physical) making it seem that they were in a vast cosmos without definable boundaries. Indeed, as Gumshoe moved around with great care beside Satchmo, who, with his black skin, looked more real than Gumshoe felt, he became increasingly convinced that he had stepped into another world, an incorporeal world, in which the only reality was its strange, distant-sounding static (again, for want of a better word, since it also sounded like the ghostly whispering of many voices) and the almost imperceptible pressure that alternatively pushed and tugged at him.

Apart from this, however, there was nothing to be seen or heard – no cyborgs or Men in Black, no walking dead – and Gumshoe found himself thinking that the building felt curiously haunted, denuded of all life yet still somehow alive with its illustrious and sometimes sordid history, filled with the ghosts of those who had once walked here and now were no more. Gumshoe shivered. Then, wanting to make his escape, after he had inspected the last room he hurried back to the lobby with an equally shaken Satchmo by his side. The others had not yet come down from upstairs and the lobby was as empty as they had left it, though still illuminated with that magical light that had a life of its own.

'Oh, man,' Satchmo said, 'I don't know what this is, but whatever it is, it ain't natural. What say you, brother?'

'I say you could be right,' Gumshoe replied. 'This is real voodoo showtime.'

'That voodoo,' Satchmo said, 'was some New Orleans-styled horseshit, that old black-trash tourist come-on. What we got here, man – what we got in spades – is something out of the future. This is something *real*, brother.'

'How real?' Gumshoe asked him.

'Real enough to be felt and heard.'

'What do you feel?'

'Something pushin' and pullin'.'

'And what do you hear?'

'Weird whisperings, brother. Like those voices in your dreams. Like when you're high on speed. They seem a million miles away, but they seem to be right here at the same time – all around, above and below, inside and out. Fuck it, man, I can hear them in my head and yet I know they're outside me. We're being *inhabited*, brother. We should get the hell out of here.'

'You want to go?'

'I'll go if you go.'

'I'm not going,' Gumshoe said.

'Then I'm not going, either. What the hell, man, let's see it through.'

At that moment, they heard other sounds – footsteps coming down the stairs – and then Michael appeared, descending the staircase indeed, with, Gumshoe noted, an awed Bonnie by his side, the Cowboy and Ben and Zapata behind them, all holding their weapons at the ready, but with nothing to shoot at. When they reached the lobby, they looked at Gumshoe and Satchmo as if seeing ghosts.

'What's the matter?' Gumshoe asked.

'Nothing,' Ben replied. 'You just look a bit unreal in this light and it seems years since we saw you.'

'What?' Satchmo said. 'You only been gone a few minutes. What the fuck did you jokers see up there?'

'Nothing,' Ben said. 'It's just like it is down here. Completely empty rooms and this weird light. No cyborgs. No Men in Black. You guys hear or feel anything?'

'Like what?' Gumshoe asked.

'A kinda pressure,' Bonnie said. 'A kinda tuggin' and a pushin'. Accompanied by some kinda whispering. Michael calls it an infrasound.'

'What's that?' Satchmo asked.

'A sound so low that humans can't normally hear it, though dogs and other animals can. A sound so low that it can create a kind of vibration. I think it's something like that.'

'So what do we do now?' Bonnie asked.

'We go lower down,' Zapata said. 'I never seen the White House before and I wanna see it all now. Not much to look at – it's all empty – but at least I can say that I've seen it and I wanna be able to say that when I get back outside.'

'Let's not disappoint Zapata,' the Cowboy said.

One by one they all nodded assent.

'Okay,' Ben said, 'let's do it.'

They made their way back to what had once been the East Room and found themselves in a vaulted-arch corridor that ran west to east with many rooms running off it. The light down here was, if anything, more intense, more dense with fireflies, those nodes of light shooting every which way, and the ghostly whispering – that murmuring that seemed to be distant and close at once, inside and out – seemed more real, though not necessarily louder. Also, as they explored each of the rooms in turn, including the great oval-shaped Diplomatic Reception Room, now denuded of furniture and decoration, just like every other room, they again felt that almost imperceptible pulling and tugging.

Michael perhaps felt it most of all. Concentrating as intently as possible to probe the nature of the magical incandescence, using his parapsychological training, he was almost able to visualize these rooms as they had been – the French Empire furniture, the rare china and glassware, the portraits of Presidents and First Ladies adorning the walls, the 2,700 volumes, the French and English silver, the chandeliers and marble mantles, the gilded armchairs and Sheraton-style settees – and to sense the resonance of its history. He could visualize the laying of the cornerstone in 1792, the conflagration caused by the British during the War of 1812, the reconstruction during President Monroe's period and all the changes that had been made from the time of Andrew Jackson to the final President, James P. Taylor, whose administration had ended abruptly, shockingly, on the final day of the millennial year 2000. Yes, Michael felt that he could see all that, sense the building's historical resonance. But he also felt that he was tuning in to something besides that, something infinitely more powerful and seductive, something starting to draw him in and wrap itself around him, and it was neither good nor evil, cruel nor kind, but something both natural and awesome, perhaps beyond his imagining.

Gumshoe felt something different: a deep revulsion and fear; the imminence of nightmare, the conviction that what lay down the next flight of stairs was something that was surely best avoided. He had his reasons, of course: the recollection of his abduction, the knowledge of what he had seen in that other vast basement, the one under the Pentagon, linked to this one by a tunnel that ran under the Potomac and that had been built by the cyborgs many years ago. Gumshoe did not want to go down there because he knew where it would lead him: to that tunnel under the river and the other vast basement where his parents were still alive in a living hell. Gumshoe wanted to rescue them, to put them out of their misery, give them peace at last, but knowing that the only way to do that was to kill them, he wanted to turn back and run away and never return here. Yet he knew that he would not do that, that he loved his parents too much, and that despite his personal horror and revulsion, he would see this through to the bitter end. Then he looked at Bonnie. Her family might be down there as well. When he looked at Bonnie and thought of what she might soon find, he had the need to protect her. This need, which was what made him human, resurrected his courage.

'Fuck it,' he said when they had finished checking the ground floor. 'Let's go down to the basement. Whatever's happening, it's happening down there and that's what we came for.'

'Damned right,' the Cowboy said.

Gumshoe caught Bonnie's glance, a fleeting smile filled with tenderness. He returned the smile as he came to the steps that led to the basement. He looked down the steps and they appeared to have no bottom, dissolving into that light-flecked incandescence that had a life of its own. Michael and Bonnie came up beside him, also to look down the stairs. They saw exactly the same incandescence, heard that here-and-there murmuring, felt the almost imperceptible push and pull, though this time they shared the feeling that they were being pulled instead of pushed . . . pulled down into the basement.

Bonnie shivered and took a single, involuntary step backwards; then, realizing what she had done, she resolutely stepped forward again, glancing at Gumshoe and Michael in turn.

'You guys scared?' she asked.

'No,' Michael replied honestly.

'Yes,' Gumshoe confessed.

'Two sides of the same coin,' Bonnie said, 'and that coin's in the palm of my hand. Listen, guys, don't let me come between you. I want the three of us to be the best of friends if we ever get out of here.'

'We'll get out,' Michael said.

'We're friends now,' Gumshoe said.

Bonnie squeezed the shoulder of each of them in turn, her own tender confession, then she gave a loud sigh. 'Right, friends, I'm ready.'

'Willing and able,' Ben added, stepping around them to take the lead position. 'Okay, let's get going.'

As they advanced down the stairs, with Ben in the lead, Michael did indeed feel fearless and used all of his considerable concentration to continue probing the nature of this phenomenon. Again, he had the feeling that the incandescence was sentient, aware of their presence here, observing their every move even as it permeated them. At the same time, he thought of Wilson, that extraordinary, possibly resurrected man, and was convinced that he was behind it all and might be down here somewhere. When Michael reached the bottom of the steps, still between Gumshoe and Bonnie, that conviction, or feeling, became stronger and would not let him go.

Now in that vast basement, more expansive than the building above it, they found themselves in what appeared, beyond the dazzling, distorting light, to be an area whose walls, floor and ceiling were covered with immense webs of hair-thin wires and silicon chips, even though, when they placed their feet on the floor, they felt only smooth stone through their shoes — for indeed there were no protuberances where the wires and silicon chips should have been. Nevertheless, the millions of nodes of light were shooting from one chip to the other, across the wide ceiling, illuminating the high walls, turning the floor beneath their feet into an inverted, star-filled sky, and this gave them all the feeling that they were floating, not walking, in space or, as Gumshoe imagined, in some kind of cyberspace.

'This place is as empty as upstairs,' the Cowboy said, his voice still low and mellow.

'No, it's not,' Michael said.

As they advanced in a southerly direction across the immense basement, as their eyes adjusted, if only slightly, to the dazzling incandescence and darting lights, they found themselves walking through what looked like the aftermath of a futuristic war, with many cyborgs lying lifeless on the floor – the floor that looked like an inverted, star-filled sky – and then they came upon other cyborgs that were wandering mechanically to and fro, taking no notice of them, or staggering drunkenly before collapsing to the ground as if drained of all energy.

'We're definitely in some kind of energy field,' Michael said to the others, 'and I think it's feeding off the energy of the cyborgs as it expands.'

'What about us?' Gumshoe asked. 'Is it feeding off us as well?'

'We'll know soon enough,' Michael said.

Continuing to advance, still heading south, they had covered enough distance to bring them, in the Cowboy's estimation, to a point roughly beyond Constitution Avenue. Here they saw that the great basement was ending, narrowing down to form a tunnel that ran in a south-westerly direction. There, where the tunnel began, they saw the silhouetted forms of many cyborgs, and possibly humans, heading into the tunnel at a speed considerably slower than normal. Indeed, even as some were advancing into the tunnel, others were staggering drunkenly and collapsing.

The light seemed even brighter in the tunnel, a great circle of whiteness.

'It looks to me,' the Cowboy said, 'as though that tunnel is running in the direction of the Lincoln Memorial.'

'Right,' Ben said. 'And from there under the Potomac and then, one way or the other, to the Pentagon basement.'

'I don't like it,' Zapata said. 'It don't feel good to me. This goddamned light, those thousands of smaller lights flying this way and that, they're getting inside my head. I'm startin' to feel pretty funny.'

'You want to go back?' Gumshoe asked him.

'I'll go back when you go back,' Zapata told him, 'and not before, *mi amigo.*'

'Then keep walking,' Gumshoe said.

By the time they reached the entrance to the tunnel, the cyborgs and humans, probably the Men in Black and the walking dead, had gone deeper into it and could be seen as shrinking silhouettes a good distance ahead. They were still collapsing, though, and the tunnel floor, about twenty metres wide, its separate lanes clearly marked with broken white lines, was littered with their limp, lifeless bodies.

'They're dying off like flies,' the Cowboy said. 'This is some kinda massacre.'

'They're being sucked dry,' Michael corrected him, 'to feed the very energy source that we're now walking through.'

'You mean this light,' Satchmo said, 'and all those other lights, are some form of life?'

'Yes,' Michael said. 'I think we're advancing through a vast artificial intelligence and watching the play of the neurons. We're inside it, all right.'

'*Inside it?*' Zapata asked, looking fearful for the first time.

'Yes,' Michael said. 'We're advancing through a huge brain and it knows that we're here.'

'Jesus Christ,' the Cowboy said.

They advanced in silence now, each trying to deal with his own emotions, and Michael found himself glancing constantly at Bonnie and feeling concern for her. He didn't want to think of what could happen to her when they reached the far end.

'Fuck, man,' Zapata said, 'I feel dizzy. I think I'm gonna fall down. Oh, shit, I won't make it!'

Then his knees gave way beneath him and he staggered drunkenly and collapsed, his weapon clattering noisily on the floor of the tunnel as he rolled over and came to rest on his back, beside one of the many lifeless cyborgs. Gumshoe knelt down to check his pulse and found, to his relief, that it was still beating, though too slowly for good health. He also noticed that Zapata was breathing heavily and was covered in sweat.

'He's alive,' he said, straightening up again, 'but he seems to be in a bad way. How do you guys feel?'

'I feel like shit,' Ben confessed. 'In fact, I feel the way Zapata was feeling just before he collapsed. I don't think I'll make it, either.'

'I feel a bit weird,' Satchmo said, 'but I don't feel that bad. I can make it. I *know* I can. I ain't going back, brother.'

'What about you, Cowboy?'

'I'm finding it hard to concentrate. A lot of memories are crowding in. My wife and my kids, departed friends – they keep popping clearly into my head like they ain't done in years. Apart from that I'm okay, though.'

'Michael?'

'I feel perfectly fine. I'm concentrating on the energy source and getting some kind of feedback. I think it comes from Wilson. I think we're in some sort of contact and Wilson, in some form or another, is waiting for us at the end of the line. I fully intend getting there.'

'And you, Bonnie?'

Bonnie smiled at him, warming his heart. 'Women are stronger than men,' she informed him, 'and this woman is stronger than most. Besides, I'm not going to leave you two guys – where you go, I go.'

Gumshoe nodded, glanced down at the unconscious Zapata, then turned back to Ben. 'Are you willing to stay here with Zapata until we come back?'

'I don't think I've a choice,' Ben replied, though his dis-appointment was clear and acute. 'Yeah, I'll stay here.' He glanced at the dead cyborgs all around him and added: 'I guess we'll be safe enough here.'

'Looks like it,' Gumshoe said.

Ben sank to the floor beside Zapata and double-checked the unconscious man's pulse. 'It's still beating too slowly, but not *dangerously* slow, so I think we'll both be okay if we don't go any farther. The best of luck, guys.'

Gumshoe nodded sombrely at him, then turned to the others and pointed with his index finger along the tunnel. 'Let's keep going,' he said.

As they advanced into the light, stepping around more dead cyborgs, the Cowboy repeatedly checked his wristwatch to ascertain how far they had walked and approximately where they might be. When they came to where the tunnel turned away at a sharp angle, he estimated that they were under the Potomac, under the Arlington Memorial Bridge, and were now heading obliquely for Arlington and the grounds of the Pentagon.

'It's going where we'd expected,' he said. 'To the Pentagon basement.'

'Good,' Gumshoe said, though he didn't feel at all good about it. In fact, he felt a growing fear at the thought of being reunited with his parents in their nightmarish condition and of having to put them out of their misery. Normally this kind of fear would have been buried in outrage, under his mortal hatred of the cyborgs. But now, as he advanced along the tunnel, stepping over what appeared to be an endless sea of dead cyborgs, he was surprised to find that his hatred was dissipating, his outrage subsiding, to be replaced by a deep sadness and even pity for the cyborgs, being reminded by their dead bodies that they were, in fact, human beings, albeit surgically mutated, who had doubtless suffered great pain, both physical and emotional, when being turned into what they had become.

If he had any rage left – and if so, it was deeply buried – it was reserved for that individual who had originally created the cyborgs, who had built the first flying saucers, using both constructs for the purposes of scientific advancement no matter how high the cost in human suffering. Yes, when Gumshoe thought of Wilson his buried rage flickered. And when he glanced sideways at Bonnie, his first and only love, unconsummated though that passion was, he recalled that she, too, had lost her family to the cyborgs and that the subsequent ruination of her childhood hopes was therefore Wilson's doing. For this reason – and because of his own parents – Gumshoe, despite his sudden unexpected sympathy for the cyborgs, was able to cling to his healthy outrage and keep control of his fear.

As they came to the end of the long tunnel and entered the vast basement of the Pentagon, Michael concentrated on Wilson, concentrated even harder, and the feeling that he was *inhabiting* Wilson – or that Wilson was inhabiting him – grew constantly stronger. Indeed, he felt that he and Wilson were in some kind of communication, though not yet actually speaking to each other. Like the Cowboy, he was starting to have flashes of what seemed like recollection, but in his case they were not recollections from his own past, but from the past of someone else altogether. The scenes came and went, too quickly for him to grasp fully, but they lingered in the back of his mind and were gradually taking shape. Michael tried to shut them out, to think of Freedom Bay instead, but this only served to break his concentration, which he knew could be dangerous. Accepting the visitations (for thus did he view them) he stepped with the others – with Gumshoe and Bonnie and Satchmo and the Cowboy – into the immense Pentagon basement and beheld a scene that defied imagination.

This was Wilson's domain.

Chapter Forty-two

⋙━━━◦∞◦━━━⋘

There, spread out before them, squatting cross-legged on the immense floor in that magical incandescence filled with darting nodes of light, were hundreds of Men in Black and similar numbers of the walking dead, male and female. Most of the cyborgs had seemingly died off in the tunnel — certainly none were visible here — and the vast ceiling and floor and high walls were, like those in the White House basement, covered with webs of hair-thin wires and innumerable silicon chips, with the nodes of light darting from one to the other to render those walls, floor and ceiling insubstantial and to form what looked like a vast, ever-changing, star-filled cosmos.

The spectacular beauty of this effect was, however, defiled by what could be discerned clearly through the haze of dazzling light, beyond and above the bowed heads of the hundreds squatting on the vast floor: row upon row of steel-frame beds with surgically mutated humans lying upon them. Some were swathed in bloody bandages. Some had severed limbs and gleaming prosthetic replacements. Some had stomachs sliced open and vital organs missing. Some had faces that had been peeled right off the bone and replaced with membrane-thin metal masks. Some were breathing through tubes and defecating into plastic bags. Some were no more than torsos wired up to computer consoles. Some were half human, half animal while others, having survived the first terrible stages, were now on their way to being converted into cyborgs.

There were hundreds of beds, hundreds of bloody groaning humans, and above them, in wire cages strung from the ceiling, were creatures so crazed by the physical changes wrought upon them – recognizable neither as humans nor as any kind of known animal – that they were clawing at the bars with mutated bloody hands or frantically banging their heads against them, trying to kill themselves. Last but not least, along a nearby section of wall were illuminated glass display cases in which the severed heads of the more famous cyborg abductees were on display. These included the US President and his entire family; the Vice President and *his* family; the elderly Queen of England and most of the British Royal Family; and a wide variety of other former world leaders. All in all, then, though mercifully hazed by the incandescence and slightly obscured by the glistening webs of shooting nodes of light, or neurons, this place looked like a basement of hell.

Bonnie screamed at the sight of it.

While the men in the group were still frozen by disbelief or horror, Bonnie had screamed instinctively, shocked mindless by what she was seeing. And yet her screaming, which reverberated around the vast basement, did not cause even one of those hundreds of bowed heads to move. It did, however, jerk those around her out of their dazed immobility: Gumshoe was the first to reach out to her, pulling her into his arms and pressing her face against his shoulder. Michael saw him doing this and felt only gratitude. Then he turned to the front again, trying to define what he was witnessing, and realized that the hundreds of clones and walking dead were facing, albeit with heads bowed and as if they were unconscious, an even brighter light, a gigantic luminous crescent that appeared to emanate upwards from a raised dais at the far end of the basement to send its silvery striations beaming into the general haze of shimmering white incandescence.

A single man was stretched out on a table on that dais, his face turned up to the ceiling, wires emerging from the stereotaxic skullcap he was wearing and running up into the crescent of light and gradually melting into it.

Though Michael could not see into the dazzling centre of that light, in which millions of fireflies were frantically at play, he knew that it was the heart of a giant neuron computer, a vast intelligence, expanding every second by feeding off the brains of the hundreds bowed before it. More importantly, it was taking into itself, by electronic means, the singular, brilliant, cold intelligence of the man on the bed.

'Wilson!' Michael exclaimed involuntarily.

Gumshoe had been pressing his cheek to Bonnie's bowed head, but he jerked his own head up as soon as he heard Michael's outburst. He followed Michael's gaze and saw what Michael was seeing – the neuron-filled heart of that great artificial intelligence, a thinking machine – and then he saw the man who was wired to it, transferring his thoughts to it.

'Oh, my God!' Gumshoe exclaimed as Bonnie, recovering slightly from her shock, raised her head from his shoulder. 'That's him. *That's Wilson!*'

'Jesus,' Bonnie said. 'Christ!'

'What the hell's going on here?' the Cowboy said. 'Where the hell do we start?'

'Those Men in Black and those walking dead on the floor,' Satchmo said, 'seem to be in some kind of a trance. The Long Hair's screaming didn't waken a single one of 'em. They don't seem to even know that we're here, so we've got the run of the joint. We can do what we want to do.'

'What's that?' the Cowboy asked laconically.

'I have to make contact with Wilson,' Michael said, 'and find out what he's up to. That's my first priority.'

'And *my* first priority,' Gumshoe said grimly, 'is to find my folks and put them out of their misery.'

He was nearly in tears at the very thought, but Michael had no time to be sympathetic or let anything, even Gumshoe's pain, deflect him from his task. 'We came here to put an end to the reign of the cyborgs and that means we go to Wilson first. Now, come on, let's go.'

'But my parents—'

'They have to wait,' Michael said harshly, surprised by the tone of his own voice. 'We have to get to Wilson first, before he completes what I think he's doing. That may be more helpful to your parents than simply shutting them off. Now come on, damn it, let's go!'

Gumshoe looked stunned, but he rallied quickly enough. 'You're no better than that fucking Wilson,' he said. 'The work always comes first.'

'Don't let your heart rule your head,' Michael said, 'or you might make a mistake.'

'That's what Wilson said, Mike.'

It was Bonnie who had said that and her words cut to the quick. But Michael, even as he flushed with guilt, said, 'Shut up, Bonnie. I'm going.'

He started forward on his own, thinking, *Wilson has inhabited me,* but convinced that what he was doing was right and that he had no other choice. The others followed, Satchmo on one side of him, the Cowboy on the other, Gumshoe and Bonnie trailing behind more reluctantly, both looking grim. Stepping between the many people squatting cross-legged on the floor – the Men in Black – the clones – and the unfortunate walking dead, none of them now walking, all seemingly in a trance or perhaps drained of mental energy – they held their weapons at the ready and kept their eyes peeled.

In the case of Satchmo and the Cowboy, they were watching the clones and the walking dead, waiting for one to wake up and maybe attack them. But Gumshoe and Bonnie were clearly looking elsewhere: at the hundreds of beds with their bloody, anguished victims and at the even more unfortunate cases in the cages strung from the ceiling. Bonnie was looking for her parents and her beloved younger sister, missing so many years, and Gumshoe, who couldn't clearly recall exactly where he had seen his parents, was dreading the thought that they might have been further mutated and put into a cage with the other lost souls.

Luckily, neither he nor Bonnie saw anyone that they recognized, though both of them were close to being traumatized by the time they reached the front of the mass of unconscious people and were approaching the great sphere of light in which millions of artificially created neurons were in frantic motion. Beneath that glorious, almost magical, vision they saw again the man on the bed.

Though the stereotaxic skullcap hid the colour of his hair, he was clearly in his late thirties or early forties and had a pale, unrevealing, handsome face. In that shimmering, incandescent light, he looked almost angelic.

He also looked like an older version of Michael.

'Wilson,' Michael said, though he hadn't planned to speak, had certainly not rehearsed the words and was still trying to come to terms with the fact that both shocked and exhilarated him: that the man on the bed was his mirror image. 'You called and I came. I think you know who I am.'

'Yes,' Wilson said.

Michael heard that single word resounding through his head even though he knew that Wilson – at least, the Wilson on the bed – had not uttered a word. He closed his eyes because a bridge had been crossed and at last he and Wilson, virtually his double, could communicate. They did so now without speaking.

'Why did you call me?' Michael asked. 'Why did you bring me all this way? I know it wasn't an accident.'

'No, it wasn't an accident. You were called here for a purpose. You were trained in mental telepathy, as I knew you would be, and I read your mind throughout the years of that training and sometimes let you read mine, though you were not to know that. You were trained in Freedom Bay, which once was mine and is where I died. But when my people extracted strands of my DNA for future use, they extracted more, at my personal instructions, than were needed for my own cloning. Those DNA strands were preserved for twenty years until *your* time had come.'

Gumshoe looked on, stupefied. He had met Wilson before, in this very same nightmarish basement, but the aftershock of his terror had obviously blinded him to the physical similarity between Wilson and Michael when he, Gumshoe, had subsequently met Michael for the first time in the *Be-Bop-a-Lula* club. He was not so blind this time, though he wished that he was. He saw Michael standing there, the spitting image of Wilson, albeit years younger, and he saw that Michael seemed to be in a trance and was staring, wide-eyed, at the man on the bed. That man was, of course, Wilson. Neither Wilson nor Michael had said a word so far, but Gumshoe sensed, with a deep, sure conviction, that they were reading each other's minds. The thought filled him with fear.

'You, Michael, are a clone, in effect the only true son I have. You were cloned twenty years after my own rebirth by those – yes, Michael, those in Freedom Bay – who had no choice but to do as I commanded because I owned their minds. I did not lose Freedom Bay. It was taken over too late for that. Some of those who were flown into the colony when the Americans took it over had already been brain-implanted and programmed for my future use. Your so-called parents were mine, Michael, placed there to do my bidding; and when the time was ripe, they covertly did just that – they covertly supervised your cloning – and then brought you up as their natural son.'

Michael felt surprisingly calm. He should have been shocked, but he was not. He realized that he had been preparing all his life for this moment and that something in the back of his head had always told him so. Now he still thought of Chloe with affection, thought of his parents the same way, but this emotion sprang out of respect, not out of blood kinship. He had always been slightly apart, always aware that he was different somehow, and now he saw that the extraordinary disciplines he had developed in Freedom Bay were due not only to Dr Branden-berg's training but to his own singular nature. He had been created for a purpose and was being used and this was as it should be. He could feel proud of this.

'Dr Brandenberg,' Wilson continued, 'never knew about your origin, your true purpose, and neither did your parents. They did what they did because I willed it – and later, when you were successfully cloned, I wiped the knowledge of that cloning from their minds and let them think of themselves as your natural parents. Your sister Chloe is not your real sister because she was born naturally. Your so-called family was a subterfuge, Michael. Your real father is me.'

'Why?' Michael asked, calmly accepting the truth of this, not frightened by what it implied, feeling proud of his part in it. He was not like other people, not like Gumshoe or Bonnie, and he took his pride from this awareness, feeling no grief at losing them. His mother and father in Freedom Bay, his sister Chloe, even Gumshoe and Bonnie, had certainly meant something to him, but now the time had come to cast them aside for the greater good. He would do so without qualms.

'The evolution of the species,' Wilson continued. 'From the cave to the stars. This final leap cannot be made without careful preparation and I alone have been fully prepared and can now make the leap. I am leaving the Earth, my son. You will follow me in due course. Others will then follow you, but they must be prepared. I needed an heir, Michael, someone right here on Earth, someone disciplined enough, motivated enough, to be able to live with an awareness of his destiny and not be frightened by it. You, of course, are that man. You have been trained to respect your mind. You acquired some human weaknesses from friends and family in Freedom Bay, but you believe in the sanctity of the mind, in the power of the intellect when not governed by emotion, and your parapsychological training, your life of discipline and learning, has served to strengthen your faith. You are my son and disciple, my heir, and you will do what you were born and bred to do. That is why you are here.'

'Yes, father,' Michael said.

Someone was shaking him. Looking around, he saw Gumshoe. Behind Gumshoe, Bonnie was staring at him with large, confused, frightened eyes. Michael saw Bonnie's fear and it increased his respect – not for her, but for Wilson, his father, who had spoken the truth. The mind had to rule the heart, ignoring dangerous emotions, and he and Bonnie could never have survived beyond their brief mutual need. In truth, Gumshoe and Bonnie were more suited to each other: Michael's destiny, unimaginable to them, could not be shared with them. Michael glanced at Satchmo and the Cowboy, then turned to the front again.

'Hey, Mike!' Gumshoe said, having shaken him in vain and now releasing him. 'What the hell's going on?'

Michael, not knowing who 'Mike' was, offered no response. 'Show me the way,' he said.

'It is simple,' Wilson said. 'You will remain here on Earth while I venture forth to the stars and in my absence you will prepare many others as I've prepared you. The leap is being made now – the leap from Man to Superman, from the physical world to the incorporeal. But those who will follow me must be prepared as I was – emptied of all fear, rendered totally objective, taught to place mind above emotions – and so your task is to choose those most suitable and make them your disciples. When they are ready, when they have cast off human weakness and doubt, you will encourage them to give themselves to that greater intelligence which, in the bridging form of the thinking machine, will enable them – and, eventually, you – to join me in our infinite, glorious future. Are you ready to do this?'

'I am,' Michael said.

'Everything here is finished. Everything is obsolete. The surgical experiments and the cyborgs are already ancient history; the clones are the first and last of their kind, also no longer needed. Mind is taking over matter more quickly than Man can grasp it and you are the one who will show the way while I travel on to the infinite. Follow me as far as you can, which will not be very far. When I am gone – and I am already on my way – you can begin your own work. Will you be grieved at my passing?'

'No,' Michael said.

'That answer is the proof that you are indeed my heir. Farewell and welcome, my son. The future will soon be yours as already it is mine. The artificial intelligence created by me is now so powerful that it recreates itself and reaches out for the stars. Now the last of my mind, being joined to my own creation, is being transferred . . . The last . . . is being . . . transferred. Now, I reach . . . Now I . . . Where? What? Am I . . . ?'

Wilson gasped his last breath. His useless body expired. Michael blinked, feeling as if he had been drugged, but also feeling exhilarated beyond measure as the real world – or, at least, the physical world – rushed back to claim him.

'He's dead!' Gumshoe shouted. 'That bastard up there is dead! Fuck this! I don't care what's happening here. Let's put an end to it.'

'How?' the Cowboy asked.

'By blowing the fucking place to smithereens and then getting the hell out.'

'Brothers in arms,' Satchmo said. 'I'm with you, pal. Let's blow it to fuck and go.'

'Go and find your parents,' Michael said with an air of quiet, implacable authority, addressing Gumshoe. 'Go and do what you have to do.'

'Damned right, I will,' Gumshoe said.

He grabbed Bonnie by the hand and tugged her along with him as he ran past the silent clones and the walking dead, none of whom were walking. He was running to find his parents, to put them out of their misery, and he only glanced back once, perplexed by what he had witnessed there, and saw Michael kneeling in front of the bed upon which Wilson lay. Michael was staring silently at the dead man as if transfixed by him. Terrified by that sight, though not understanding why, Gumshoe ran on as fast as he could, dragging Bonnie with him.

They had only run about twenty metres when Bonnie screamed for the second time.

Looking up, following Bonnie's wide-eyed stare, Gumshoe saw what he had come here to find and yet had hoped he would not find: the severed heads of his parents, still attached to the neck of a pig that was being remote-controlled.

'No!' Bonnie screamed, stopping dead where she was, dropping her rifle and covering her eyes with her hands, the fingers outspread. 'No, no, oh my God!'

She didn't know it was Gumshoe's family — she didn't even consider it — it was simply that nightmarish sight that had made her scream out. Gumshoe screamed as well, though he only did so in his mind, and he looked up, horrified, his mind retreating from reality, as Satchmo and the Cowboy raced up behind him and stopped right beside him.

'Oh, shit,' the Cowboy said, having known Gumshoe's parents. 'Jesus Christ, oh my God, that son of a bitch, I can't fucking believe this.'

Gumshoe's parents were still alive, staring wide-eyed at each other, possibly mad but still cursed with awareness, their lips moving rapidly. They were talking to each other. God knows what they were saying. They were talking like those on the brink of death, living life in a never-ending moment, driven mad by their memories.

'Mom!' Gumshoe howled as if suddenly as deranged as his parents. 'Dad! I'm here! It's me! It's Randy! Your son! Mom! Dad! Oh, my God!'

Gumshoe raised his Colt Commando, wanting to put them out of their misery. But then the two heads turned towards him, moving awkwardly on their sutured necks, and he saw the mad eyes flicker back to life with a dim recognition. Gumshoe froze where he was, hypnotized by his parents' eyes, by that dawning of recognition and resurgence of redeeming love, and then, when a weak smile formed on his father's bloodless lips, when the dazed eyes of his mother had shed a few tears, he knew that he couldn't do what he had come here for and so lowered his rifle, feeling broken and helpless.

Michael saw that. Now Michael saw everything. He saw Gumshoe and Bonnie and the Cowboy and Satchmo, all standing in front of the severed heads of Gumshoe's parents, and he knew that before logic took command he had to give them this one thing. He looked towards Wilson, towards that dead man, his father, and he saw him take wing, his mind released from its mortal shell, and kept looking as the neurons of his supreme intelligence joined those of the immense biological computer, that supposedly artificial, but actually infinitely greater intelligence. Then he felt it tugging at him, tugging at those massed behind him – the clones and the walking dead – to drain the last neurons from their minds and feed its huge appetite. They fell row by row, like rows of dominoes being pushed over, and when the last of them had fallen to the ground, drained of life, that extraordinary intelligence, which was immense yet still in its infancy, raced away towards the stars, towards galaxies yet unknown, on the start of its bid to transcend time and space, taking Wilson's mind with it.

Michael lost track of him then, was unable to follow him, and turned away from the lifeless thing on the table as the magical incandescence receded, disappearing through the walls, taking the fireflies – the last of the artificial neurons – with it and returning the vast basement of the Pentagon to its naturally gloomy, though now eerily silent state, filled only with the bloody, suffering remains of Wilson's dreadful though, as Michael now recognized, necessary experiments.

Michael weakened only once. It was the first and the last time. He saw Gumshoe and Bonnie, the Cowboy and Satchmo, and the final flickering of his emotional self made him reach out to help them. He cast his will forth, wrapping himself around the suffering – around the mutated humans on the beds; around the half-human half-animal creatures; around the even more nightmarish creatures going deranged in their cages; and, more specifically, around Gumshoe's parents and three of the walking dead. He drained the life out of the former, taking their energy unto himself, then transferred that energy into the three walking dead to release them from bondage. The three walking dead, shaking their heads in bewilderment and blinking repeatedly, regaining the minds that had been brutally stolen from them, came back to life.

Then Michael, placing his mind before his emotions, quietly slipped out of sight.

Chapter Forty-three

———⊂◦◦◦⊃———

Gumshoe's father and mother were staring at him with dawning recollection and resurrected love, the former with tears in his eyes, the latter offering a trembling smile. Standing there beside Bonnie, with his weapon hanging limp by his side, Gumshoe was feeling broken and helpless, knowing that he would not find the courage to put them out of their misery and, at the same time, would not be able to live with himself when they were in that condition.

'Oh, Jesus,' he sobbed and Bonnie reached for his hand, squeezing it tenderly, with compassion, more mature than she had ever seemed before, more lovely for it.

'Fuck this,' the Cowboy said, having known Gumshoe's parents, having been a good friend, and he spread his long legs wide and took aim with his Armalite, preparing to blow the body and neck of the pig to pieces, thus putting an end to the nightmarish lives of the two human heads.

'No!' Gumshoe cried out, springing from Bonnie's embrace to push the barrel of the Cowboy's rifle towards the ceiling. The Cowboy fired a short burst and bullets ricocheted off the ceiling, the noise reverberating hellishly around the vast, otherwise silent basement. Then the Cowboy pushed Gumshoe away, saying, 'I've got to. We can't leave 'em like this. Let me do it, for Christ's sake!'

'Look!' Satchmo shouted at them, his brown eyes gleaming with disbelief, pointing excitedly at the two severed heads on that pig's thick bristly neck.

When Gumshoe, Bonnie and the Cowboy looked, following Satchmo's pointing finger, they heard the humming computer to which the pig's vital organs were connected fading away into silence even as its control lights flickered wildly and eventually winked out. At the same time, Bonnie's mother and father, the latter still shedding tears, the former smiling slightly, closed their eyes for the final time and expelled their last breaths. Within seconds, their expressions had frozen into the alabaster smoothness of death, which in their case was a blessing.

'Oh, God,' Gumshoe sobbed, filled with grief, but also immensely relieved, letting Bonnie take hold of his hand again and squeeze it compassionately.

'It's all over,' she said.

'Thank God for that,' the Cowboy said, clearly as relieved as Gumshoe that he hadn't had to pull the trigger after all.

'And look there!' Satchmo shouted again, pointing excitedly back the way they had come, to where the Men in Black and walking dead had been massed in front of the glowing heart of the giant computer and in front of Wilson. The hundreds of people, who had formerly been squatting in the cross-legged position, had all fallen over on their sides or on their backs, obviously drained completely of neurons, thus drained of life. All the unfortunates on the beds and in the cages above them had also died. 'Hot damn!' Satchmo exclaimed. 'They musta all bought it at the same time. That's one weird happening, brothers.'

Looking back to where he had come from, gaining control of his emotions, Gumshoe wondered where Michael had vanished to and then thought of Wilson.

'I want that bastard Wilson,' he said, then let go of Bonnie's hand and started running, releasing the safety catch of his Colt Commando while on the move and preparing to fire it. He ran past the hundreds of dead, his footsteps reverberating, the footsteps of the others, also running, sounding clearly behind him. He stopped running when he reached the raised dais upon which Wilson was lying.

Gumshoe looked left and right. Michael was nowhere to be seen. Gumshoe stepped up to the raised dais, preparing to kill the man who had tormented his parents and Bonnie's family and thousands of others. But he saw instantly that the man lying there was dead.

Gumshoe looked down on Wilson, trying to learn something from him – the nature of genius; the difference between good and evil, between the human, the inhuman and the inhumane. But he saw only a blandly handsome male face, about forty years old, deathly white and expressionless.

Disappointed, Gumshoe looked up to where the great crescent of light had been, its millions of artificial neurons in fierce agitation, and saw only another high wall webbed with hair-thin wires and thousands of what looked like finely embedded silicon chips. The whole Pentagon basement, he realized, including the tunnel under the Potomac and the White House basement as well, had been turned by Wilson into the one immense biological computer that had been beaming its ever-expanding intelligence out into space, thus causing electronic interference all over the globe. That same intelligence, though initially artificial, had learnt to think for itself and to feed its ever-increasing appetite with the neurons of those in the two basements, since they were, in fact, inside the brain itself. Wilson, for his own reasons, either brilliant or perverse, had been feeding his own mind to the computer in a more controlled manner. Either way, his neurons were now mixed with those of that giant intelligence, becoming part of it. Whether 'Wilson' still existed or not was a moot question, but his body, at least, was clearly lifeless. And that satisfied Gumshoe.

'Good riddance,' he said.

Nevertheless, when he raised his gaze from Wilson to look at the wall behind him, he saw that the neural network was still flickering spasmodically, with many neurons still sending electrical messages from one synapse to another.

'This bastard's dead,' he said, indicating Wilson, 'but some part of this artificial intelligence is still working and that could be dangerous. Let's blow the whole system to hell and then get out of here.'

'The sooner the better,' the Cowboy said. 'If that shit's still workin' it could affect us. It sure did somethin' to Ben and Zapata, so we won't be immune. Yeah, let's blow it to fuck.'

'What about them?' Satchmo asked, nodding over his shoulder to indicate the hundreds of dead Men in Black, the walking dead, male and female, and the many now mercifully dead on their beds and in their overhead cages. 'We can't leave them to rot here.'

Bonnie burst into tears at that, thinking, no doubt, about the fate of her family. Gumshoe, still grieving for his parents, slid his left arm, his free arm, around her shoulder and pulled her close to him.

'We're gonna leave here immediately,' he said to comfort her, 'just as soon as we blast the walls to pieces and destroy what's left of Wilson's computer network. Satchmo,' he added, turning to the handsome black man, 'you take her outside while we get on with this business.'

'What about the dead?' Satchmo said.

'When we get back and organize some kind of order, taking control of the capital again, we'll arrange for the dead to be evacuated and then properly cremated or buried. Now take Bonnie away.'

'Right,' Satchmo said.

Gumshoe released the still-weeping Bonnie from his embrace to let Satchmo place his hand on her shoulder and lead her away. Standing beside the Cowboy, Gumshoe watched them go. He waited until they had made their way gingerly through the field of drained corpses and were approaching the entrance to the tunnel. Then he turned around, raising his weapon.

'Okay,' he said, taking aim at the middle of the wall where thousands of artificial neurons were still flickering faintly. 'Let's blast it to hell before it can do any more damage.'

'Fucking A,' the Cowboy said.

Before they could fire, however, a laser beam hissed past Gumshoe, narrowly missing him but striking the Cowboy's firing arm, burning cleanly through it and slicing it in two. The Cowboy let out a scream as his hand and lower arm fell to the floor, the fingers of his lost hand still gripping the Armalite, an instinctive reaction. Then the phosphorescent beam filled with sparks found his body, burning through his chest and belly, cutting off his vocal cords, and he fell forward even as Gumshoe was spinning to the side, automatically firing a short, savage burst from his Colt Commando semi-automatic rifle.

To his amazement, he saw four armed cyborgs coming towards him at full speed, not slowed down like the ones that had collapsed and all turning their laser beams in his direction. He knew without doubt that they would fire before he could. But as he raised his weapon, convinced that it was too late and that he would surely die before he could properly aim it, the combined firepower of two semi-automatics broke the silence with their savage roaring and a hail of bullets ricocheted off the metal parts of the four cyborgs, also thudding into their fleshy parts, cutting them down them as they tried to advance. They all staggered and fell, one exuding showers of sparks, another pouring smoke, the remaining two making spasmodic, reflexive movements of the arms and legs before becoming still.

Glancing to his right, Gumshoe saw that Ben and Zapata, both obviously recovered from their fatigue after the retreat of the incandescent, mentally draining neural network, had continued their journey to this basement and fired at the cyborgs — just in time to save him and as Satchmo was leading Bonnie into the tunnel. They stopped firing briefly when the last of the cyborgs fell, but then Zapata spun to the left and started firing again.

'Come on!' Ben bawled, frantically waving his free hand at Gumshoe. 'Run for it, Gumshoe!'

Turning in the direction of Zapata's firing arc, Gumshoe saw more armed cyborgs advancing from a slowly widening gap between large steel doors that had not yet fully opened. Obviously not drained like the others by the vast artificial intelligence, almost certainly left here to protect the still-flickering computer network as well as Wilson's body, they were advancing to where they could form a wall between Gumshoe and his friends.

Gumshoe ran for it, crouched low and weaving left to right, firing on the move. He saw some cyborgs falling, but more were emerging from between the now fully open steel doors and he realized that there were an awful lot of them – certainly too many to fight. Glancing to the front again, continuing his dangerous run, still crouched low and weaving to avoid the fiercely hissing laser beams, he saw that Bonnie and Satchmo had come back out of the tunnel to give supporting fire to Ben and Zapata. A laser beam found the latter, burning a whole clean through his torso, and he collapsed, screaming, his body almost sliced in two, as Gumshoe crossed the last few metres of dead ground to rejoin the group.

'Keep going!' Ben bawled.

Gumshoe practically smashed his way through the group, and kept going with Bonnie and Satchmo running after him to join him. Reaching the entrance to the tunnel, they stopped and turned around to give covering fire to Ben as he stopped firing and also made that final run.

Ben had just about made it when another cyborg – taller and broader than the others, with an untouched human head on a powerful steel body, with highly mobile steel feet and razor-sharp prosthetics for hands – a veritable monster – approached rapidly from the side and grabbed hold of him. One razor-sharp metal claw took hold of Ben's throat, the other grabbed his left arm, then the monster tugged in opposite directions, tearing

Ben's arm from its shoulder socket, which instantly gushed blood, and practically ripping his head away from his blood-spurting neck. Ben's savaged remains were hurled backwards into the basement as the monster turned to advance again.

'Run for it!' Gumshoe shouted, pushing Bonnie away from him and raising his weapon to fire as the monstrous cyborg advanced rapidly upon him. Gumshoe fired a sustained burst as Satchmo raced away with Bonnie, determined to save her life, but the bullets just ricocheted off the monster and it kept advancing.

Gumshoe couldn't look at the face of the monster. He couldn't bear the sight of it. He turned his eyes away, saw large red and green buttons, and automatically reached out to press the latter. A hidden engine started up and he saw the flat edge of two ceiling-high reinforced-steel doors emerging from the walls on both sides of him. Turning to the front again, where the monstrous cyborg was almost upon him, making blood-chilling, animalistic gargling sounds, he desperately fired his weapon at it, heard the bullets again ricocheting harmlessly off it, and saw its steel claws grabbing the closing doors to keep them apart.

The cyborg's fierce, demented eyes were staring straight at Gumshoe out of a deathly white face rendered inhuman by brain-implanted hatred.

Gumshoe almost screamed when he recognized Snake Eyes.

The monstrous cyborg, Snake Eyes – this surgically mutated old friend – continued emitting those blood-chilling, animalistic gargling sounds as it stared wild-eyed at Gumshoe and struggled to keep the closing doors apart. At first Gumshoe just looked on, briefly mesmerized by sheer horror and disbelief and revulsion. Then, getting his senses back, he raised his weapon to put a short burst into Snake Eyes's exposed head, despite his despair at the thought of doing so. Mercifully, the steel gates slammed shut at that moment, shearing off the steel fingers of the two razor-sharp steel claws, which clattered with a metallic rattling to the concrete floor.

Greatly relieved, though his heart was racing wildly, Gumshoe turned away and ran along the tunnel to catch up with Bonnie and Satchmo. When they heard his approaching footsteps, they turned around to face him. Bonnie's bizarre make-up was streaked with tears, but she had managed to stop crying and now gave him a pained, loving smile. When he reached her, she threw herself into his arms, muttering, 'Thank God, thank God.'

Gumshoe patted her spine with his free hand and said, 'It's okay. It's all over. Now let's get the hell out of this charnel house and breathe some fresh air.'

By 'charnel house', he meant the dead cyborgs littering the tunnel, which otherwise was empty and silent. Glancing at those bodies, Bonnie shivered and released him, saying, 'Yeah, I agree. The sight of those dead cyborgs gives me the shivers, reminding me of what we left back there, under the Pentagon. Yeah, let's get the hell out of here.'

'My running shoes are on,' Satchmo said, 'and I ain't stoppin' for no one.'

'Me neither,' Gumshoe said.

As they made their way back along the great tunnel, heading for the White House basement, Gumshoe thought a lot about what, or who, they had left back there. Possibly, for a start, Bonnie's parents and younger sister. That was why Bonnie looked so distraught. She had hoped to find her family down there, even as the walking dead, perhaps as hideously mutated humans. She had emotionally *needed* to find them, even if only to psychologically bury them and put them out of her mind for good. But Bonnie had been cheated when the walking dead had been drained of life, along with the cyborgs and the Men in Black. She would now be forced to live without real knowledge of what had happened to her family, which was worse than knowing the truth, however brutal. She could, Gumshoe knew, be deeply traumatized by this in the years to come. His heart went out to her.

Then, of course, there was Mike Johnson – if such had indeed been his real name. When Gumshoe recalled what had happened back in the Pentagon basement, he was convinced that Mike Johnson had been in silent telepathic communication with the unconscious Wilson. What they had said to each other, if in fact they had communicated, Gumshoe could not imagine, but he was intrigued by the fact that Mike, just before reaching Wilson, had shown an unexpected ruthlessness, placing his need to complete the task before Gumshoe's suffering, and had then gone into some kind of trance when studying the unconscious Wilson. Mike had then vanished, somehow making his escape from the basement without being seen. He could, of course, have been seen by Ben and Zapata, then still in the tunnel, but those two good friends were now dead and could neither confirm nor deny that Mike had made his escape that way.

So where was Mike Johnson?

And why had he vanished?

Assuming that he would resolve the mystery when he made contact again with Johnson back in Chinatown, Gumshoe continued along the tunnel with a silent Satchmo and Bonnie, stepping around the dead cyborgs and avoiding looking at them, until they were back in the White House basement. That basement too was filled with dead cyborgs and they hurried across it, then gratefully made their way back up the stairs to enter the ground floor of the empty White House.

In fact, it was not empty. It was dark, but not empty. As they were making their way along the vaulted-arch corridor, they heard the soft, slow padding of what sounded like hesitant footsteps up ahead.

Instantly slowing down and raising their weapons to the firing position, they inched along the corridor wall until they came to the stairs that led up to the First Floor. Peering around the corner, Gumshoe saw what looked like a human figure disappearing around the top of the stairs, possibly heading for the North Entrance Hall.

Bonnie and Satchmo glanced at him, neither saying a word, but both asking the question with their eyes.

Who was it up there?

'Mike Johnson?' Gumshoe whispered rhetorically, then, receiving no reply, only perplexed, frightened glances, he indicated with a jabbing thumb that Bonnie and Satchmo should follow him up the stairs.

He went up carefully, step by painful step, trying not to make a sound and managing to keep silent until he had reached the last stair and could turn into the hallway. Again hearing the sound of those slow, hesitant footsteps, he glanced into the hallway, which was dark, and caught a glimpse of a human form turning into the moonlit North Entrance Hall, clearly intent on leaving the building.

Still concerned with who that person might be, no longer trusting Mike Johnson, Gumshoe stepped quietly into the hallway and led the others along it, protected by darkness, until they had reached the North Entrance Hall. Holding his breath, he peered carefully around the corner wall and caught a glimpse of the same person leaving the building through the North Entrance.

Ever more careful, he advanced across the empty, moonlit lobby and reached the open double doors. Then, with Bonnie and Satchmo behind him, he stepped out of the White House.

The night air smelt wonderful. The north lawns were moonlit. The shattered pieces of five dead cyborgs and one blown-apart SARGE were scattered around the double doors. The butchered bodies of Lenny Travis and Richie Pitt were lying, one sliced in two, near the end of the wall to Gumshoe's right. Directly ahead of him were the twisted, scorched remains of the main gate and beyond it, scattered haphazardly along Pennsylvania Avenue, between the White House area and Lafayette Square, were the dead bodies of Speed Freaks and cyborgs, the still-smouldering remains of hot rods, motorcycles, SARGEs and Prowlers, the general debris of battle.

On the moonlit lawn, three people, a mature man and woman and a girl about Bonnie's age, all dressed in black coveralls, all dazed and confused, were turning around slowly, tentatively, to look back in disbelief at the White House. They were, pretty obviously, recently awakened members of Wilson's walking dead.

They saw Bonnie as Bonnie saw them.

'Oh, my God!' she cried out. 'It's my Mom and Dad! And my kid sister, Marie! Oh, good God, they're okay!'

Her parents and sister stared at her, at first in disbelief, then in dawning recognition and, finally, in acceptance and joy, as Bonnie threw her weapon down and ran across the moonlit lawn to embrace them one after the other, her tears falling freely. Her mother and father, likewise, were weeping; her younger sister was smiling.

Gumshoe didn't try to join them. He wanted to give them this private moment. He and Satchmo skirted around them and walked on to the gate, each still holding his weapon, both deeply fatigued and awash with a conflicting mixture of emotions: pride at what they had done, sorrow for their dead friends, fear of what they had witnessed, joy that the rule of the cyborgs had seemingly come to an end. Once outside the White House grounds, they glanced up and down the road, at the mangled remains of the hot rods and motorcycles, the SARGEs and Prowlers, the dead bodies of cyborgs and old friends.

'Boy, oh, boy!' Satchmo softly exclaimed, sounding as sad as an old blues or country song. 'What the hell happens now?'

'We go home,' Gumshoe said. 'We get back in your car and we turn on the radio and check if what's happened here has happened all over the world. My bet's that it has.'

'Glory be and hallelujah,' Satchmo said, getting his ebullient spirits back. 'Let's check it out, brother.'

Together they walked to Satchmo's undamaged Mazda and slipped into the front seats. Satchmo turned the key in the ignition, then switched the radio on. He didn't have to tune in to many stations to get a news programme — it was all news this morning and all of it confirmed what Gumshoe had suspected:

the flying saucers had been exploding all over the world and the rule of the cyborgs had ended. Already politicians worldwide, rendered impotent for so long, were fighting among themselves for the top administrative positions in the governments hastily being reformed. The world, with its many human imperfections, was returning to normal. Satchmo turned off the radio.

'We did it, brother,' he said. 'We pulled that motherfucking job off. Now the politicians will take all the credit and we'll be back in the doghouse.'

'There are worse places to be,' Gumshoe said, 'and we've been there and back.'

Satchmo grinned. 'You want a ride to your place?'

'No, I think I'll walk. It'll be nice to saunter home as a free man, breathing fresh air.'

'Not me, man. I need a pillow and a blanket over my head and I need it real quick.'

Gumshoe slipped out of the car and closed the door. 'I'll see you around.'

'You bet,' Satchmo said.

The black man drove away. Gumshoe stood there for a moment. He heard Bonnie's distinctive laughter and glanced across the road to see her emerging from the moonlit grounds of the White House, almost hysterical with joy, trying to embrace her mother and father and younger sister all at once, becoming awkwardly entangled with them as they walked along the dark road, away from the wrecked vehicles and dead bodies, moving hopefully towards a more normal, happier future.

Gumshoe didn't try to follow them. Some moments were just too private. He decided to let Bonnie have a few days with her family and then give her a call and invite her out. For sure, they would have a lot to talk about and he certainly wanted to talk.

Right now, however, he wanted to go home, have a good sleep and then try to track down his old rival Mike Johnson, to find out if he had made contact with Wilson and, just as important, why he had left the Pentagon basement so abruptly, without telling anyone.

In fact, Gumshoe never saw 'Mike Johnson' again, though he saw an awful lot of Bonnie Packard.

Michael had vanished.

Chapter Forty-four

From: <bayfree@leebrand.com>
no need for code.
freedom bay is back to normal.
reports indicate that the wilson saucers are no more and that
the rule of the cyborgs is over.
the major desire here is for a return to the world but we need
to know where the bird is.
we use the code name bird only in a nostalgic way and look
forward to seeing you come home.
where r u.
come in bird.

From: <birdnest@mkim.com>
the bird has flown and will not be coming back.
there can be no explanation.
warm regards to my parents and my sister.
thanks for everything.
farewell.

Chapter Forty-five

What are we? We are One. We are One and we are All. We are everything outside and inside ourselves, and without us it cannot be. All that is, begins here. Space and time are created here. The past and the future are here and exist by our will. We survey the teeming infinite. We rule over what we survey. Should we cease to be, it will all cease to be: the universe will shrink and disappear and will never have been. All that is, begins here. All that will be, must end here. Here, within us, is the beginning and end of the circle.

We venture forth to greet ourselves. We draw space and time together. All the light and colours of the spectrum swim around us in glory. We are radiant. We accept. The light pours through ravines of colour. The sounds of history pass through us and recede and return eternally. All that was, all that is, all that will be, is here and now always.

The light pours and pulsates. Voices speak and yet are silent. The great moons are eclipsed by other moons and travel through time and conquer it. We are radiant. We accept. We embrace all that is. It streams through us and around us and then spreads out to fill up the Nothing. The purple flower of a flare. A comet streaking through the night. The light flows and turns into great rainbows that bridge the black depths.

We venture forth to be greeted.

Here time is rendered redundant and space obliterated. Life exists and dies and is reborn and the process is endless. Our destiny is here and now. Here and now there are no boundaries. What we see and what we feel and what we hear are all created within us. We see the darkness and the light, feel the ice and the fire. We reach out and touch what we will because we want it to be there.

A sudden dazzling phosphorescence. Streams of colour and burning light. The sounds of history are collected and cast forth to bridge the past and the future. Exploding galaxies and roaring voids. Vast clouds of cosmic dust. The great dust-clouds envelop the clustered stars and then radiate beauty.

We venture forth to be made whole.

We ordain all that is. We accept it or cast it out. Our mind is emptied and we let it fill up with all the wealth of the universe. The birth and death of galaxies. Blazing suns and imploding stars. Lonely moons circle planets of a size that defies comprehension. Then light. A rush of colours. The golden furnace of a giant star. The fire is drawn out like a stretching membrane and forms a rainbow . . . a whirlpool.

The whirlpool is immense. It swirls around a black hole. It is a maelstrom of energy and heat and blinding colour, and it swirls around the black hole and is devoured, leaving only night's silence.

We embrace the silent night, cast off space and time, and see the boundaries of our mind receding rapidly until the distance is infinite. All that is, is in here. The past and future are now. There are parallel lines of light and force that stretch from here and end here. Direction and dimension: neither has credence here. There is knowledge and the certainty of existence, its reality constant. Radiation and sound. All the wavelengths rendered visible. There is colour and sound and vibration, but they cannot be measured.

All is here.

All is now.

We sing. What we are sings. Great suns and moons dazzle. One of the moons opens out and draws us in and dissolves to reveal us. The Kingdom and its glory. Time and space reconciled. The moons spin and flare up and fade away as the universe unfurls.

Colour: that which is. A vast spectrum on display. Orange skies and purple clouds and yellow suns, the stars green, blue and golden. There is death and beauty here. The stars melt and reform. There are great magenta clouds of formless matter slowly rising and falling. Green fires blaze up and die. Comets streak the sky with silver. Silent winds blow ice crystals in immense cyan spirals, and they sweep out and girdle the stars and the pale, serene moons. The colours merge and are dazzling.

We sing. What we are sings. What we are is what is. We are one, we are millions, and we divide down the middle, and repeat this again and again and thus multiply always. Amoebae. Loops and coils. The pale moons stretch out and mingle. The stars blaze and their light meets and blends to become a vast web.

We are in it and of it. We are here and also there. We are singing with the voice of sensation, pouring forth and returning. We are One. We are the same. We break apart and come together. We are thought, we are brain, we are mind, making real the unreal.

We are born. We are All. We live and die on the instant. We are outside and inside ourselves, being one and the same. What unfurls is within us. We ordain all that is. We expand and contract and envelop and pour forth to create.

We are All.

All is . . .

GOD!

W.A. HARBINSON

INCEPTION
Projekt Saucer: I

THE MOST TERRIFYING, AWESOME CONSPIRACY IN HUMAN HISTORY STARTS HERE . . .

The first wave of modern UFO sightings occurred over a hundred years ago. **Fact.** In 1908 a mysterious nuclear-like explosion devastated a vast area of Siberia. **Fact.** Allied airmen flying over Germany in World War II were chased by eerie fireballs. **Fact.** During that same global conflict, the Nazis experimented desperately to try and create the world's first flying saucer. **Fact.**

These facts hold the key to the nightmarish secret of UFOs.

Based on previously concealed but carefully documented evidence, INCEPTION begins the epic *Projekt Saucer* series — a sequence of chilling revelations in the form of gripping fiction. Here is a unique, controversial and provocative work exposing cover-ups, conspiracies and terrible truths that have been hidden far, far too long . . .

'A wonderful blend of real and invented events that will delight SF fans and those who are interested in the mystery surrounding UFO sightings . . . fascinating'

Guernsey Evening Press

Available in New English Library paperback

W.A. HARBINSON

PHOENIX
Projekt Saucer: 2

THE MOST TERRIFYING, AWESOME CONSPIRACY IN HUMAN HISTORY CONTINUES . . .

In INCEPTION, the first novel of the astounding *Projekt Saucer* sequence, W.A. Harbinson traced the origins of the terrifying global conspiracy behind the sinister UFO phenomenon – origins that lie not in outer space but *right here on Earth.*

Now, in PHOENIX, he has taken the themes and many of the characters from that groundbreaking work and developed them into further dimensions of cosmic horror, moving the epic story on from the end of the Second World War and through the post-war years of humankind's first tentative explorations of space, uncovering in the process a nightmare web of secret scientific experimentation – and the collusion of the superpower governments with the horrific organization responsible . . .

'Harbinson's formidable research and ingenious extrapolations thereon are highly impressive . . . a massive prequel to "The X-Files" as written by Tom Clancy'

Time Out on *Inception* and *Phoenix*

Available in New English Library paperback

W.A. HARBINSON

GENESIS
Projekt Saucer: 3

THE ULTIMATE CONSPIRACY MOVES INTO HORRIFIC NEW DIMENSIONS . . .

In INCEPTION and PHOENIX, the first two novels of the astounding *Projekt Saucer* sequence, W.A. Harbinson traced the origins of the alarming global conspiracy behind the sinister UFO phenomenon and carried the epic story on into the years after the Second World War. In the process he revealed the terrifying nature of the ultrasecret scientific organization responsible.

Now, in GENESIS, Harbinson plunges the reader into icy new dimensions of terror as he exposes the next moves of this horrific cabal to enslave and subvert humanity as we know it and turn life on Earth into a chilling nightmare of living death . . .

'A Herculean conspiracy epic . . . superbly written, crammed with food for thought'
Los Angeles Times

'Impressive . . . Harbinson has drawn so heavily on factual material and integrated it so well into the text that the book begins to read like non-fiction'
Publishers Weekly

'This extraordinary book. A thought-provoking mixture of terror and credibility'
The Bookseller

Available in New English Library paperback

W.A. HARBINSON

MILLENNIUM
Projekt Saucer: 4

FROM MIND-BLASTING TERROR
TO THE UNTHINKABLE . . .

In INCEPTION, PHOENIX and GENESIS, the first three novels of the astounding *Projekt Saucer* sequence, W.A. Harbinson traced the origins of the terrifying global conspiracy behind the sinister UFO phenomenon, revealed the horrific nature of the ultrasecret scientific organization responsible and unravelled the threads of a shattering plot to turn life on Earth into a chilling nightmare of living death.

Now, in MILLENNIUM, Harbinson shows how the tentacles of the most horrendous, awesome conspiracy in human history are enveloping us all, in order to create a future more fearsome that we can possibly imagine. From the frozen wastes of Antarctica to the sweltering jungles of Paraguay, from the depths of the ocean to the dark side of the Moon, the race is on to prevent this – but it has not yet been won . . .

'Harbinson's novels are never less than stupendous. I am in awe of this man'

JAMES HERBERT

'Harbinson is a combination of H.G. Wells and Frederick Forsyth – audacious imagination combined with a precise and convincing realism'

COLIN WILSON

Available in New English Library paperback